Still Waters

A Contemporary Southern Novel

Kim~
Enjoy Edisto...
I love it as much
as Berry!

by Lindsey Brackett

Lindsey P. Brackett

FIREFLY
SOUTHERN FICTION
LIGHTHOUSE PUBLISHING OF THE CAROLINAS

STILL WATERS BY LINDSEY BRACKETT
Published by Firefly Southern Fiction
an imprint of Lighthouse Publishing of the Carolinas
2333 Barton Oaks Dr., Raleigh, NC, 27614

ISBN: 978-1-946016-23-2
Copyright © 2017 by Lindsey Brackett
Cover design by Elaina Lee
Interior design by Karthick Srinivasan

Available in print from your local bookstore, online, or from the publisher at:
lpcbooks.com

For more information on this book and the author visit: lindseypbrackett.com

Brought to you by the creative team at Lighthouse Publishing of the Carolinas:
Eva Marie Everson, Jennifer A. Slattery

Library of Congress Cataloging-in-Publication Data
Brackett, Lindsey
Still Waters / Lindsey Brackett 1st ed.

Printed in the United States of America

PRAISE FOR *STILL WATERS*

Lindsey Brackett's debut novel *Still Waters* is poignant, heartwarming, and romantic! The Lowcountry coast comes to life with the skill of Brackett's writing, and the cast of compelling characters moves right on in to your heart. So much more than a romance, this is a story of family and faith and forgiveness that will settle over your soul like a warm ocean breeze.

~Carrie Schmidt
ReadingIsMySuperPower.org

Still Waters was lovely and wonderful and I wish I could sit on that screened-in porch and drink tea with Nan. Brackett set up such a lovely sense of place. She made me want to be there. I loved it.

~Hannah Hall
Bestselling author of the
God Bless Us series

I found *Still Waters*, the brilliant debut novel from Lindsey Brackett, full of reality, restoration and romance! Who cannot help but sympathize with a family who has multilayers of relationships and regrets? Our community centers around a vintage family cottage on Edisto Island Beach, where both nature and nurture are battling for happy endings. But recent graduate Cora Ann is hesitant to deal with her past, even if it's the only way she can embrace her future. Along the way, we end up rooting for the handsome builder and preservationist, the independent young woman who must make hard choices, and the feisty grandmother orchestrating everything from her perch on the porch. This story was both intriguing and delightful. It left me wanting more from this fine novelist. I'm eager to discover where the path leads for these stalwart southerners. Enjoy *Still Waters* and look out for Lindsey Brackett.

~Lucinda Secrest McDowell
Author of *Dwelling Places*
EncouragingWords.net

With as style as fluid as Edisto Beach waves, debut novelist Lindsey Brackett has written a story that draws you in and doesn't let go until the last page is turned. I loved it.

~**Ane Mulligan**
Bestselling author of
Chapel Springs Revival

Still Waters invites you to sink into the serenity of Edisto Beach. On this picturesque island forgiveness is as warm as the summer sand, grace swirls as gentle as the tide's ebb and flow, and love is as healing as the salty sea breeze. This stunning debut from author Lindsey Brackett promises rich stories to treasure for years to come.

~**Heather Iseminger**
Award-winning author and blogger
PetalsofJoy.org

The story told in *Still Waters* not only runs deep, it burrows inside your heart with engaging characters and a touch of mystery firmly set in Lowcountry culture. With its exquisite writing and multifaceted themes, Lindsey Brackett's novel may elicit a few tears and that dueling "I can't wait to get to the end/I don't want this story to end" feeling. It's truly one of my favorite contemporary romance novels.

~**Johnnie Alexander**
Award-winning author of
Where She Belongs

Lindsey Brackett has truly captured the complexities of a family, revealing the baggage each one carries that make up the dynamics of a family that loves deeply, endures and comes through the hurts, and learns to forgive and let go.

~**Susan Reichert**
Editor-in-Chief
Southern Writers Magazine

Set against the backdrop of a small beach town, *Still Waters* is a beautiful story of enduring love, forgiveness and the unpredictable storms that can lead us home. Brackett's moving debut will linger in your memory long after you've turned the last page.

~Connie Mann
Romantic suspense author & boat captain

My heart ached with longing at how sweet and genuine the author depicted Edisto Beach, and how its magic helped a girl find herself, her love, and her Lord. Remarkable debut novel. A very pretty story.

~C. Hope Clark
Author *The Edisto Island Mystery Series*

Lindsey Brackett weaves a story so beautiful in its telling, you'll ache for more when you reach the last word.

~Bethany Jett
Award-winning author of
The Cinderella Rule

Still Waters starts out as a sweet, predictable romance, but each chapter leads your heart into deep waters of forgiveness, healing, and faith. Lindsey Brackett writes with a Southern warmth that wraps you up in a blanket of wisdom and strength. Her charm and smile graced each page and left me wanting to read her next book.

~Andy Lee
author of *A Mary Like Me: Flawed Yet Called*

Still Waters is a charming story of brokenness, healing, and the beauty of a pursuing, enduring love. Like the slow swell of sunrise over the ocean, Brackett's heroine, Cora Anne takes a gradual dawning from the darkness of her past to the beauty of forgiveness when the love of a good man and the wisdom of a caring grandmother force her to meet her past and future, head-on. A sweet story with a tender premise and some breathtaking kisses.

~Pepper Basham
author of the *Penned in Time* and *Mitchells Crossroads* series

ACKNOWLEDGMENTS

If it takes a village to raise a child, it takes the whole tribe to raise a book. People about fell over themselves to help me with this project, and there are no words enough to extend my gratitude.

Bits and pieces of this story are my roots, spread wide as the live oaks in the Lowcountry soil of Colleton County and Edisto Island. The people there took me in and called me local because of my mother and aunt and uncle and their parents whom we lost far too early. Which is really what made me choose this setting—that pervading "what if" they'd still been around to see all their grandchildren rising toward adulthood. I hope we'd have made them proud.

Many, many thanks to the Edisto Historical Society and Museum and Mrs. Gretchen Smith, who answered so many of my questions and helped me maintain authenticity. John Girault, Executive Director of the Edisto Island Open Land Trust, works tirelessly with volunteers and staff to preserve this beautiful place, but he still found time to drink coffee with me and offer insight into Tennessee's efforts to do the same. Jim Ramsay and family, owners of the Chaika House, gave us a great deal on a week's stay in 2016 so I could finish edits and research the rest of my trilogy. Bill Smoak, a longtime family friend and the only shrimper who still docks on Edisto, inspired Lenny's character—but he also gave me a great gift the day he let us tour the *Sarah Jane*. One look at my toddler boy and he saw my grandfather Tom, reinforcing my belief that God's gift of genealogy is oh, so good. I hope he doesn't mind I borrowed his boat for this book.

I'm often asked how I found a publisher, and truth is, I owe it all to my friend Amy Ivey who asked me to attend a writer's conference with her in 2014. There I met Eva Marie Everson, the first person to see this fledgling manuscript—and the first to tell me I had talent. She must have seen something on those early pages, because she offered me her suggestions, and after I went and applied those, she acquired it. Eva, you have believed in me since that first day, and I am honored to call you my friend and mentor. Thank you, also, for sharing Jessica with me to answer questions and make this process more navigable.

Thank you a thousand times over to Jennifer Slattery, my editor, who made me probe deeper into the characters and draw out their idiosyncrasies. You made my writing stronger and you always, always pointed me back to God's great purposes.

Many friends saw this book in its early stages and helped shape it into something infinitely better. Much love to Brooke Barksdale, Leslie Terrell, Willene

Keel, Elaine Piniat, my Word Weavers group, and any others I've neglected to call by name who truly helped make this novel readable and Cora Anne likeable.

My writer soul sisters—Sarah, Taryn, Heather, Kim, and Hannah—thank you for praying and talking me off the ledge a time or two.

My publisher, Eddie Jones, the realism behind the dream, answers my questions and has even dropped a compliment or two, and believe me, I know how special that is. Thank you, Eddie, for believing LPC can reach more than the choir.

Finally, I humbly offer gratitude to my family. My Mama, Daddy, brother and sisters, who first inspired me to write; my cousins and extended family, with whom we've stayed in nearly every house on that beach (and Jocie for those beautiful photos!). Madelynne, Annabelle, Amelia, and Gus who love Edisto and love their mama, even when I ignore them to work on my computer. My husband, Joshua, who has always encouraged me and who embodies my greatest example of Christ's love on earth—this story would never have happened without you refusing to let me run away.

To the One who knows my heart, and has made writing the work of my hands, *eucharisteo*. Always.

For my family
in celebration of Edisto summers and peach ice cream.

Chapter 1

Cora Anne knew she needed more than a cherry limeade. The floorboards of her tiny Honda Civic practically groaned, loaded down as they were with books and clothes and the paraphernalia of college. Pressed between her laptop and her planner was her diploma—Bachelor of Arts in History. With the *magna cum laude* seal, nonetheless.

And the best she could do was an icy drink with an extra wedge of lime that stuck to the straw when she pulled on the last of that syrupy sweetness.

Hurricane Katrina had wrecked more than New Orleans when it surged through the fall before. That storm waitlisted her for the graduate program at Tulane University.

The whole mess got worse when she slammed the brakes at the bottom of her mother's sloping drive. Her purse with its organized compartments tumbled to the floorboard as the remains of her big splurge landed in her lap. She ground her teeth as her twelve-year-old triplet brothers negotiated the turn from driveway to street with skateboards tilted.

"Thanks a lot, boys," Cora Anne called, leaning out her open window.

The boys waved and flashed wide dimpled grins before speeding off toward the neighborhood's community house, where they would undoubtedly ignore the posted regulations about no skateboards on the tennis courts.

With a groan, she scooped melting ice off her shorts and back into the cup. Her favorite running shorts were soaked, and rivulets of the sticky red drink trickled down her leg, which matched the nervous perspiration running down her back.

The Civic strained up the drive's incline. Dad had offered to help her move right after graduation, but she'd needed that extra week to let go of her routine. The University of Georgia's schedule was no longer her safe place, even if she wanted to return. Without a graduate assistantship available, UGA didn't solve her financial problem.

So home she'd come, despite the plans she'd made.

Inside the simple brick bungalow, her mom and brothers had their own routine going now. Life here had gone on now for four years without her or Dad, but hopefully, she'd fit in.

Arms full, she headed through the garage to the back door. The mudroom strewn with her brothers' sneakers and their half-hearted attempts to hang their book bags on the wall hooks smelled, as always, of laundry detergent and Pine-Sol. Towels had been folded and stacked on the dryer, but the utility sink was full of soapy water and the boys' baseball uniforms. She rolled her eyes. Her mother never gave up trying to keep those white pants clean from game to game. Cora Anne hung her purse and left her bag on the bench under the hooks.

"Mom?"

"Cora Anne, there you are." Lou rose from the breakfast table stacked with paperwork and her school-issued laptop. "I figured traffic might get you." Her mother's petite stature often fooled her students into believing they had the upper hand. She had what looked like chemistry lab reports in her hand and a red pencil stuck between her ear and smooth, bobbed hair.

Cora Anne leaned in for the quick embrace.

"What in the world happened?" Lou pulled back and grimaced at her now damp khakis.

"Your sons happened." She threw her empty cup in the trash and washed sweat and stickiness from her hands. Relieved of that mess, she smoothed her dark hair, tucking back tendrils that had escaped on the drive from Athens to Marietta. Early May in Georgia meant possible heatstroke in a car with no air conditioning, though, so down the windows stayed despite the tangles in her curly hair.

"They startle you, coasting down the drive on those neck-breaking skateboards? I'd say I hate that your father bought those things, but truth be told, it burns off some of their endless energy." Lou tried to make eye contact, but Cora Anne avoided her gaze.

"I'll bet so." She reached for the dishtowel and knotted her hand over the monogram. Every time she came home, she was surprised it still hung beside the sink. As if nothing had changed.

"I'm sorry this isn't a big-deal homecoming, but there's a pot roast in the crockpot, and your brothers might be gone long enough for me to finish grading, which means I'll actually be able to focus on something else."

"Like what?"

Her mother bent back over her paperwork. "There's a letter for you."

"Really?" She snagged the pale blue envelope from a wire basket of mail on the granite countertop and recognized the formal spidery script immediately. "It's from Nan."

"I know. My mother likes to remind everyone that handwritten correspondence isn't dead."

Cora Anne worked the flap open and glanced at her mom to see if she was interested in the note's contents. Lou wrinkled her forehead as she marked another report. The late afternoon sun filtering through the windows caught more glints of silver in her chestnut hair than Cora Anne remembered.

She read through the note without unfolding the enclosed check. When finished, she stared at her mother. "I don't understand."

Lou looked up. "What does it say?"

The request made no sense. "My dear Cora Anne," she read. "I regret so deeply I was not able to attend your graduation and see you receive a diploma that represents far more than achievement. It is, I know, the embodiment of your first life goal, and I hope you will know I am so very proud of you for attaining it. Please allow me to make it up to you by sharing this last summer of freedom—"

Her voice hitched but she shook off the emotion.

"I would like to offer this gift of good memories to overshadow the despair you harbor, for both our Edisto home and your delayed dream. Come stay with me, my dear, to learn about our history and delight in our past, so you might truly be ready for your future. I have enclosed a monetary gift as well. If you come, I will match these funds at the end of the summer in order to offset any loss of income you might experience. With all my love, Nan."

Lou raised her eyebrows. "How much?"

Cora Anne opened the fold and gasped. "Five thousand dollars ..." Stunned, she handed it to her mother, who had left the lab reports behind.

"I'd say she really wants you to come." Lou handed the check back and tapped her pencil against her palm.

"Did you know about this?" She stuffed the stationery and money back in the envelope.

Now Lou avoided Cora Anne's gaze. "Yes. She called me last week."

"What am I supposed to say, Mom?" She would have appreciated a warning. "I hate Edisto and never want to come back?"

"You don't hate Edisto." Lou crossed her arms.

Cora Anne mimicked her. "Well, it hasn't exactly been all sandcastles and suntans, now has it?"

"Did you bring that attitude home with you? Because I think I'd like you to pack the sass back off to Athens."

She tossed the letter on the counter. "Why now? Why would she ask this of me *now*?"

Lou raised her eyebrows. "She told you. Because it's your last summer."

3

"What if I've already made new plans? Yesterday, I talked to the curator at the history museum. This"—the panic rising made her gesture wildly about the kitchen—"doesn't have to be my only option."

Her mother sighed as though this argument made her tired. "Did it ever occur to you that we're not all out to ruin your life? That maybe your grandmother is trying to share something with you she thinks you might actually enjoy, even though it hasn't been pre-approved and prescribed into your perfect timeline?"

"My timeline isn't perfect." A hurricane had seen to that. "But it's mine, so yes, I think I should have a say in 'pre-approving' changes to it." She stepped back in mock capitulation. "But that's fine. I'm used to everyone else making plans without me."

"Cora Anne …"

She watched her mother and waited. She would rather stay here and be a stranger than go back to that place. Did Lou sense that? Evidently not, because her mom relaxed her stance and shrugged.

"I think Edisto and Nan could be good for you."

Cora Anne spun and headed back outside. She had a car full of dirty laundry, a schedule to make, and no intention of spending the entire summer with her grandmother at Edisto Beach.

Lou shook her head at the remnant of pot roast left on the platter in the middle of the dining room table. She'd tried. "Well, boys, guess I'll have to buy a bigger one next time."

"Or make more rolls," J.D. suggested around a mouthful of Sister Schubert yeast roll.

"More potatoes." Cole scraped the serving bowl to get the last of the mashed potatoes.

"Aw, Mama, it's just 'cause Cor is here now. Once she leaves, we won't have to hold back." Mac patted his belly. "Maybe I'll lose a couple pounds letting her have my share, and then I can run the bases faster."

"If that's what you call letting me have your share, I think I'll be the one losing weight." Her daughter tousled that brother's dark hair. Mac was the only triplet who shared her thick waves. Lou had seen them bond more over their humidity-induced curls than anything else.

"Boys, clear your plates, please, and then I want you upstairs. Showers and homework. Inspection's at eight sharp."

"Mama, are you ever going to stop acting like we're in boot camp?" J.D. rose and picked up his plate and glass.

"Are you ever going to stop acting like you need boot camp?"

They grinned at one another and cleared their plates. Lou and Cora Anne sipped the remainder of their sweet tea amidst the clatter of dishes in the sink and the tromp of footsteps as the boys raced one another up the stairs.

"Like a herd of wild elephants." Chin propped in her hand, Cora Anne handed her plate to Lou's outstretched hand.

"I've actually down-graded them to a pack of wild hyenas." When Lou returned for the serving dishes, she found her daughter stacking the stoneware bowls and platter.

She gathered the linen napkins that were a vain attempt to teach the boys manners. "Thanks. It's nice having a little help."

Cora Anne shrugged and went into the kitchen where she opened the dishwasher in silence. Lou came beside her and began rinsing.

She ran a scrub brush over mashed potato remains and debated. Start easy. "What are your plans for tomorrow?"

Her oldest and most stubborn child—no matter she was now a college graduate—simply loaded the plates without looking up. "Why don't you tell me?"

So much for easy. She tried another tactic. "Your dad wants to see you, I'm sure."

"I'll try to squeeze him into my schedule."

Lou jerked the faucet off. "That's enough. You don't have to make the time you're here miserable."

Cora Anne shut the dishwasher with a click and snatched a towel from the counter. "I know I deserve nothing but misery because of Edisto, but I didn't think you'd be so cold as to actually send me back."

Lou gripped the sink. "You are not the only one who suffered, Cora Anne. But you can't lay blame on a house or an ocean."

"Because I only need to blame myself."

"Maybe not if you go and stay with Nan." She touched her daughter's shoulder. "She wants to help you understand."

Cora Anne shrugged off Lou's touch. With a sigh, Lou stepped back. She picked up the pitcher of tea and opened the fridge.

"What does she expect me to do all summer?"

The question raised Lou's hopes. "I'm not really sure. All I know is she wants to do some work on the beach cottage."

"She didn't rent Still Waters at all?"

"No, said she's closing up the farmhouse and staying at the cottage until the fancy strikes her to go home." Lou filled the crockpot insert with hot water and soap.

Cora Anne rounded the island and sat on a barstool. In her old high school track t-shirt and Adidas shorts, she could have been the same girl who sat there

5

and moaned about trigonometry while eating chocolate chips straight from the Tollhouse bag. Even then, she'd been guarded, but the wall that existed between them now was so thick, Lou wasn't sure she'd ever find a way to break it down.

"She's hinted about a reunion." Lou let that seep in and watched Cor's shoulders tense. "But I really think she wants company. She's lonely, you know, since your grandfather died."

"Are you trying to make me feel guilty?"

"No, just needed."

Cora Anne scuffed her bare toe against the pockmarks on the pine floor. Indentions left by years of the triplets and Matchbox cars. Lou waited for the inevitable.

Her daughter lifted her chin, her voice a controlled calm. "If she wants us there for old times' sake, then I don't see why we can't all go."

Lou pursed her lips. Her mother had been adamant Cora Anne come alone, at least for the beginning.

"I'm teaching summer school, and the boys are signed up for baseball camp. We've got a busy June and July, but if she really wants a reunion, we'll come for that. Maybe I can come early while they're with your father. Spell you a bit."

Her daughter huffed at the wisps of hair that had fallen in her eyes. "What about Hannah or Aunt Caro?"

"It's wedding season. You know that. No way either one can get away for more than a day or two." Cora Anne rolled her eyes, and Lou resisted the urge to agree. Planning weddings might seem frivolous to her, but that business was the bread and butter of her sister Carolina's life.

"So I'm all who's left to go." Cora Anne stood, arms folded. "Back to Still Waters on Edisto, where the ocean is anything but still and tragedies always happen."

"One tragedy." Lou's voice lowered with her downcast eyes. Tears pricked their corners. "That's all. The rest was just life." Her voice caught. "And someday, you will have to make peace with it."

"Have you made peace with everything? Because I don't see you spending idle summers at the beach anymore either."

The words cut Lou's heart. She may not have wrestled all her demons either, but it was worse watching her daughter allow past sorrows to steal her happiness.

She raised her head. "I learn over and over, every single day, how to live with my decisions. Life's a fight for joy, Cora Anne, and you're not even in the ring."

Her daughter spun and strode toward the stairs. Lou waited until she'd gone before she dropped her head in her hands and sobbed, shoulders quaking in the quiet.

Chapter 2

Not even the smells of coffee and bacon lured Cora Anne out of bed the next morning. She hid under the comforter that had been hers since middle school and tried to shut out the sounds of her mother and brothers readying for school.

She buried her face in the down pillow, knowing she should apologize to Lou. But words were never enough to undo all the past hurt.

Her stomach churned. Hunger or nerves? Only one way to tell. The house had gone blessedly quiet. She emerged and crept down the stairs.

In the kitchen, Cora Anne poured a cup of coffee and dosed it liberally with cream and sugar. Her eyes strayed to the wall between the window and the stairs, where a set of four framed photographs hung. Memories of their better days at Edisto.

In the top left frame was a sunset view from Still Waters, her grandparents' beach cottage. Indigo ocean and deep purple sky streaked orange as the sun's orb sank low on the horizon. Next was a dawn shot of the cottage taken in soft, hazy light. A classic beach bungalow with the Atlantic in the background and sea grass waving in the breeze. She gripped her cup tighter. She'd taken that picture herself the summer she was ten years old.

The other two photographs were her grandparents' Lowcountry farm, barely fifteen miles inland. There was the farmhouse with its strange array of peaks and porches, a testament to her grandfather's knack for adding on until the space felt right. The last shot showed an arbor with heirloom yellow roses climbing the sides. Her grandmother Nan's pride and joy.

Two different homes in the same place, serving two different purposes. One brought her family there. One took them away.

"You can't blame a house or an ocean ..." Her mother's words echoed in the stillness. Cora Anne sipped her coffee and pondered.

The plastic laundry basket dug into her hip where she'd hefted it to go upstairs. With the company of *Good Morning America*, Cora Anne had spent the better part of her morning washing and folding. At least she didn't have to worry about drawer space for newly acquired items. Instead, she would return everything to the duffel she'd unloaded the afternoon before. The phone rang as she reached the stairs. Let the machine get it.

Her mother's brisk voice informed callers to leave a message. "Hey, Cor? You there? It's your old dad and I'd love to talk to you—"

She dropped the basket when she swiveled and grabbed the cordless from the hall table. Silent curse as tank tops and underwear toppled into a heap at her feet. "Hey, Dad."

"Well, there's my baby girl. You made it in all right?"

"It's not a bad drive. Just feels long."

"Well, I know you hate driving on that interstate. You settled enough to come have cafeteria food with me? There's nothing on today's docket aside from some big sendoff for the soccer team when they leave for state this afternoon." Dad had taken the assistant-principal job at a rival high school the summer he moved out. Overnight, he'd become a stranger who monitored curriculum rather than the grades of his football players.

She tried to put some enthusiasm in her voice. "Sure, I'd love to. One okay? I've got some errands to run first."

"Sure thing, sweetheart. Just buzz my cell when you get here."

"Okay, Dad. See you then."

"Your mother thinks you should do *what?*" Her father wiped his hands on a wad of paper napkins.

Today's school lunch consisted of pulled pork sandwiches dripping with sauce, limp fries, and a rounded scoop of slaw. Cora Anne had opted for the salad bar, and now she poked at her cherry tomatoes and marveled that despite a steady diet of cafeteria food, Dad was as trim and fit as she'd ever seen him. No doubt the result of after-school pickup basketball games with his staff. His dark blond hair had yet to thin—or even gray—and he wore it cropped short, making him look younger than his late forties. In contrast to her mother, David Halloway hadn't let the divorce age him.

"It's just for the summer. To help Nan out. Apparently, she wants to work on the beach house, and I guess she figures if I'm going to be an independent woman I need to learn to swing a hammer?"

Her dad narrowed his eyes at her joke.

She lay down her fork. "I don't really understand … but Mom was pretty insistent I should go."

Dad pressed his lips together. "Your mother always bows to the wishes of her mother. It doesn't have to be your legacy too, honey. If you don't want to go, don't go. And if that's a problem, come stay with me." His hazel eyes twinkled. "There's a pool and I see kids your age hanging out there all the time."

She rolled her eyes. "Really? You want me to bum around at the pool? At least a summer on Edisto will help finance my career."

Dad sighed. Cora Anne knew he'd pay for grad school if he could. She cocked her head, listening to the energetic buzz of the cafeteria. She'd never been that high school kid without a care beyond the next algebra test. They ate without speaking until her dad's last bite of soggy sandwich dripped sauce on his tie.

"Sheesh." He grabbed a napkin and blotted at the grease. "Always making a mess."

She giggled, some of her tension seeping out with this familiar scene. "Well, at least we know where the boys get it from."

He laughed too. "Bet they were excited to have you home." Dad reached for her hand, but Cora Anne moved it to her lap and kept the conversation light.

"Oh, yeah. They demonstrated that excitement by trying to run me over with their skateboards."

Dad smiled. "Your mom still hate those things?"

"You better believe it."

"Well, nothing I've ever done suits her. But at least I can make you and the boys happy."

She lifted her drink and forced her own smile. "I got my degree, so I'm happy."

"You'll get to Tulane. This waitlist is just a bump on the road." He sipped his tea, and Cora Anne fidgeted with her napkin.

"I don't know what else to do." The confession rushed out. Dad listened. He always had. "I don't want to go back to UGA ... but that's the most practical choice."

This time, she didn't pull away when he took her hand and squeezed. "Sometimes, the practical choice is the best way to get what we want."

"Mom thinks I just want distance." This admission came out before she'd thought it through.

He squeezed tighter. "I'm sorry your mom and I let you down."

Cora Anne pulled her hand back, the moment of affection swiftly gone and replaced by the sting of rejection she'd felt for so many years. "Yeah, well, she also says that's just life, and I need to learn to live with it."

"How consoling of her." Dad's sarcasm was sharp.

"So, I'll go help Nan with Still Waters." Her father's eyes were soft, unlike the steel she saw in her mother's sometimes. "If I can make peace with Edisto, maybe I'll take my advisor up on his offer."

He raised his eyebrows. "Interview at the College of Charleston?"

A bell rang, signaling the end of this lunch period. The noise around them swelled as students clattered trays and shouted last-minute goodbyes. Cora Anne nodded affirmation to her father. No reason to speak above the din and over the lump in her throat.

"You always loved Edisto." He leaned close for this gentle reminder.

She dropped her gaze. "A long time ago. I was different then."

"Not really." Dad reached over and smoothed an unruly dark curl behind her ear. "I think my carefree child is still in there somewhere."

Always the optimistic one. She shrugged. "Maybe she is, Dad."

The garage door burst open and the triplets announced their presence with war whoops and thuds of backpacks hitting the floor. Cora Anne winced at the noise. Those boys had come into this world at Christmas, when she was ten, and she'd never quite gotten used to them. They'd been loud and rowdy even then, as infants in the NICU who took all her mother's time and energy.

She steadied her hands on the counter. Memories belonged in the past.

"I smell cookies!" Cole parked himself on the bar stool directly in front of a cooling rack of chocolate chip cookies.

"Great! I'm starving." Mac went straight to the fridge and brought the milk to the counter.

J.D. entered with an open book in his hand. "Hey, leave me some."

"If you read, you may not feed." Cole laughed as he stuffed a second cookie in his mouth. The oven timer beeped.

"Where's Mom?" She took out another pan of cookies and silenced the timer.

All three boys looked around, shrugged in unison, and went back to the cookies. Mac poured milk, and J.D. read with a cookie in one hand and a full glass in the other.

She glanced at the title. "*Tuck Everlasting*? I had to read that in sixth grade too. It's beautiful."

"It's boring." Mac's full mouth sprayed crumbs as he talked. "But we have to read it and pass the test to watch the movie."

"Done!" J.D. triumphantly closed the book and grabbed another cookie.

"You gonna tell us how it ends?" Cole guzzled his milk and, setting down the glass, burped loudly. Cora Anne shook her head. The boys always ate like it was their last meal.

"Coultrie Halloway!" The sound of Lou's voice from the doorway startled them all.

"Excuse me," mumbled Cole. He glanced sheepishly at Cora Anne under eyelashes that were far too long for a twelve-year-old boy, and she fought back a smile. Annoying as her little brothers could be, they were always good for a laugh.

Lou lowered her leather bag onto a chair in the breakfast nook and brought a stack of mail to the counter. "I sure appreciate you all helping me get the mail, bring in the trash can, clean out the car …"

The boys scrambled to their feet.

"On it, Mama."

"I call trash can!"

"Man, you realize you have to roll it back up the hill, not skate it down, right?" J.D. crammed a final cookie in his mouth and gave his brothers a shove toward the mudroom door.

The garage door slammed. Lou cast her eyes upward and then at the counter. "Bribery?"

"No." Cora Anne poured her mother a glass of milk. "Peace offering."

"How ironic of you." Lou sat on one of the abandoned stools and sifted through the stack of mail. Opposite, Cora Anne leaned on the cool granite and broke a cookie in half.

"I'm only going because I need the money for grad school."

The corner of her mother's mouth lifted in a half-smile. "We both know that's not true."

She nibbled her cookie. "Well, it sounds true. Grad school is expensive and research hours only pay so much." A new worry hit. "Where's Nan getting that kind of cash anyway? I'm not taking a chunk of your inheritance."

"I wouldn't worry about that. My mother and father always saved for a rainy day. They were children of the Depression, squirreling away money like those days might come again. If she's offering, she has it set aside for you."

Cora Anne rubbed her temples. "What if something happens?"

To her surprise, her mom reached over and touched her shoulder. "Bad things only happen in threes, right? I think you're good."

She pressed fingertips to her eyes. Faith and superstition. Her mother's Edisto upbringing had blended both. Too bad she hadn't also learned how to balance family and work. But that was an old argument for another day. Right now, Cora Anne just wanted to be sure what she would encounter.

"So Nan just wants some company? Nothing else is going on?" Nan's cancer had been in remission for almost four years. Since the last time Cora Anne had stepped foot in that Edisto beach cottage.

Her mother shrugged. "Still waters run deep, Cor, but they don't always precede the valley of death." Lou glanced over her shoulder at the photograph of the beach cottage. "Your grandmother always liked a metaphor."

Cora Anne pressed her palms on the counter. "If I get there and something happens …"

"Now don't go borrowing trouble." Her mom took another cookie. "Besides, you know she's right. We can't carry past despair—or fear—into the future."

Cora Anne propped on her elbows. "Fine, then." She leaned into her mother and whispered. "I'll work on mine, if you work on yours."

Lou raised her eyebrows, but Cora Anne smiled at her for the first time since she'd pulled in the drive.

Chapter 3

The Monday after Mother's Day, Cora Anne sat at the breakfast table with the Bible her mother had left beside a half-drunk cup of coffee. Louisa Coultrie Halloway was stamped in the corner and she traced the golden letters with reverence. A gift from Nan, the Bible had lain on her mother's nightstand in the same place for years. Now, as she sipped hot tea, Cora Anne saw her mom had finally taken to using it. Bookmarks dangled from the spine and the book flipped open easily when she tugged at one. Among the Scripture lavishly highlighted in yellow and green, she stumbled upon a verse that had been underlined and starred as well. *Give thanks in all circumstances.*

Cora Anne huffed. Thanks in all circumstances? Not hardly. What about the Katrina floodwaters? The derailed plans she'd worked so hard to achieve? Or living while someone else died? She shut the Bible, put her cup in the dishwasher, and loaded her car for Edisto under clouded skies.

Rain drizzled while she passed through Atlanta and its early-morning snarl of commuters. Low-hanging clouds cloaked the whole city in dismal gray. If staying here, she'd have counteracted the smog-thickened air with quiet cool at the history museum in downtown Marietta. Instead, she followed the interstate signage onto I-20 and headed toward the oppressive humidity of the Lowcountry.

The long drive stretched ahead in miles of pine-lined interstate. Cora Anne fidgeted in the quiet and cranked up the radio to her favorite local station for a mix of classic rock and current chart-toppers. When the signal gave out twenty miles from Augusta, she hit auto-select. Country music with its familiar rhythm and twang came through the speakers. She hummed along until the song's iconic beat dredged up reminders of summer days spent with Uncle Jimmy's boombox on the deck of Still Waters.

She changed the station.

The strumming ring of her cell shattered the quiet when she crossed the South Carolina border.

Her cousin Hannah's name lit up the screen. "Hello?"

"I was going to text you, but then I remembered you still think we're in the

Dark Ages." Hannah wasted no time with greetings.

"Talking is better. Texting seems cold."

"It's efficient. As in—are you almost there?"

"Just crossed the border. Rain held me up in Atlanta."

"Well, that's what you get for living in that city. Be safe. Call me tomorrow. Miss you and wish I could come too."

"That's all you called to say?"

"Yes. I only have five minutes before Bridezilla, bless her heart, comes in for her consult."

"Do you know you call all your brides that?"

"Do you know it's 2006 and there's this new-fangled option called texting that helps me check on you without being rude and cutting our conversation short?" Hannah talked far too fast for a Charleston debutante.

"I never think you're rude."

"Then you're the only one. Now, have fun relaxing." Hannah's voice softened. "It's time, Cor. Really."

"You too? Why is it everyone's mission to get me back to Edisto?"

"Because I don't like to drink margaritas alone. Oh—gotta go. Bride's here." Hannah hung up.

She tossed her phone on the seat beside her. With Hannah, everything from bridal-gown fittings to empty iced-tea pitchers constituted a state of emergency.

Despite their differences, her cousin was her best friend. They shared their grandmother's blue eyes, their mid-July birthday, and, once, a love for Edisto Beach.

The place hadn't scarred Hannah like it had Cora Anne.

She shrugged off the memories and drove into the early afternoon, stopping in Walterboro at a busy station near the new Walmart. Even amidst the gas fumes and rubber tires baking in the heat, she could smell the change in the air. The Lowcountry had a perfume all its own, salt and marsh and farmland. Cora Anne breathed deep.

Home.

A cracked county highway snaked its way across the island. She passed trailers on cinder blocks and tiny homes belonging to those stubborn enough to scrape out a living here. An invitation to linger hung in the Spanish moss and the twisting branches of live oaks edging the highway. Cora Anne hadn't let herself linger anywhere in years.

Her grandparents had met on one of these dirt roads that left the highway. "Things like love have a way of being in the last place you're likely to look," her grandmother said once.

Cora Anne startled when her cell rang again. She glanced at the name and her finger hovered over the answer button almost a moment too long. "Hey, Nan. I'm almost there."

"Well, good thing, darling, 'cause I can't wait to hug your neck." At the sound of her grandmother's voice, tears pricked the corners of Cora Anne's eyes. Had she really intended to stay away from Nan for so long?

She steeled herself with a change of subject. "Need me to stop at the Pig on the way in?"

The Piggly Wiggly was Edisto's only grocery store, a somewhat convenient reminder of simplicity.

"Oh, honey," Nan's Southern drawl was perfect, a coating of honey and muted syllables. "I got everything you need right here."

Chapter 4

Tennessee heard the car before he saw it. He crouched on the roof of Still Waters, a ridiculously tall palmetto tree blocking his view. He ought to cut it down before a hurricane did, but Mrs. Annie refused to let him.

He knew Cora Anne was coming, and he wondered if he ought to go on ahead and call it a day. Otherwise, he risked getting roped into some sort of reunion. He put glue down for a loose shingle. He'd better talk to Mrs. Annie about replacing this original asbestos-laden roof pretty soon, too.

The car's engine quit. He leaned forward and looked through the palm fronds.

The last time Tennessee had been this close to Cora Anne Halloway was the night his father drowned in a riptide off the beach in front of Still Waters. He'd been fifteen, which made her what? Maybe eleven?

Twelve years was a long time to hold onto the image of a quiet girl with dark braids. But he'd never forgotten how sorrow and guilt had darkened her eyes that night.

Now she was fresh out of college and all grown up. *Hair's still long*, he noticed. Dark and shiny, it was pulled into a messy knot atop her head. She'd grown into her curves but tried to hide them under her Georgia Bulldog t-shirt and running shorts.

She didn't bound up the steps and immediately greet her grandmother, as he assumed she would. Rather, she stood back and gazed at the house with her hands propped on her hips.

Mutiny crossed her pretty features. How well he understood that. But then, her shoulders relaxed, and she wrapped her arms around herself and bowed her head. Resigned. He knew that too.

She turned and trudged to the car's trunk.

Tennessee let go the breath he'd been holding. Somehow, in that short moment, he'd crossed the line from curiosity to appraisal.

And he'd liked what he'd seen. Enough to get a little more comfortable with the idea Mrs. Annie had planted in his mind when she first told him Cora Anne would be coming for the summer. Maybe she was finally ready to talk about what really happened.

He expected her to haul out matching luggage, probably in that floral fabric that seemed so popular with girls these days, but instead, she slung an old duffel across her body. After leaning back in the trunk, she came up with a crate of books. When she headed for the stairs, Tennessee realized he needed to get off the roof, stop ogling, and offer to help. After all, she was an old family friend.

With the grace and skill of one accustomed to heights, he scooted across the shingles and dropped neatly onto the worn planks of the cottage's back deck. His sudden appearance went unnoticed because of the reunion he could see through the big picture window.

Anne Coultrie hugged her granddaughter fiercely with the affection Tennessee often longed for from his own grandmother, who instead, merely greeted him with a cool brush of lips on his cheek. Feeling stupidly out of place—did he really want to see the girl who'd cost his father's life?—he began to gather his scattered tools so he could make a hasty exit.

But Mrs. Annie saw him and waved. She tugged her granddaughter with her and opened the creaky door that led out to the deck.

"Tennessee, there you are, young man. You remember Cora Anne." She slipped an arm around her granddaughter's waist. Her bright blue eyes probed, and her lips twitched, as though she knew he'd been spying from the rooftop.

He shifted the hammer to his left hand and held out his right. "I remember."

As they shook, Cora Anne pressed her lips into what might have been a smile—if it had reached her eyes. Her heart-shaped face still bore a childlike sprinkling of freckles on her nose, and her blue eyes were still the color of the ocean where it meets the sky on the most perfect summer day. He clenched his jaw and fought back the grief-filled memory. And the attraction.

"Nice to see you again." Her hand was warm in his, making his pulse quicken.

"You too." She pulled back. "Thanks for helping Nan look after the place." Her smile deepened then, showing off the dimples he remembered. "Guess we'll find out if I'm any good with a hammer, now, won't we, Nan?" She looked away from him.

"Hmm ... perhaps not, dear." Mrs. Annie's eyes danced between them. "Since you seem to be finished for the day, Tennessee, I won't persuade you to stay for a late lunch. I'm sure you've got other jobs, and I really need to help my girl settle in."

"Right." He nearly dropped his hammer shifting it back to his other hand. "I'll see you later, then, Mrs. Annie. Cora Anne."

He intended a nod of acknowledgement but it felt more like a spastic jerk of his head. The women crossed back into the beach house, leaving him free to be disgruntled.

What was that? He'd dated plenty of women far more beautiful than Cora Anne Halloway. So why in the world was he having a gut-punch attraction to a girl he hadn't seen in years?

Sure, he'd wondered how she'd turned out, but that was just the idle curiosity of old family friends.

Right?

Hand still tingling from her touch, he haphazardly tossed tools into the box, too disoriented to bother with his usual careful packing. Other girls didn't shoot electric currents up his arm when he shook their hands. Though it hadn't been a shock so much as a warmth, like how the afternoon sun felt on his back as he worked the loose roof tiles.

He snapped the clasps shut on his toolbox and blinked at the sun glinting off the Atlantic, calm now at low tide but tumultuous once the waves rose. He wondered if Cora Anne still harbored guilt over his father's death.

The look in her eyes had suggested she did.

He had a sudden urge to blow off the rest of the afternoon, head down to the marina, and throw back a couple of beers with whoever was hanging around. Drown out the memories. But he was no longer a rebellious, fatherless teenager. He had obligations now that didn't afford him the luxury of wasted time.

Or pretty blue-eyed girls, for that matter. Especially a girl with more baggage than she would pull out of the trunk of that Civic.

He jogged down the rickety back steps. There was another Still Waters project that would have to wait for another day. He heaved the toolbox onto his truck bed with renewed vigor. Time to check on the window-repair crew out at the Campbells' place on Jungle Road. And the Bells on Myrtle needed their deck braced. He set his mind back to where it belonged and backed out of Still Waters drive without another glance at the dusty silver car.

Chapter 5

"I'm going to get the rest of my stuff inside." Cora Anne dragged her old duffel to the narrow staircase in the front corner of the living room.

"Of course, dear. Can I help?"

She shook her head. "No way, Nan. You just stay in the cool." Surely climbing those steps again and again would calm Cora Anne's nerves. The more trips the better.

"All right, then. I'll just finish my solitaire." Nan retreated to the sun porch.

But it took only two trips to haul in the material wealth of Cora Anne's life. Upstairs, she dropped the last bag in the center of her old room with its peaked roof and view of the ocean. Legs quivery and stomach knotted, she sat on the edge of the bed, picking at the quilt Nan had made years ago when summers at Edisto were simple and uncomplicated by sadness.

She'd been prepared for the memories ... but not for Tennessee Watson himself. She flopped back on the bed with closed eyes.

He'd matured into a gracious young man. He ought to hate her—and this place. But there he was, on the back deck of Still Waters, helping fix the cottage. Polite. Jovial. He'd been her first crush for all those reasons.

The memory burned. Twelve years ago, Tennessee had sat with her on the beach while she sputtered and shook. It was an act of forgiveness and protection she didn't deserve and had never forgotten. Then today, he'd taken her hand and the embrace had been as warm and familiar as that long-ago July night.

"Darling, are you coming back down?" Nan's tone was patient, as if she could wait all day.

"Coming."

She opened her eyes and wrinkled her forehead. Her room was different. The original pine paneling had made it cozy but dark. Now the walls had been stripped and stained the color of honey. With the afternoon sun streaming through the windows, the planks glowed. Bright-colored throw rugs dotted the buffed and polished hardwood floor. Everything seemed tinted with gold, and the changes made her smile.

And frown. Her grandmother wasn't capable of work like this.

She descended the stairs, but not two at a time like she and Hannah had done as children, much to the chagrin of their mothers. Nan was in the kitchen. Her white hair was finger-waved to shoulders that stooped a bit more. Otherwise, in her floral capris and linen blouse, glasses hanging from a beaded chain around her neck, she was the same woman who'd always made Still Waters a summer home.

"There you are." Nan peered over the top of the refrigerator door. "Like your room?"

"It's ... lovely." Moving around the counter, Cora Anne took an avocado-colored Tupperware container from her grandmother's hands. "You sprucing this place up for somebody special?"

"Of course I am." She retrieved a salad already assembled in her blue willow bowl and hip-bumped the fridge door shut. "You're pretty special."

Cora Anne just shook her head. "I don't know if I'm special enough to be changing things for." They carried the food to a corner of the long dining table, which had always sat parallel to the sliding glass doors and the vast ocean beyond the back deck. Sunlight glittered on the sapphire sea and gulls cried along the beach below.

"Well, it's not just for you." Nan peeled saran wrap off the salad bowl. "Oh, go fetch the plates. I'm sure you stopped for lunch, but I'm also sure it was something terrible served in a paper bag."

She found the plates on the worn butcher-block countertop. "So what made you hire Tennessee Watson?" She rubbed her thumb along one shell-patterned edge and hoped the question seemed casual.

"Tennessee is building a business of his own, and you know your Granddaddy and I always believed in supporting local folks. Edisto has to function in the off season, too, you know." Her grandmother lowered her glasses and fixed Cora Anne with a direct gaze, as if she were single-handedly responsible for the welfare of Edisto's local businesses.

Cora Anne dropped her eyes and unfolded a napkin in her lap. "So he took over his dad's business? I'm sure that made his mom happy."

"Grace is quite pleased he's settling down, yes." Nan opened the Tupperware full of boiled shrimp. "Already peeled these for you. Remembered how you hate their legs."

She smiled and held out her plate for what was sure to be a large helping. Nan didn't believe in moderation. "Thank you."

"Besides, Tennessee is just so handy, and so nice to look at, that I kept coming up with more jobs."

Cora Anne rolled her eyes. "Really, Nan? You're keeping him around just to look at?"

"There are worse reasons to keep someone around."

She shook her head. "You're impossible." Poking at her pale pink shrimp, she asked the nagging question. "So it's not hard for him, being here?"

"No." Nan pursed her lips. "Is it going to be hard for you?"

She sensed she was being watched carefully, as if she were one of those delicate mollusk shells that washed up on the beach and must be pried open gently so as not to damage the creature inside.

She forked a piece of lettuce and shrugged. "Of course not."

Nan stood. "I'm going to pour us some sweet tea. You sit and rest." She patted Cora Anne's shoulder. "Enjoy that shrimp. I got it fresh off the boat this morning."

Cora Anne ate her salad and watched the sky and the ocean through the glass doors and picture windows. At the edge of the sea, a dark line of clouds gathered, an afternoon storm blowing in for humidity relief.

"Do you want to see my list?" Nan asked.

"Sure."

Her grandmother had written the list on the back of a flyer advertising the return of summer bingo nights at the Lions Club.

"Looks doable." None of the projects appeared to require knowledge of power tools, so surely her contact—if any—with Tennessee Watson would remain minimal. Nan wanted fresh paint and linens, new pictures on the gallery wall, and closets purged and organized. The only task that gave Cora Anne qualms was the garden.

"What do you need a garden for, Nan? Between King's Market and George and Pink's, you can get all the produce you need. Support local business, you know." She twitched her eyebrows at her grandmother, who chuckled.

"I'd just like to grow my own tomatoes again, is all. Maybe some peppers and squash, too." She rose and stacked their plates. "You don't have to worry, hon. Tennessee said he'd be happy to help."

Cora Anne pressed her lips together and nodded.

Later that evening, when she went downstairs to the ground-level laundry room, she saw the beach towels already folded in a wicker basket. A smile tugged at the corners of her mouth. Nan had always provided their beach towels, usually whatever cartoon character or superhero was the current obsession.

Those lazy summer days spent searching for snail shells, playing cards on the screened porch, and begging for a third helping of homemade peach ice cream had been the very pulse of her life as a child.

Where was the old wooden ice cream churn? She shoved aside a plastic basket of sand toys and peered into the narrow closet. When she did, a red bucket tumbled over and landed at her feet. She froze.

The image swam before her eyes, the bucket bobbing on the white-capped waves, the sky behind growing darker with each moment. Somehow, that summer she turned eleven, her mother had time to dig dirt with babies but not swim with her.

She had lost it one day and thrown a hissy of a fit right there at the edge of the Atlantic Ocean. Kicking and screaming and throwing those pieces of plastic junk into the water as far and hard as she could until—

Her hand went to her cheek. Sometimes, she could still feel the sting her mother's slap had left. Sometimes, she could still hear the screams after she nearly drowned chasing that stupid red bucket after it reappeared later that evening, bobbing like a talisman on the rising waves.

Using her toe, she nudged the bucket into the closet. Best to forget it was even there. Better yet, she could toss it out when Nan added *organize laundry room* to her lengthy list.

Cora Anne leaned her elbows on the washing machine and dropped her head to her hands, trying to remember the good times. Like the beach towels. She caressed the coral and mint threads of one. Her mother would whip those towels in the breeze and grumble as sand blew back in her face. *Let it be*, Nan would say. *Sand in beach towels is such a trivial worry.*

Of course, back then, before she'd ruined it all, every worry on Edisto had been simple and trivial.

Chapter 6

She waded into the water. The waves were heavy and the sand was already pulling from beneath her feet, but she kept going. Someone screamed at her to come back, but she ignored the plea. The foam crashed over her head and she struggled to right herself. She was waist-deep and determined. Wet braids plastered against her back, and she fought her way. Just a little farther and she'd show them …

Suddenly, she was under and didn't know which way was up. She kicked and thrashed and tried to get above the crushing weight of water. Her toes sought purchase on the sandy bottom that was being sucked back into the sea. The riptide was strong, and she was weak. She would drown because she was a stupid little girl seeking attention.

An arm encircled her waist, and a hand forced her head up and over the crest of tormenting waves. He told her to swim and she did, parallel to the shore like all the signs on the beach showed. He was with her, and she felt another wave buoy her up and send her home. No longer was she being drug back into the depths. She stumbled, gasping, onto the shore. More arms pulled her over the line of pulverized shells that scraped her knees. She was safe, but there was still so much screaming …

Cora Anne always woke with the screams. She lay stiff in her narrow twin bed and panted shallow breaths. She closed her eyes and whispered the words she'd always used, even though they'd never seemed to work. "I'm sorry. I'm so, so sorry."

She breathed, slow and deep. Opening her eyes, she noticed that even in this hour before the dawn, her little room no longer seemed dark. She glanced over her shoulder at the new alarm with its CD player and glowing green numbers. Exactly six. Perhaps the sunrise would force her fears back to their depths.

"You're up early." Annie entered her kitchen while belting her light-blue cotton robe. She appraised her namesake as Cora Anne expertly poured steaming water into the pot of an old-fashioned tea set.

"I thought we could have tea on the deck and watch the sun rise."

"Well, now, sounds like someone's remembering what this place is really good for."

Her granddaughter lifted the wicker tray with its bounty of porcelain and banana bread.

"Found yourself a snack, did you?" Annie followed her over to the glass doors that welcomed sunlight and ocean views into her home at every meal.

Cora Anne bent her head over the tray as she inhaled. "Banana bread might be my only weakness, Nan."

"Oh, sweetheart, if only we all had but one." She flipped the bolt and tugged at the door. "It sticks sometimes," she said by way of explanation when Cora Anne raised her eyebrows.

Of course, it didn't help this was an old door, swollen heavy with years of humidity, and she was an old woman with hands swollen stiff with the pangs of arthritis.

Outside was quiet and calm. The rhythmic beating of waves on the shore sounded beyond the bank of sand dunes. Still Waters sat on a large lot, and a yard with sandspur-laden grass stretched between the deck and the dunes. There was a faded gazebo, and a hammock swung in the slight breeze beneath a couple palmetto trees. A buckling old boardwalk linked the narrow path over the dunes to the back steps of the deck.

Annie pointed to the boardwalk as Cora Anne set the tray on a side table. "Tennessee says we should replace that."

"He does, huh? Bet there's a lot around here he thinks we should replace."

Annie watched her girl settle into a rickety Adirondack chair and tuck her right leg under her knee. Making her nest. If only her little bird felt safe here …

Annie poured the tea and watched her granddaughter watch the sun rise. It began with a slow, burning glow that was more orange than pink, and edged timidly over the horizon. The palmettos and sea oats in the foreground were black against the light. Then, in the time it took Annie to slow-blink, the ball of fire eased up and streaked the sky a deep wash of purple.

The sunrise always reminded her of giving birth. How one moment there was just pushing and glimpses of a crowning head, and then in a breath, there was life. She looked away from the sun to the vista before her of still-dark sea and sand. She thought she saw movement on the beach, a man with a fishing pole perhaps? But the tide was high and so were the dunes, so she couldn't be sure. Her Thornton used to like fishing at dawn. She'd always suspected it was less about the fish than it was the quiet clean of a new morning.

Annie leaned back and ran a hand over the worn armrest of her chair. She'd asked Tennessee about refinishing this furniture, too. Maybe best not to mention that yet.

"It's peaceful." The words were a whisper, as though Cora Anne couldn't believe them herself.

Annie smiled gently. "I've been telling you that for years."

"I just …" She tilted her head against her shoulder and sighed deeply. "I just always wonder now, what awful thing will happen next?"

Annie laid her hand with its gnarled knuckles and simple gold band on the child's knee. "Darling, there is a time to weep and a time to laugh. I think it's about time I heard you laugh again."

Her granddaughter slipped her hand into Annie's. "I promise I'll try. That's the best I can do."

Annie squeezed her knee. "Well, you better. Otherwise, I'll have to get Hannah over here, too, and then we'll never hear the end of how many weddings we ruined."

She chuckled. "You'd think she was a surgeon or something with the way she and Aunt Caro are about that business."

"Exactly. But I put my foot down this year. We're having a reunion. A real one with everyone."

The teacup twisted in her hands. "Do you think they'll all come, really?"

Annie nodded. "Oh, yes. That's why you're here now, dear. To help me get this old house ready and guilt everyone into coming."

"A real reunion …" She shoved her unruly hair behind one ear. "It's been a long time, Nan. You sure you're up for all that?"

"Do I look like I have one foot in the grave? It's time. Been long enough without, and I've got things to say that I'm only saying once when everyone can hear." Annie picked up her tea and cut a glance at this stubborn granddaughter. "Are you going to help me?"

The smile almost reached her eyes. "Do I have a choice?"

Chapter 7

"Nan, why in the world is all this in here?" Cora Anne stood on a stepladder and tugged another box free from the front closet. Nan had called these mementos. Looked more like junk. "You have a plenty big enough house at the farm."

"Well, it's full, dear. We've lived there over fifty years, you know."

She bit her tongue as she always did when Nan casually slipped. Fifty years was a long time to have been a *we*. Her grandmother was entitled to forget occasionally.

"You know," Nan peered into an old box emblazoned with Stride Rite on the side. "I think I put some of this up there when your mama was young and bossy like you."

"Ha, ha."

Nan pulled out a stack of scalloped black-and-white photos. "I'd forgotten all about these."

"Let me see." She stepped down and leaned over Nan's shoulder. The picture showed two young girls on the old front steps of Still Waters. The cherubic little girl with blond curls, wearing a smocked dress with a lace collar and neatly folded socks, had to be Aunt Caro. Beside her, in a matching dress with an untied sash that hung below her knees and no socks in her mary janes, had to be Lou.

"I believe my mama was a hot mess back then." But *mess* would never describe Louisa Coultrie Halloway now.

"She was." Nan's brows drew together as she brought the photo up to her nose. "She hated that dress, so I bribed her with ice cream. Believe we were headed to a singing at the church that night." She dropped it back in the box and picked up another. "Look at this."

Even in an old, creased photograph, the mischief sparkling in Uncle Jimmy's brown eyes reminded Cora Anne of the triplets. This would be the perfect project for her to execute this summer.

"Nan?"

"Yes, dear?" Her grandmother lifted the lid on a box marked "Louisa".

"Can I catalog these? Organize them by years and put them into albums?"

Nan looked up, a spark in her blue eyes. "That would be wonderful. I think …" She replaced the lid on what appeared to be a box of letters and flipped through a stack of glossy black and whites. "Yes, I used to be real good about writing dates." She showed Cora Anne the penciled date on the back of one. "See, 1958. Our first new car." A young couple sitting on the hood of an old car, the dirt road tunneled by live oaks. With a sheepish shrug, she said, "I guess I was just no good at actually putting them someplace safe."

Cora Anne eyed the dated images Nan had hung as a gallery wall, and then shifted her gaze to the worn furniture draped with crocheted afghans. She'd been sitting there, tucked in the corner of the sofa under that blue blanket, the night her father told her he'd be moving out when they returned to Marietta. She blinked and glanced at the threadbare armchair where her grandfather had been sitting one minute, teasing her about school, and then slumped over and never spoke again.

Through the bank of windows along the back of the house, the ocean glittered, a constant reminder of how quickly life and tides changed.

For two straight days, Cora Anne sorted the disarray of pictures, paperwork, discarded games, and general family hodgepodge the closet had contained. Now, organizing and cataloging the pictures would keep her hands and mind busy. Far too busy to dwell on the recurring nightmares.

"I think you've breathed about enough of this dust for today." Nan plucked a stack from Cora Anne's hands and laid it out of reach at the far end of the table.

"I'm on a roll here."

"Nope, you're on a break. Let's go to lunch."

Cora Anne sighed and chewed her lip. She didn't need a break. Or lunch. Or small talk with the locals.

But of course, when she and Nan climbed the worn wooden steps into McConkey's Jungle Shack, Tennessee Watson sat hunched in the corner of the deck under a red umbrella. With his head bent over paperwork, he'd never have noticed them if Nan hadn't called out, "Yoohoo, Tennessee! How are you, dear?"

Cora Anne cringed. He looked up and grinned—a wide, expansive smile that jolted her back to carefree days.

"I'm wonderful, Mrs. Annie. How are you?" His eyes slid over Nan and landed on her.

"We are right as rain and hungry as the gulls." Nan leaned over and mock whispered, "I told my girl the secret about these fish tacos."

His laugh was the same. A rumbling chuckle that gently quaked his broad shoulders. "Pull up a chair."

Now they had gone too far. Cora Anne tugged Nan's elbow. "We don't want to intrude." She jerked her chin at his scattered paperwork. "You look busy."

"Oh, I'm never too busy for lunch with pretty ladies." Smoothly, he cleared the table. Nan settled herself across from him, leaving Cora Anne the plastic chair between. She perched on its edge and busied her hands with a menu. His eyes kept flicking to her and the familiar tangle of knots started in her stomach. Nan prattled on about the weather and renovations.

"I'll get that boardwalk replaced by the weekend, no problem. We're between big jobs right now, so I've got crew to spare." Tennessee looked at her again. "That okay? Or will we be in the way?"

He seemed so calm, so sure of himself, not the man wracked by life and left to struggle she'd always envisioned.

Cora Anne twisted a loose strand of her hair. "No, I've got work in the house to do." Untangling her finger, she drummed the tabletop. Where was a server? "Actually, Nan, let's go over the list and pick up a few things while we're out."

Nan's hand reached for Cora Anne's fidgeting one. "Work, work, work. Can you believe I haven't even let this girl go down to the beach yet?"

Tennessee's brown eyes shadowed for a moment, but then he grinned. "Well, now, Mrs. Annie, let's fix the boardwalk so we can do something about that."

After the server took their orders, Cora Anne excused herself. Tennessee watched her retreat, wishing she'd let her long, dark hair swing around her cheeks again instead of pulling it up in that knot.

Mrs. Annie said with a sigh, "I've got her here. Now it's up to her and the good Lord to make peace."

Tennessee stretched his long legs under the table. If nervous cues were any indication, peace was pretty far from that girl's agenda. "I'd like to help her, you know. Get to know her a little bit. But I don't get the impression she wants me around."

"You're a reminder. Cora Anne doesn't like reminders unless they're already written in her planner."

Tennessee leaned forward. "How much have you told her, Mrs. Annie?"

"Not enough and already more than she can handle."

He raised his brows. "But I'll have a crew out at your farmhouse through late June, at least."

"No reason we need to go there anytime soon. I'll tell her when the time is right." Her hand shook a bit as she lifted the plastic cup of tea. "And you've drawn up paperwork for the other?"

"Yes, ma'am. That's a beautiful piece we'll be able to preserve."

"Preserve?" Cora Anne had returned to the table.

Her grandmother's face smoothed of worry. "Tennessee here was telling me about the land trust's latest conquests. He's a member of the board, you know. Quite an honor for one so young."

Cora Anne's eyes shifted between them, and Tennessee felt uneasiness curl in his belly. Clearly, Annie Coultrie had no intention of letting her family in on this secret either.

The server delivered baskets of fish tacos to the women and set a hamburger and fries down for him. Lacing his fingers together, he offered to pray.

"Yes, please." Mrs. Annie bowed her head, but Cora Anne's gaze lingered on his with a touch of accusation. Her grandmother should watch out for that intuition.

He prayed succinctly and with conviction, "Father, thank you for this food, this company, and this blessing of life. Amen."

Mrs. Annie echoed his amen, but her granddaughter shifted her attention to the tacos and didn't speak again until everyone was halfway done.

"What's the land trust?"

Tennessee wiped his mouth. "Edisto Island Open Land Trust. It's a non-profit organization committed to preserving tracts of undeveloped property so the island can maintain much of its natural state."

"Like the National Registry of Historic Homes, but for property?"

"That's a good comparison. Ownership remains intact, but together, we place certain restrictions on the land's development and cultivation."

"That's a good idea for this place." She seemed genuinely interested. "Keeps it unchanged." But then her demeanor shifted. "At least for those who appreciate it."

Tennessee cocked his head. Her grandmother was right. Cora Anne had shut herself off from this world.

"You know"—Mrs. Annie dabbed her mouth— "once that boardwalk is finished, we can tackle my garden."

Cora Anne crossed her arms. "Nan, you know Tennessee's not running a handyman business." Her tone dared him to contradict.

"Well, for some folks, I am. Mrs. Annie's a lot less demanding than people who just buy property here for the investment."

She rolled her eyes. "I think I can handle planting a few tomatoes."

"Ah, but can you build me some of those fancy boxes—what are they called?" Mrs. Annie furrowed her brow.

"Raised beds?" Cora Anne's smile revealed affection, for her grandmother at least, must still linger despite her hardened persona.

Mrs. Annie clapped her hands. "Exactly. Can we plan for next week?"

"Whatever you want, Mrs. Annie."

"Cora, dear, you'll have to drive me to town for seedlings."

"Whatever you want, Nan." She actually grinned at him a bit as she parroted his words.

"You know …" Mrs. Annie turned that innocent gaze between them. "Tennessee has been blessed to work a variety of jobs. Maybe you should talk to him about what all he's been up to since you were children."

He shook his head. Incorrigible, that's what this woman was.

"I'm sure he has enough work to keep him busy." Cora Anne pulled a list from her back pocket. "And so do we. Thanks for letting us join you." She stood and slipped a hand beneath her grandmother's elbow.

"Well, all right, then." Mrs. Annie shook a bit as she stood. "Tennessee, we'll see you soon."

Cora Anne grimaced but covered it with a tight smile when he caught her eye. Nudging her grandmother along, she flicked her hand at him in farewell. In return, he tipped his Citadel ball cap like a proper Southern gentleman.

He sat a few minutes after they'd left, eyes settled on the strip of sea glinting beyond the Piggly Wiggly's parking lot and Edisto's front-row houses. He'd fix that boardwalk and plant a garden. Maybe ask a few questions, see if he could break through Cora Anne's shell and find the girl he remembered.

Chapter 8

After Cora Anne backed out of the drive Monday morning with Nan in the passenger seat, jotting a list, Tennessee pulled in. She raised a few fingers in acknowledgement without letting go of the wheel. Yesterday, in a brief conversation during his break from repairing the boardwalk, they'd agreed. He'd build the beds while she took Nan over to visit Uncle Jimmy at the nursery in Walterboro. Since he'd proven himself so efficient, Cora Anne bet Tennessee would be done and gone before they returned. At least, that was her hope.

Too bad she didn't set much store in hope anymore.

They returned in the early afternoon, stomachs full of the buffet lunch from Duke's Barbecue. In the backseat nestled tiny green shoots of tomatoes, squash, peppers, and basil, because Nan liked the smell.

"It's been years since I've bothered with fresh herbs," she had confessed, inhaling the fragrance. "But who knows? Maybe I'll be inspired."

Cora Anne had shrugged. "Maybe." Then she'd loaded the plants and listened to Uncle Jimmy's advice about watering.

When they returned, Tennessee's truck took up half of the drive, so Cora Anne had to scoot Nan's sedan around him to park in the cool under the house. Still Waters sat too low for his massive Dodge, but just right for her little Civic and Nan's hardly used car.

She held her grandmother's arm as they walked around back to check the progress. Nan seemed a little wobbly after their long morning and Cora Anne felt worn out herself. Must be the sugar crash from Duke's sweet tea.

In the backyard, tucked up next to the concrete patio that led into the downstairs storage, Tennessee had built three rectangular boxes of lumber. He emptied another bag of potting soil into the last one as they rounded the corner.

"Oh, these look wonderful." Nan pulled her arm away and stepped carefully over the sandspur-laden grass. "Can't you just see me picking tomatoes from here? I won't have to bend over at all if these plants grow like Jimmy promised."

"Glad you like them, Mrs. Annie." He tossed the empty bag with the others in the yard and smiled over Nan's shoulder at Cora Anne, who stepped back.

Why did he always seem glad to see her?

Perspiration darkened the edges of his blond hair and ringed the collar of his old Citadel t-shirt. The knees of his carpenter jeans were green with grass stains. When he swiped a gloved hand across his jaw, a smudge of dirt got left behind.

She drew her breath. He'd been working hard, and she ought to be more grateful Nan's list didn't put him out.

"I'll bring the plants around and work on getting them in the ground." She offered a nod of thanks toward Tennessee and patted her grandmother's shoulder. "Why don't you go on upstairs and rest?"

"You know, I believe I will." She started up the back steps with a firm grip on the rail. "Oh, Tennessee ..." She paused, and he looked up from gathering the trash. "Why don't you help Cora Anne with those plants? I wouldn't want my tomatoes damaged just because her mama never taught her right."

"Sure thing, Mrs. Annie."

Cora Anne strode back to the car. Fine, then. Nan could trust her with irreplaceable photographs of family history but not a few tomato plants.

She hefted a flat of the seedlings and nearly collided with Tennessee coming around the corner of the house.

"Whoa, there, girl." He put his hands on her shoulders. They were warm and steady.

Heat rushed her cheeks. "Sorry." She pulled away and sidestepped him. Apologies were all she would ever have to offer this man.

In the corner of the yard stood a small garden shed her grandfather had built. She pulled open its doors in search of gloves and a small shovel. The shed was in as much disarray as the closets had been in the house. She added it to her mental checklist of plans that would keep her hands busy and her mind occupied. A set of worn gloves peeked out from an old sand bucket on a shelf, so she grabbed those and pulled them on.

"That place could use a good clean-out unless you want to worry about snakes."

She spun around and set her gaze on Tennessee, perfectly at ease with a flat of plants under each arm.

"I'll take care of it. Nan does trust me with inanimate objects." Though snakes were another matter ...

He grinned and shook his head, blond hair falling over his bandana, just as it had when he'd been a teenager. "Wow."

"What?"

"Who'd have guessed you'd grow up to be so surly?"

She propped hands on her hips. "Who'd have guessed you'd grow up to be my grandmother's handyman?" A prickly nature kept people from getting close. She'd figured that out a while ago.

He held her gaze. Where was his anger—simmering below the surface of that easy, confident grin? And why was he still here, anyway? She'd have gotten as far from Edisto Beach as possible.

Breathe. She only had to get through the next thirty minutes. How long did it really take to plant a tiny garden anyway?

But there was that dimpled grin again. "I enjoy the company." He cocked his eyebrow. "And the paycheck."

Of course. Nan probably paid him twice what was necessary. Guilt twinged. Technically, Nan paid her too. "Just tell me what to do so she doesn't complain."

"So she doesn't complain, or so she thinks you did a good job?" Tennessee drew his brows together. "Because that's not the same thing."

She blew out a breath. Sweat trickled down her back.

"Because you seem like someone who'd be more concerned with a job *well* done versus just done."

She eyed him. How did he know that? "I'm listening."

He helped her set out the seedlings, lifting them gently in their compostable pots and loosening the roots so the tiny sprigs would find purchase in the soil. He didn't ask her any questions, just offered straightforward guidance in a no-nonsense manner. He wasn't overly friendly, but he wasn't cold either.

When Cora Anne set the last of the plants in the shallow hole and covered it over with dirt, he nodded. "From boogie boarding to garden planting." That grin again. "Looks like you still take directions well."

The composure she'd built up weakened. He'd bestowed that same smile on her so many summer afternoons of their childhood. "You always were a good teacher."

He rocked back on his heels. "Listen, Cor, we should really talk about—"

"Is Nan calling me?" She stood quickly and clapped the rich, black soil from her gloves before peeling them off. "You go. I'll finish up."

He stood. Thank goodness, he could take a hint. "Sure. But want me to water?"

"No, I got it. I'll come back out in a bit."

"Okay, but don't wait too long."

She nodded, moving toward the porch. Yes, Uncle Jimmy had said that too. Make sure to water. Surrounded by the ocean, but the seedlings would die of thirst without fresh water.

"Cora Anne?"

She glanced over her shoulder where he stood in the fiery glow of the low-hanging sun. For a moment, she saw his father as he'd last looked, backlit by the sunset and shouting at her to stay out of the water. Then he shaded his face with a gloved hand and grinned up at her, no shadow of a ghost.

"Even if you forget, plants are pretty forgiving. Just soak 'em good."

Her feet fumbled on the steps as she wondered—surely people weren't as forgiving as plants.

Chapter 9

Her internal alarm nudged her awake the next morning. Cora Anne lifted her arms above her head and stretched, toes touching the end of her narrow twin bed.

A worn copy of *Savannah* borrowed off her grandmother's shelf slid to the floor. She had read herself to sleep with distraction—and trepidation—the nightmare expected with Tennessee's warm smile in her consciousness.

But sleep had been deep and uninhibited. For the first time since graduation, she felt truly rested. Outside her window, Edisto stirred awake. Suddenly, she wanted to see if everything else really had stayed the same.

On the front steps, Cora Anne laced shoes that hadn't seen pavement since she'd left Athens. Better take this slow. Stretching quickly, she settled into a jog. This morning, the sun would rise at her back as she explored a path she'd almost forgotten.

Gulls cried, swooping into the outgoing tide. But she left the ocean and let Edisto Street take her down to join the bike path that hugged the curve of the island. A fisherman with tackle box and pole in one hand, a chair slung over his shoulder, and a soft brimmed hat hiding his eyes, nodded briefly when she passed him on his trek to the surf.

When she turned down Jungle Road, the silence hung heavier. Homes here nestled among the oaks, scrub pines, and yucca plants. Soon, she approached a row of modest townhomes, sheltered by the shade of thick palmettos and ancient oaks. Spanish moss draped over winding limbs.

Now these were something new.

She turned down the narrow, freshly graveled street. The homes faced the marsh and, painted subdued hues, contented themselves as part of the landscape.

A widow's walk caught her attention and as she looked up, her right foot twisted in the loose gravel. She landed knee-first with a jolt that stung more than stunned. Groaning, she pushed herself up and saw the cause. One of those far-reaching live oak roots. Thank goodness no one saw that display of grace.

A door clicked closed and she whipped her head around.

Tennessee Watson leaned on the porch rail of the home she'd just passed. "You all right?" One corner of his mouth tilted up.

Did the man have to laugh every time he saw her? She inspected her scraped and throbbing knee.

"I'm fine. Just wasn't watching my feet."

"Well, that was obvious."

Shading her eyes with her hand, she winced at him. "Well, construction zones are hazardous."

He grinned even wider, which only irritated her more. She could accept—even expect—his resentment, but she didn't know how to contend with this friendly demeanor.

He spread his arms. "This isn't a construction zone. It's all finished and move-in ready."

"Of course it is. As long as you don't mind tripping over tree roots in your driveway." She glanced at a sign in the yard. Watson Custom Homes. How had she missed that? And she'd been headed right toward his big white truck parked at the end of this little street.

"I guess you built these?"

He trotted down the steps, his boots echoing in the still morning. Standing in front of her, he blocked the sun that beamed through the screen of tree limbs overhead. "Actually, my crew did. I drew the plans and oversaw construction in between all the little jobs I had." He smirked as he hooked thumbs in his belt loops. "Like rebuilding boardwalks and planting tomatoes at your grandmother's place."

She crossed her arms. "No one said it had to be you doing all that. You have a crew. Send them if you don't want to work at Still Waters."

Tennessee drew his eyebrows together and squinted at her. "Why would I not want to work there? Still Waters is one of my favorite places on the beach, and Dad always said it was a solid place he loved maintaining."

At the mention of his father, Cora Anne hugged herself tighter and looked away across the marsh.

"So what do you think of these?" He swept an arm toward his handiwork. Cora Anne heard the pride in his voice and willed herself to be friendlier. After all, he hadn't lashed out at her. Not yet, anyway.

"I think they look cozy and homey." She gazed at the tranquil surroundings, and her shoulders relaxed. "They blend in well here."

"Well, good, because that's what I was going for. They're locally sourced and eco-friendly, too. See the solar panels?"

She nodded mutely. Since living here was nowhere on her life's agenda, she didn't really care.

His smile became sheepish. "Well, anyway, I just like reminding folks what Edisto gives."

"Right ..." He seemed so happy, so content. For a moment, his father's laughing face flickered in her mind, and she spoke without thinking. "But Edisto takes away, too."

His eyes flashed, and she shut hers. *Stupid.*

"I'm sorry." She spun on her heel, hoping to make a hasty exit.

Tennessee reached out and grabbed her arm. She didn't see that coming, just like she hadn't seen the tree root. His hand felt warm for so early in the morning, and she caught her breath.

"I think ..." He paused, and she bit her lip. Here it came. The long overdue anger. "You need to know I'm all right."

Not what she'd expected. Then again, Edisto never was. Cora Anne swallowed hard. "Good, then." She tried to duck away, but he still held her arm.

"Please look at me."

She lifted her head and met his eyes, deep brown and searching hers.

"It wasn't your fault, and I've never been mad at you."

His kind words were still a punch in her gut. "Is this really a conversation we want to have first thing in the morning?"

"Guilt's been written all over your face since the night my dad drowned, and I'm tired of seeing it there. You've grown up far too beautiful to let this haunt you anymore."

Tears pinpricked her eyes. She broke his gaze and pulled away. "I appreciate that, really. But we can't go rewriting history, so I guess we'll just both have to go on living with it."

He sighed. "Fine. We'll talk later."

She shook her head. "Later?"

No way was she having this conversation.

"Yeah, I'm headed back over to Still Waters this afternoon. Promised your grandmother I'd paint the deck chairs."

"She didn't tell me you were coming over again."

His lips curled. "Well, now, Cora Anne." He said her name with the slow drawl of the Lowcountry, *Corr-aa E-an.* Almost musical. "Don't you know life is full of surprises?"

"I'm not really good with surprises." She turned before he could ask more. "Got to get back." Her knee throbbed as she jogged away. Nothing about this morning was going as planned.

"Are you running the bike trail?"

"Yes." She stopped and rubbed her joint.

"The whole thing?"

"That was the idea."

"It's five miles."

"I know." She pushed wisps of sweaty hair out of her face. At this rate, she'd be walking for sure.

"I just never figured you for the type who runs five miles for fun."

She tossed her ponytail. "Well, life's just full of surprises isn't it?" That came out more flirtatious than she'd planned.

He waved, shot her a smile, and she could feel the dazzle even fifty feet away. Ducking her head, she picked up her pace, refusing to acknowledge Tennessee Watson's smile gave her the same feeling of homecoming she'd experienced driving onto Edisto the week before.

Chapter 10

In the kitchen of Still Waters, Cora Anne grabbed a bottle of water and climbed on a barstool at the peninsula. "I ran into Tennessee Watson over on Jungle Road at those new townhomes."

Her grandmother stood at the stove, cracking eggs in a bowl, determined to fix a proper breakfast since she decreed cereal to be a waste of good milk.

"What were you doing there?"

"Admiring."

"Him or the homes?"

"Nan!" Cora Anne felt heat creep up her chest. "The homes, of course. Anyway, he said you lined him up for another project." She took a long sip of water. "Painting the deck furniture? Really, I promise I could watch a YouTube video and do it correctly."

Nan poured the eggs into her cast iron skillet. "When one has a job to do, it's best to have someone with expertise do it." She sprinkled salt and pepper over the pan. "That's why I've asked you to chronicle family history, and I've asked the professional to paint my deck furniture."

She scowled. "He's a *builder*. And a pretty good one from what I can tell."

Nan gave the eggs a stir and opened the cabinet for plates. "Tennessee Watson is many things these days, dear. I told you already, get to know him a little better and find out. I'll bet he could use a hand scraping those chairs."

She doubted he needed her help with anything. "If you want me to, I will. But I'm here to help *you*."

With fluttering eyelashes, Nan patted her arm. "Would you help me out today by making sure Tennessee Watson knows I want my deck chairs sanded smooth as a baby's bottom?"

Water caught in her throat, and she sputtered. "Well, that's *not* the phrase I'll be using." Narrowing her eyes at her grandmother, she said, "Why do I get the feeling this is a set-up?"

"Because it is." Nan scooped scrambled eggs onto plates. "I'm just saying— he's a cute, nice boy. You're a sweet, beautiful girl. What's wrong with having a bit of fun?"

"Seriously? With Tennessee Watson?" She took a drink to clear her throat. "He's at least five years older than me, we have next to nothing in common, and let's not even mention the obvious."

"What's that?" Nan picked up the plates and started to the table, but Cora Anne jumped up to take them from her.

"Would you let me help you already?" She heard the harshness in her voice and hung her head. "I'm sorry. It's just I came all this way and changed all my plans so *I* could be the one you need."

Early morning joy depleted, she carried the plates to the table and pulled out her grandmother's favorite chair. Nan came up beside her and slipped an arm around her waist.

"Having you here is all I wanted, baby girl." She waved her hand at the cluttered table. "Look at what you've already done. I can't believe all this was collecting dust in the closet."

As they ate, Cora Anne sifted idly through a pile of pictures, checking the backs for dates. An old three-by-five photo with the soft sepia tones of the early seventies caught her eye. Setting down the rest of the stack, she peered more closely at this one. A young woman with dark hair and a serene smile, wearing a sweet dress of green chiffon and a corsage of baby roses on her arm, leaned into a young man. He was tall and trim, with honey-gold hair and laughing eyes. Cora Anne recognized them both, but it made no sense. She laid the picture down in front of her grandmother and spoke softly.

"That's my mother."

Nan scrutinized the photo beneath the slender lens of her reading glasses. She laid it back on the table and met Cora Anne's eyes. "Yes, it is."

"And that man she's with ..."

"That is Patrick Watson, yes."

She rubbed her chest. How was he everywhere?

Nan scooted closer and put her hand on Cora Anne's shoulder. "They were college sweethearts … I would have thought your mother told you sometime."

She breathed in, slow and deep past the tightness in her chest. Just like when she'd run that morning. "No." Pressed fingers against her temples. "I guess that's why she took it so hard, then." Listened to her grandmother's even breathing for a clue. "When he drowned. Do you remember how inconsolable she was?" *And how my father could do nothing to calm her?*

Nan kneaded her shoulder gently. "I do. I'm sorry, sweetie. I guess your mama figured that was a piece of her past you didn't need to share."

She picked up the picture again. "They looked happy." Something she hadn't seen in her mother in a long time. "What happened?"

Nan chuckled. "Well, dear, I would think you'd be glad that didn't work out. Otherwise you wouldn't be here."

She chewed her lip. What if she learned Lou had loved Patrick and her dad had only been a consolation choice? Maybe her mother's guilt was the answer to why her parents had ultimately split.

Cora Anne knew a thing or two herself about living with a daily burden. "I'd like to know."

"Well, for that answer, you're going to have to ask your mama. She never really told me."

Of course not. That was Lou, always silent. "But you know anyway, don't you?"

"I have my speculations."

She scrutinized her grandmother's innocent expression. "Is this why you keep pushing Tennessee and me together?"

The sparkle came back into Nan's eyes. "Just because things didn't work out for your mama, doesn't mean you don't deserve the opportunity for a little happiness."

Questions swirled in her mind. She needed to categorize, calculate before seeking answers. But—she slumped in the chair. "You really think I'll find some getting to know Tennessee Watson?"

Nan laid her palm, cool and smooth, against Cora Anne's cheek. "I really do, sweetheart. I really do."

Chapter 11

By the time Tennessee knocked on the back-door glass that afternoon, Cora Anne had done as her grandmother asked and "prettied up." Meaning she'd showered and put on a clean tank and shorts.

He looked the same as he had that morning in paint splattered t-shirt and old jeans. But his smile when she tugged open the heavy door was even more radiant than it had been in the early morning sun. She felt butterflies in her belly. His father died, but he'd said he was all right. Perhaps that was true, and he didn't resent her. But she couldn't see how.

"Hey." He leaned in but didn't cross the threshold. "Garden's looking good."

"Well, it's only been one day." But she'd soaked the plants according to instruction and decided that garden would thrive, no matter what.

"First few days are important." He glanced around. "You care to let your grandmother know I'm getting started out here?"

"She asked me to give you a hand." Cora Anne shrugged, hoping he got the impression this hadn't been her idea. "But I'll let her know." She stepped back, leaving the door open. To her surprise, he stepped inside and shut it smoothly behind him.

"You want anything?" She retreated toward the kitchen. "A drink, a snack?"

"No, I'm good."

So it would seem. She hurried down the short hallway off the kitchen to poke her head into Nan's bedroom.

"I'll be outside." Cora Anne purposely left off *with Tennessee*, but Nan's eyebrows rose just the same.

"All right. Don't get too hot." She turned a page in *Southern Living*. "Oh, and sweetheart, don't forget you're not ten years old anymore."

Cora Anne gaped, but Nan read her magazine as though she found an article about biscuit-making far more interesting than this conversation.

Back in the main room, Cora Anne found Tennessee studying the table of photographs with undisguised interest.

She moved to his side and slipped the photo of Lou and Patrick out of sight before he noticed. "You ready?"

"Sure." But he continued looking. "This is quite a collection."

"I'm trying to win Nan over to photo albums. She prefers to immortalize walls, and apparently, shoeboxes in the closet." She waved at the now-bare wall where she'd taken down previously framed photographs. Holes stood out on the wood she'd polished that morning while arguing mentally with her mother. She'd almost picked up the phone but remembered Lou would be teaching summer school all day.

Chuckling, he pointed to a five-by-seven of a young girl proudly holding up a string of fish, dark braids on either side of her head, eyes squinted at the sun. "This is you, right?"

"Yeah, I was like eight or something."

"Or something. I remember those braids. You used to chew the ends of them when you were nervous." He arched a brow. "Which was every time I took you out at high tide to ride the waves."

A blush crept up her neck. "Well, I used to be afraid of the big waves." Now, she just stayed out of the water. "Are we going to paint deck furniture or stroll down memory lane?"

He shrugged. "I figured both. You Coultrie kids were always multi-taskers. For instance, eating a popsicle while searching for shark's teeth."

"Yeah, that really qualifies." Her heart hammered. He wasn't in a hurry and she wasn't prepared for small talk.

But once outside on the wide back deck, he was all business. They covered the old floorboards—soft green worn silvery gray—with past issues of *The Press and Standard*. He explained Nan wanted the two Adirondack chairs and matching side table converted from their weathered stain to a crisp coastal white so they matched the newer patio set Uncle Jimmy had given her a few Mother's Days ago.

She nodded. "Whatever she wants. That's the plan this summer."

His brow creased as though he had a question he wasn't going to ask. They started sanding the remnants of stain off the chairs. "So, Atlanta, huh? That's where y'all still are?"

She scrubbed a little harder than necessary on the chair's arm with her sander. "Marietta, actually. That's where my parents and brothers are." She looked up at him. "Different houses, you know, now."

"I know. Your grandmother told me." He stood. "This one's pretty wobbly. I'm going to brace it some."

"Well, this furniture's nearly as old as the house, so that's no surprise."

He crossed to the bench that ran the length of the deck and popped open a drill case. "Your grandmother told me her father bought the land in the 1946 auction."

"That's right. When lots sold for as little as $250." History, she could talk. As long as it wasn't hers.

"Now, that's a steal." He looked out over the beach. "Bet he paid closer to five for it, though, because it's waterfront and here on the point. One of the pricier pieces."

She nodded in rhythm with her sanding. "Somebody knows his real estate."

"Comes with the territory." He fit a screw onto the driver and pressed it, whirring into the wood. He'd always been good at fixing things. "It true they met because she was lost?"

"My grandparents?" How did he know that?

He fitted another screw. "My dad told me that once."

"Oh …" *Wonder what else Patrick told you.* "Yeah, that's how they met. She ran into my granddaddy off Brick House Road while he was bundling pine straw. When he learned her name, he told her some Jenkins family history and took her to see the Brick House ruins."

Cora Anne paused and swiped the back of her hand across her forehead. She wanted to get the story right, but telling it made her ache for her grandfather. "Anyway, he hooked her with the notion she belonged here, so she broke her engagement and married him a month later. Caused quite the scandal, but …" She bit her lip. "Guess you could say it all worked out in the end."

"I'd say so. Profitable local business, nice family, house at the beach. What more could one want?"

She avoided looking at him. "Seems like you're all set then."

"Well, I'm still working on the family part. My mom is already dropping hints about grandchildren."

The sander fumbled right out of her hand. That part of any plan was so far away she couldn't even comprehend it. But obviously, he could.

She forced lightness into her voice. "Oh, yeah? Got some lucky girl in mind for that venture?"

Tennessee leaned over, his arms brushing hers so he could give her chair a good shake to check its stability. He tipped his head and looked down at her. "Maybe."

Breath strangled in her throat. He was entirely too close, too warm, and too handsome to look at her like that. Not to mention too tangled into her past. She stood up and put some distance between them. "Wow, it's hot already."

"Supposed to be a scorcher come mid-June." He had evidently judged the chair to be sturdy because he moved over and resumed sanding. "What we need is a good hurricane."

She raised her eyebrows. "That's funny coming from someone with a lot invested in hurricane-front property. All the work you've just done would go to waste."

He rolled a shoulder, working the sander over the chair's arms. "It's a fact of life. You need a storm every now and then to clear out the junk."

"I hardly think New Orleans believes that."

He rocked back on his heels. "Probably not. But they'll rebuild stronger. We always do."

"Or we just move on because there's nothing to fall back on."

"I get the feeling this is about more than a hurricane."

She huffed and swept wisps of hair back from her sweaty face. Between the humidity and this conversation, her shower had been useless. "I got waitlisted for Tulane. Not enough assistantships available for history research this year. Had to take a few cutbacks, you know. Focus on getting the school back up and running."

"I'm sorry."

Leaning against the deck rail, she studied him. He meant it. "Thanks."

"So no Plan B?"

She waved her sandpaper at Still Waters. "You're looking at it."

"You know, Cor, storms are facts of life. Sure as death and taxes. And sometimes they destroy what you spent your whole life building." He stood.

She noticed he no longer towered over her. As a girl, she'd tipped her chin to the sky in order to see his face. As adults, they could nearly look each other in the eye.

"Rebuilding's always possible." He nodded toward the cottage. "You just have to change your perspective. After Hugo, my dad helped your grandparents preserve the past and prepare for the future."

She followed his gaze over the little cottage. In the early nineties, after Hurricane Hugo, the porches had been rebuilt and expanded, and all new storm-hardy windows had been installed, though they'd salvaged the old awnings. That year, the cottage had gone from dingy gray to bright white with sage trim. Preserving the past. Planning for the future.

Evidently there *was* more to Tennessee Watson these days than a tool belt and hammer.

Tennessee kept the conversation peppered with light, surface-level questions throughout the afternoon. He told stories about growing up on Edisto and talked exuberantly of both his mother and father.

"She's from the hills, you know. How I got my name."

"Seems fitting. She didn't want to forget where she came from." *But I do.*

"Kinda like your grandpa and Mrs. Annie. He got her believing she belonged here."

She thought about the photograph of Patrick and her mother. Is that what happened? Lou didn't believe she belonged? Or maybe—she didn't want to stay?

"Did you stay because your mom did?" She wanted to know what kept him here.

He looked out across the Atlantic this time instead of looking at her with those frank brown eyes that had already probed too deep that day. "No." The answer wasn't swift, but it was curt. She took the hint.

"You still have that jet ski?"

His eyes crinkled when that lazy grin resurfaced. "Girl, I sold that thing years ago. Needed a trawling motor for running the creeks."

"Still catching your own supper?" He and his father used to bring them creek shrimp and buckets of blue crabs. He'd tease her by waving the claws at her nose and her mother would reach over and snatch the crab, dropping it in a pot of steaming water and slamming the lid.

"Sometimes. Want me to bring you something?" He winked and she turned away before he could see her blush.

Over the can of white paint, its fumes reminding her how easy it was to make something look new, he said, "You know, Cor, sometimes Plan B works out okay."

She scruffed the bristles of her brush through her fingers. "So it's working out for you?"

"You can run away from a place"—he swirled the paint—"but your past will still be there. Just because you leave it behind doesn't mean it's going anywhere."

The past doesn't have to go anywhere. It just has to stay here. Her hands shook as she dipped paint.

He bathed the chair with firm, even strokes of the paintbrush. "And this isn't my Plan B. It's the life I never knew I wanted."

She wanted to ask how he'd gotten to this place of peace—how he became this settled, steady man who could forgive her selfishness. But before she could say anything, the back door creaked open and Nan appeared.

"I've got cookies in the oven and lemonade, soon as y'all finish."

Tennessee ate six cookies, drank three glasses of lemonade, and told Nan she'd just paid him better than anyone else all year. She tossed her white curls, and Tennessee met Cora Anne's eyes over Nan's shoulder. Her heart fluttered a bit. His easygoing manner with her grandmother was admirable. Most young men she knew treated grandparents with a mixture of disdain and aloofness, disguised by sugarcoated formality.

When he picked up his toolbox and started down the back steps to his truck, Nan sidled over to Cora Anne. "Gracious, dear. Help the boy load his things. Manners, you know."

"Manners or matchmaking?"

"Well, you could use a little of both."

Cora Anne picked up the paint cans and bucket of brushes, partly to appease Nan, but mostly because today, she and Tennessee had almost bordered on friendliness.

Tromping down the stairs so Nan could deplore her lack of poise, she set the items on his tailgate.

"Hey, listen." He squatted in the truck bed securing his toolbox.

"Yes?"

"I'd feel wrong taking the full fee for the chairs. You did half the work."

"Don't worry about it. She probably should pay you more for watching me like a hawk so I wouldn't splatter the deck with paint."

And every time she had caught him watching her, she'd expected him to drop his gaze in embarrassment. Instead, those dimples deepened, and she was the one who looked away first.

"Sorry about that. Guess I'm still getting used to you being all grown up."

"Yeah, well, that happens. Time marching on and all that." She chewed her lower lip before exhaling slowly. This was too hard. "We're not kids anymore, Tennessee. We don't have to be friends just because our parents were."

"Good thing, because I'm not really interested in being your friend."

The words stung but she'd anticipated them since her first day back. Of course he wasn't because—

"I'd like to take you out. On a date. Not a friendly reunion."

Blinking, she stepped back. *This is not happening.*

He jumped down from the tailgate and stood in front of her. He raked his fingers through his hair, making it stand up in blond spikes. Maybe she wasn't the only one quaking at his request.

Nan's words came back to her—*You're not ten years old anymore.*

This time, the smile he offered waned. "If you don't want to, that's okay. I just thought we might have fun."

He'd offered her an out. She should definitely take it. But maybe—

"More fun than painting deck furniture?" She swallowed over the lump in her throat. His olive branch might give her, if not peace, at least a tolerance for this place.

He grazed her arm with the barest of touches and her pulse quickened.

"Absolutely more fun than painting deck furniture."

"I guess, then, it's a date." Those butterflies quick-stepped again in her belly.

His eyes brightened. "I'll pick you up tomorrow around eight. I like to work as much daylight as possible." He held out his hand.

"Eight's good." She put her hand in his. A perfect fit. He ran his thumb over the inside of her wrist in a gentle gesture both familiar and unsettling. She pulled back first, locked her arms behind her, and backpedaled toward the deck stairs.

"I better go check on Nan."

He waved, and Cora Anne climbed the stairs slowly, controlling her urge to run away. From Tennessee Watson and Edisto Island and everything about this place that reminded her, it was the last place she belonged.

Chapter 12

"Of course I don't have anything to wear, Hannah. I came here to help Nan, not date her handyman." Cora Anne jerked a shift dress out of her closet and held it up for scrutiny.

On the other end of the phone line, Hannah giggled. "I can't believe you're going out with Tennessee Watson. It's like a fairy tale."

"Or a nightmare. Depends on your perspective."

"Take it from the expert in this industry, Cor. You're destined for happily ever after."

With a huff, Cora Anne hung the dress back in her closet. She'd worn it to graduation and her dad had commented idly that it was shorter than usual, which set her mom on the defensive.

But Dad was right. The dress was a little shorter than necessary, which hadn't mattered under her black robe. But it might matter on a date she probably shouldn't be on.

"Do you still have those earrings I gave you?" Hannah's manicured nails must be drumming on the phone.

"The long dangly ones that get caught in my hair?"

"You mean the fun, sexy ones you should wear on a date? Put them on."

"With what? I can't just wear earrings."

"Well, you could, but I probably wouldn't on a *first* date."

"You're not helping." Cora Anne shoved hangers aside in the narrow closet. She shifted the phone to her other ear. "How about this?"

"What exactly am I telepathically seeing?"

"Jean skirt. Forgot I even owned it. But that's cute and classic, right?"

"Hm … don't you have a white blouse we bought in Charleston last year? Kind of a hippie thing?"

"Are you criticizing or suggesting?"

"I think that will work. Take a picture of yourself and text it to me."

"I'm not sure I know how that works."

Hannah huffed. "Sheesh, Cor. Get out of the past and into the twenty-first century, please."

Cora Anne found the shirt Hannah mentioned and fingered the crocheted edge of the linen. "Don't you think I'm trying?"

An hour later, having been pronounced suitable by Hannah and beautiful by Nan, she perched on the edge of an armchair and twisted a strand of hair around her finger.

Nan reached over and stilled Cora Anne's quivering knee. "Usually, we have hurricanes, dear. Not earthquake tremors."

She clasped hands in her lap and thought of the photograph on the table. "This is a bad idea."

"Why? Yesterday, you seemed to like Tennessee."

"I don't like him! I mean, I do, but not like, *like* him, like him." This wasn't a date, no matter what he called it. More like an apology. Which she should do over and over again until her soul absolved of guilt. She started pacing, arms crossed tight against her chest.

"Sometimes you remind me so much of your mama, I'd swear it was 1968 again," Nan said.

She stopped mid-turn. "I'm not sure that's a compliment."

Nan rose and came to her. The hands she placed on Cora Anne's shoulders were strong from years of farm work but soothing from decades of knowing how to love. "You let him see you for who you've become."

"But—"

Nan shook her head. "He's not afraid of that any more than he resents the child you were."

A timid knock sounded on the front door. Her grandmother patted her cheek. "Your grandfather would be proud of you, facing this fear." Nan ambled over, twisting the knob, opening the door, and pushing out the screen before Cora Anne had fully collected herself.

"Evening, Mrs. Annie." Tennessee Watson filled the doorway. He embodied confidence and ease in his khaki shorts and golf shirt, but when he looked at her, a muscle twitched at the corner of his mouth. Not so confident after all.

"Wow, Cor." How easily he slipped into the old nickname. "You look nice."

The appreciation in his eyes said more than his words, and she let herself smile. When he placed his hand casually in the small of her back as they went out the door, Nan calling goodnight, the warmth slowed her hammering heart.

Tennessee drove with both hands on the wheel because he was sure if he didn't, he'd give in to his ridiculous urge to hold Cora Anne's hand.

He glanced at her profile in the dimming twilight. Tendrils of hair curled around her face and she kept her lips pressed in a thin line. So he wasn't the only one with nerves. Reaching up, she fiddled with one of those dangly earrings that suited her better than he'd have imagined.

"These new?" His gesture flipped the silver dangle—and grazed her chin—but he put his hand back on the wheel before he risked touching her skin again.

"Hannah gave them to me last year. For our birthday." She tugged one. "We have different tastes. These are definitely more her than me."

"Well, they suit you just fine." He remembered Hannah, an imp with a daredevil nature. Always surprised him Cora Anne had been the one in the water and not her.

He slowed at the oak-sheltered intersection for a family on bikes who waved their thanks. "What's Hannah up to these days?"

"Working at her mom's bridal boutique. Aunt Caro says she can't wait to retire and leave it all to her."

"She like that? The kid I remember was always up to mischief."

"She's calmed down a bit." The edges of her mouth softened. "Happy the weddings aren't for her."

"Single and loving it, huh?" He steered into a drive just before the Yacht Club's entrance. Sailboats dotted the river's landscape and in the marsh beyond, a heron soared, no doubt in search of supper.

"Something like that …" Her voice trailed as they parked. "This isn't the Dockside."

"No, a buddy of mine opened this place recently. Dockside can fry shrimp, but this place has ambiance." Impulsively, he winked at her and was rewarded with another more tentative smile. He'd brought her here because he was serious about getting to know her. And letting her know him. At least, as much as he could.

In contrast to Dockside, the oldest eatery on Edisto near the bustling marina, this setting was intimate and serene. The large white cottage overlooked the water where Scott Creek flowed into Big Bay. A tasteful sign hung from the porch, *The Hideaway,* and under it in small script, *Casual Fine Dining.*

Cora Anne slipped out of her seatbelt. "This is beautiful. Can't believe I didn't notice it when I ran by yesterday."

"Well, it's called The Hideaway for a reason."

She reached for the door handle.

"I got it, hang on." He hustled around the truck and opened her door. "I'm supposed to have the manners of a southern gentleman, right?"

"If you insist." She stumbled climbing down from the truck, and he grabbed her hand.

Her face flushed. "I promise, I'm not as clumsy as it seems."

"Don't know what you're talking about. I just figure you find me irresistible." This time, he got a laugh. He seized the opportunity and held her hand a moment longer.

"Irresistible, yeah, that's it." She wiggled her fingers, so he let go. But she fell in step beside him, their shoulders nearly touching, as they climbed the wide stairs. She wasn't the child anymore who had tagged along, trying to match his teenage strides across the sand.

And he wanted to know the young woman she'd become.

The Hideaway's sign might have said casual, but its interior said exquisite. Simple square tables, draped with white cloths and topped with votive candles nestled in glass bowls of shells, filled the dining room. Hardwood floors and walls the color of raw honey alluded to the rustic style of original beach homes. Picture windows surrounded three sides of the center room, and a bar ran the length of the fourth wall to their left. A screened deck off the back offered a spectacular view of the sun setting over the marsh and river.

The blonde young woman at the hostess station waved. Unlike the servers in classic black and white, she wore a bold print sundress that complemented her bright smile.

"Hey, Christy." He approached before the interrogation began. "This is Mrs. Coultrie's granddaughter, Cora Anne."

Christy cocked her eyebrow—he was going to pay for this surprise later—but simply said, "Welcome to The Hideaway, Cora Anne. Porch all right?"

They followed her out to the deck, where she seated them at a corner table Tennessee knew had the best view.

"I'll bring y'all some tea, and Tennessee ..." Christy gave him a mother hen look. "Ben's in the kitchen."

"Well, I figured." Still, he didn't offer her any more information, so she spun, skirt swirling, and strode off. Five minutes was probably about all they had before the inquisition. Curse and blessing of small towns and old friends.

Cora Anne darted a glance after Christy, but he figured, treading the waters of a first date, she wasn't about to ask. When she looked back at him, he told her. "High school."

"Oh ..."

For someone who planned to make a living digging through history, she sure didn't seem interested in his.

He plunged ahead anyway. "Christy's brother and I went to school together. She was right behind us a couple of grades, but that didn't stop her from hanging around and being a bit of a pest."

Cora Anne glanced toward the hostess station where Christy greeted an older couple affectionately. "Looks like she grew out of it."

"She did, but I might as well tell you." He sighed and opened his menu, keeping his eyes on Cora Anne's. Keeping it light, for now. "Once, she had an enormous crush on me."

That got him a purse of her lips. "Poor girl. How did she ever get over it?"

"Oh, she met a pro golfer one day, married him within a year, and has since produced the two most beautiful kids I've ever seen." He enjoyed the way her mouth fell open and her eyes grew wide, first with surprise then disbelief.

"She doesn't look any older than me."

"Yeah, she's blessed like that. Speaking of high school …" He leaned back to acknowledge the waitress who held sweet tea in mason jars and wore a sparkly new diamond. "Hey, Maria. How's Duncan doing with the old ball and chain?"

"Hey, yourself." Her black ponytail swung as she tossed her head. "He's loving it, of course. Ben said to tell you he's coming out in a minute." She beamed like a cheerleader at Cora Anne. "Gotta watch out for these island boys." She headed for another table.

Cora Anne cocked her head, studying him. Good. "So, you're the high school anomaly because you're still not married."

He winced. "Ouch. You sound like my mom."

"Just trying to figure out what you've been up to for twelve years." She unrolled her napkin, creasing it before placing it in her lap.

Fidgets when nervous. In the truck, she'd twirled a strand of hair the whole time.

Unable to resist the urge, he reached across the table and caught her left hand, silencing fingers that were beginning to drum. "For twelve years, I've been wondering what happened to *you.*"

She inhaled sharply and withdrew her hand as Ben, in khaki cargos and an untucked button-down, swaggered up to their table. "Hey, Watson, how about a heads up when you're bringing a date over?"

Though Tennessee stood, his closest friend didn't wait for an introduction. He clasped Cora Anne's hand with vigor. "Benjamin Townsend, the brains behind the brawn. And you're Cora Anne, granddaughter from the Coultrie place, Still Waters." He gave Tennessee a sideways look when she nodded. "That's a nice piece of property. Great decks, big yard, renovated cottage." Crossing his arms, he shook his head of summer-cropped brown hair.

Tennessee rolled his eyes and addressed Cora Anne. "Ignore him. He's a real estate tycoon with an eye for anything he doesn't—or can't—have."

"That's right. And that's why I'm a proud small business owner of actual buildings, but Tennessee here, he's just a handyman." Ben thumped Tennessee's shoulder and trained his hazel eyes on Cora Anne. "So, tell me, what manner of desperation made you come out with this guy?"

"Well, so far, no better offer has come along."

Ben's guffaw had other tables looking up and smiling at the inside joke they didn't know. "Sweetheart"— he patted Cora Anne's arm—"you just call me up when you're done taking pity on my poor business partner."

Her eyebrows shot up, but Ben didn't appear to notice. He turned to Tennessee. "I gotta go run this place, but I'll be back to check on you. Shrimp came off Lenny's boat this afternoon, so you better like it, or I'll tell him." He clapped Tennessee on the shoulder, chuckling as he left.

Tennessee eased back down, ready for the scrutiny in Cora Anne's blue eyes. "Obviously, there's more to Watson Custom Homes than new builds and renovations."

"Obviously. This is one of your ventures?" She swept her arm around.

"Yes, first time we've tried the restaurant business, but Ben had a vision, so I helped execute it."

"You did a beautiful job." Her words sounded sincere, but she'd lowered her gaze.

"Does bringing you to a place I own—where everyone knows me—negate this as a date?"

He knew that word made her nervous. She dug elbows into the table, lacing her fingers open and closed like that old finger play game of church his mama had taught him. "No. But you are a fixture here, which is obvious and intimidating."

"Why?"

She lowered her arms and leveled her gaze on his. "Because these people are like meeting family."

The shock she'd realized so quickly made him sit back for a moment. He kept his eyes on hers, wondering how she'd seen what so many didn't. Even folks like Maria, who had known them for years, didn't always understand his and Ben's mix of friendship, partnership, and passion for the Island's preservation. But Cora Anne pinned it. Family. For all those reasons and more.

She dropped her eyes and twisted her hands. "It's nice, knowing you belong somewhere."

He leaned forward again. Did she not believe she belonged here too?

"You know"—he reached across the table and laid his hand on hers—"tragedy can tear down, or it can forge bonds."

She tried to pull away, but he wasn't about to let her hide from reality. Instead, he fixed his eyes on hers, willing understanding. "Lenny is Ben's stepdad, and Christy is his sister. They helped save me after—" He stopped. She knew.

She stared at the grip he still had on her hands. "What happened to Ben's dad?"

She needed distraction—and perspective. He gave it to her. "Something far worse than a freak accident. He traded his family for a heroin addiction."

"Oh, how awful."

"Yeah." He let her hands go. "But if I've learned anything, it's to lean on those who understand." And when she was ready, he had every intention of letting her lean on him.

Chapter 13

Over platters of boiled and beer-battered shrimp, fresh crab legs and mussels, sides of steaming grits and tangy slaw, they talked the balmy evening away. Cora Anne removed shrimp shells with an agility she'd forgotten, relieved she had enough food to keep her hands busy. Kept her from worrying about her nervous system's response when his fingers brushed hers over the basket of hushpuppies.

"So why research and not teaching?" Tennessee pried open a mussel. "Trying to break the family mold?"

"No." She dipped a shrimp in and out of cocktail sauce. "I've always been in awe how a teacher—like my mom or dad—can be such an influence in someone's life." Propping her chin in her hand, she added, "Maybe someday."

"Don't want all that responsibility?"

"Responsibility is my middle name." She scoffed and popped the shrimp in her mouth. Responsibility she could handle. But the vulnerability relationships required?

"Guess I've been calling you the wrong thing all along, Cora Anne." He stretched the syllables out again with that Lowcountry twang. He must have stretched his long legs with her name, because he nudged the bobbing foot she'd been using as an outlet for nerves. She jumped, tea splashed from her recently refilled glass, and her cheeks burned.

He shifted his legs away and asked, "How's life with triplet brothers?"

"Chaos, from day one." She regrouped with the subject change. "Their preschool teacher nicknamed them the mischief-teers because she was too nice to call them little terrors."

He laughed, and she marveled at how easily laughter came to him while searching her memory for a funny story. The triplets had done more than their fair share to keep her life from being morose.

"When I was in middle school, my dad put one of those chain locks on my door, you know the type?"

He nodded. "But we only children never had to worry about things like that."

"Well, I did. We were trying to keep them out of my black nail polish because they had already painted my bedspread."

"I can't envision you with black nails."

"Didn't you hear me say middle school? The early nineties treated none of us well."

A shadow crossed his face. "True."

Way to go. She'd inadvertently referenced the date for the very topic she wanted to avoid. What had Tennessee been up to while she'd been despising her brothers and wearing grunge?

She clasped her hands in her lap and rushed through the rest of the story. "Well, the lock worked for about a week, and then one of them, probably J.D.— he's the problem-solver—figured out if they stood on a chair, they could reach it. So, I come home one day from school, and there they were, covered in lipstick and nail polish."

His shoulders shook with laughter.

The moment had passed, thank goodness. She continued. "They told Mom they were wild Indians who needed war paint. She said in that case, they were in captivity. Then she shut the door and chained it. Made them so mad and scared they never messed with my stuff again." She crossed her arms. Even now, so many years later, she felt the exasperation. The triplets had always been more than a handful.

His leg bumped hers again, but this time, she didn't jump. His eyes were serious, prying gently. "But you love them like crazy, mischief and all."

She looked out over the creek where a johnboat motored slowly down the waterway in the gathering dusk. There had been a time, but ... "Yeah, I do."

He went back to his shrimp. "I'd have loved a sibling. This place got pretty lonely. That's why Ben's like a brother. Lenny used to take us out on Saturdays to help haul in the catch. Christy would whine and stomp around their kitchen until one day, he finally let her go." His smile widened, open and unguarded. "Made Ben pretty mad, because turns out, little sis was a better shrimper than him."

She pressed a fist to her mouth, stifling her own laughter. "Poor Ben. There's nothing worse than being one-upped by a younger sibling."

He arched his eyebrows, but she looked away. No reason to elaborate on the jealousy she'd long harbored for her brothers.

Tennessee took the hint. "Yeah, drove him nuts, but I reckon that's some of what drives him now. Determination to prove that, while he may not be able to troll the waters or coax back the land, he can leave a legacy his own way."

Now they were getting to it. How he'd found a life to live for, after all.

"So what exactly does this business partnership of y'all's do besides build houses and fry Edisto shrimp?"

"Best you've ever had, isn't it?" He rolled his unused spoon through his fingers. "Ben went over to Charleston and stole a sous chef. One of his wiser decisions."

"There have been less successful ones, then, I take it?"

His smile wavered, and he scrubbed a hand through his hair, nodding. "But those townhomes you liked, those are proving pretty wise, too."

Maybe he was more guarded than she'd initially thought. Her turn to pry. "How's that?"

"We're trying to encourage our generation to stay here, rather than moving to Charleston or Walterboro—or somewhere worse, like *Atlanta*." He said it with such mock disdain, she almost choked on her tea. "But to do that, there's got to be jobs and affordable housing. Ben and I wanted a design that had old Edisto appeal but modern convenience."

"I'd say you accomplished that."

"Yup. And we had buyers for two of the five before we even finished. Both locals, which is good, because here on the beach side, we're usually dead come October. Locals can keep businesses from becoming completely dependent on tourist season and ease the worry that one bad storm could set us back months, or even years, financially."

"I thought you said we need a few storms now and then to 'balance things out.'" She air-quoted him.

He chuckled. "Guess I did, and I meant it, too. Sometimes, the storm's what clears out the junk, so you can better deal with what's left standing."

She looked away. What had she left him standing with after his father died? Financial struggles? A business they almost lost? But somehow, he'd gotten from there to here.

The din of other conversations had died away as they sat on the porch, and when she glanced around she noticed they were nearly the only patrons left.

Maria came by and lifted Cora Anne's empty plate. "Y'all want coffee? Dessert?"

"Sure thing." Tennessee handed over his plate. "Bring us some of that key lime pie, please, ma'am."

Cora Anne grimaced. "How can you still eat?"

He leaned back and patted his flat stomach. "Practice. Years and years of it."

She crossed her arms on the table and looked over the water where a moon was rising, waxing to near full. "I'm surprised you stayed." The words slipped out.

"You know, it surprises me you didn't have a list of schools waiting after Tulane turned you down."

She leveled her gaze on him. One evasive maneuver, and he'd turned the conversation back on her. "Yet another moment in my life when I made a bad decision based on emotion."

"So you do let go occasionally."

"And it doesn't turn out well." She ignored his raised brows. "I applied to Tulane, UGA, and because my advisor insisted, The College of Charleston."

"You didn't get in?"

"No, I did. But because I wanted to wait on Tulane, UGA filled their assistantship positions."

"And Charleston?"

"I don't want to go to Charleston. That was an appeasement."

"Why not? What's so special about Tulane?"

"My plan is to study historic preservation, with a concentration in architecture." To her relief, he didn't remark on the irony of her wanting to preserve other people's history. "They have one of the best programs around."

"So does Charleston. And we're older. And prettier."

"Touché. What makes you the expert?"

He sat up straight and saluted. "Citadel. Class of 2001. Civil engineering, minor in history, but I interned with the Historic Charleston Foundation's neighborhood revitalization."

Surprise made her sit back. "I'm sorry. I had no idea."

"Here you go." Maria set down wedges of pie and porcelain cups of fresh-brewed coffee.

Tennessee thanked her, but Cora Anne sat blinking. She should have realized. The care he took with the beach house, those townhomes, the way he spoke of this land and its protection.

This is why he'd stayed. Because he never doubted the purpose that bound him to Edisto.

He tapped a finger against the furrow in her brow. "You know, my mama used to say, better be careful or your face will freeze like that."

Nerves skittered up her neck with a flush. She brushed his touch away, unable to think with his skin against hers. "I'm glad your life really has turned out … all right."

"Well, took me a bit to get here, but yeah. It's all right, now." He leaned forward and spoke softly. "And none of it was your fault."

There was no answer to that. Everything about the night his dad died had been her fault.

"Still not ready to talk about it, huh?" He rapped his knuckles on the table. "Maybe you need a come-to-Jesus meeting like I had."

"Church?" Was he serious?

"Or a shrimp boat. That's where Lenny held mine."

She wrinkled her nose. "Think I'd prefer church."

"Well, sweetheart …" His exaggerated southern drawl was back, making the endearment colloquial rather than personal. "That can be arranged."

Chapter 14

The phone rang just as Annie finished steeping her tea.

"Morning, Mama." On the other end, Lou sounded as though she needed something stronger than her morning cup of coffee.

"And it's a good one here, though you seem otherwise." The cord trailed as she eased slowly back over to the table.

"Spent all day yesterday at a ball tournament. My shoulders are more burnt than they ever got at the beach."

"Well, aren't you the one always spouting the benefits of sunscreen?" Annie lowered herself back into her chair. "Maybe you should listen to your own advice."

Yesterday, Cora Anne had stacked all the photographs into neat piles and affixed sticky notes to the table, designating years. Annie hoped her shaking hands wouldn't fail her and spill tea all over everything.

Lou huffed. "I wore SPF 50, Mama. Just didn't do any good." She rattled something, frozen waffles in the toaster, likely. "Is Cora Anne around? I have a question for her."

Annie swallowed tea and cleared her throat. "She's still in bed, I believe. Had a late night."

"Oh, yeah? Y'all play an extra card at Bingo or something?"

"No ... she went to dinner with Tennessee Watson."

Sharp intake of breath. Annie had expected that.

"Mama, you didn't ... "

She'd expected that too. "Didn't what, dear?"

Now the deep sigh. "I know you were heartbroken when things didn't work out with me and Patrick"—Annie cast her eyes to the ceiling as Lou lectured—"but you can't push our children together."

"I'm not pushing. He just wants to help her find some peace, that's all." She could see Lou now, drumming her fingertips on that cold granite counter. "Speaking of finding things, she's been going through old pictures. Found one of you."

The rustling over the line stopped. "You're telling me she knows?"

"What she knows isn't nearly enough." Annie shifted the phone. Old thing was getting heavy.

"She's never been ready to listen."

Annie raised her brows as Cora Anne entered the kitchen fully dressed, but not for a day at the beach. "I don't know. She might be getting close."

Cora Anne wore a simple linen sundress, pale blue, with pearl earrings and, when asked, simply said she thought Nan might like some company for church. She spoke briefly with her mother about the weather, Nan's appetite, and how, yes, she'd appreciate it if Lou forwarded her mail. Then she drove her grandmother and herself back up Highway 174 to the white-columned Presbyterian church.

Flanked by sprawling live oaks and a 300-year-old cemetery rumored to be haunted, the ancient Presbyterian Church of Edisto Island suited her passion for history, if nothing else.

The sanctuary filled with an eclectic group of faithful worshipers and visiting tourists. Years had passed since she'd last gone to church with her grandparents. Their roots were deep here, and she recognized aged faces of distant relatives. But she ignored how they put their heads together in speculation, surely discussing how Annie Jenkins Coultrie had finally gotten one of her wayward ones to come home.

The pews, with quaint doors that opened to allow in parishioners, and the curved mahogany stairs leading to a raised pulpit, were reminiscent of a time Edisto had been settled with the landed gentry. But for her, the polished wood and quiet reverence evoked memories of many Sunday mornings with her grandfather. He'd always insist on church first, then catching fresh flounder for a Sunday fish fry. In the years following the accident, when she couldn't beg out of the annual beach pilgrimage, she'd spent most of her time with him. Fishing tidal creeks meant she avoided the ocean.

Nan's cool hand, with its lines of blue veins and knuckles swollen with arthritis, covered Cora Anne's clenched ones in her lap. "I'm glad you came."

"Me, too."

Maybe. Church always reminded her of what she didn't deserve: life everlasting when she'd taken life from someone else.

She shifted in her seat as the service came to order. When she lifted her head after the prayer, there sat Tennessee Watson on a stool down front, a guitar on his knee. He strummed a few chords and then looked out into the sea of worshippers and caught her gaze.

Beside him, Christy sang, "Come thou fount of every blessing, tune my heart to sing thy praise ..."

Nan's soprano warbled in with others. "Streams of mercy never ceasing, call for songs of loudest praise ..."

She looked away from Tennessee and down at the hand of her grandmother still in her lap. But the gentle music washed over her, and she closed her eyes so that no presence could distract her from the words being sung.

"Here I raise mine Ebenezer;
hither by thy help I'm come;
and I hope, by thy good pleasure,
safely to arrive at home.
Jesus sought me when a stranger,
wandering from the fold of God;
he, to rescue me from danger,
interposed his precious blood."

After the service, she left Nan talking pleasantries on the porch and wandered out to the graveyard. The words of that hymn still reverberated in her soul, and she needed a moment of quiet.

Just behind the church, a fence surrounded the graves of the prominent Seabrook family and the monument honoring patriarch William Seabrook, a man who had been the richest planter on the Island.

She paused. Once, this man had wealth unimaginable, but lost it all to war and reconstruction. History told of his endurance with a home still standing, well preserved and loved for generations. She ran her fingers across the iron gate. Perhaps it was possible to lose everything and still find happiness.

She left the Seabrook plot and wandered beyond the church, to where the newer grave markers nestled under the spread branches of live oaks. There lay her grandfather's ashes, and a few rows over, she found fresh flowers on Patrick Watson's grave. She knelt and traced the date. July 28, 1993.

Cora Anne rose and crossed her arms. *You're not ten years old anymore.* Then why did she still feel like that child?

"There you are." Tennessee came striding across the cemetery. "Looking for someone?"

She couldn't help the smile. "I think he found me."

He glanced at his father's grave and then took her arm, tugging her back toward the front of the little white church. "You enjoy the service?"

A guitar case swung from his hand, and she nudged him with her elbow. "You could have told me you're a man of many talents. Where'd you learn to play?"

"Aw, this?" He swung the case with ease. "Just a little something I picked up during the college bar scene."

She gaped at him, unsure if he was making another joke, and he tilted a half-smile her way. "We've all got a history. Some more colorful than others."

They had paused at the edge of the gravel lot, and now she looked across it for Nan. She found her at the bottom of the porch steps, being embraced by a woman with soft blonde curls and a face too youthful to be middle-aged.

Cora Anne stepped back and Tennessee snagged her elbow to keep her from falling. Again. Blasted oak tree roots.

"What's wrong?"

She fisted her hands against her stomach. "That's your mother."

"Yeah, I know. She and Mrs. Annie have become good friends." He peered at her. "You're white as one of these supposed graveyard ghosts."

"I haven't seen your mother since … since …" Her chest constricted and she forced a deep breath past the tightness. "Can you please tell Nan I'll be in the car?"

"Here." He shoved the guitar case at her. "Why don't you do me a favor and take this over to my truck? I'll meet you there."

She backed away without arguing and found his white Dodge Ram easily among the sedans and midlife crisis convertibles. Setting the case inside, she leaned on the open door. Grace, it seemed, would be harder to face than her son.

She looked back up as he bounded over the lot with Nan's floppy straw hat in his hand.

"Your grandmother said to put this on."

She took it hesitantly, fingering the brim. "Why?"

"Because she said your cheeks look pink." He leaned past her and swung the case into the narrow backseat of his extended cab. "And because I'm taking you for a drive."

Chapter 15

Back pressed against the seat of the cab, Cora Anne tugged a strand of that long dark hair. "I don't think—"

"This is a good idea?" When he pulled the truck out on the highway, the woven bag she'd set on the seat between them toppled over, and a spiral-bound planner slid out. "*I* think you worry too much."

She tucked the book back in her bag. "Where are we going?"

"I want to show you something."

He drove them down to King's Market and bought crab salad, fresh chunked watermelon, and a damp bag of boiled peanuts. He figured she was all in when she added two Cokes in glass bottles to the pile on the counter.

But when he left the highway and started crisscrossing the island's rutted dirt roads, she started twisting her hands in her lap.

"Relax, Cor. I'm not kidnapping you. I told your grandmother where we're going."

He turned in a drive lined neatly with pecan trees. One of the signs affixed to the gate said Cooper Creek Plantation. He drove all the way down past the old plantation home and caretaker's cottage, parking in the grass that led down to the dock.

Now she spoke. "I guess we're ignoring that No Trespassing sign."

He grabbed the bag of food and opened his door. "Yup."

She climbed out the other side, wariness in her eyes. "Who lives here?"

"Millionaires from Chicago. They love to buy up our Lowcountry plantations. But they aren't down for the season yet."

He traipsed through the grass that was due for a cutting and let her follow, because he figured curiosity and hunger would outweigh her fear of breaking rules. On the dock, he kicked off his boat shoes and dropped, feet dangling over the tidal creek that would rise with the tide. Cora Anne sat primly, legs to the side, like any good Southern girl in a church dress.

He jerked his thumb to the plantation. "So this is where I grew up."

Her eyes swept over the house that rose behind them on a knoll. Three stories atop brick pilings, four chimneys anchoring the roof.

"Not there. In the caretaker's cottage."

She turned toward him. Listening.

Taking out the bag of peanuts, he grabbed a few and passed it to her. "My grandmother was half Cooper, half Ravenel—still is, despite marrying an outsider."

She pressed her lips together in a slight smile, and he knew the idiosyncrasies of Charleston's gentry were not lost on her.

"But when my daddy said he'd rather be a carpenter on Edisto than a lawyer on Broad Street ... well, that didn't go over so well." He nodded toward the house. It overlooked this section of Store Creek, and from the gable in the attic, his father used to say, one could see almost to the spire of St. Michael's in downtown Charleston. "My grandmother sold the plantation so he couldn't inherit."

She tossed empty peanut shells into the blue-green water. "That's dramatic."

"I know. Dad said the rest of the family about had hysterics. His uncle begged him to reconsider, but he must have gotten his stubbornness from her, you know? He walked, and the new owners came in here with a yacht-sized dumpster and gutted the whole place—"

"Surely not." Her eyes widened. "That's a piece of Greek Revival architecture."

He nodded. "Even ripped out the hand-carved banister because the wood was gouged—gashes left by Yankee soldiers during the occupation."

"Where was the historical preservation society?"

He lifted a shoulder. "Happens all the time when an old home is sold. See why it gets my goat?"

Her eyes narrowed. "Why are you telling me all this?"

He leaned back on his elbows and watched the clouds scuttle across the powder-blue sky. Her dress was the same color and her eyes were a shade darker, and all he knew was when he looked at her, he had an overwhelming need to make her understand. But he couldn't. She had to want to.

He gazed out over the creek to the spartina grass waving in the slight breeze, an unbroken vista that, thanks to his efforts, no development would ever touch. "Just figured you'd find it interesting."

She leaned back beside him, her grandmother's hat shading her face. "It is interesting—and sad."

"This is why I joined the land trust. Only way I could save some of what he left behind."

She shifted a bit, putting more space between them. "I'm sorry." Her words were barely a whisper on the breeze.

He snagged her hand before she could get up. "I know."

She didn't pull away, just watched as he passed his thumb over her palm. "You must miss him all the time."

"I do, but I know he'd be proud of what I'm doing now. A few years ago, not so much." He let her hand go and sat back up. "I had to get out from under those waves of grief and learn to live with what I had."

"How—" She pressed her lips into a thin line. "How did you get out?"

"Remember that last summer, when I took you and Hannah out at high tide?" He pulled his knees up, wrapped his arms around them, and watched her.

She nodded, clasping her hands in her lap. "I couldn't get my footing, and I was scared to death." She kept her eyes down. "But you held my hand and told me what to do. Let the wave—"

"Carry you into shore. Let the wave do the work."

"When I got out, my knees were all scraped up and my mama was yelling because she and Aunt Caro had gone to the store, and she couldn't believe our dads had let us in that water with you." She met his gaze.

He grinned. "And you had the biggest smile I'd ever seen, you were so proud of yourself."

She looked away, and they both sat for a moment, breathing deep the scent of pluff mud and salt breeze. Remembering.

He relaxed and pressed his hands into the soft wood of the dock. "We were just kids back then, both of us. Invincible." She sniffled quietly and he watched her out of the corner of his eye. "I don't know why you went in the water that next night, Cor." He held up his hand to keep her from interrupting. That part had never mattered. Not to him. "But I do know I'm to blame for getting up your confidence, and if my father hadn't been there, I'd have been the one who'd gone in after you, and I believe we'd have both been lost." She'd been too close to the rocks. They had been the final culprit. Not her. Not the riptide. But she didn't seem to remember that.

She swung her legs over the creek and tucked her hands under her knees where they bent at the edge. For a moment, she leaned forward so far, he thought she was jumping in the water, just to get away from him and this conversation.

"I feel that way all the time." She didn't look at him as she spoke. "Like I'm still being sucked in by that ocean and I'm never going to make it back to shore."

"I fought that current, too, in all the wrong ways. But when I finally let the wave do the work and wash me on in, there were folks waiting to pull me out."

She raised her brows and he told her about Ben and Christy, and their angel of a mama. And Captain Lenny. "When I wouldn't listen to the parent I had left, when I was sure I could drown all the pain and guilt in a bottle of beer or"—he sucked in a deep breath and dropped his gaze for a moment before leveling it back on her—"the arms of any woman who would have me, they pulled me back. They're the only reason I graduated the Citadel and wasn't kicked out for dishonorable behavior."

"I can't imagine you being dishonorable."

"I was different then. Angry, hostile. Much worse when I'd been drinking. I had no peace, you know?"

She nodded.

"I kept trying to find it in all these other places. After 9-11 happened, I figured this was it—better put all that cadet training to good use, so I told everyone I was headed for the Marine Corps." He shook his head. "Foolish, hot-headed, guilt-ridden young men don't make thoughtful decisions. So Lenny, he put me on his shrimp boat one morning, just me and him. Took me way out to sea and we had that come-to-Jesus meeting."

She prompted him with raised brows.

"Told me that his family, and my mother, and he reckoned the good Lord too, were tired of seeing me waste the life and legacy my father had left."

"Ouch."

"Then he quoted the blessing my father would speak over a home he'd just finished. Reminded me that Patrick Ravenel Watson christened his life's work with prayer."

She pressed her lips into a thin line.

He figured, for her, answered prayer had been as elusive as peace. "Want to hear it?"

She shrugged, and Tennessee figured that was good enough. Straightening his back, he closed his eyes. "Heavenly Father, you are always so good. May this home be blessed. May it be full. May it be a place of mirth and not of strife. May it give You glory and remind these folks of all You have created. In the precious name of Jesus, amen."

"That was beautiful." Cora Anne was blinking back tears.

He folded his hand into hers. Strong enough now, God-willing, to bring her out from under the wave and set her on the shore.

"I can never apologize enough to you and your mother—"

"Shhh." He squeezed her hand. "You do not need our forgiveness, because there's never been anything to forgive. It was a tragedy, but it was an accident. Pure and simple."

"I think your father would be so proud of the man you've become."

He quirked a smile at her. Her eyes sparkled with unshed tears. "He'd like you, Cora Anne. All grown up and serious. But he'd tell you to cut loose every now and then."

She laughed, the sound like church bells ringing. "Oh, yeah?"

"Yeah. Life's too short for planning everything."

"Maybe …" She wet her lips. "Maybe that's true."

He almost warned her then, what was coming. But she pulled her hair over her shoulder and smiled—a glimmer of hope in her eyes—and he changed his mind.

Summer was too short for fixing everything.

Chapter 16

The bucket must've gotten caught in the groin and the tide washed it back in. She could almost reach it if she stretched a little more—her feet went out from under her and the sea pulled her in dizzying circles. Up was down and down was up—

Gasping, Cora Anne jerked up in bed. She drew up her knees and pressed her forehead down. She'd forgotten the rocks. And Hannah dragging her to the edge of the groin, claiming the shark's teeth would be plentiful there.

Currents were always worse off those pilings of rocks and wood. An approaching storm had already begun stirring the ocean. No wonder Tennessee and his father had screamed at them to stay out of the water.

But she went in anyway.

On Tuesday afternoon, while Cora Anne peeled the backing off dozens of tiny photo tabs and affixed pictures in scrapbooks, Hannah burst in the front door of Still Waters. She wore a floral dress and a sunhat bigger than Nan's.

"I have come" dramatic sweep of her arm—"at the request of our mothers. And"—She made a stop gesture and Cora Anne froze rising from her seat—"to play bingo because this girl's feeling lucky tonight."

"Well, hello to you too."

Her cousin skipped across the room and engulfed Cora Anne in a hug. "How are you? And what have you done with Nan?"

"She's done nothing I haven't asked for," their grandmother called as she made her way down the hall. Hannah bounded over and hugged her with less fierceness. "I've missed you."

Nan patted Hannah's cheek. "We've missed you, too, dear. And how are all the weddings?"

"Ugh." She grabbed water from the fridge. "Hot, because no matter what I say, brides will not be convinced that garden weddings in June are a bad idea."

"Speaking of gardens, you should see what Cora Anne and Tennessee have done with mine." Nan pressed a hand to the small of her back as she meandered over to the sofa.

"Yes, let's do speak of Tennessee." Hannah smirked.

No doubt her cousin had heard an ounce of truth and a pound of speculation. Cora Anne shrugged. "Nan hired him."

"Mmm-hmm. That's not all *your* mother told *my* mother."

"And you think texting is efficient."

"It is true, no method of communication will outdo family gossip." Hannah flopped on the sofa beside Nan. "Give me the scoop."

"I thought you came to play bingo." Cora Anne started tidying up her mess.

Hannah consulted her watch, more a statement than timepiece. "We've got at least two hours, so dish, Cor."

She tapped a dozen three-by-fives into a neat stack with her palm. "There is nothing to dish. We're just friends." Patrick and Lou's smiling faces peeped out of the stack. They'd been just friends too. Right?

Hannah rolled her eyes.

Tennessee's friendship to her was miracle enough. "Ask Nan."

Their grandmother pursed her lips and shook her head. Quite the effective secret-keeper Nan had proven to be. She had yet to divulge any details about the photograph, even though Cora Anne kept leaving it out in plain sight.

Hannah pouted. "Fine, then. If I win tonight, you talk."

She crossed her arms. "And if I win?"

"Then I'll buy you a new dress for your next date."

Folks started lining up for bingo an hour before the doors opened. By the time they made it into the concrete building that housed the Lions Club, the humid air buzzed with chitchat and electric fans.

Nan seemed unaffected by the clinging warmth. She pulled at the light sweater around her shoulders and settled into a folding chair between Cora Anne and Hannah.

They were discussing the reunion—really which July wedding was least high maintenance so Aunt Caro and Hannah could get away—when Cora Anne felt the tug on her ponytail.

Tennessee beamed at her. "Look what the cat drug in."

She bit her cheek to keep her smile in check—Hannah didn't need anymore fuel. "More like the cousin."

He reached across her to shake Hannah's hand. "Hey, there. Long time, Hannah."

"Sure has been." She fluttered her lashes. "I hear you're well? Business is good?" She spoke to him, but her eyes watched the hand he'd propped on Cora Anne's chair.

"No complaints." He touched the brim of his Citadel cap. "Have a good one, ladies." His fingers brushed her shoulder, and Cora Anne looked down, fighting the blush and her quivering stomach. He navigated the room easily, shaking hands, and took his place with the other volunteers. Of course he'd be a member of the Lions Club, too. Good for business.

Hannah was indeed feeling lucky that night. She won a round of the twenty-dollar jackpot and outlasted their entire table during the Stand Up game. For the rest of the evening, she squirmed with glee. Cora Anne figured her cousin put a crick in her neck with all the craning she did, trying to keep an eye on Tennessee, whose eyes flicked their way far too often. Once Hannah got an idea in her head, she hung on with a tenaciousness to rival any deep-sea fisherman.

Cora Anne knew she was on the hook.

"Let's go down to the video store and get some ice cream," Hannah suggested after bingo as she slid into the backseat of Nan's sedan.

"Y'all go on and have fun, but take me home first. I'm ready for a rest after all that excitement." Dramatically, Nan lay her hand on her chest. "I'm wilting like a magnolia."

At home, she got Nan up the stairs because Hannah wanted to rummage the storage area for the old bikes.

"Faster than walking and more fun than the car," her cousin proclaimed when Cora Anne came down and found her testing a rusty old Schwinn.

Since protests were useless, she followed Hannah through the dimming twilight of the bike path down to the shopping center that housed Edisto's only ice cream shop. At the video store, probably the last remaining place in South Carolina one could actually rent a VHS, they got cones. Strawberry for Cora Anne but Moose Tracks for Hannah. They pushed the bikes one-handed, eating ice cream and crossing under the fluorescent lights of the Piggly Wiggly parking lot out to the pier on the beach. Hannah leaned far over the rail to see the waves breaking hard and fast against the pilings as the tide came in.

Cora Anne hung back. She had again grown used to the sound of the ocean from the back deck of Still Waters, but here, under her feet, the sound pounded through all her limbs.

Hannah grinned over her shoulder. "Remember coming here as a kid? We used to spend all our money on nonsense like shell rings."

"Yeah."

"You recall everything, don't you?"

She tossed the rest of her cone in a nearby garbage can. "Enough."

"That's why you're the smartest person I know about books, Cor. But you've got a lot to learn about life."

"Oh, really? This coming from the girl who hates working for her mother and living in her parents' guest house?"

Hannah popped the last of her cone in her mouth with a grin. "See, that's the difference between us. I'm doing something I expect to be short-term and making the best of it. You, on the other hand, have a short time to make things right and you might be wasting it."

"Wasting what?"

"This, you dummy!" Hannah, prone to big gestures, cast her arms wide as if she could embrace it all—the great indigo sky dotting with stars, the waves slapping the shore, the old pier stretching lights out across the darkness. "Do you like him?"

She turned her face away. Unlike her cousin, who could both mask and play emotions, she could only shut hers down. But, so far, these had refused temperance. "More than I should."

"Accept it, Cor. This is a gift. A shot at once-in-a-lifetime happily ever after."

"You're crazy."

"Nope. Prophetic. Get out of your own way and you'll see."

Chapter 17

Tennessee parked in what had become his spot, a patch of sandy grass between the cottage's pilings and that blasted palmetto tree leaning precariously toward the roof. He appreciated the shade in the heavy heat of a Lowcountry June, but that tree needed to come down.

Still Waters had come along nicely these past couple weeks. Cora Anne had kept the raised beds watered and tomatoes were just beginning to fruit. This early evening, the scent of basil mingled with the salty air and revived his tired senses. Over the yard and dunes, the boardwalk stretched, an expanse of clean yellow boards. Would only take a few summers before they faded to a weathered silver gray. He smiled and scrubbed his hand through his hair. A job well done. Appreciated for years to come.

As for the present … well, he'd been appreciating finagling Cora Anne's company every chance he got.

She had this way of listening to him, as if she were trying to hear beneath what he was saying. As if she knew the story that lay in the unspoken. She feigned exasperation with her grandmother's plans but always went beyond Mrs. Annie's expectation.

He looked through the backdoor glass as she rubbed a cloth over the heart pine walls. Her hair was braided in one long plait over her shoulder, softer than the pigtail style of her youth. She'd topped it with a blue kerchief, ends secured at the nape of her neck. Loose curls bobbed with her vigorous polishing. The carefree girl was emerging from the stoic woman, and he wanted to snatch her away before she went under again.

And he wanted to kiss her senseless. He'd pretty much lost the debate with himself about that.

She scrunched her nose and narrowed those cobalt eyes—her concentration face. She scrubbed harder at some unseen spot.

He grimaced. No amount of polish was going to erase her past in this place. But together, they could make those memories bearable.

Tennessee rapped his knuckles on the glass. She waved the rag at him and he shoved the door open, mentally adding WD-40 for those hinges to his list.

"Hey." Her shoulders softened and the corner of her mouth lifted just a bit.

"Hey, yourself. I like this." He tugged at the kerchief, and for once, she didn't shrug off his touch. The tang of lye and lemon tickled his nose. "Murphy's Oil Soap, huh?"

"Oh, yeah. Nan said if I'm going to put up new pictures, then the wall better look new too." She traced her fingers over a knot in the wood. The planks dated the beach cottage as one of Edisto's oldest and represented the type of craftsmanship Tennessee hoped his company embodied. "I hear it's trendy to paint, but these walls are part of the character and charm of this place."

"Living with history." He knew she'd catch his meaning.

"Learning to." She capped the soap and nodded toward the roll of paper in his hand. "What've you got there?"

"Mail call." He held up a packet of envelopes and magazines looped together with rubber bands. "Your grandmother had me drop by the farm." She didn't seem to find anything odd about that. Well, Mrs. Annie would have to come clean sooner or later. Straddling a barstool, he spread the blueprints on the peninsula. "And something new."

She leaned her elbows on the counter. "Is that our laundry room?"

"Yup. Your grandmother asked me to draw up some plans for converting it a bit. Said this place could use more beds." He outlined the drawing with his finger, showing her. "See, if I move the washer and dryer to this corner and build closet doors and shelves, then you'll have plenty of room for a couple of bunks. Especially since we can open up this wall between the laundry and the owner's closet."

She wrinkled her brow. "I thought those old walls were concrete blocks."

"Not this one. It's drywall. I helped my dad put it in after Hugo." The line between her eyes deepened a bit, but she didn't withdraw. He added, "Originally, the walls were pine like up here, but the flooding ruined 'em."

"Huh." She propped her chin in her hand. "I guess I don't remember that."

"Don't remember what?" Mrs. Annie came in the kitchen, a long sweater engulfing her slender frame. "Hello, Tennessee. Have you had supper yet?"

"No, ma'am. I just dropped by to show you those blueprints you asked for." *And to see your granddaughter.* But he didn't have to tell her that. Annie Coultrie had lit the match to this fire, and from what he could tell, she was quite pleased with herself.

"Well, why don't you tell me all about those plans. Cora Anne can warm you up some of that chicken I taught her to fry this afternoon. Would you believe her mama buys it in a bucket most of the time?" The old woman pursed her lips and shook her head. "I swear I raised her better than that. When she was a child, we could just go out in the yard and wring a bird's neck if Cora Anne's granddaddy got a hankering for fried chicken."

Cora Anne giggled as she pulled Tupperware out of the fridge and a plate out of the cabinet. "From my understanding, he got that hankering *every* Saturday night."

Mrs. Annie accepted his assistance onto the other barstool. "That he did. Now, young man, show me what you've got."

They perused the plans, and then she shook her head. "Looks like an awful lot of tearing down."

"No more complicated than the other job—"

"Told you he wasn't a handyman, Nan," Cora interrupted, sliding a plate of supper across the counter.

Mrs. Annie's gaze implored him. Best not to mention the crew he had working at the farmhouse. So in that moment, he chose.

This secret wasn't his to tell. But he wouldn't let her heart be broken again, either.

Chapter 18

Cora Anne caught one corner of the ratty, plaid beach blanket and Tennessee the other as they spread it in the sand just beyond the dunes of Still Waters. The sun had barely dipped under the horizon and the waves beat the shore in perfect cadence as the tide receded. She closed her eyes, willing herself to see this moment—Tennessee asking her to sit on the beach and stargaze—rather than the one from twelve years ago. In that one, he shouted from the shore and she waded deeper into an ocean that wouldn't play fair.

"You all right?" He'd flopped on the blanket and lay on his back, hands flat over his stomach.

She grinned. His very full stomach. That man could put away food as well as her brothers.

"Yeah, I'm just tired." She sat crisscross beside him. "Nan's plans get bigger and her lists get longer, no thanks to a certain someone." She wagged her eyebrows.

He propped on his elbow with a smile. "At least this job comes with benefits."

"Like supper?"

"You know what they say about the way to a man's heart …" He leaned over and sniffed the sleeve of her t-shirt, the stubble of his five o'clock shadow tickling her arm. "Mm … you still smell a little like chicken."

"It's the latest perfume. Southern Fried Delicacy." His nearness made her stomach do flip-flops. When he leaned back, head lifted to the dusky sky, she bit her lip. Nan and Hannah might think a summer romance worth the trouble, but Cora Anne disagreed. At least she did when Tennessee wasn't sitting beside her, hip to hip in the surrendering twilight.

Overhead, tiny silver specks of iridescent light appeared and then winked out again before returning to burn with vigor. Often, she and Hannah had sat on the back deck with Granddaddy and watched the stars emerge, playing a game of who could be first to find the dippers and the belt of Orion.

Except for the first summer the triplets had been around. As babies, they'd been colicky and restless, demanding the attention of every adult available. She and Hannah had retreated to the hammock in the yard and played MASH instead, opening and closing the folded paper and dreaming of mansions and movie stars. After Patrick drowned, she'd lost interest in the stars. And she'd lost precious time with her grandfather.

"Can I ask you something?" Tennessee's voice stirred the memories.

She gave him a sidelong look. "That depends."

"On?"

"What you want to ask."

He shifted a little on the blanket, settling more into the packed sand. He'd left his boots at the house and disdained flip-flops, telling her he knew there were no sandspurs or splinters on that nice, new boardwalk. Now he dug his heels in the sand and watched the waves.

"You been in the water since?"

She tensed and sat up straight, tucking her ankles under her. "No."

When he sat up and leaned his shoulder against hers, she pushed back. He took the hint. "I could go with you, if you ever want."

She linked her fingers together, then pulled them apart. "I'm all right." Even offered a small smile to prove it. "I mean, lots of people don't like to swim in the ocean. Salt and shells make you all sticky, and then, you know, there's jellyfish. At least …" She lifted a handful of sand, let it trickle through her fingers. "That was always one of my mom's excuses."

He tipped his head toward hers. "I remember that. You'd beg her to go in, and she never would. That's why your dad let me take you out that time. He thought you'd be distracted."

A knot formed in her throat. Words wouldn't get around it. So that was how she and Hannah got a boogie board lesson from fifteen-year-old Tennessee Watson.

"Did it work?" He nudged her shoulder again.

"Yeah." She pursed her lips and forced herself past the memory, sandy hand unclenching. "I think it's still working."

He grinned and reclined again. "I do love distracting a pretty girl. Especially on Saturday nights."

"Is that an invitation?" Stretching out her legs, she leaned back too, reveling in his *pretty girl*. And he might like the cloying smell of fried chicken grease and furniture polish that permeated her t-shirt, but she'd rather fill her senses with the scent of sawdust and sunscreen that always clung to him.

"Depends. You going to help me tear down drywall?"

She laughed. "Well, since we're on a schedule, I guess I'd better."

"Think everyone's really coming to this reunion?"

She worked her toes into the soft sand. They'd set the date for the end of July, and Nan had insisted on sending handwritten invitations. "So they say. There's great lure in the promise of new window screens and deck stairs that aren't rotten, you know."

The edges of his brown eyes crinkled. "Glad to know my work is appreciated."

More than you know. He helped her see beyond what she remembered. But not everyone might. "I'm guessing my mom will lament all the changes we've made and tell me what I should have done instead. For someone who doesn't come all that often anymore, either, she sure hates change."

"Maybe she'll just be glad change makes you and Nan happy." He crooked his pinky finger and captured hers.

The slight touch sent tingles up her arm. "Maybe ..."

"And maybe everyone will realize this time's a treasure you won't have much longer."

She jerked away. "What are you talking about?"

Tennessee held his hands up in mock surrender. "Whoa. I'm just saying your grandmother is getting along in years. That's all."

"Nan is fine. She's always been in perfect health, except for ..." She bit her lip.

"Except for the cancer right after your grandfather died."

She swiveled her head to look at him. "How is it you know everything?"

"Because Edisto Beach is really nothing more than a small town. And my mother has always gone to church with your grandmother. And because I pay attention to details."

"What's that supposed to mean? That I don't?" Uncertainty bubbled in her gut. Lou had admonished her to keep an eye on Nan.

He slid his arm around her shoulders. Despite the mugginess of the evening, gooseflesh crawled her arms. Worry tempered by anticipation.

"I'm sorry." He ran his fingers lightly up and down her arm. "Really, Cor. Should've thought before I spoke."

She couldn't think—or speak—with him this close.

"Your grandmother might be the most stubborn woman I've ever met. And if you ever meet mine, you'll know that's saying something." He'd slid his hand under her braid and lightly kneaded her neck. "I hear stubbornness runs in the family."

"Evidently ..." Her voice rasped out and she swallowed hard. "You hear a lot of things."

Tennessee traced her cheekbone with his thumb, and she closed her eyes. He hadn't kissed her yet. Whether he was waiting for the perfect moment or just waiting, she wasn't sure. But she had lain awake every night since Hannah's lecture playing *what if*, all while telling herself that the last thing she needed was a summer fling that could go nowhere come fall. *But what if it could?*

"Do you ever hear anything? About me?" He murmured the question, and her eyes fluttered open to meet his.

"Why? Are you afraid I might hear you have a different girl every summer?" She meant it as a joke—he'd made it clear at the plantation those days were long gone—but when he dropped his gaze from hers, uncertainty bubbled again. She turned her face away.

"Don't do that." He cupped his hand behind her neck and leaning in, said, "Cora Anne Jenkins Halloway, the only girl I've ever wondered about every summer since I was fifteen, is *you*."

The kiss came before she could catch her breath and, succumbing to it, she thought she'd finally let go of her role in the haunting nightmare that was their history.

His hands slid from her neck down her back to rest on her waist, and she leaned into this moment of surrender. Warmth radiated from him, skimming across her arms. Wrapping her in safety. When they broke apart, he rested his forehead against hers, his breathing labored.

"We better slow down before this gets out of hand." His palm grazed the curve of her hip.

Her thoughts scrambled to restore their reliable order. But the balmy night cloaked their embrace with the promise that life could be as steady as the tide. A promise she wanted desperately to believe.

Caressing his five o'clock shadow, she kissed him again, slowly. Treasuring the memory of this first, perfect kiss with a man who seemed to know her better than she knew herself.

"Cora Anne …" His breathing ragged, he pulled back. "As much as I would like to stay here all night, I'm going to take you home now."

She felt the smile slipping from her face. "Why?"

He leaned back into her. "Because if I don't, you'll have sand in places it doesn't belong and your grandmother will kill me." He kissed her again, with an urgency that told her why he was right.

"Besides …" He stood and pulled her up with him. "I want to spend a lot of time kissing you." He wrapped his arms around her waist and grasped her in a tight hug. "And it's best if we take it slow."

"Mm …" She put her hands behind his neck and tugged his head down. "Slow is overrated."

"Says the girl who likes plans and schedules." But he kissed her again, softly and sweetly. Then, tangling his fingers with hers, he walked her to the back door of Still Waters, and left her again with the jumbled feeling that, if things were different, slow and steady Edisto might actually be where she belonged.

Chapter 19

On Saturday, they tore down drywall and snuck teasing moments—and a few kisses—when Tennessee's two crew members weren't watching. But on Sunday, they went to church and he slipped in the pew at her side and held her hand when they walked out.

She suspected that was less proclamation and more insurance she wouldn't run away from his mother.

Under the sprawling live oak, Grace Watson took Cora Anne's hand. The older woman's eyes, barely lined with middle age, betrayed no resentment. "How lovely you've grown up."

"Thank you, Mrs. Watson." The name croaked when she forced it through her tight throat.

"It's just Grace, hon." His mother had the same frankness as Tennessee. Honey-colored hair with no streaks of gray rested gently on her shoulders. "No pretentions here, not among friends." She squeezed Cora Anne's hand, lightly but with significance. "And we should be friends."

This was the woman who had cut gum from her hair when she was eight, who brought fresh bread to Lowcountry boils, who had wept beside her on that darkening beach. *This can't be easy.*

But Grace made it seem so. Turning she said, "How are you, Annie? And when are you coming by to see me? 'Bout time for a set?"

Nan fingered the white wisps of hair coming out from under her straw hat. "I'll get by, but I've been keeping to the beach cottage lately. Making sure your boy does his job."

Grace eyed her son with a half-smile. "From what I understand, he's made you his primary client."

A hot blush crept up Cora Anne's neck, but Tennessee remained cool as a cucumber—a cliché she'd never really understood until now.

"Actually, Mom, I thought we could all go to lunch." The words were as smooth as the arm he hooked around Cora Anne's shoulders.

She had to crane her neck back to look at him because he was studying the sky as though he hadn't been planning this exchange all along.

"If it's not an imposition, we'd love to." Nan looped her arm through Cora Anne's and squeezed gently.

Hemmed in on both sides, she had no choice. "Of course."

A short time later, they were being seated at a long wooden table on the back porch of The Hideaway. The smell of fresh bread mixed with the briny breeze from the river, where sunshine glinted off the masts of sailboats taking advantage of the slight wind.

Cora Anne chose a seat facing the water and asked Grace, "Isn't this too much of a table for just the four of us?"

"Oh, no." Grace sat next to her. "Tennessee, I'm taking your seat so I can talk to this beautiful girl." She scooted up and then added, "Ben's family will be along shortly. We do this every Sunday the restaurant's open. Then, when it's not, I have to host because I have the biggest kitchen." She added in a whisper, "A bigger house isn't all it's cracked up to be, but don't tell my son."

"My mom says the same thing." Cora Anne crossed her legs and jiggled her foot. A server filled water glasses and nodded at Tennessee in recognition.

"I'll tell you, it's really just more to clean is all." Grace smiled proudly at her son. "And sure enough, I wanted those granite countertops and new appliances he put in, but honey"—she swiveled to face Cora Anne—"have you ever had to clean fingerprints off stainless steel? It's a losing battle, I tell you."

Before Cora Anne could question whose fingerprints needed cleaning, Grace started waving.

"Over here, y'all!" In a conspiratorial whisper, "There's the fingerprint culprits."

She turned and saw Christy, the hostess from the other night, navigating tables, a child's hand clutched in each of hers. Patrons—who had to be regulars—called hello and ruffled the hair of her little boy. Behind Christy followed a woman in her mid-fifties with a salt-and-pepper bob and the same smile of genuine delight. Cora Anne increased her jiggling foot's tempo.

Under the table, Tennessee lay a hand on her knee until the shaking stopped. He murmured in her ear, "They're excited to meet you."

Christy came straight to them with arms outstretched and to Cora Anne's shock, the young woman embraced her first. "We're so glad you came. Tennessee wouldn't let me talk to you the other night, selfish man." She pulled back and admired Cora Anne's vintage A-line sundress. "Love this. Now don't mind my hooligans." She waved toward the kids climbing into chairs at the other end of the table. "That's Colby and Elizabeth. We'll sit down there and keep our mess to ourselves, right, Mama?"

"Jeanna Townsend, dear." The other woman squeezed Cora Anne's offered hand. "And yes, we'll do our best to contain them. They think they own the place, you know."

As the table shook and the kids settled, Ben set down heaping baskets of cheddar biscuits and stated the Sunday brunch special was spinach and artichoke quiche, sliced ham, shrimp and grits, and seasonal fresh fruit.

"Take it or leave it." He patted his mom's shoulder.

"We'll take it, then." Jeanna beamed at her son.

"I have some strawberries for you if you're good." Ben tickled his nephew's belly. "Hi-ho, hi-ho, back to work I go …" he sang as he headed back to the kitchen.

Elizabeth ducked her head and giggled. "Uncle Benny is so funny."

Cora Anne sat back, listening to the easygoing banter of this family. Jeanna kept up a steady stream of conversation with Nan and Grace about Tennessee and Ben's latest real estate adventures and the plans Nan had in mind for Still Waters.

"I think it's just lovely you're reclaiming the old place, Annie. Get those girls of yours back down here and remind them how much they miss the pace of Edisto." Jeanna sighed contentedly. "I don't know how anyone who has it in their blood ever stays away for long."

"Mama, that's because you aren't having to work two or three jobs like other people just to be able to hang onto a sliver of family land." Christy glanced at her son. "Oh, honey, color on the picture please." Beside Colby, Elizabeth colored placidly, the giant pink bow in her auburn hair bobbing gently.

"Give him to me," a voice boomed.

A sinewy and tanned gentleman, with a shock of coarse gray hair, made his way around the table. He scooped up the squealing toddler and bounced him easily on his hip before dropping a kiss on Jeanna's cheek. Then, leaning over the table, he extended his hand to Cora Anne.

"Hey there, I'm Lenny."

"You're the famous shrimp boat captain." She shook the hand of this man Tennessee credited with saving his life and marveled at the strong grip and easygoing smile. Shrimping could be the most taxing and frustrating industry on the island, what little of it was left, yet this man appeared completely content.

Lenny chuckled. "I don't know about famous, more like infamous probably." He addressed the group. "Sorry I'm late, went out this morning to see if I could keep up with the demands of a certain restaurant owner."

"And I appreciate it." Ben saluted his stepfather and delivered a plate of sliced strawberries to Colby's place. Behind him, servers bore coffee carafes and pitchers of sweet tea. At his mother's insistence, Ben promised to join the group when the entrée came out.

"He works too hard." Jeanna stirred cream into her coffee. "Wouldn't you agree, Tennessee?"

"He's pretty driven," Tennessee conceded. Jeanna raised her eyebrows. "Okay, okay. He's a workaholic. But that's all right. Keeps him busy and out of trouble."

"Keeps you both busy and out of trouble." Lenny broke a biscuit in half for Colby. His gaze wandered over and met Cora Anne's. "Though I think Tennessee here has found something besides work to occupy his time."

She flushed, and Christy swatted at her stepfather. "Don't tease them, Lenny. We don't want to scare her off."

"Who's hungry?" Ben returned with servers and more food than "anyone needs for a month of Sundays" declared Nan as he spread the bounty.

After everyone ate their fill and boxed the leftovers so no dinner had to be cooked that night, Tennessee put his arm over the back of Cora Anne's chair and whispered, "Having a good time?"

"I really should be mad at you for not telling me about this," she whispered back.

"But you're not."

"No, I'm not. But I'll get you back." She let the smile play on her lips. Being around him meant it came more easily.

"Oh, yeah?"

"Mmm-hmm. Remember that big family reunion you're getting the cottage ready for?" Satisfied when his eyes widened in realization, she added, "This is tame by comparison." She winced to make her point, and because as the reunion loomed closer, so did memories she'd rather not dredge up. But Tennessee's calm presence might keep those at bay.

"Well, in that case …" His breath tickled her ear. "I guess I better keep you to myself for as long as possible."

"I think we could make that happen."

He smiled so wide the edges of his eyes crinkled, and with a jolt, Cora Anne remembered the sepia picture she'd tucked into an album for her mother. Their families seemed destined to be entwined, but without a happily ever after.

Her mother always called on Sunday afternoons, so when the phone rang shortly after they returned from lunch, Nan raised her brows at Cora Anne and didn't rise from her seat on the sun porch.

She lifted the receiver gingerly. "Hello?"

"Did Edisto freeze over? Can't believe you're answering the phone." Lou's voice came through sharp and clear despite the crackly old line.

"I answer my phone."

"No, you send me text messages in response to voicemails."

Cora Anne shrugged one shoulder, then realized her mother required an auditory response. "We've been busy."

"So I've heard. But did you decide?"

"Decide about what?"

Lou's huff came through the miles of phone line loud and clear. "About Tulane. I forwarded the letter two weeks ago."

"What?" She snatched the packet of mail off the counter. She hadn't even bothered to open it since Nan said Uncle Jimmy had set up all her utility bills to auto draft and she had little use for AARP circulars.

"I told your grandmother to forward the mail from the farmhouse to a PO box you could check more frequently."

"I'll get right on that." She'd found the letter. A thin envelope that ripped easily. Inside was a single sheet of letterhead and a succinct statement that an assistantship had become available and she'd been moved from the waitlist, pending receipt of her deposit. "Ohh …" She fumbled for a barstool and sat heavily.

From the porch, Nan called, "You all right, dear?"

"I've been accepted." The words set like a stone in her stomach, rather than fluttering like the feather she'd imagined.

"I thought as much. You're going to take it?"

"I … " She swallowed hard. "Of course I'm going to take it."

"Cor"—Her mother's voice lowered and became almost gentle—"if you've changed your mind, that's okay."

"No." She bit her lip. "I haven't changed my mind."

Chapter 20

"So you finally kissed her, huh?" Ben tilted back his beer and grinned at Tennessee. "Moving a bit slow for you?"

He glared at his old friend. "You know my life's not like that anymore."

"Obviously, but from the signals you two were giving off the other night, I'd have thought kissing was old news by now." Ben chuckled.

Tennessee knew his friend well enough to know the guy enjoyed pushing his buttons. He stared out at the marsh from the impressive second story veranda of Ben's newest acquisition. The man bought up property the way women bought shoes.

Sipping his bottle of green tea, Tennessee wondered what Cora Anne had thought of their first kiss. If the subsequent ones were any indication, she'd enjoyed it as much as he had.

Ben propped on the railing. "I'm just saying, man, you two were sizzling like a burger at Whaley's."

"I prefer to think of it as a slow simmer—like that she-crab soup you promised your mama you'd add to the menu."

Ben raised his bottle. "Maybe I should come along on some jobs with you. I might get lucky too."

"It wasn't luck." He shook his head. "And, by the way, Cora Anne *is* the one."

Ben dropped the second beer he was pulling out of the cooler and pivoted around to stare. "Who are you and what have you done with Tennessee Watson?"

"I'm not kidding."

Ben sat in the other plastic chair the former owners had left behind and leaned forward. "Look, the Tennessee I know doesn't drink beer with me anymore, writes bigger checks to charity than himself, and always makes rational decisions. Rational, not rash."

"Who's being rash? All I said was she's definitely the one."

"Now it's definitely? How do you know?"

"When it's right, you know." He grinned at Ben's furrowed brow. "Guess you've never known."

His friend went back to the cooler and retrieved his bottle. Flipping the lid onto the porch floor, he took a long drink. One hip rested against the porch railing and both eyes rested on Tennessee.

He knew Ben's caution had nothing to do with Cora Anne and everything to do with the history—and the present. Those deals that had been made before she'd ever stepped foot back on this island.

He spoke softly. "She doesn't even know."

Ben held up one hand. "You are not about to tell me she doesn't know about the money."

He ducked his head.

"Oh, man." His friend turned his back. "You have to tell her. And the house, the easement, the job—"

"You know, we already have enough baggage without dragging all that into it." Tennessee cracked his knuckles. "And I promised her grandmother."

"You promised—" Ben sputtered. "Do you hear yourself? When she finds out, she's going to think you played her."

"She's not ready to hear about it." He used the same tone when they closed a deal. Ben wouldn't push him.

But there was a first time for everything.

"Maybe she's not." Ben tipped his bottle toward him. "But you are."

"So?" Hannah flipped through bolts of toile fabric in a fancy home décor shop on King Street. "How's it going with Tennessee?"

Cora Anne pressed her lips together and lifted a bolt of bold turquoise. "Pretty good, I guess." She glanced around the shop and spotted Nan fingering the spines of antique books a few feet away. Lowering her voice, she added, "He kissed me."

Hannah squealed and bounced on her toes—which earned her a disapproving glare from the spindly clerk at the counter.

"Shhh …" Cora Anne put a finger to her lips and pretended to consult the fabric choices again. They were shopping for the downstairs bedroom remodel.

"Was it fantastic?" Hannah's brow furrowed. "Surely it wasn't awkward—"

"Now, Hannah, nice girls don't kiss and tell." Nan had snuck up behind them and both girls jumped. "Child, you nearly match this swatch." She held out a patch of fire-engine red dotted with white sailboats.

Cora Anne rubbed at the flush creeping up her neck to her cheeks.

Hannah scoffed and tossed her head, making the beads on her earrings sway. "Nan, you really expect us to believe you didn't tell your best girlfriend about it the first time Granddaddy kissed you?"

"Given that my best girlfriend was the sister of the man whose ring I'd just returned, it hardly seemed fitting." She shook a little as if the memory were a cobweb clinging to her body. "But never mind that. What do you girls think of this?"

Cora Anne flipped it over and glanced at the price tag. "I think my brothers aren't worth that much a yard." She showed Hannah who gave a low whistle. This time, the clerk cleared his throat. Loudly.

Hannah rolled her eyes. "I think this family might be better suited to the Pottery Barn clearance shelf."

They left the shop and headed down King Street, the heart of shopping in downtown Charleston. The day was already heavy-hot, so they stayed on either side of Nan, who moved slowly. But she also stopped every few feet to admire a new window display of vintage silver or woven bags or local art.

At a corner was a small store specializing in benne wafers and Charleston gourmet. Nan paused again and closing her eyes, inhaled deeply.

"You all right?" Cora Anne hooked her hand beneath her grandmother's elbow. Had they pushed her too hard this morning?

Nan opened her eyes and laughed. "You girls worry too much. I'm just savoring that sweet smell. Been a long time since I indulged in a benne wafer."

"Then let's get some." Hannah pushed open the jingling shop door.

Inside, the sweet, nutty scent enveloped them. Hannah bought a bag of the delicate, crisp cookies and three bottles of water. Nan sipped and sighed.

"Seems like a good thing you have a check-up this afternoon." Cora Anne untied the ribbon on the cellophane package.

"I told you, I'm fine. It's tough work keeping up with you two young things."

"Speaking of keeping up ..." Hannah draped a napkin over her skirt. Despite the heat, she remained un-rumpled in her pressed linen shell and peach cardigan. "I think I'll have the juicy details about this kiss."

Nan reached across the table and pinched Hannah's arm.

"Ow!"

"Remember how you were raised."

Cora Anne giggled. "Thanks, Nan." She attempted to smooth her own frizzy hair back into its once-neat coif. Her cotton top and shorts were already wrinkled and sticky. She couldn't keep her appearance in order any more than she could her life. "There's nothing to tell, Hannah. He kissed me and walked me home."

Her grandmother coughed and said, "Think I'll have to start waiting up for these flustered walks home."

The flush crept up her neck again.

"Nan, you may need to start chaperoning these walks. She's awfully red for someone who got a chaste kiss under the moonlight," Hannah teased.

"So, we're dating, sort of. But it's just a summer romance. Remember? I told you I got into Tulane."

"But you haven't accepted the position yet. Maybe you want to stay?" Hannah lifted her brows so high they disappeared beneath the trendy long bangs of her latest hairstyle.

"I—" Cora Anne bit her lip. "I just haven't had time to make the call yet. There's a lot of details to work out."

"As a researcher, you're usually more on top of the details."

"And as a debutante with good breeding, you're usually not so nosy."

"Ooh, touché." Hannah popped a wafer in her mouth and smiled. "Let's see what other secrets we can uncover today."

Chapter 21

Annie smiled as her granddaughters bantered. Cora Anne's pinked cheeks were a reminder of her own experiences with moonlight kisses on Edisto Beach.

She admired Hannah, so professional and poised, even if she had no use for the coming-out her parents had put her through four years ago. Her granddaughter swiveled that head of newly highlighted hair and probed. "Finish the story about yours and Granddaddy's first kiss, Nan."

Annie lifted her shoulders and winced. The girls probably thought the memory pained her, but it didn't. Not anymore. "What about it? He asked me to marry him, and then he kissed me."

"And you had no friend to share it with?"

"Well, we could hardly remain best friends after I broke her brother's heart." Annie's heart had broken, too, when she realized Charlotte Cooper would never again be part of her life. But Thornton Coultrie had been worth it. Now, perhaps, time had righted old wrongs. She shifted slightly. Too much would spread the ache from her chest to her limbs.

And the girls might notice.

Hannah propped her elbows on the table, chin in her hands. "That's our Nan, breaking hearts and eloping on the beach." She sighed. "I'm definitely eloping. This wedding business is cra-a-zy."

Annie studied Cora Anne's still-pink cheeks. Her girl definitely wrestled with more than just the flutters of a first kiss.

"Did I tell y'all about how I saved the day at Middleton Place last week when the sheep thought they were invited to the ceremony ..."

Annie listened to Hannah with one ear while studying her other granddaughter. The girl had fallen hard, and Annie wondered how long before Tennessee told her the rest of the story, and how she'd feel when she learned just who this Edisto boy had truly become.

After a visit to the Pottery Barn, and a leisurely lunch at Poogan's Porch, Hannah headed off to a consultation with a bride. Cora Anne drove Annie across town to the stately brick offices of her oncologist. Once signed in, they made themselves comfortable on a leather sofa. A coffee table strewn with a variety of reading material would pass the time.

Cora Anne picked up a glossy local magazine while Annie sat and leaned her head back. "I'm just going to rest a bit."

The day had worn her out, though it was always lovely to be out with her granddaughters. There would not be many more opportunities. She expected they would soon realize the enemy lurked, and this time, it would not be scared away with a bag of chemicals that dripped into her veins and stole more life than it gave.

The last time, food became like the beach sand in her mouth, nothing but grit. The sun had burned, so she hadn't been able to drink her morning tea on the porch or putter in her garden for months. Grief and the cancer threatened to eat her alive, but not this time. She couldn't win, but there was more to fighting than doctors knew.

The cool air of the office seeped through her capris and light sweater. An outfit perfect for the warmth of shopping on King Street and having alfresco lunch, but now she shivered with cold and trepidation. She couldn't go home until these children understood.

"Nan?"

"Hm?" Annie opened her eyes.

Cora Anne's brows were knit together. "What's this about?" She pointed to a picture in the magazine.

Annie took it and studied the photograph. Tennessee, in a sport coat and tie, presenting a check for ten thousand dollars to the Edisto Island Open Land Trust. The caption identified him simply as a local entrepreneur and owner of Watson Custom Homes.

"I'd say that's about Tennessee giving back." Annie settled against the couch again.

"But—" Her voice dulled. "I'm confused. I know he supports the trust, but that's a lot of money. I guess I just thought ..."

"That he's been struggling all along? Hardships come in more ways than finances, dear."

"I know that." Her granddaughter huffed. "But after he showed me the old plantation, I assumed things had been difficult for him and his mother."

Annie closed her eyes so she wouldn't have to explain more.

Cora Anne ignored the hint. "I know you're not telling me something."

With a sigh, Annie opened her eyes. "Darling, if he hasn't seen fit to tell you about his financial standing, then it's certainly not my place to do so either."

"You know, I'm getting tired of secrets and old pictures. You won't tell me about my mother and Patrick Watson, and now you won't tell me about Tennessee either. That's not fair."

Her plea reminded Annie of that awful summer, when the child had been ten but acted like a tantrum-throwing three-year-old. Life hadn't been fair then, and life wouldn't be fair now. This world didn't work that way. High past time someone reminded her of that.

"You're exactly right. It's not fair how you want to delve into everyone else's histories but avoid your own." Despite the sheen of tears she saw her blinking away, Annie nodded firmly. "You should be asking Tennessee—and your mama—these questions. And you should be thinking long and hard about the secrets you might be keeping from yourself."

"Mrs. Coultrie?" A nurse appeared in the doorway.

Annie acknowledged her with a wave and stood slowly. Cora Anne looked as though she might crumple up and cry—or possibly throw that magazine at someone. Given the circumstances, Annie would have liked to see her actually break and do the latter.

She patted her granddaughter's shoulder. "Now don't sit here and stew the whole time, dear. Just use that fancy cell phone and call your young man."

"Oh, no." She tossed the magazine back on the table. Well, better than tossing it at the nurse. Or Annie. "If he didn't feel the need to tell me, I won't be the one bringing it up."

Annie adjusted her purse and stepped toward the door. "Yes, you will, dear. Because good historians don't believe in leaving things buried." She walked away from the scowl. She no longer had to worry about Cora Anne discovering *her* secret today.

"Good afternoon, Beverly." Annie greeted the nurse with kind brown eyes. "How have you been?"

"Right as rain, Mrs. Coultrie. How are you feeling today?" Beverly escorted Annie down the hall. These checkups were futile, Annie knew. Sometimes, there was nothing a person could do but believe in a higher plan.

Cora Anne called Hannah, of course, while Nan was with the doctor. Hannah's quick Internet research revealed Tennessee was indeed heir to a million-dollar trust fund that had been his father's. The details on why the money hadn't been used by Patrick Watson himself were sketchy.

She pinched the bridge of her nose and frowned. "Then why is he working all the extra jobs at Still Waters? He obviously doesn't need the money."

"Maybe he enjoys the company," Hannah said, ever the optimist.

"Then why didn't he tell me?"

"Tell you what? Hey, I'm a millionaire because my dad died, but no big deal. Except it is a bigger deal because of who *you* are."

"You think I'm being overly sensitive."

"Cor, I'm sure he was waiting to tell you when he was sure it wouldn't scare you away."

Then he'd had ample opportunity. At the plantation. The cottage. The beach. She leaned her back against the smooth bark of a dogwood that grew outside the doctor's office. "I don't scare that easily."

Hannah paused, then said softly, "Yes, you do. You're looking for a reason this isn't going to work—especially since Tulane came through—and now you think you've found one."

"So you think I'll run?"

"You don't run, you retreat. But you know what, I don't think Tennessee's going to let you do that this time."

"Well, it's not really up to him, is it?" She hung up, more conflicted than before.

The drive back to Edisto was silent. Nan kept her eyes closed, but Cora Anne wasn't sure if she was napping or praying.

The charm of coming in under the canopy of live oaks was gone from this return. Rather, Cora Anne felt smothered.

She drummed her fingers on the steering wheel, out of tune with the music. Sliding over a glance, she caught Nan awake, staring out the car window, longing and sadness etched in the droop of her mouth and the lines on her face. Today had to have been more than an annual check-up.

Nan eyed her back. "You're awfully fidgety this afternoon."

"You're awfully quiet."

"That boy will tell you the truth about anything you ask, so you might as well get it off your chest." Nan rubbed her arms. "Turn down this air, will you?"

Rotating the dial, she added, "Anything *you* want to tell me if I ask?"

"I'll tell you anything I think you need to know."

"What did Dr. Kelly say?"

"Fill these prescriptions." Nan indicated the white paper sacks sticking up out of her purse on the floorboard.

"I don't suppose you'll tell me what they're for?"

"Sure I will, hon. Old age."

"Haha. You're hilarious." She cut her eyes over to her grandmother where a smile now lurked at the corner of her mouth. She relaxed her grip. Surely Nan was fine. It was her own nerves that wreaked havoc.

"Those pills are a little something to keep my energy up. I told Dr. Kelly how you all are going to be descending upon me in another month."

Cora Anne forced a smile. The reunion. The reminder.

On their right, the small grey building housing King's Market came into view.

"Go ahead and pull over here. I'd like to stretch my legs and buy my handyman a key lime pie."

"You sure he deserves one?" But she eased into the gravel drive.

"He deserves better than you prying into his personal affairs without asking, that's for sure."

Her mouth fell open. "How did you know?"

Nan tugged at her door handle. "I'm old, child, not senile. And while we're here, why don't you go ahead and call your mama and report on me like I know you're going to do anyway?"

Her grandmother strode into the market. Their argument must have invigorated her. Cora Anne stayed outside in the setting sun, leaning against her car door. The sweet scent of fresh earth and baked goods wafted through on a warm breeze that tickled her neck. A blue minivan loaded with beach gear, chairs on the roof and bikes on the hatch, pulled beside her. Peals of laughter sounded as children spilled out and ran inside, calling about ice cream.

Had her family ever been like that? She could remember the simplicity of coming to Edisto before the triplets, and the heartache of coming after, but never the sense of abandonment she saw playing out before her. Perhaps some of those answers to *why* lay with that old photograph back at the beach house.

She should call her mother. Lou would want to know about the appointment and how Nan was getting along. But she wouldn't want to talk about the past. She never did.

Cora Anne chewed her lip and glanced at the magazine page she'd torn out and tucked in her purse. Maybe Tennessee could tell her about more than his wealth. After all, he'd said Edisto was nothing more than a small town.

Nan pushed through the screen door, a pie balanced in both her hands. A child ducked out behind her—a dark-headed little girl with a fudge pop in one hand and a bag of boiled peanuts in the other.

"Look, Mama!" The girl bounced on her toes and ran to the side of the minivan where her mother jiggled a toddler on her hip. "Just what I wanted."

Cora Anne smiled and opened the car door for Nan. Questions and phone calls could wait. The day was slowing down and, despite her resistance, Edisto was kneading the tension out of her heart.

Chapter 22

After a morning working a house gut on Myrtle Street, Tennessee knocked on the back door of Still Waters and waved before letting himself in. Cora Anne sat cross-legged on the sisal rug, surrounded by old photographs and frames. A quick glance up and a nod as he came in, but she was clearly focused on her task.

"Hey." He knelt beside her, intending a kiss, but she averted her face. He didn't miss the look though.

"Something wrong?" He stood and looked around. "Where's Mrs. Annie?"

"Napping. She does that a lot these days."

He squatted back down and watched her swap a small picture from its narrow gold frame into a thick wooden one. "So shopping went well?"

"Shopping was fine."

He shifted back on his heels. Wait this out or wade on in? Patience wasn't a virtue today. "You going to tell me what's wrong?"

Her shoulders dropped as she exhaled. Pushing to her feet, she crossed to the table still littered with stacks of pictures. He followed.

She handed him a photograph. Sepia toned, scalloped edges. "What do you think of this?"

An old picture, like the ones in his mother's photo album of her first summer on Edisto. Except that wasn't his mother. But the laughter on his father's face made him grin. That infectious smile was one of his strongest memories. "This is great. You should show your mom."

"But …" She took the picture back. "Nan says they were a couple. Did you know?"

"Sure, didn't you?"

"No, she's never told me." She shook her head. A ponytail today that settled on one shoulder. "I thought they were just old friends."

"Well, they were." Tennessee hooked thumbs in his belt loops. "I think the fact they stayed friends says something, don't you?"

"But what happened? Do you know?"

He shrugged. His father had never elaborated much on his relationship with Louisa Coultrie. Hadn't seemed like a big deal, but Cora Anne appeared to believe it was. "I guess they just wanted different things. I mean, my dad wanted to build a life here and have this business. Your mom wasn't interested in that, was she?"

"I don't know. I've never really asked her why she didn't stay." She fingered the edge of the photograph. "I guess I always assumed it was because she met my father."

He offered the suggestion he knew she'd dismiss. "Maybe you should talk to her."

Cora Anne propped a hand on her hip. "Maybe she should just tell me things."

"Aren't you the one who says you have to ask the right questions to get the right answers?"

She tried to turn a glare on him, but he grinned and grabbed her around her waist. Bit by bit, he'd wear down that wall she had built up.

"Fine, I'll talk to my mother." She put her arms around his neck and let him kiss her. But then she pulled back and pushed his hands away. "I have another question."

"Hit me."

She leveled her gaze on his. "Were you ever going to tell me about your trust fund?"

He sucked in a deep breath. She might as well have thrown a punch. "You know?"

She held up another picture. This one torn from a magazine. "Reading material at Nan's doctor's office. Picture's worth a thousand words, you know." She glanced back at it. "Or in this case, ten thousand."

"I'm a little wary of making it a first-date revelation."

"Good thing we've had—" She ticked off on her fingers. "At least four dates. Unless demolishing drywall doesn't count."

He laughed. "If you say it counts, so do I."

"I want to know what you're really about, Tennessee."

He arched a brow at her. "I thought you did." He'd taken her out to the plantation, which wasn't exactly hiding the family legacy. "Here's a hint. I'm not society and money."

She sank into one of the ladder-back chairs. He bit his cheek. That had come out too harsh.

"I know you're not." Her voice was small.

He knelt beside her. Mrs. Annie had told him to wait. But this part, she could handle. He was sure. "The money was inheritance. My grandparents didn't give it to Dad while he was alive because they harbored so much resentment that he chose this life over the one they expected. But when Dad died ..." He rolled his shoulders.

"It was the only way they knew to extend forgiveness, for me at least." He squeezed her fingers. "I guess you could say it's one of the good things that came out of his death. It reconciled our family."

She pulled her hands from his. "You didn't tell me because it's my fault you have money instead of a father."

"I don't believe that, Cor. And you know it." But of course, she believed it. He had known she would. He put his hand under her chin and turned her face toward his. "You have to forgive yourself. You're the only one who can change how you remember that day." She twisted away, and he let her. Maybe she wasn't ready.

"All I can do is be here." He spoke to her back. "And tell you that while I'd give anything in the world to have my father back, I know he's in a better place. Someday, I'll understand why."

She turned back to him, slowly. "Community and compassion."

"What?"

"That's what you're about."

He rose and pulled her up with him. She got it. He'd hoped she would. "Cor, you need to understand. I didn't want to bring it up and give you another reason to talk yourself out of this."

She chewed her lip. "What exactly is *this*?"

"This!" He gestured from himself to her. "We already have *something*—and you're scared."

"I am not scared, Tennessee Watson." She crossed her arms. "I'm practical. It's June. My family's coming in July, and I'm leaving in August."

"Going where?"

She faltered now, arms falling to her side.

"What?"

"I got moved off the waitlist."

"Tulane?"

She lifted her chin. "Yes."

"Congratulations." He ground out the word.

Her head ducked again and he regretted his temper. Reaching for her hand, he passed his thumb over her palm. "Then we should make the most of the time we have."

Her lashes fluttered as she looked up at him. "Did you have a reason for coming over?"

"I don't know ... Is kissing a good enough reason?" He traced a line from her temple to her jaw with his lips. Her hair smelled like fresh coconut.

"Mm ..." She pulled back. "I think we might need an activity that will require us to use both hands."

"I can think of a few."

"Want to help me hang pictures?" She wriggled free. Keeping distance got harder every time he touched her. And now she was going to leave?

"Too pretty a day for inside jobs." And too tempting to keep kissing her until Mrs. Annie woke up. "Want to see if there's enough crabs in the traps for dinner?"

Handling pincer-happy blue crabs should give his hands plenty to do.

But she looked at him askance. "I have never liked crabs unless they come in cake form."

"Edisto's in your blood and no one ever taught you to love crabbing? Now that's a crying shame." Maybe just one more embrace ... He pulled her back and wound his arms around her waist. "It's now my mission to have you try new things. What about shrimping? Want to go out with Lenny on the boat?"

She laughed and fisted her hands in his shirt, tugging his head down so she could kiss him sweetly. "Tennessee Watson, I think you've already got me trying things I never have before. But let's wait on the shrimp-boat excursion."

Lighter. This girl was lighter. She'd slumped in that chair but bounced back. He wondered if her Tulane revelation was the cause, or if he dared hope he might become her safe place.

Despite the secrets he still harbored.

Chapter 23

T he truck bounced over the rutted dirt drive that twisted between the pine trees. He was taking her to his home.

Cora Anne spotted a herd of deer, their white tails up in flight as they circled the last bend in the road that opened to a clearing. A tributary of Steamboat Creek glittered in the background, and his mother's house stood on pilings that rose above the flood plain. But the drive wound beyond her screened porches and carried them a football field's length away to a little A-frame tucked back among the trees. Tomato and pepper plants grew in canisters on the steps, and the porch boasted a view of the water as it flowed back toward the sea.

"Home sweet home." He cut the truck's engine and swung his wide grin her way. "Dock's just over there."

She followed him up the steps and around the porch. Stacked beside his back door were five-gallon buckets, fishing poles, nets, and coolers.

"Here." He handed her a vintage Igloo. "There's a bag of ice in the freezer. Fill 'er up."

She pushed open the back door. Unlocked. As open with his possessions as his life. In the tiny kitchenette, she filled the cooler and surveyed his living area.

A bookcase shoved full of books about carpentry, home improvement, and Edisto history took up most of one wall. The television was on a low stand next to it, a large map of the island tacked above. There was a bachelor's futon, but the neatly folded quilt told her he'd let his mother offer a few things. This place spoke of independence and a man comfortable in his space.

She'd never had a place of her own. Even the apartment in Athens had been shared with three roommates and the common area had been furnished with oversized chairs and shiny tables. In fact, helping Nan with Still Waters was the first time she'd ever put her own stamp somewhere.

Maybe she would be leaving a piece of herself behind, after all. Tossing off the twinge of regret, she headed back the way she'd come.

"Hey." He stood in the shadowed hallway. "Find everything okay?"

"Kind of hard to get lost."

The hall was so narrow, he filled it completely. "Living, bath, bedroom …" He jerked a thumb toward the neat room on her right. Shaker-style dresser, masculine bronze lamps, plaid duvet cover. "Pretty much it."

"Not sure you need much else."

He slipped a hand under her ponytail and smiled. "I'm not so sure about that."

This kiss, like all the others, woke up her senses. She smelled the cedar wood he'd used to plank the walls and saw the dappled sunlight streaming through the bedroom window. There was a pull in her belly, tantalizing her with wanting and waiting.

She put the cooler between them and pushed him back toward the porch. "Maybe we should stay out here."

His cheeks reddened. "Definitely should."

She helped him gather the gear—buckets, nets, weighted lines, and bait— with the newfound knowledge that, despite what he said, Tennessee Watson might desire more than just a casual summer romance.

And so might she.

She couldn't let her emotions wreck her practicality. She was here to help Nan and then be gone. But as they strode through the spartina grass, she gripped a bucket until her knuckles whitened.

Standing on the dock, the ebbing tide carrying the creek back toward the sea, Cora Anne tugged on the brim of the cap he'd loaned her and tried not to inhale the brine and sulfur scent of pluff mud. Some said the thick gray ooze smelled of promise, for it was here that Lowcountry creek life had its beginnings.

She only smelled death.

And the rotten chicken parts Tennessee was tying onto leaded strings didn't help.

"C'mon, Cor." He dangled a line in front of her and she was reminded of the teasing teenage boy he'd once been. "You can do this."

"Just drop it in the water and wait? Like fishing, right?"

"Not exactly."

They spread a couple of old beach towels, and then he lay on his belly at the end of the dock and settled the line in the water. "Come watch." She scooted beside him.

A whole ecosystem teemed in the shallow water beneath. Minnows swam in circles and fiddler crabs, their one big claw giving them a lopsided appearance, scuttled over the drier ground among the reedy grass. A turtle, diamonds patterning his back, hauled himself from the water's edge and into the sun.

And the Lowcountry's trademark blue crabs were already nipping at the line he'd dropped in the water.

He winked at her. "They love a good chicken neck."

"You know, last week, Nan taught me how to sauté those and make gravy."

"Sounds like she's equipping you for domesticity instead of a university. Heads up!" In one fluid motion, he pulled the line and whisked the net underneath. "See, that's all there is to it."

She peered at their catch. "Sure, that's it. What now?"

"Now you put it in the cooler."

"Or I watch *you* put it in the cooler."

He laughed. "Okay, but you're going to learn to work the net."

Working the net was simple. She trailed it in the water—"Don't block the sun," he cautioned— and swooped it under the crab when he pulled the line taunt.

"You're a natural." His gaze lingered on hers.

She looked away, the pull she'd felt before now a tingle. "You're a good teacher."

He cast the line again and again until they had almost a dozen crabs of keeping size. She noticed he studied their undersides before he shook them into the ice.

"What are you looking for?"

"Sooks." At her puzzled expression, he added, "Females. Can't keep a sook crab with an egg sac."

She wondered if all kids raised in the Lowcountry grew up on these lessons. How to tell male and female crabs apart, how to hold a line in the water at just the right time of day, how to navigate a small boat down a narrow creek while the tides rose and fell. She knew without asking he'd learned most from his father. But how much had he been forced to glean from others?

Despite the bounty, Tennessee said they ought to check his traps just in case. "As hard as they are to pick, it's always best to have more."

"Going out on the water?" She swallowed hard. She hadn't been on the creeks since Granddaddy died. And even then, the small waves rocking under the boat had made her lose her lunch more than once.

"It's low tide. You'll be all right." No condescension tinged his voice.

There was water in the bottom of the johnboat that seeped over her old sneakers as soon as she stepped in. Cora Anne flinched despite its warmth.

They cast off and headed up toward the wider channel of Steamboat Creek, with Tennessee pointing out landmarks and other docks belonging to locals. Confederate flags flew from some, and others sheltered boats that looked far too fancy for these backwoods.

"Want to drive?" he asked when he slowed the motor and approached a bank.

"Think I'll leave that to the expert."

The boat listed a bit when he stood. "Trade places with me. See the line?"

A mud-slickened rope was tied to an old tree stump, and she waited until he grasped the line to ask the question nagging her. "Sure you're not trying to train me for something besides a university?"

He kept his back to her, grunting as he pulled. "I just want you to appreciate where you came from, Cor." The wire crate broke the surface and he tossed a grin over his shoulder. "Now that's a catch."

Another half dozen crabs snapped at one another inside the trap. Tennessee shook them into the cooler and then bent down with a furrowed brow. "Uh oh." He reached in and snatched up one of the angry crabs. "Look here."

She leaned back as he held it out.

"She's not going to get you," Tennessee said, laughing. "See her egg sac?" He held the crab higher, and now Cora Anne could see the orange sac protruding from her abdomen. "Got to throw her back. " He extended his arm again. "Want to do it?"

"I don't know ..." But she reached out cautiously anyway.

"I'll help you. Hold her here, where the claws can't get you." She clasped the crab's back and Tennessee let his fingers go. His hand dropped to her waist. "Just give her a gentle toss."

She flicked her wrist and the crab let go, tumbling into the water.

"See?" Now he slid his arm around her in a hug. "That wasn't so hard."

No, she thought, leaning into his embrace. It wasn't. If only she could go back to where she belonged as easily.

Nan was on the screened porch, piecing her quilt, when they returned to the beach house.

"Hey, there." Cora Anne dropped a kiss on her grandmother's powder-scented cheek.

She wrinkled her nose. "You smell like pluff mud and fishing bait."

A combination more delightful than she'd expected. "But we brought dinner home."

"Then the smell's worth it." She left her sewing and plodded toward the kitchen. Slow but steady, like a loggerhead turtle returning to shore.

Her grandfather's voice whispered in her head. He'd shown her a loggerhead once on a long ago summer night. *"Those mamas will come back to the same shore their whole life, baby girl. And their children will return to the same sands on which*

116

they were born. Now don't go telling me there's not some great Creator behind all that. We know our way back home."

Home wasn't so easy for her to define. Couldn't be the Marietta house without Dad. Certainly wasn't his third-floor apartment. Or Edisto, where all her memories crowded together in a way that wouldn't let her separate the good from the bad anymore.

Thumps on the back porch announced dinner had been brought up.

The back door scraped open as Tennessee came in. "Hey, there, Mrs. Annie. Brought along some supper company, if you don't mind."

Ben entered with a tote bag full of fresh corn and, trailing behind, Grace, who bore a large plastic-wrapped bowl.

Nan gasped like a child. "How lovely! This house was meant for company. Let me take that, Grace, dear." She reached for the bowl. "What a beautiful salad."

"Thank you, Annie. I remembered how you like my toasted pecans, so I tossed in those as well."

Over his mother's head, Tennessee winked at Cora Anne. He'd assured her Nan would love the impromptu dinner party. She'd be irked he was always right, but seeing her grandmother's delight pushed away any reservations.

Nan peered into a kitchen cabinet. "One of you is going to have to haul out this big pot for steaming those crabs."

"If you'll hand me a bowl, I'll take care of shucking this corn." Ben sniffed the browned tassels. "Sure am glad other folks like farming."

"I'm just glad other folks can run The Hideaway on occasion." Grace patted Ben's arm with a mother's familiarity. "Why don't you let me take care of that?"

"Oh, no." He hefted the bag. "These days, I'm an expedient expert at corn shucking."

"Plus, he's got to earn his keep." Cora Anne slipped beside her grandmother.

"Says the girl who stood on the dock and shrieked, even though all she had to do was hold the net." Tennessee hip bumped her as he came over to wash his hands. *Told you so*, his eyes said.

"Like I said, crabs are best in cake form." From among the discount and discarded dishes, she wiggled out the deep, blue pot Nan wanted.

"Then you better get that water going if you plan to eat before midnight." Nan nudged the dislodged clutter back into the cabinet. "Crab cakes are a labor of love, right, Grace?"

"Yes, ma'am. Lucky for me Tennessee's usually too busy these days to check his traps."

"And he's about to get busier." Ben took the bowl Cora Anne handed him.

"C'mon, partner, we got a new proposition to discuss."

Tennessee dried his hands on a worn towel printed with seashells. "I already told you we're not buying the foreclosure on Ebb Street. We've got enough going on."

Ben rolled his eyes. "No, this is a new trust opportunity. Got a call today about that place on Russell Creek."

"Near Nan's farmhouse?" Plunking the pot in the sink, Cora Anne put Edisto's water to its best use.

"Sure is." Tennessee slipped behind her and helped lift the full pot from sink to stove, his hands lingering on hers longer than necessary. A hot blush swept her cheeks when she turned and saw Grace watching.

He kept on. "Say, your grandmother wanted to put a conservation easement on some of the farm property, right, Mrs. Annie?"

Clearly, they'd been talking. Nan pursed her lips and shrugged. "Perhaps."

"And it butts up to this other piece. That'd be seventy-five acres big development can never touch."

A crash and an avalanche of dishes spilled from a cabinet. Cora Anne shook her head. "Forget land easements. There's enough work to do right here."

"What you need," Tennessee interjected as everyone helped pick up the disarray, "is some good carpentry work for storage. I could put a lazy Susan in that corner cabinet. It'll make a huge difference."

"Really?" Nan raised her eyebrows. "Without tearing my kitchen to smithereens?"

"Sure. I'll go fetch my tape and take some measurements right now. Benny-boy can handle the corn."

"Nan, you know more storage isn't an excuse for keeping all this junk down there." Cora Anne pulled her head out of the cabinet she'd been restacking. "That waffle iron Grace is holding has to be at least thirty years old."

"If it still works, why would I get rid of it?"

"Because there's two more down here."

Grinning, Grace handed over the appliance and helped Nan, who seemed to have wilted a bit, ease onto a stool. "Why don't I pour you some tea, Annie?"

"With lemon, please."

"I'll get it, Grace." Cora Anne took down three transparent blue glasses. These shelves held the entire set of glasses, plus a mismatched collection. Plastic cups leaned in towering stacks alongside kid-sized ones emblazoned with sea creatures, and plastic tumblers that kept their sweet tea cold, even on the beach. "I'd say this needs an overhaul, too. Why don't you deed over cabinet organization instead?"

"Look at you, ready for another project when your first one still lies all over my living room."

She eyed the mess. "Tennessee promised to help me hang those tonight." Thank goodness she'd already tucked away that picture of Lou and Patrick. Grace didn't need any more reminders of what her husband had meant to this family. Pouring tea from a red Tupperware pitcher she suspected was older than her, Cora Anne added, "So, you've talked about this trust idea?"

"A bit. Now, don't squeeze those lemons too hard, please." Nan sipped. "Ahh, I let myself work too long without a break."

Grace picked up her glass with a glance between the two. "I believe I'll go monitor the boys and let y'all catch up."

Cora Anne nodded at this patient woman who embodied her name. *Grace.* An idea, like forgiveness, that had long been elusive in her life of controlled moments.

"So are you going to do it?" she asked her grandmother. "Deed over the farmland?"

Nan lifted one shoulder. "Perhaps. Edisto is part of this family, but hard decisions will have to be made when I'm gone."

"Oh, yes, years from now, we'll have to figure out how to pay the taxes." Cora Anne tapped a finger on her glass. Taxes had been Lou's primary concern after Granddaddy died.

"That, among others." Nan folded her hands. "I take it you and Tennessee have reconciled."

"I wish you'd just told me."

She sighed. "I advised him to take things slowly, skittish girl that you are."

Skittish. Like the crabs crawling the sides of their trap, looking for a way out. Cora Anne winced. "I think the water's ready," she mumbled and went to fetch help.

While Tennessee measured the cabinet, Grace lifted the pot lid and expertly dropped the crabs in. Cora Anne blinked, another memory grazing the surface of her thoughts the way the net had skimmed crabs from the creek.

Grace, and Patrick with her, stamping the lid on that pot each time he dropped a crab in. Her mother, laughing and calling him a show-off as he snatched the crabs one by one from the cooler, never pausing long enough to get pinched.

Cora Anne glanced at her grandmother, wondering if she remembered those times. Nan, a hint of something sad creasing her eyes, merely sipped her tea and watched the ocean.

Chapter 24

June melded into the first of July with thick heat and wisps of clouds that offered occasional relief. At least when paired with a cold drink and the sweep of an ocean breeze.

From the screened porch, Annie watched Cora Anne and Tennessee swinging in the hammock strung between two palmettos. Despite the dry ground and brilliant sun, she had insisted on new flowers in her front beds—red and white roses alongside the blue hydrangeas—honoring the July fourth celebrations tomorrow. The two had mulched and planted all afternoon, finally finishing after Tennessee installed a drip line. They deserved this little break.

She watched the hammock rock and listened to her granddaughter laughing. A nice sound, especially in contrast to the thrashing Annie heard early in the mornings when the girl woke from her nightmares. Sometimes, it seemed, they subsided after Tennessee's company. Other times, like after the dinner party the other week, memories were triggered, and Cora Anne ducked back inside her shell.

Until Tennessee prodded her back out.

Intimate familiarity had come easily to them, as Annie had hoped it would. Their courtship reminded her of another summer long ago, when she had been barely twenty-one, young and naïve enough to know her own mind and heart. One wrong turn down that old dirt road blanketed with long leaf pine straw, and she ran straight into the arms of a man right in all the wrong ways.

She thought, perhaps, Tennessee might be right for Cora Anne in all those same ways. And then, what would *his* grandmother have to say about that?

A glance from the hammock down toward the shore showed her a man, in a shirt the color of the sky, fishing at the water's edge. Annie drew a breath—not so deep as to hurt—and ambled back to the wicker sofa.

She sat on the seat cushion of faded roses and thought of the farmhouse up the highway where she and Thornton had raised three children and crops of tomatoes before he started the nursery business. Jimmy had promised to look after the gardens, and since it was likely he sent over an employee, rather than coming himself, she didn't worry about him going into the house. But to be on the safe side, she'd told him her housekeeper aired it once a week so he needn't worry. In the Lowcountry, humidity could do more damage than a storm.

But she might need her Dutch oven when teaching Cora Anne to make gumbo. Annie picked up her quilt piece but looked out the sunroom's windows instead of at the pattern. The fisherman was still there. Cora Anne and Tennessee would need to leave that hammock soon and put away the scattered yard tools. Maybe someday, when all else on her list was finished, they'd have time to take care of that cluttered little shed.

She flinched when a stab of pain cut under her ribs. Maybe not.

The sun hung low in an azure sky. It was too late for a drive out to the farmhouse, and she was too tired to answer the questions.

Annie closed her eyes until her breathing eased. She would ask Tennessee for the favor in a few days and let Cora Anne draw her own conclusions from what she'd see. Secrets always lingered around an old home place, and this one begged to be set free.

"Two weeks to finish the downstairs. Should've told her the kitchen could wait." Cora Anne elbowed Tennessee's work boot. They lay at opposite ends of the hammock, soaking up the late afternoon sun filtering through the palmetto fronds.

"How could I do that once she started talking about needing enough time to make pound cake?" Tennessee grinned. "She's much easier to please than my grandmother. No tie, just the tool belt."

"Pushover. You don't want her to get mad and stop inviting you to supper."

"Babe, as long as you're the main feature, I'm gonna do anything she asks."

She poked his arm with the toe of her Chaco sandal. He knew she hated being called *babe*. At least that's what she told him. Secretly, a little thrill curled in her belly every time he employed the term.

"So …" He tickled her ankle and she jabbed his ribs in retaliation.

"So what?"

"You didn't answer my question this morning."

"It was a dumb question. I already told you not to get me anything."

"Not happening. You've got to give me some ideas, Cor, or you'll wind up with a birthday hammer wrapped in a big red bow."

"Hammers are useful. I could hit you with it for not listening to me."

"I've seen you swing a hammer. I'm not scared."

"Well, maybe you should be. My brothers will be here by then, and they have good aim. With anything. Baseballs, dishes, books …."

"Books? You, the bibliophile, let them throw books around?"

"I don't *let* them do anything. It's hardly my fault they wanted to celebrate the beginning of summer vacation one time by chucking books into the neighbor's pool."

"I think I'm going to like these brothers of yours." This time, he circled her ankle with a fingertip. "So besides books, which you have plenty of, what makes a good birthday present?"

His touch sent shivers up her leg. She jolted up. "Surprise me." The sudden movement made the hammock rock like his johnboat when they hauled in crabs. Which he'd now taken her to do three more times.

He sat up too. "Surprise it is." Cupping his hand behind her head, he drew her close before she could retract her statement. Surprises rarely ended well. But, instead, she surrendered to his kiss while the hammock swayed gently with the ocean breeze.

The phone rang as she bounded up the back steps after bidding Tennessee goodbye later that evening. Her mother was on the line and she didn't resist a comment about Cora Anne's breathlessness.

"I'm surprised you get anything done with that boy around." In the background, she heard her brothers start up a teasing chorus of the kissing in a tree song. Lou leaned away from the phone to shout, "Boys! Go get showers, right now. That tournament starts at eight a.m." She returned with a huff. "Sorry."

"Tennessee's here working."

"On something, I'm sure."

Cora Anne twisted the cord around her finger and kicked off her sandy shoes. Now she'd be in trouble with Nan and her mother. "What do you need, Mom?"

"Just checking in. Usually, your grandmother answers this time of night."

"She's ... " Cora Anne glanced around. Where was Nan? "She's gone to bed early, I guess."

"Don't let her overdo it, you hear? I know she has all these grand ideas for the reunion, but I'll be there a few days before to help."

"Like how early? For my birthday?" She hadn't meant to sound disappointed.

"Well, I thought you might like that." Her mother's voice took on an edge. "But I guess you might want to do something with Tennessee Watson instead."

She twisted the cord tighter. "We haven't really talked about it."

"To hear your grandmother, you two are pretty serious. And Hannah already has your Aunt Caro dreaming big."

Her heart skipped. Aunt Caro and Hannah had no reason to even consider *that*. There were plenty of other weddings out there, for couples without issues like dead fathers and distant graduate school. She used the line on Lou she kept telling herself. "Well, they can keep dreaming. We're just having fun." She bit her lip. "He's got a whole life here, and I've got plans."

"Oh, and I know how you hate to have your *plans* disturbed." Lou's sarcasm stung.

She clenched her teeth. Her mother was one to talk about derailed plans. "Anyway." She worked her jaw loose. "Nan's adamant about fixing up the cottage. She naps every day, but other than that, she has more energy for all this than I do."

"I know." Lou sighed and her tone softened. "She's amazing. Always has been. She'd teach all day, come home and work in the fields if Daddy needed help, then cook supper, clean house, and grade papers before she went to bed." The wistfulness in her mother's voice was new. "Sometimes it's all I can do to get your brothers home before they eat all the chicken I picked up at the KFC."

Lou had never admitted to feeling less than adequate.

She considered that before saying, "Mom, you know Nan's had me organizing old pictures."

"So I heard." Curtness returned.

"Anything I should know about those?"

Her mother's breath quickened. "Don't read too much into things, Cora Anne. Not every old picture tells a story." The words weren't clipped, but heavy, as though the telling would be too much right now.

They finished up with a few quick remarks about the weather, the boys' travel ball, and their arrival on her birthday. She hung up the phone and stood in the kitchen, resisting the urge to do exactly what her mother had discouraged—study that photograph again for the story that lay beneath. For the secret of who her mother had really loved. For the answer of why Patrick Watson had even cared she'd been in the water that night.

She padded down the hall and peeped in Nan's open door. Her grandmother sat in a rocker beside the window, the room's only light coming from the pale moon. Just enough to illuminate her face and the tears glistening on her cheeks. Nan's eyes were closed, so Cora Anne turned and tiptoed away, feeling she'd intruded on a private moment her grandmother wouldn't have wanted her to see.

In the kitchen, she counted the days until her mother's arrival on the wall calendar from Coultrie Nursery. Then she realized. Today was July third. The anniversary of her grandfather's death.

Amidst all the projects, she'd let herself forget—long ago, she'd learned busyness helped. Recollection seeped through. That year, the boys had wanted to decorate their bikes and ride in the annual Edisto Beach parade. She'd wanted to stay home and work her summer job. Lou had threatened to call her boss and demand Cora Anne's time off, so she'd come to avoid embarrassment.

And she'd watched her grandfather die of a heart attack before the ambulance could make it. Massive. Sudden. A clutching of his chest and a convulsion that sent him to the floor.

The memory morphed and she saw Patrick Watson fighting the waves with one arm, his other a vise around her chest.

Cora Anne jerked her shoes back on. She'd go walk down Pointe Street. Anything to escape this house and that beach and the nightmare that was coming.

Chapter 25

The morning of July fourth, Annie beat Cora Anne to the porch for the sunrise. She sat in the Adirondack with its slick new paint and sipped her tea with fresh mint. That little garden plot had come along nicely.

Cora Anne pushed the heavy door open with her hip, and then a kick when it caught on the weather stripping. "Nan, maybe the door should be next on Tennessee's list." She settled into the chair beside Annie's and cradled her cup of tea with a slice of lemon floating on top. "You're up early."

"Seemed a waste of time to be sleeping when there's all this glory." Annie tilted her chin toward the pinking sky. The sunrise never failed her. "And I already asked him to fix the door. Said he'd try to get to it today. Can't have a sticky door with all these folks coming in and out."

Once, Independence Day had signaled her family's return. For the whole month of July, her children, their friends, and relatives she saw maybe twice a year, even though they lived just over the bridge in Charleston, would tromp through the house and over the boardwalk. Her kitchen counters would overflow with watermelon slices and pound cake, while big pots of Lowcountry boil would steam on the porch alongside churning peach ice cream.

Thornton had always loved this holiday, and she could honor that after her grieving yesterday. She only had to wait a couple more weeks for everyone to come. Annie smiled. They would have a weekend of games and beach-sitting and fishing. Thornton's old fishing gear sat taking up space in the closet downstairs, and she intended the triplets to use it. This reunion would be the perfect ending. Or beginning. Depended on one's perspective.

"What are you so content about over there?" Cora Anne had finished her tea and now sat with her knees tucked under her chin, arms wrapped around her legs.

The child never fully relaxed. She'd jumped when children shrieked on the beach or clutched the back of a kitchen chair when a siren wailed in the distance. Even after all these weeks, she still carried tension in her shoulders. But sometimes, her eyes softened. It was then, Annie thought her girl saw the beauty of this place and not the hardships.

"Thinking about having all my chicks under one roof again." She sighed without pain this morning. "When you get old, dear, you'll understand just how short life is. How quickly it comes and goes through its seasons."

"I think I've already experienced that a bit, Nan." Her granddaughter's voice held none of the bitterness that tainted it the first few weeks. Instead, she slumped her shoulders and laid her cheek upon her knee in quiet reflection.

"Have you given staying any thought?"

Cora Anne lifted her head. "Why would I do that?"

"Well, if you don't know, sweetie, I can't tell you. But I know I'd like it if you would. Fall's the best time for the beach. Sun's not so strong and the hordes leave us locals to enjoy ourselves."

Her girl dropped her knees and bent to adjust her shoelaces. "Come fall, I'll be at Tulane." Annie heard the resolve. "It's what I've worked for and where I'm going."

"Well, all right, then." Annie sipped her cooled tea. She knew when it was time to leave well enough alone.

Cora Anne gave up her jog halfway down Jungle Road. The freshness of the morning—how she'd hoped to move past her night of grief—spoiled by Nan's reminder that summer coasted toward its end.

The notion of staying on Edisto, with Tennessee, was idyllic and romantic, but she wasn't that girl. They shared a past that couldn't be undone. She wasn't her grandmother, for whom leaving everything had worked. Or her mother, for whom it clearly hadn't.

She scuffed her shoe on the pavement. Lou needed to tell her about Patrick. Doubts that her mother had ever loved her father had plagued her since she'd found that picture.

Now she might be ready for the truth.

Looking up, she realized she'd let her feet carry her down Marsh Lane to the same spot she'd first listened to Tennessee offer her forgiveness. And she'd accepted.

So why did she sometimes still feel so heavy?

Especially when she thought of leaving.

But Tulane was the plan. Four years of perfect grades and internships, so she could be a graduate assistant at a prestigious university. So she could discover projects she wanted to study. Or perhaps, so she could simply discover herself.

New Orleans needed rebuilding, and she could be of use there, helping preserve what had almost been lost to Katrina's waves. Helping strangers hold on to their past would be far simpler than living with her own.

And if she left, she could *choose* to come back. Returning, perhaps, without resentment. She remembered Nan's check. Or coercion.

She wandered over to the steps of a townhome and sat, staring at the marsh. A crane, long legs and wide wings in perfect formation, rose and flew over the ebbing water to roost in a twisted tree. She should fly away too. Soon. Before it was too late and this place reminded her once more how she could never deserve to call it home.

When she came around the corner of Point Street onto the dirt lane, she saw Hannah's car looking like a bridal shop on wheels. The back hatch of the small SUV was open, and tulle spilled out among white boxes and bouquets of silk gardenias. Cora Anne grinned. A visit from Hannah would be just the distraction she and Nan both needed.

Hannah threw open the front door and enveloped her in a hug before Cora Anne stepped over the threshold. "Where have you been? I've got coffee, real lattes from Starbucks that I packed in a cooler with a towel just to keep hot for you. And scones my mama made. They are to die for." She talked a mile a minute and drug Cora Anne into the house. "And what in heaven's name have you been letting that boyfriend of yours do to this place? Our mothers are just going to have a conniption." She dropped, gasping, at the kitchen table and held out the trademark green and white cup.

Cora Anne accepted and then set it back down quickly. "It's still hot."

Hannah rolled her eyes. "Told you so." She drank from her own and raised her eyebrows. "Well? Sit down. Eat. Don't runners need to carb load or something?"

Cora Anne sat. "You want to tell me what you're doing here and why you brought the whole boutique?"

"Like I told Nan—"

"Wait," Cora Anne held up a hand. "Where is she?"

Hannah cocked her head. "Deck. Has barely moved since I got here. Said she's resting."

"She's been sitting there since I left an hour ago."

"I don't know. I just got here." Her cousin handed over a blueberry scone. "Eat. So I can talk. I have a little wedding for a patriotic bride over in Beaufort this afternoon, so Mom sent me by here to check up on you, Nan, and reunion shenanigans."

She swallowed a bite and silently cursed her Aunt Caro for baking such melt-in-her-mouth concoctions. "Don't you think the place looks great?"

Hannah glanced around the room. Her eyes lingered on the kitchen. Cora Anne had talked Nan into removing the cabinet doors and embracing open upper shelves that displaced the hodgepodge of dishes with surprising panache. Tennessee had taken down the upper cabinets over the peninsula and the whole room appeared bigger and brighter as a result.

"Good job. Still Waters has never looked better, but that's not why I'm here."

This time, Cora Anne nearly choked trying to swallow. She put down the scone and brushed crumbs from her fingers. "Good job? That's it? Nan and I have worked ourselves to a frazzle—"

"No, you haven't. You've been hanging out with Tennessee Watson under the guise of doing remodel work on this house. It's a ruse, Cor. I know it. Nan had *that* planned all along. Shame she didn't pick someone out for me too." Hannah leaned back with her latte and flicked her wedge sandal on and off her foot.

"What are you even talking about?"

"Nan. I'm talking about Nan." Her cousin leaned back in. "She's sick. Can't you see?" Hannah broke a corner off a scone. "So, what are we going to do?"

"Why do you think"—she sipped coffee that burned all the way to her stomach, but at least it cleared her throat "— she's sick?"

Hannah licked icing from her fingers and ticked off a list. "She's lost weight, you said she's sleeping a lot—"

"She's tired from all this planning and work. And she doesn't eat much. Says she's not hungry because one of her meds makes food bland, and sand's not worth eating."

"Cora Anne." Hannah stopped the tirade with a raised hand.

She hunched and crossed her arms. Thoughts she'd had for weeks rambled forth. "She spends a lot of time staring at the beach but doesn't go down there. Says she likes to watch the fishermen because they remind her of Granddaddy."

"There's no fisherman on the beach right now."

"Well—what?"

"She's sitting out there, staring at that beach, and there's no fishermen."

"So?"

"So," Hannah scooted her chair closer. "I think she's sick but doesn't want us to know."

"That's why she's so insistent on the reunion ..."

"Probably."

"Should we warn our mothers?"

Hannah's eyes widened. "Absolutely not. We might be wrong."

"But you just sat there and said—"

"I know what I believe, Cor, but you've been here all summer."

Breathe. In through her nose, out through her mouth. Calming. For once, Hannah exhibited patience and waited for Cora Anne's composure.

"I think, as always, this place is full of secrets and sadness." She bit her lip and decided. "But Nan doesn't want that to be what we remember."

Hannah nodded. "I've got to handle today's event, but then I'm headed back. Mom needs to train the help, and I need a break from demanding people."

"Well, you're not going to get that here." She swept her arm around the room. "Think all this happened because she asked nicely?" But relief coursed through her. Hannah would lighten this load.

Her cousin laughed. "I can handle Nan. At least she knows the difference between peonies and hydrangeas."

Later, after they'd sat on the front porch watching Edisto Beach's annual July Fourth Golf Cart Parade, and bid Hannah goodbye, Nan pulled out her list. She'd taken to keeping it with her wherever she went, and the tattered edges testified to the past six weeks of work.

"Well, now, what sorts of projects should we give our Hannah?" Her fingers shook as she scratched *plant flower beds* off the list.

"How about all the dishes and grocery runs?" Cora Anne forced herself to stop watching the road for Tennessee's truck. Hannah had been right. His presence and these projects kept her from paying attention.

"If Hannah goes to the store, I fear we will have to survive on Oreos and sangria." Nan tapped the pencil against her smile. "Though I do enjoy a good Oreo. This will be just like old times, right, dear?"

"Just like when we were kids, Nan. I promise." She squeezed her grandmother's swollen knuckles and noted her milky pallor. No more distractions.

Life had a habit of happening when she wasn't paying attention.

Chapter 26

B y the time the whirlwind of incorporating Hannah into their simple routine subsided four days later, Cora Anne longed for those innocent childhood days again. Back then, she and Hannah had been united in their attention to details, hunting unbroken snail shells or mollusks with perfect bore holes for twining into a necklace.

Now Hannah's focus was primarily aesthetic—she insisted on rehanging the gallery wall, not so the pictures were chronological, but so they were symmetrical—and she delighted in the knickknack décor that drove Cora Anne's practical mind mad with clutter.

"But Cor, Nan's had these sailor men on the mantle for years. They'll look adorable on a shelf in the boys' room."

Then there was the matter of Tennessee Watson. The morning after Hannah arrived, he'd stopped by to say he'd be pretty busy all week with the Myrtle house punch list. She hadn't seen him since, and the downstairs bedroom was now sectioned off by half-finished drywall. It was unlike Tennessee to leave a project undone for so long.

And she missed him, a realization that settled deep in the pit of her stomach right alongside the recognition of Nan's deterioration.

Nan panted coming downstairs to give an opinion on the rug they'd found at a thrift store in Walterboro. She barely made it back up and then lay down for two hours. Her habit of early morning tea eased into mid-morning. Her laugh had become brittle, as though the action pained her.

Cora Anne hated admitting Hannah was right about more than design choices.

Late in the week, after a simple dinner of ham sandwiches and cucumber salad, Nan gathered her quilting basket and sat on the screened porch settee with Hannah beside her. Cora Anne perched on a chair and cast idle glances from the quilt to the windows overlooking the street, telling herself she wasn't watching for him.

Nan handed over her quilting frame to Hannah and tucked a light afghan around her legs, despite the warmth of the late evening sun. She advised a stitch, and then asked the question Cora Anne figured she'd been chewing on for the last few days.

"Hannah, darling, how did you really steal away? Your mother always reminds me summer's the busiest wedding season of them all."

"It is, but I needed some time off." She finished the stitch with flourish and grinned at Nan. "Besides, Mom is thrilled you're domesticating me."

"She's been trying that all summer with me." Cora Anne slid from the chair's arm down into the lumpy cushions so she couldn't watch Point Street. No more pining. "I've learned to fry chicken and make crab cakes and boil shrimp. But quilting's not taking."

"That's because you're too much of a perfectionist, dear. You have to be willing to take out the stitches and start over, instead of becoming angry and giving up."

She curled into the chair, arms wrapped around her knees. "I don't get angry."

"Yes, you do." Hannah and Nan spoke at the same time.

"Is this some sort of intervention?"

Hannah rethreaded the needle. "Nope. Just stating the facts. You want everything to be perfect all the time, but it's not." She lowered the needle and met Cora Anne's gaze. "Sometimes, we mess up."

"I know that." She shifted and shook her foot. No one had to remind her life wasn't perfect. "But sometimes, you can't clean up a mess. There's nothing wrong with doing things right the first time."

"Absolutely not." Nan adjusted her afghan. "Now, Hannah, if I'd known you wanted time off, I'd have invited you down here too. But, then again, I am glad I haven't had the both of you scrutinizing my every move all summer long. I thought that day on King Street was enough." She arched accusatory brows.

Despite the gravity, Cora Anne grinned. Nan had always seen right through them. Her smile faded as she studied her grandmother's watery eyes. "You do seem pretty worn out."

"We're just a tad worried about you," Hannah added.

Nan blinked and tossed her head with more spunk than she'd shown in days. "Girls, as long as you are here to enjoy yourselves and my company, you are more than welcome. But if I needed, or wanted, a nurse, I'd have hired one."

Stabbing her needle through the quilt, Hannah didn't look up. "So, you're admitting you're sick, then?"

"Isn't everyone in this old broken world sick? Of course, I'm old, so mine's a bit more acute."

"Nan." This charade fatigued Cora Anne. "In a week, the whole family will be here, and my mother and Aunt Caro, for sure, are going to notice you're not yourself. Might as well tell us what's going on."

Nan pursed her lips and winked. "Why don't you tell us what's going on with you and my young handyman?"

Cora Anne closed her eyes briefly. She'd much rather not. "That's our own personal business."

"And this, my dear, is mine." She stood without leaning on the armrest for support. "Now I'm going to rest since I am, as you said, a bit tired. You girls tidy up." Regal as a queen, she left the porch.

"Well, that's an avoidance technique if I ever saw one." Hannah had the needle poked through the fabric, but made no effort to pull it through.

Cora Anne strode to the window and stared out at the street. A flock soared over the back row of houses. Must have come up from the marsh. *Fly away before anything bad happens …* Maybe they were wrong. They had to be.

"Nan's fine. We're just so used to tragedy, we can't accept simple aging." That argument helped her sleep at night. Kept the nightmares at bay. Bad things only happened in threes. Patrick Watson. Granddaddy. Her parents.

"Let's get out of here for a while, go down to Whaley's and clear our heads." Hannah tossed the quilt piece atop this month's issue of *Southern Living*.

Lou still liked to remind everyone how she'd pull a wagon between Still Waters and Whaley's to get ice when it was the only convenience store on the island. Now, it was a popular bar and grill Cora Anne figured would be loud and crowded this time of night. She grinned at Hannah.

"I've got a better idea."

At The Hideaway, Christy found them a quiet table in the corner and apologized to Cora Anne that the porch was already full. Over her menu, Hannah raised her eyebrows.

She shrugged. "It's the only place I've sat when I've been here. There's a great view."

"Obviously, you've been here a lot, since the hostess hugged you like a long-lost friend."

"That's Christy, Ben's sister. Remember I told you about her?"

"The golfer's wife with the kids? She doesn't look any older than us."

Christy must have heard her. "Island life agrees with me," she said, setting down goblets of ice water. "You must be Hannah. It's lovely to meet you."

Hannah shook Christy's hand. "I think we'll have to get together so you can fill me in on any secrets my cousin might be keeping."

Christy laughed. "I'll tell you anything you want to know, and don't worry"—

she put a hand on Cora Anne's shoulder—"all of it will be a glowing endorsement for Tennessee Watson. Now, y'all just holler if I can get you anything." She left the table and greeted the next wave of customers.

"So this is Tennessee and Ben's place, huh?" Hannah's head swung back and forth as she assessed the restaurant. "Would make a great reception site. I'll have to keep that in mind." She flashed a smile at Cora Anne. "Money aside and no matter what he pretends, Tennessee is hardly just a handyman."

"He's hardly just anything."

Hannah pored over the menu and suggested glasses of a local wine from a vineyard in Charleston, which Cora Anne countered with the shrimp dip appetizer. By the time a harried waitress took their order and set down glasses, Ben had emerged from the kitchen. He worked the room like a celebrity, shaking hands and accepting bear hugs from folks who had, Cora Anne was sure, known him his whole life. She noticed Hannah watched intently as he made his way to their table.

"Cora Anne Halloway." Ben patted her on the back as if they were old buddies. "Where's the main man?"

"You tell me. I haven't seen him in days because of that house on Myrtle Street."

Ben puffed out his chest. "Want to run off with me, then?"

"You're incorrigible."

He turned a dazzling smile on Hannah. "Since she's already taken, I think I'd like to meet you."

"This is my cousin, Hannah." Cora Anne smirked, as Hannah fluidly tossed her hair from her eyes. "Hannah, Ben Townsend."

Ben bowed over Hannah's offered hand, like a Southern gentleman of old. "How can I be of service to you lovely ladies?"

Hannah's eyes sparkled and she propped her chin on her knuckles. "I'm sure we can think of something."

No way could Cora Anne sit here and be third wheel. "If you two will excuse me, I believe I'm going to track down Tennessee." Sitting here while Hannah and Ben flirted would only make her agonize more over Nan and leaving and ... missing him.

"Tell him I said to get on down here." Ben commandeered a chair at the table. "I promise not to talk business."

Cora Anne grabbed her cell and headed for the front porch. Leaning against a column, she pressed the phone to her ear.

He answered on the first ring. "Hey, babe, everything okay?"

She caught her breath. *Babe.* "Yeah, we're fine. Just haven't seen you all week."

"I know ... I'm sorry. Work has been crazy, and I figured you and Hannah might want some time. But I've missed you."

Tangible relief made her press a hand to her stomach. And confess. "I miss you, too." She bit her lip. Maybe this could work past summer? "Want to come hang out with us at The Hideaway? Ben's here."

Phone calls weren't hard. But impromptu dinners when she was hundreds of miles away would be.

"Oh, yeah? He proposed yet? I tell you, Cor, I think he's just after your money."

That irony made her giggle—like the love-struck girl she kept telling herself she wasn't. "You mean my grandmother's beach house?"

"To him, they are one in the same."

"Well, he did invite me to run off with him, if that counts."

"I'll be there in five."

"Don't break your neck. I turned him over to Hannah's charms. If we work this right, we could wind up with an evening to ourselves."

"I'm in my truck."

"See you soon." She ended the call and lifted her eyes to the sun sinking low over the marina. One more day gone.

When she got back to the table, Hannah and Ben had their heads together in deep discussion.

"Tennessee's coming, if y'all want to be left alone." Cora Anne dropped into her seat and took a sip of wine, hoping for an immediate calming effect. A bit fruity. This, she could drink.

Hannah smiled coyly at Ben. "He's filling me in on growing up with Tennessee. Bet I know something you don't know."

"Seems there's a lot around here I don't know." But she could play along. "Hm ... could it be that Tennessee has a million-dollar trust fund?"

Hannah rolled her eyes.

"Could it be that he has more ex-fiancées and girlfriends than I want my father to know about?"

Ben almost choked on his Corona. "That's a good one, Cor. He's loosening you up." His smile was genuine and his hazel eyes were bright. "I like it."

Hannah shrugged. "You're not even trying." She spread dip on a cracker and lifted it toward Ben. "What if I told you the two fine upstanding gentlemen you've been keeping company with this summer were once part of the graveyard tour?"

"So? We only went on that once because—"

Ben moaned softly. At seventeen, that sound had sent chills down Cora

Anne's back.

She glared at him across the table. "Wait a minute. Are you telling me the mausoleum haunting was staged?" She whacked his arm. "You and Tennessee scared me away from that graveyard for years. I could barely stand to go to church there."

Hannah laughed so hard tears gathered in her eyes. "I told him. You nearly wet your pants."

"What's so funny?" Tennessee stepped behind Cora Anne's chair and pecked her flushed cheek.

"Oh, no." She scooted back. "Seriously. You and Ben were props for the graveyard tour?"

"Knew I could never leave you alone with him." Tennessee gave Ben a light punch. "Thought we agreed to take that secret to our graves, man. Pardon the pun."

Ben held up his hands. "I surrendered to the spell of a pretty lady with questions."

Tennessee slid his arm around Cora Anne and leaned over so his stubble tickled her cheek. Hannah's eyes danced and she mouthed, *Told you so. Fairytale.*

But even fairytales have darkness. In this mirth-filled setting, she could laugh it off, but the night they went on that tour, Cora Anne had lost her supper in the bushes of Still Waters and Patrick Watson had haunted her dreams.

"If you want, I'll take you back to that graveyard and prove there are no ghosts." Tennessee's whisper in her ear sent a different kind of chill down her back.

"That sounds like an excuse to get me alone with you."

"Oh, we'll let them come along, too. So if there are any haints"—he mock-whispered the Lowcountry term— "we have a better chance of escape."

"Whatever." Hannah tossed her head and leaned closer to Ben.

The four sat in the restaurant, laughing and talking for over an hour. When Ben heard Hannah and Cora Anne shared their birthday, he insisted they bring the family to The Hideaway for a little celebration. Obviously, he'd been smitten already, and Hannah didn't seem far behind.

In the parking lot, Tennessee wrapped his arms around Cora Anne's waist and hugged her. "So you missed me, huh?"

She tilted her head back and saw the rounded moon hanging low over the banks of the Edisto River. It would wane away before month's end. Would be easiest if this did, too. But the warmth of his embrace seeped through the thin cotton of her shirt, and she let herself meld into his kiss. Even the moon waxed full before diminishing.

When she buckled herself in behind the wheel, Hannah sighed, and Cora Anne tucked her hair behind her ears with shaking hands. "I know, you think we're destined for happily ever after."

"I do think that, Cor, and it's beautiful." Hannah's smile held a hint of sadness. "But I never realized how much I've missed this place the last few years. It's easy being here, because it's home, too, you know?"

Cora Anne lowered her window so the breeze could blow on her warmed skin. *Home.* What would it be like to believe that?

Chapter 27

B etween beach walks with Tennessee and Ben, Nan's never-ending to-do list, and Hannah's exuberance for Pottery Barn, Cora Anne found no time for dwelling on the impending countdown toward summer's end and leaving. By the time Tennessee and his crew finished the remodel downstairs, they had barely a day to pull the room together before everyone would arrive.

Now new sheets graced the bunks stacked against the freshly painted walls Hannah had accented with local art prints. On the new shelves in the laundry area, they stacked beach towels beside a basket of extra sunscreen, goggles, and snorkeling masks. Their final task was to stock the small pantry with snacks, canned drinks, and paper products, all in anticipation of a certain band of twelve-year-old boys.

On her birthday morning, Nan met Cora Anne on the deck with tea and a hug. "We did it." There was still firmness in her arthritic hands squeezing Cora Anne's shoulders. "Thank you."

Cora Anne pulled her into a hug, resting her chin on the soft spot in her grandmother's clavicle. Like she had as a child. "Thank *you*." Maybe it was the busyness, or maybe something more, but the cottage felt different now. Lighter. No longer the harbinger of bad memories.

Even her nightmares had faded to only a lingering worry she could shake away with the morning. Perhaps they, too, were waning away as she gave the cottage new life.

Nan sniffed. "Anyway." She eased away. "It's nice to see you happy again. Now, how about a special birthday breakfast?" She squinted at the sky. "Sun's already strong."

Cora Anne perched on a stool at the peninsula and assessed her grandmother's graceful and efficient movements. "You seem to be feeling better."

"Nothing like a little celebration to perk up these old bones." She cracked eggs into buttermilk and then beat the mixture so that none spilled over the sides of the measuring cup.

"Why is everyone so chipper this morning?" Hannah grumbled as she plopped onto the stool beside Cora Anne.

"Someone's not a morning person." Cora Anne elbowed her cousin.

"And someone else should learn life's little indulgences. Such as sleeping late."

"Happy birthday to you too. I made coffee, and Nan's making blueberry pancakes."

"Really?" Hannah leaned over the counter and snagged a handful of blueberries. "Thanks, Nan."

"Anything for my birthday girls." Nan poured batter onto the hot cast iron skillet she'd recently taught them how to season.

Hannah went around the counter to fetch her coffee and mimed behind Nan's back with elaborate gestures. Cora Anne ducked her head to hide her laughter. Yes, she seemed much better.

"Calm down with those pancakes, Nan." Hannah stepped beside her. "You're just feeding us, and I still have to fit into a bikini."

"In that case, you better eat more." Nan nodded as a knock sounded on the back door. "Now, here's company that appreciates my efforts."

"I hear something about birthdays and pancakes?" Tennessee poked his head inside, and Nan waved him over.

Hannah grinned at Cora Anne. "Should've known it wasn't just about us."

Nan ignored that and tilted her face up to Tennessee for a kiss on the cheek. "You sure did, sugar. Now tell your sweetie pie to scoot over and share till I get this batch ready."

He dropped a kiss on her cheek, and then leaned over to steal a bite of Cora Anne's pancakes.

"Hey! Get your own fork, at least." Cora Anne snatched hers back. Nan's narrow shoulders quivered as she chuckled. All summer, he'd fit into this small part of her family, indispensible as fresh water.

But today, things changed.

"Think I'll just wait for my own." He came behind her and kneaded the tension gathering at the base of her neck. "Yours are liable to put me into sugar shock. And happy birthday." He kissed her forehead when she leaned her head back in relief. She'd promised herself the birthday gift of not thinking about tomorrow. That had worked for Scarlett O'Hara. Sort of.

He propped on the other stool and grinned. "Mornin', Hannah. Happy birthday to you too."

She lifted her mug. "Want some coffee?"

"Honey, I'll get it."

Hannah's sidestep thwarted Nan's attempt. "If my mama gets here and finds out we've been letting you do all the work, I'll never hear the end of it. I can pour coffee. You tend to Tennessee's pancakes before he starts nibbling on Cora Anne."

Glaring would be more effective if the hot flush hadn't already crept up her face.

"Now, don't tease the girl. She's already the same color as my tomatoes." Nan pressed a finger to her lips and turned her back. "Hand me the milk, please, Hannah."

Tennessee, evidently taking Hannah's suggestion to heart, put lips to her ear and whispered, "Any chance I could get you to myself for a few minutes?"

"Want to make a break for it now?"

He sat back. "And miss breakfast?"

"I see where your priorities are."

After breakfast, Tennessee watered the raised beds while she picked the tomatoes. Her hands wrapped around the handle of Nan's garden basket. The afternoon they had staked these plants together suddenly seemed long ago.

He stretched the hose from its coil and came to stand beside her. "Why are you nervous?"

She hated—and appreciated—he could read her so easily. "Just feels strange. Like our bubble is about to burst."

He sprayed the beds with a gentle cascade. The water fell on the parched plants with the softness of rain, and stalks perked up right before their eyes. He gave her that half-smile that deepened his dimple and reminded her so much of that old picture she planned to ask her mother about again.

"Doesn't take much to perk up thirsty ground." He switched the hose to his other hand and reached to thread his fingers through hers. "And it's all right to bust our bubble and let me meet everyone, Cor."

"You say that like you've never seen them before."

"I haven't, not in this territory."

She cocked her head. So he wanted to tread these waters.

Tennessee released the handle and the water died to a trickle. "You think it's a big deal talking with your mom before your dad?"

"That depends. What are you talking about? The weather? The boys' behavior? Paint colors for the bathroom upstairs?" She took her hand from his and pulled a plump tomato off its stem.

"Don't be evasive."

"I'm not." She picked another and deliberately turned her back.

"If you don't face me, I'm going to spray you with this hose."

She spun around. "You wouldn't."

"Dare you to make me." The smile tickled the corners of her mouth, and she bit the inside of her cheek to keep from giving in. He tucked his free hand under his other arm and let the hose dangle. "You going to talk now?"

"About what?"

He lifted the hose and took a step toward her.

She backed up. "I don't know what you want me to say. I don't think it's a big deal if you see my mom before my dad. We don't know there's ever going to be a reason for you to meet him anyway."

He advanced again and this time, sprayed the ground at her feet.

She yelped and jumped back. "What in the world is the matter with you?"

"What in the world is the matter with you that you think there wouldn't come a time I'd want to see your father?" He aimed the hose at her, and she backed into the palmetto tree in the corner of the yard.

She held up her hands. "Truce?"

He sprayed a light mist that dampened her face.

Sputtering, she spat out, "I can't believe you did that."

He leaned in, one arm on either side of her body, and pinned her against the tree. "Do you surrender?"

Her heart ricocheted. "Why? Are you afraid I'm going to run away?"

"Yes, but I figure I can catch you."

"Oh, really?"

"Oh, yeah. I can chase you all the way over to Louisiana if need be."

She opened her mouth, and then closed it. She had no retort. Would he really follow her to Tulane if she asked?

"Guess I have your attention."

"I guess so."

He leaned his forehead against hers. "I love you."

Of all the things she had expected, this wasn't it. The days of pretending this was just a fling were over. She'd walked into deep water with this man, and this time, she really might drown.

But for a moment, she closed her eyes, and reveled in the security of his admission. When she finally looked deep into his, she saw passion and turmoil and fear.

"So, happy birthday." The muscle in Tennessee's jaw twitched.

Her hands cramped in their death grip around the handle of the old basket. Dropping it to the ground, she laid her hands on his chest.

"I think ... I think I love you, too." *And I'm terrified of what that means.*

His smile radiated like the sun. She had to tell him. "But I don't—"

"Shh." He put a finger on her lips. "We'll figure it out. Together."

Nodding, she blinked back tears. He lowered his head and kissed her, his thumbs skimming her cheeks. When she opened her eyes and looked into his, they were now as tranquil as the still waters of the St. Helena Sound lapping beyond the ocean.

Chapter 28

By late afternoon, the cottage was spotless, but Cora Anne's stomach considered revisiting the bushes like the night after the graveyard tour.

"You need to calm down." On the table, Hannah folded beach and bath towels into teetering stacks.

"I can't." So she paced, adjusting Nan's bowls of shells on the end tables and flicking a dust rag over the television.

"Seriously, Cor. Your mother is hardly someone to worry about."

"She's going to be furious with me if Nan's really sick." She kept her voice low, even though Nan napped with her bedroom door closed.

"Well, count on the fact that you're in lo-ove to keep her from overreacting." Hannah placed the last towel and then tucked the stack under her chin so it didn't fall. "I think it's my feisty mom we should worry about. Maybe tomorrow we can relocate to one of those townhomes?"

Cora Anne walked over and took half the towels. "I'm sure if you asked him, Ben would find you a place to stay."

Her cousin pursed her lips into a pout. "He's cute and all—"

"Don't forget the part about being a self-made businessman."

"But I hardly have time for romance, right now."

"Yeah, like I do."

Hannah smirked. "Well, you sure made time, didn't you?"

A car door slammed, and they both jerked. Her stomach had filled with sludge—like pluff mud between her fingers.

"Chin up." Hannah opened the door to a cacophony of catcalls and whistles. "Sheesh, your brothers are the definition of ruckus."

Cora Anne peered around her. The boys leaned out the open side doors of her mom's minivan, which seemed to sag under the weight of them and the bicycles on the roof.

"Hey, sis! Where's your boyfriend?"

"Hannah! You the lookout?"

"Cora and Tennessee sittin' in a tree—K-I-S-S-I-N-G—" All three sang at the top of their lungs.

She uttered a silent prayer for patience. What a show for the afternoon foot traffic heading to the public beach access down the street.

"J.D., Cole, Mac—stop that right now or you won't set one foot on the sand of that beach this afternoon." Lou's authority cut through the serenade.

"Aw, Mom!"

"Can't we even have a little fun?"

"He's not here, anyway. Do you see a big truck?" That was J.D. Always thinking.

"Hey, guys." Cora Anne joined Hannah, leaning on the porch rail to enjoy the spectacle. "Thanks for letting Edisto Beach know you're here. The public warnings we put out probably weren't being taken seriously enough."

Lou cracked a smile up at her.

As one entity, the boys barreled up the stairs and engulfed Cora Anne. Cole grabbed her from behind, while Mac and J.D. squeezed from each side.

"Can't—breathe—" She puffed through the ferocious hug. But her prayer must have worked because she felt strangely endeared to them and their lack of subtlety.

"Hey, sis, miss us?" Mac asked when they let her go.

"Yeah, I always miss being squeezed to death." She ruffled his hair. Already, the humidity made his dark locks swirl. "Mom letting y'all get long, huh?"

They grinned and J.D. tossed his stick-straight honey-colored bangs back with a swoop. "Yep. She hates it, but says you gotta pick your battles."

That sentiment had kept Cora Anne on peaceful terms with her mother during their weekly phone calls.

"Boys!" Lou climbed the stairs weighed down with a bag on each shoulder and a laundry basket of groceries. "Come down and unload this van before I start throwing bags in the ocean."

The boys thundered back down, skirting their mother along the way.

"Hannah, you be ready for a proper greeting when we get back," Cole called as he brought up the tail.

She laughed. "You guys make my brother look serene."

"Personally, I find Matthew's behavior refreshing." Lou huffed up the last step.

"Hey, Aunt Lou, I've got this." Hannah took the basket so Cora Anne could welcome her mother. After the boys' bear hug, Lou's quick embrace seemed stiff.

"Happy birthday."

"Thanks."

Her mother's appraisal raked over her simple sundress and sandals. "You're looking awfully nice today."

"Don't start, Mom. The boys are right. He's not even here right now."

"Well, then, I'll anxiously await his arrival."

Cora Anne followed her into the cottage. Nan had emerged from her bedroom and was in the kitchen, directing Hannah with the groceries.

"Mama!" Lou lingered on the hug she gave her own mother. "How are you?"

"I'm fine, Louisa. Just fine. Now, where are those wild hoodlums? All that bedlam woke me from my nap."

"I'm sorry. I'll calm them down."

"Why? They bring a lot of life to this place."

"Nan!" J.D. came through the door and dumped his duffel in the middle of the floor, Mac and Cole right behind him.

"Don't squeeze her," Hannah cautioned as the boys greeted Nan.

They heeded her warning and clasped cautiously.

Nan laughed and pulled them closer. "I'm not going to break. All these girls worry about me too much." She bent her head, and the boys huddled with her. "Now, you three are growing into such good-looking, polite young men, that I know when your sister's beau arrives, you will behave with the utmost decorum. Anything else could result in a loss of house privileges."

She looked at all of them, and they grinned sheepishly.

"Um, Nan?" Cole pushed hair back from his sweaty forehead.

"Yes, dear?"

"What are you talking about?"

"What she's trying to say, mischief-teers, is that when Tennessee gets here, you better behave, or she won't feed you." Cora Anne hefted a duffel to J.D. "Now, move this stuff downstairs or I'll follow through on Mom's threat."

"You mean we hauled all this up here, and we gotta take it right back down?"

"Yep."

"Where are we sleeping? In the laundry room?"

"Head downstairs and find out." She ushered them toward the hall.

Nan eased herself into the armchair. Her lips pinched as though the sheer volume of family greetings had pained her. "Cora Anne, take your mother, too." The pep left her voice and she spoke almost breathlessly. "So she can see the improvements."

Lou followed them down the narrow interior stairs, though Cora Anne could sense her reluctance. Her mother wanted to stay upstairs and scrutinize Nan.

"Well, this certainly looks different." Downstairs, Lou circled the room. She opened the accordion doors to the laundry and studied the shelves Tennessee had built into the walls. "Must have taken him weeks to do all this."

"Well, Hannah and I did most of the details."

But Tennessee's mother deserved the credit for donating an old gaming system that made the boys' faces light up. Duffels hit the ground and Cora Anne wished Nan had negotiated the steps to see their appreciation.

"This is more than just details." Her mother narrowed her eyes. "It's a complete remodel."

Cora Anne crossed her arms. "He's an efficient worker. Got most of it done over the last week, actually."

"Definitely efficient, then. Tell me, has that man worked any other jobs since he discovered you were here?"

She took a deep breath and glanced at the triplets who were engrossed in studying the games. "What, exactly, are you trying to say?"

Lou lifted her chin and shrugged. "I don't know. All I know is you came here to help your grandmother, not to chase a relationship that doesn't suit your future."

Her mother's words stung, despite their accuracy.

"Of course," Lou added, "to hear Nan tell it, he's the one who did the pursuing, and you resisted the idea at first. But I'm sure she encouraged you. Probably found it a good distraction so you wouldn't notice."

"Wouldn't notice that she's obviously not well? I've kept you updated, Mom."

"Not well enough." Lou hugged herself and rotated, appraising the room again with the same critical eye she'd given Cora Anne. "Don't you see what all these improvements have been about?"

"She just wants the cottage to be a home again. A place we want to come instead of avoid."

"I don't think so. It looks to me like she's had Tennessee distract you all summer so you wouldn't notice she's getting it ready to sell."

Cora Anne sucked in a breath with such sharpness it stabbed her side. "How can you say that? This place is supposed to be yours and Aunt Caro's someday."

"And we told her last year we wouldn't be able to keep up with this house, but she said she'd hang onto it until the day she died, and then we could do whatever we want." Lou pressed her lips together. "Either she changed her mind, or that day's coming soon."

Cora Anne reached for the support of a chair. "You think she's dying. You've been here five minutes, Mom, how can you say that?"

Lou placed her hands on Cora Anne's shoulders. For the first time in a long time, she sensed her mother meant the gesture for comfort.

"I'm sorry. He's done a wonderful job. *You've* done a wonderful job." Lou dropped her hands. "But all this … my whole life, she's hardly changed a thing about this place. Then all of a sudden, she wants it to be fresh and new. You understand why I'm concerned?"

"She wanted me to love Still Waters again." Her voice sounded small and felt tight. Had she really missed Nan's plan? Tennessee had quipped once that this was more than just a simple reunion. He flipped beach homes as a business. But his eyes when he'd told her he loved her …

"Do you?"

"Do I what?"

Lou lifted a shell off the dresser and rubbed it like a talisman. "Do you love it here again? Did you find your peace?"

She answered with only a tremor of less confidence than she'd given Nan that morning. "I've been happy."

Lou put the shell back on the dresser. "Then I guess that's all that matters for now, isn't it?"

Chapter 29

Lou settled herself onto the old green bike. Pushing her toes against the sandy ground, she felt the stretch through her hamstring all the way up her lower back. She ached from the six hour drive and the tension that had built more steadily the closer she came to the island.

When she found the nearly empty bag of White Lily flour in the kitchen cabinet, she had announced to her mother she was biking to the store for a little fresh air and essentials. Like biscuit flour and maybe a six-pack of Palmetto Ale.

Twenty-six blocks to the Piggly Wiggly. Enough time to get the salty sea breeze tangled in her short hair. The knots along her spine loosened with each pump and pedal. So, maybe her daughter had found the peace this simple down-home place always gave.

The bike bumped off the curb and Lou balanced herself. She'd never regretted leaving Edisto, not until that first summer with the triplets. The summer Patrick drowned saving her daughter.

She rolled away memories of the past with each pedal of the bike down the cracked sidewalk in a place as familiar to her as breathing. Rounding the last curve, she crossed the highway into the cramped parking lot of the small store.

Lou parked the bike next to a golf cart still bearing its Fourth of July streamers and grabbed her wallet from the basket. Pushing her sunglasses atop her head, she blinked against the sudden brightness, and for a moment, thought she was having a heat-stroke hallucination.

A young man exited the store, tall and sandy-blonde. Muscular build and confident walk. She watched him cross the lot and climb in the cab of a white truck. She didn't need to read the logo on the truck's side to know who he was. Tennessee Watson was the spitting image of his father.

No wonder her daughter had fallen hard.

Lou shook her head to clear it and went inside to buy her flour. But on her way out, she collided with someone headed in.

"Oh, sorry, I—David?" She gaped at her ex-husband. "What are you doing here?"

He stepped back and hooked his thumbs in the pockets of his cargo shorts. Sheepish, like his sons when they were caught red-handed. "Hey, Lou. I came to wish Cora Anne a happy birthday."

"Did she know you were coming?" She hoped not. Surely her daughter would have given her a heads-up.

"No, spur-of-the-moment decision." He moved aside so other shoppers could enter. She stepped beside him.

"Don't you think you should have called?" She rubbed her sweaty palms on her shorts.

David lowered his Ray-Ban sunglasses and let them dangle on the cord around his neck. She bit her lip. After the divorce, he'd taken on this persona of someone hip and cool. Made her feel like a loser wallflower at the school dance.

"I wanted to surprise her." His gaze wandered over her wrinkled shorts and old t-shirt. "Did you just get in? Because I figured you'd have come earlier."

"The boys had baseball practice because of the tournament down at Disney next week. I told you about that." She reverted back to the clipped tone she always used with him. Better he think her an ice queen than a remorseful ex-wife.

"That's right. I marked it on my calendar. So, you just got in?"

"That's what I said." She walked to her bike. He followed. She put the flour in the basket and turned to face him. "Do you need something else?"

He shrugged.

"Well, you know where the house is." *Be kind.* She sighed. "We're going out to dinner. I'm sure Cora Anne would be happy to have you join us."

He tilted his head, and she tried not to wince when he looked at her. He still made her heart race when his hazel eyes met hers. But she'd told him to leave. That she was tired of trying.

Really, she was tired of feeling selfish.

"Will it bother you if I'm there? I can drive to Charleston, come back tomorrow."

Because, with one exception, he had always been the selfless one.

"No, it will be fine." Her standard comeback, even though nothing about this had ever been fine. "You know about her boyfriend?"

His eyes rounded and Lou sighed. Cora Anne hadn't told him. At this rate, she'd be spending the whole evening extracting her foot from her mouth.

"There's a boyfriend? Who in the world could she have met? Oh." His eyes narrowed and studied hers. "She did mention Tennessee Watson has been doing some remodeling work for your mother."

"Yes. They've practically redone the whole place." Lou swung her leg over the bike. "It looks good. You should check it out while you're there." Sweat trickled down her back. Gas fumes mingled with the smell of hot tar, obliterating any sea breeze that might calm her stomach.

"So he's the boyfriend, huh?" David stepped back, arms crossed, eyes cold. "Well, like mother like daughter, they always say. I'll see you later, Lou."

She nodded, her throat too thick with tears to speak. David went into the store with his back straight and his head high, but she hung hers and barely looked up the whole ride home.

Despite the aura of stiffness her parents brought to this birthday, opening the cottage door to find her dad had been a pleasant surprise. Cora Anne took him all around the cottage, showing off her and Tennessee's handiwork without pausing long enough to reflect on the last time they'd all been at Still Waters.

The last time they'd been together as a family before he moved out.

Her mother hadn't shared in the enthusiasm, but she'd been tolerable, at least. And Cora Anne suspected the charm of the Hideaway might soften her even more.

For this birthday dinner, Ben had employed his mother and sister to decorate the porch, though Cora Anne suspected Hannah's influence. On the tables, tea lights floated in glass bowls, and shells rimmed place settings with linen napkins.

"This is just lovely," Nan sat gingerly at the table's head. "Isn't it, Lou?"

"Indeed." Her mother fingered the edge of a sea-grass mat. "I love these. Mama, didn't you used to have some like this?"

"Exactly like these," Cora Anne said. "I found them in the hall closet. Told you we should use them more, Nan."

Tennessee pulled out a chair for her beside Lou, but then he stepped aside and indicated to her father that he should sit on her other side.

"Cool! Look at this boat." Cole and the other boys were glued to the railing, watching as Lenny brought the *Sarah Jeanne* into port. She smiled. Now this was the kind of moment she wanted to cherish.

"That's Ben's stepdad. He might take you out sometime if you ask." She grinned wider when the boys swung around as one to pin Ben with pleading gazes.

"I'll tell him to sign y'all up for the dawn duty." Ben nodded. "Now, these women picked quite a menu when you're all ready."

Cora Anne saw her mother studying Ben, his arm casually propped on the back of Hannah's chair. Aunt Caro was going to get plenty of details when she and Uncle John finally made it over in the morning.

"Go on. We all know you're bursting with pride to show off." Tennessee's dimple winked as he teased his friend. She welcomed the return to his familiar demeanor. He'd greeted her mother with only cordial formality, no doubt trying to be as respectful as possible. Though she had a feeling that, given permission, he'd treat Lou like an old friend. Which, in a way, they were.

"It wasn't all him." Hannah insisted tipping a smile at Ben. "We got to pick the sides."

"Yes, as long as cheese grits and tomato pie were included." Cora Anne darted a look down the table at Tennessee. He met her glance and she knew they were thinking the same thought.

If they were a fairytale, Hannah and Ben were a romantic comedy.

Ben clapped his hands and announced, "Tonight, for your dining pleasure, The Hideaway is pleased to provide locally caught shrimp prepared fried, broiled, and in cheese grits. Per request of the birthday ladies"—he smiled broadly at Hannah—"we have fresh flounder on the grill. Sides will include more of our almost-famous cheese grits, tomato pie, fresh green beans, sautéed squash, and all the hushpuppies you can eat."

"Sounds delightful." Nan beamed. "I couldn't have planned a finer menu myself."

"Maybe you should have this young man cater the reunion," Dad suggested. "Then you don't have to argue with Jimmy about the importance of actually cooking a burger versus just searing its edges."

Nan laughed. "You and Jimmy never did see eye to eye about that."

On Cora Anne's other side, her mother lowered her eyes and picked at the mat again. Cora Anne knew she didn't understand how Dad and Nan had maintained an amicable relationship. Truth be told, she didn't either, but she appreciated their efforts.

The food came quickly, tantalizing and heaped high in glazed bowls. Ben nodded at Hannah as he set down the tomato pie in a piece of ocean-blue pottery. "Someone has a good head for business. Customers love these, and the gift shops downtown are turning a nice profit."

Lou leaned into Nan, but Cora Anne heard her whisper. "Really, Mama, did you intend to set these girls up this summer?"

Nan pursed her lips as if suppressing a smile.

"Oh, Mama." Her mother's voice trembled. "What if none of this works out?"

"You just need to quit projecting your own unhappiness onto others, dear." Nan eyes slid to Cora Anne, who looked away. "All good things come around eventually. You'll see. Now have some of these grits. I need you to tell me what that boy's chef puts in them that makes them so much better than mine."

"No one makes better grits than you." Lou took a bite, swallowed, and then raised her eyebrows.

Nan grinned. "I told you so. Now what is it? Besides heavy cream?"

Ben leaned over to fill their tea glasses. "Family secret. We'll never tell."

Lou scoffed but Nan laughed, and Cora Anne felt some of the tension ease away on the evening breeze.

During dinner, they engaged in conversation about the summer's activities, Ben's Charleston chef, and her plans for graduate school. She let herself have this lull, this semblance of family again, even if her parents managed to never actually speak directly to one another. Only Tennessee, who rolled his shoulders and clenched his jaw when Dad asked about her leaving date, showed any signs of apprehension.

When dusk settled her cloak over the marsh, Ben lit the candles and brought out dishes of praline ice cream. The group sang an off-key chorus of Happy Birthday that had Hannah in stitches but left Cora Anne pensive. She hadn't celebrated a birthday with her parents together since the divorce.

His bowl empty, her father rose. "Better be heading on. Figure I'll drive up the interstate some, stop at a hotel in a few hours. Breaks it up a bit."

Cora Anne grabbed his hand, the impulse to make him stay strong. "Dad, I hate for you to leave. This was far to come for just a few hours."

"Well, my girl is always worth it." He squeezed her hand.

She spoke without looking at her mother. This would be Nan's decision. It was still her house. "You could stay in the basement with the boys. There's an extra bunk."

Beside her, Lou bristled. She set down her tea goblet and nudged Cora Anne's elbow. "I'm sure your father prefers better accommodations."

But the triplets had joined the plea. "Dad, it'll be great."

"You can even have the top one if you want."

"And Nan said she'd make waffles for breakfast."

"Yeah, can you believe Cora Anne wanted her to throw away the waffle iron?"

Dad shushed them and put his hand on Cora Anne's shoulder. "I don't think that's the best idea, kids." He darted a glance at Lou. "I'll be fine."

Tennessee stood. "Mr. Halloway? If you'd like, you're welcome to crash at my place. I can always sleep at my mom's." His eyes found hers and that muscle in his jaw—his one nervous trademark—twitched.

Dad looked at Lou again, and then extended his hand to Tennessee. "All right, then. I appreciate that. And it's David."

She smiled at Tennessee as her father pumped his hand. This would work. If he could be with her after their past, surely Lou could handle having Dad around one more day.

"Well, if you're staying tonight, you might as well come on over tomorrow and help Jimmy grill those burgers." Nan sat back, folded hands in her lap.

When her father looked at her mother in question, Cora Anne expected an immediate contradiction. But Lou gave a quick nod, lips pressed tight. "It's a reunion, after all."

Chapter 30

Tennessee's heart hammered as he unlocked his front door for Cor's father. It wasn't until after he'd made the offer that he'd realized what that meant. Her father—the man who potentially held more influence over her than any other—would be coming into his home.

"Something wrong with your lock?" David swatted at a palmetto bug.

Tennessee let out a breath he didn't realize he'd been holding. Better to just get this over with.

"No, sir. Come right on in." He opened the door, stepped over the threshold, and flipped a light switch. The interior of his A-frame bungalow, with its pine paneling and sparse furnishings, had a polished look and smelled faintly of lemon Pine-Sol.

Thank goodness he'd inherited his mother's housecleaning habits.

David stepped around him, and Tennessee pulled the screen closed against the bugs. But he left the door open, letting in the night air tinged with the brackish smell of the creek.

"Nice place you got here." David admired the skylights in the ceiling. "You build it yourself?"

"Sure did." Tennessee moved three strides into the tiny kitchenette. "It's not much, but it suits my needs."

"Keeps you out from under your mama's thumb." David nodded. "Your father would have liked this."

The reference caught Tennessee off guard. Somehow, he never thought of David as having known his father. Lou, of course, but David had always seemed on the outskirts of memories he had involving summer events with the Coultries.

"Thank you, sir." He indicated the coffee pot and fridge. "Help yourself to anything you like. I'm sure my mom will want to send over a hot breakfast in the morning."

David shook his head. "No need. I told my boys I'd be back for waffles. Don't think it made Lou happy, but ..." He shrugged and looked up again at the peak of Tennessee's ceiling. "You really did some fine work in here, son."

"Guess when it's a passion, you do it well." He shifted his weight and shoved his hands in his pockets. *What now?*

"Bedroom down there?" David pointed at the hallway.

"Yes, sir. I'll make sure it's straightened up, grab a few things, and be out of your hair."

"Thanks." David turned his attention to the gallery of Edisto photography behind the futon.

In his bedroom, Tennessee quickly changed the sheets and made an attempt at pillow fluffing that seemed ludicrous. He put a change of clothes in a small bag. He didn't really need anything. The bungalow was so small that half his life was still stored at his mom's house, but if he went back in the main room, he'd have to make small talk and he didn't know what else to say to Cora Anne's father. She didn't talk about him much, and aside from knowing he'd been the one who left, Tennessee's knowledge of the man pretty much ended there.

He stepped back into the main room.

David sat on the futon, reading the newspaper. He looked up. "This land trust group, you're on their board?"

"Yes, sir. Just started my term."

"Pretty interesting idea. Maybe Annie would think about it. I know she's concerned about Lou and the others keeping up the old farm after she's gone." He raked his fingers through his hair. "Course, that's no never mind to me now. Any chance you got a beer?"

Surprised, Tennessee nodded. "Probably. Ben leaves some here on occasion." He pulled open the fridge door and found half a six-pack in its cardboard packaging. "Here you go."

David took it and popped the lid with his key ring. "Want to join me on the porch?"

"Sure." He got himself a bottle of green tea and followed him out. He shut off the light so the bugs would head elsewhere. David had sat on the top step, so he joined him there.

"You don't drink?" He indicated the bottle in Tennessee's hand.

"Not anymore."

"There's a history, I guess."

"Something like that." Tennessee sipped his tea. How much should he tell him? He waded in. "A while back, a few of those turned me into someone you wouldn't recognize."

"I'd reckon any man who watches his father die saving someone else has two choices." David set his quiet eyes on Tennessee, who straightened. "He either loses himself or he takes up that mantle of nobility." He tilted his bottle toward

Tennessee's. "Or both."

"If that's a compliment, I'm taking it, Mr. Halloway."

"It is, so do. And tell me"—he leaned back—"what exactly are your intentions of nobility regarding my daughter?"

Tennessee nearly choked. He should have seen that coming. He swallowed and told the truth. "I'd like her to stay here, sir. And I'd like to marry her."

"I figured as such. She know that?"

"I'd like to think she does, but I don't know. She's like a dog with a bone over this Tulane business. Won't even entertain a different plan."

"She's a lot like her mama in that regard. Makes up her mind, and it takes a lot to change it." His low voice hinted at remorse.

Tennessee looked across the yard to his dock, barely perceptible in the dim light of a waning crescent moon. "Maybe I can."

"Well ..." David drained the bottle. "I say keep at it, son. I think you've got at least half a chance, which is a whole half more than me." His grin faded.

He nodded. Regret was something he understood, and David Halloway's had been obvious tonight. "Thank you, sir. Means a lot."

"I'm going to turn in now. Long day, and I expect tomorrow will be longer." He stood. "You've never been to a Coultrie reunion, have you?"

Tennessee rose as well. "Once, I think. When Cor and I were kids. Mrs. Annie invited us, I guess."

David clapped him on the shoulder. "Well, let me guarantee you, this isn't going to be like when you were kids. Good night."

"Good night." Tennessee leaned against the porch rail and heard the door click shut. No, nothing anymore was like when they were kids.

A splash sounded in the creek, and he watched the ripples carry to the shore. He should tell Cora Anne everything now—all the plans already in motion—while the news could dissipate as it broke. Rather than waiting for the wave that might take her under again.

Chapter 31

Reunion day dawned gloriously beautiful—and mercilessly hot. Cora Anne figured if humidity was any indicator, this time, the forecasters were right about an evening storm.

She'd woken sticky with sweat, the nightmare the worst it had been in almost a month. Patrick's laughing face over the crab pot became contorted as he hauled her to the shore, the rocks and waves trying to trap them in the sea. Showering, she'd tried to wash away the clinging guilt, but it persisted.

Breakfast became a distraction as Hannah and the boys planned the day's strategy. She concentrated on ignoring the undercurrent of tension between her parents.

Her mother refilled her father's coffee and ignored his thanks, instead fixing her gaze on Cora Anne. "When can we expect our other company?"

She knew Lou didn't mean the aunts and uncles. "Tennessee got a call from an irate realtor. Renters complaining about a shaky back deck. He'll be here later."

"So, he's off saving Edisto Beach, one shaky deck at a time."

His offer to put up Dad must have irritated her mother more than she'd let on.

"You know he does more than renovations, dear." Nan pushed away the waffle she'd barely touched. Cora Anne gave her a grateful smile.

"He told me a little about this land trust board last night." Her father sipped his coffee. "Seems like a worthy cause."

Lou huffed. "Sure, get landowners who've held onto family property for generations to give it up for nothing more than a tax write-off. Very worthy." Her sarcasm chilled the room.

Cora Anne figured she ought to try and dispel her mother's misconception. "The land trust doesn't—"

"Is it all right for the boys to bait the seagulls?" Hannah interrupted, peering out the window over the sink.

"What?" Lou jerked open the back door and the room seemed to exhale as she left.

Nan patted Cora Anne's hand. "She pretends otherwise, but we all know your mama just doesn't like change. Am I right, David?"

His eyes trailed out the windows to the back deck where her mother admonished the boys. "No, she'd like to believe if she pretends hard enough, everything can stay the same." He stood abruptly when she came back in. "Think I'll keep the boys in check while y'all finish."

"Well, that would be nice." Lou sat, drinking her coffee in silence.

Nan pursed her lips as though she wanted to say something. Cora Anne traced wood grains on the table and wondered what all her mother might be pretending.

"Hey, Cor." Hannah tugged her ponytail. "Let's go fill the floats, okay?"

Under the back deck, they unfolded classic red-and-blue canvas squares.

"Why don't you quit worrying and relax?" Hannah said. "Nan invited him here, so she must be pretty confident your parents can behave like grown-ups."

"He really puts her on edge, right?" She crossed her arms. "Lou's all worried I've been harboring bitterness, but maybe she should take a look in the mirror."

"He makes her nervous." Hannah flipped on the air compressor. When the roar subsided because the float was full, Cora Anne exhaled. She'd forgotten that sound—how it reminded her of water rushing in her ears.

"You getting on one of these today?" Hannah tested the float's buoyancy with her foot.

"Not a chance."

Her cousin examined her nails as though operating the air compressor might have chipped her manicure. "You ever tell Tennessee why you really went in the water that night?"

She closed her eyes and forced the memory to recede. "No, and I don't think I ever will."

"Now who's keeping secrets?"

She swallowed hard. Not a secret, just an old wound not worth reopening. He'd offered forgiveness. She had to let the past be.

But the present could be addressed. "Why do you think Dad makes her nervous?"

"Because Aunt Lou is not a flutterer by nature, but she's been fussing over every detail like a bride on her wedding day."

She wrinkled her brow. "I think she just wants Nan happy."

"Nope." Hannah unfolded another float. "She wants your dad to be happy."

Her cousin's perceptions tended to be accurate, but her mother had cared little for Dad's happiness over the last few years. Flopping on the inflated raft, Cora Anne shielded her face from the sun. "This is weird."

"Wouldn't be a reunion if it wasn't." Hannah flipped the switch again, and this time, Cora Anne embraced the deafening roar.

Once the floats were done, they organized the triplets into a caravan of beach gear and set up for the day. Cora Anne and her father dug deep into the sand so umbrellas wouldn't blow over in the strong breeze. He'd volunteered for this task, just like he had at every other reunion she could remember. Lou had looked relieved, but whether it was because this job kept him out of the house, or because she was grateful not to shovel herself, Cora Anne couldn't tell.

But her father liked being here, even as he fought that old blue umbrella with its trademark South Carolina logo of palmetto and crescent moon. The corners of her mouth twitched into a smile.

"What are you laughing at?" Dad wrestled the umbrella into the hole. "And why didn't you throw out this monstrosity when you were doing all that cleaning?"

She packed sand around the base. "It's Nan's favorite. You know that. That's why you always set it up and never give Uncle John a chance to help."

"Think I'm trying to stay on your grandmother's good side?"

"Aren't we all?" She grinned and patted the sand down until solid. "There. Think it will hold all day?"

"Guess we'll find out." He turned the crank to raise it. "Rusted old thing." The gear stuck halfway, so he maneuvered underneath and lifted the canopy. "There, got it." He swiped at the sweat already gathering at his temples. "Where's Tennessee? Figured he'd be here already, all underfoot trying to prove he's helpful." His tone teased.

She leaned on the shovel. They were alike—her father and the man she loved. "You know he's helpful, Dad."

"So I gathered from the cottage's work. Is there anything in there he hasn't touched this summer?"

She laughed. "He's only done what he's been paid to do."

"Well, I'm thinking this is the best paying job he's ever had." Her father cupped his hand under her chin. "He's been good for you."

She met his eyes. He understood, though she didn't know why. "Yes."

"All right, then." Dad stepped back.

"You're okay with him?" The question burst from her chest. Tennessee would always be Patrick Watson's son.

He picked up the other shovel and jabbed at the sand. "Long as you and I are good, that's all that matters."

She wanted to ask what he remembered but bit her tongue. The day was hard enough already.

By mid-morning, Aunt Caro and Uncle John arrived. When Uncle Jimmy rolled in a few moments later, Hannah squealed. "You remembered!" An old tractor tire inner tube loaded down his golf cart.

Uncle Jimmy adjusted his baseball cap with an impish grin. "Figured I'd better let Susan in on the secret of just how redneck we really are." His new wife waved from the seat.

Cora Anne bit her lip and waved back. The tractor tire. Another beach tradition she'd skip.

By noon, the sun was high and hot on the beach. Hannah offered to walk Nan back to the house despite her protests that she wasn't a toddler and didn't need a nap every day.

"But you go on by all means, dear." Nan adjusted her large straw hat and studied Hannah. "You're getting a little pinkish on parts of your body that ought to be covered up."

Hannah propped a hand on one perfectly proportioned hip. "Well, I hate to leave everything to the imagination."

"Why not? Mr. Ben Townsend's not here right now."

Cora Anne choked on her Pepsi. Nan was in rare form today.

Her grandmother thumped her back. "You all right? Hannah will be happy to take you up to the house if you're not."

She coughed into her beach towel and rubbed her watering eyes. "I'm fine. Just fine."

"Well, go on up anyway and wait for your young men. If you two are going to tell your mamas on me and my napping habits, I'm going to tell secrets on you. Now scoot."

Hannah pulled a sheer cover-up over her bikini, and Nan said, "Do you really think that's going to do any good?"

"Oh, you." Hannah leaned over and kissed her papery cheek. "You wore bikinis back in the day. Cora Anne showed me the pictures."

"Did y'all dig out all those old pictures she's been storing away for years?" Aunt Caro squirted more suntan lotion on her legs. "We should get them organized."

"We definitely should. Then *you* girls can tell *your* girls all about your wild days." Nan sipped lemonade from her tumbler and raised her eyebrows at Cora Anne.

"Mom! Look what we found!" Down the beach, Cole hollered and held up a piece of driftwood. A clear blob hovered on the end, tentacles swinging.

"What the—" Lou bit off the end of her sentence when Nan shot her a look.

Cheeks flushed, she stalked to the surf's edge where the boys were with Dad.

Cora Anne followed, trepidation building.

"What are you doing, David? Do you want them to get stung?"

"Relax, Lou. It's dead." Her father sounded weary.

Her mother leaned into him, arms crossed, tone clipped. "Why do I always have to be the responsible parent? Why can't you just say no?"

"Why can't you stop being in control?"

"Someone has to be. You—"

Cole's yell had Cora Anne scrambling.

"Now see what's happened?" Her mother always had to have the last word. Cole hopped on the sand, supported by the other boys. "Let me see." Lou bent and examined the red welt. "Got you good."

Cora Anne took his arm. "I'll take you up to the house, Cole. Get some vinegar on that."

"I have some in my bag." Her mother stepped back and glared at Dad. "Someone has to be prepared."

Her parents following, Cora Anne led her limping brother back to the umbrella. "Bet you won't pick up any jellyfish again."

Cole shook his head, but he darted up a glance from under his long lashes. Would take more than a sting to keep that boy down.

"You okay?" Dad ruffled Cole's wet hair, sending splatters of water onto Lou.

"Do you mind?" she snapped, dousing the vinegar again.

Her father held up his hands. "So sorry. I forgot you're the only one who ever does anything right."

Cora Anne's cheeks burned like the slash across Cole's ankle.

Hannah pulled at her arm. "C'mon, Cor. Let's go get some more drinks." Her cousin led her up the path through the dunes to the boardwalk. Her parents' angry voices carried over the sand. "They say when people argue like that it's because they still have feelings for one another."

"Are these the same people who say children recover more quickly from divorce than their parents?"

"Probably." She looped her arm through Cora Anne's and squeezed. "It'll be all right."

Would it? Her family hadn't been all right in years. Secrets on that beach seemed buried too deep for the tide to wash away.

As they reached the house, Tennessee climbed out of his truck, still in his work clothes, with an apologetic smile. She went straight into his arms and buried her face in his chest. Sawdust and sweat, but she didn't care. He rubbed her back lightly and kissed her messy bun of hair.

"That bad, huh?"

"What were Nan and I thinking asking my father to stay? I guess I was crazy enough to think Edisto magic worked."

He smoothed tendrils of loose hair back from her face. His soothing touch flamed her cheeks again. "Well, it might yet. Day's still young."

"Lou had a conniption because he let the boys catch a jellyfish. Accused Dad of being irresponsible."

"Well, jellyfish sting. Even when they're dead."

"We know." She sighed and dropped her head back on his chest.

He gave her a brief, tight hug. Leaning in the cab of the truck, he emerged with a small duffel and a bouquet of daisies.

"Figured these made a good apology for being late. Or maybe I just knew you'd need to be reminded of my thoughtful qualities."

She brought the flowers to her nose and breathed the simple, grassy scent. "Thank you."

"You're welcome. Now, what are the chances I can change and meet you on the waves?"

"Hm …" She glanced back toward the shore. Aunt Caro had her arm around Lou, leading her away for what must be a walk down the beach, which meant things had probably cooled down. The tide pounded as it rose. Soon, it would encroach on their chairs and umbrellas and wave riding would be optimal.

If she wanted to get in the water.

"I'll watch you teach the boys how to really use that old tractor tire of Uncle Jimmy's."

"Good enough." He took her hand as they headed for the stairs. "And Cor?"

"Yes?"

"You know, sometimes folks argue because they don't know any other way to communicate feelings they've kept buried pretty deep."

Chapter 32

Waves dumped her brothers on the crushed shells rimming the beach, but the knot in Cora Anne's stomach eased watching them struggle back out and coast back in. Fighting those waves had once been a simple thing. She remembered how hot the black rubber of that tire would be under her suit. How inevitably, the valve always scraped her leg at least once during the times she and her cousins drug it out past the limits of their mamas' hollering.

By late afternoon, the waves became too choppy for fun, and everyone worked to take down umbrellas and other beach gear as the wind's momentum increased.

"Looks like a storm." She shook a towel and then blinked against the sand that stung her eyes.

"Sky's been threatening for days and there's been nothing," Tennessee said as he lowered the blue umbrella in one fell swoop. Lifting it from the sand, he propped it on his shoulder and flashed her a grin.

Beside her, Dad whispered, "That was impressive. But don't tell him I said so." She laughed, and he hugged her to his side. "I like him. But don't tell your mom."

"Oh?" She concentrated on dusting sand from another towel. "Why not?"

"Because she has a habit of disliking my suggestions." He closed a beach chair. "But we'll get her to come around. You wait and see." He glanced at Tennessee, who had loaded himself down with more than his fair share of gear. "She's always liked those Watsons."

Her chest tightened, but she nodded, the words between them unspoken. The edges of her father's mouth had creased, and she wondered how long he'd known. Before or after Patrick died saving her? And for the first time, she realized how hard it must be for him to see her with Tennessee.

She wasn't the only one suffering through memories.

"Come on, folks. Those burgers aren't going to cook themselves." Uncle Jimmy hefted two chairs with one arm, pulled a cooler with the other, and led the charge up to the boardwalk.

"If Jimmy's grilling, those burgers aren't going to be cooked at all." Uncle John fell into step with her father, who nodded his agreement.

For a fleeting moment, when Cora Anne came downstairs after changing, everything seemed like it had once been. Her mother, grandmother, and aunts were in the kitchen, slicing tomatoes, tossing slaw, and sprinkling paprika on deviled eggs. On the deck, she saw her father sipping a beer while Uncle John gave Uncle Jimmy grilling tips he was ignoring.

She knew how the evening would unfold. Jimmy liked his burgers just this side of mooing, but after he filled the platter, Aunt Caro would hand it right back to Uncle John to finish. Jimmy would complain about being unappreciated, but her mother would hand him a beer in a Clemson koozie and tell him not to set a bad example for his nieces and nephews. Then he would sit on the bench and argue football with her father until time to eat.

The last one to make a plate and find a seat would be Nan, because she would be making sure everyone else was settled and didn't already want seconds of her almost-famous potato salad.

Consistency had once been the heartbeat of Edisto summers.

Her mother glanced up briefly when she came around the corner. "Can you go downstairs and make sure your brothers aren't using the outside shower as their personal bathhouse? Last time we were here, I had to remind them that public nakedness stopped being acceptable when they came out of diapers."

She cut through the kitchen and stole an egg off Aunt Caro's platter, not because she was hungry but because it was something she always used to do. Downstairs, all three boys lounged on the rug, still in their swim trunks while they played Nintendo. At least their public decorum was intact.

"Hey, mischief-teers. Mom said get cleaned up."

The game continued. Cora Anne shrugged. She wasn't her mother. They could come to dinner in what they had on for all she cared.

She left through the screen door and found Tennessee hosing floats in the yard. "You hiding from the family?"

"Are you?" He mocked spraying her again, and she pretended to flinch.

"Maybe I was looking for you."

He arched an eyebrow at her and then resumed rinsing. "You holding up all right?"

His question felt heavier than it should—like when the floats got holes and took on water. She crossed her arms. "Everything's almost the same."

"And that's a problem?"

"Yes." She brushed sticky strands of hair from her face. "Because nothing can ever be the way it was."

"So you learn a new normal, Cor. Let yourself move on."

The early evening air, thick and hot, strangled in her throat. Patrick's face swam in her mind. "How can I do that when this place still gives me nightmares?"

Tennessee tossed the hose aside. "What are you talking about?"

"Every night." She shouldn't be telling him something he couldn't fix, but she plunged ahead anyway. "I dream about that night he drowned. And every day with you, I think I can push past it but then … "

He'd grabbed her by the upper arms and now he squeezed lightly. "But then what?"

"Then it comes back."

He dropped his forehead to hers. "Oh, Cor, you should have told me." He ran his fingers up and down her arms. "We need to talk."

She shook her head against his. "I'm tired of talking." Slipping her hands behind his neck, she tugged his mouth to hers. In these moments, she could forget. She could.

He pulled back. "I talked to your father."

Her eyes snapped open. "About what?"

"Eloping to Vegas."

Before she could suck in a breath, he pressed his lips to hers.

"I'm kidding."

She wasn't so sure, but she was too busy trying to breathe to contradict him.

He wrapped her in his arms and sighed. "But I did tell him I'd like to go along with whatever plans you have, even if you think they don't involve me." Eyes, brown and warm and steady, fixed on hers. "You know. Plans like graduate school far, far away …"

"What are you saying?"

"What do you think I'm saying?"

She pressed her hands to her temples. For once, she didn't have the capacity to plan beyond today.

He tightened his grip on her waist. "I have to tell you something—"

"Hey, Cor!" J.D. hung out the basement door. "Woo hoo, don't let me interrupt. I'll just tell Mom you were too busy kissing to help set the table."

"Go away, J.D., or I'll tell Mom how she really got that dent in the van."

Her brother darted off. Tennessee's lips twitched and his shoulders shook. She slipped her arms back around him. "You really want to hang around with this crowd?"

He tossed his head back and laughed, giving her a gentle push toward the stairs. "I'll finish rinsing. You better go."

She went, but mostly to avoid the intensity she'd seen in his eyes. Whatever he wanted to talk about was probably something she didn't want to hear.

Inside, her mother and Aunt Caro stood hip to hip and arranged lettuce, tomato, and cheese slices on a pewter platter shaped like a swordfish.

"I can't believe we still use this ugly thing. Cora Anne, we should've made you a list of things to throw out." Aunt Caro grimaced as she covered the fish's protruding eye with a tomato. "There, that's better."

"I can hear you. You know that was a wedding gift from your great-aunt Amanda." Behind them, Nan lifted the lid on the simmering beans and popped in a spoonful of brown sugar. "That's right, you smell divine. But this will be even better."

Hannah glanced at her and Cora Anne glanced at her mother and, for once, laughter between them came easily.

"What?" Nan waved her spoon at them. "You think it's funny I talk to the food, but sometimes it needs a little coaxing. Just like my plants." She put the spoon on the clean oyster shell she used for a rest and picked up a spray bottle to spritz the African violets on her kitchen window shelf.

"Oh, Mama." Aunt Caro lifted the offensive tray and leaned over to kiss her mother's cheek. "You are a prize."

"Why, thank you, dear. I'm sure glad to know someone still thinks so."

"Think this came from great-aunt Amanda, too?" Hannah stuffed forks in an old wicker caddy with a swordfish wired to its side. "If so, she's not getting an invite to my wedding."

"No worries, darling. Amanda died eons ago." Nan meandered around the table. "Believe I'll have a sit down."

"Mama, we're about ready to serve." Lou's voice carried an edge as she set out the big bowl of potato salad.

"Well, go on. You and Carolina can handle it, I'm sure. I just need a little rest. Y'all wore me out today."

Cora Anne met her mother's raised brows with a shrug.

"We told you to take a nap, Nan." Hannah beamed a told-you-so smile around the room as Uncle John came through the back door with a platter of burgers.

So much for hoping everything hadn't really changed.

Chapter 33

Dinner was lively, a throwback to when time together had been relatively uncomplicated and unshadowed. The triplets begged childhood stories from Uncle Jimmy. Lou served Nan's almost-famous potato salad without fuss.

Seeing her grandmother hand over a treasured task gave Cora Anne that quivering feeling in her stomach again. If she left, would Nan still be here to come back to?

Tennessee's fingertips grazed her shoulder blade when he slipped his arm around the back of her chair. No doubt he'd be here. He could say what he liked about wanting to follow her, but he belonged in Edisto. And she did not.

"Anybody want anything else before dessert?" Lou stood and began gathering plates.

"Presents!" Hannah got up, laughing. "Because, seriously, I can hear that ice cream churn slowing down, but if I don't stretch there'll be no room."

"I've always got room for ice cream." Cole leaned back and patted his belly.

Dad poked it. "I don't think so. It's rock solid in there."

"That's probably because he needs to—"

"Malcolm Halloway, don't finish that sentence." Her mother's voice cut sharply across the table, and Mac's ears reddened.

"So, presents?" Uncle John, ever the peacemaker, tossed his napkin on the table and stood.

Tennessee whispered in her ear, "I got you a present just like you told me to."

"I believe I told you *not* to get me a present."

"You know," he drawled, "sometimes, I'm real hard of hearing. It's all the hammering."

She rolled her eyes. "C'mon." They stood behind the sofa where the triplets piled in eager anticipation. Unable to resist, she leaned over and tickled two of her brothers behind their ears. They yelped and flopped about in mock misery.

"Louisa, control your children, please." Nan's teasing smile belied her words. She clapped her hands together like a child on Christmas morning. "Now, we all know yesterday was a special day for the girls."

Melodramatic moans and whines from the triplets. "It's always about the girls—"

"But, as always, there's a little something for everyone since this is the only time we're ever all together." Nan beamed and dramatically pulled away the beach towel draped over a large basket of presents.

"Mama, you didn't have to go to all that trouble." Lou spoke over the whistles of the boys.

Nan smiled gently. "Yes, I did."

"So it's birthdays plus Christmas in July, huh?" Tennessee hooked his arm around Cora Anne's shoulders. "I can get behind this tradition."

"Then how about you help pass out those gifts?" She shrugged loose. "Go on, eager folks are waiting."

He glanced at her mother as he stepped around the couch. A smile tugged at one corner of Cora Anne's lips. Already, he understood the nuances of this family. Lou's barely perceptible nod was all the permission he needed.

"Now, how does this work?" He knelt beside Nan and read names on tags. "You guys all rip in at the same time?"

"Of course. We lost all sense of patience years ago," Nan said. "If we wait for everyone to open their own, we'd be here all night and never get the chance for a good card game."

"Except birthday girls," interjected Hannah. "We get our own turn." She grinned widely at Cora Anne across the room, pointed at Tennessee, whose back was turned, and laid a dramatic hand over her heart.

Cora Anne shook her head. *What?* Hannah must know about Tennessee's present. He handed Lou the last gift, and then the triplets ripped in. The adults opened theirs meticulously, with Aunt Caro and Lou discussing what to do with saved bows.

The boys promptly donned the masks and tubes of their snorkeling sets, while her mother peeled the paper off her box.

Brow furrowed, Lou lifted the photo album from where it had been nested among tissue paper. She seemed to sense this gift was for more than just fun. Her thumb rubbed the cutout on the front—Nan had suggested the picture of Lou in a debutante gown for that. "Think I'll enjoy this later."

"Oh, Lou, it's wonderful." Aunt Caro paged through hers, laughing. "I'd forgotten all about those times we dressed Jimmy up in Mama's sunhats."

Everyone chuckled, except Lou. She found Cora Anne's gaze across the room and held it. This time, Cora Anne offered the small nod. She'd tucked that picture in there without Nan's permission. Maybe now she'd get some answers.

"Birthday time!" Nan called, clapping her hands.

Hannah snuggled herself onto the couch with the boys. "Place of honor, you know." She elbowed Cole aside. "Come on, Cor. Jump in."

"Think I'll move." J.D. settled on the floor, still wearing his snorkeling mask. "This is just a little too much family togetherness for me."

Cora Anne squeezed in between Hannah and Mac. "We'll barely have room to open our presents."

"Good thing they're so small." Hannah nodded toward the stack of gifts Tennessee was holding.

"Let's see ... I guess since technically, Hannah is the oldest, she goes first? That how this works?" He glanced over his shoulder for confirmation from Nan.

"Whatever my birthday girls want."

Cora Anne leaned on Hannah's shoulder as she gently peeled tape from white paper tied with a concoction of blue and silver ribbon. From the tissue paper, Hannah lifted a white linen swimsuit cover up with a hood and lacy detail on its edges. "Nan, it's gorgeous!"

"Well, it will help keep you decent at least." Her eyes twinkled and everyone laughed at Hannah's pout.

Her next present was a tacky Edisto Beach t-shirt from Cora Anne who grinned and said, "I just knew you'd especially love the giant sea turtle."

"I'm pretty sure I bought you that same one about fifteen years ago at The Edistonian." Aunt Caro held the bright pink shirt up for inspection. "Yup, I definitely remember that turtle."

"Well, I love it. I'm going to wear it right now." Hannah stood and pulled the shirt on over her sundress.

"Look at that," said Nan. "It's longer than her skirt."

"Nan, you are so mean." But Hannah leaned over and kissed their grandmother's soft cheek.

They opened gifts from their parents and even the triplets produced a slightly squashed package from under the couch.

"Last one." Tennessee handed Cora Anne a gold box festooned with purple ribbon.

She took it warily, her heartbeat ricocheting. "This isn't a hammer."

"No, it's not."

She swept a glance at the room full of family and studied the tiny box in her hand. Surely he wasn't planning ... not right now. Not here.

"Open it already," Hannah begged.

She tugged off the ribbon and lifted the box lid. Inside, nestled on a bed of soft cotton, lay a simple ring of pale pink shell. She paused, unsure of this gift's significance.

But quite sure her heart might jump out of her chest.

Tennessee shrugged as though this gift were no big deal. "You told me to get you a souvenir. Hannah said you two used to buy shell rings all the time at the Pavilion."

Breathe. She must remember to breathe.

Hannah rolled her eyes. "But I don't think you bought this one for a dollar at the Pavilion."

Tennessee shoved his hands in his pockets. "I'll never tell."

She would believe he was jesting if his eyes weren't so earnest and fixed on hers.

Nan pushed herself up. "Are you going to show off that pretty bauble or just gawk over it?"

Cora Anne found her voice. "I'll show it off." She took it from the box and attempted to slide it onto the middle finger of her right hand. It wouldn't pass her knuckle, so it went on her ring finger instead. "There, see?" She wiggled her fingers without looking at Tennessee again.

"It's just lovely." Nan took her hand and squeezed it. "Now, I think I hear that churn telling me the ice cream is ready."

"Hey." Tennessee slipped out the back door.

"Hey, yourself." The wind whipped her hair and she wrapped it impatiently with the band on her wrist. Already, the sun had dipped below the horizon, leaving behind a darkening sky.

He propped his hip on the railing next to her. "So you didn't like my present, huh?"

He stood so close, her arm brushed the corded muscles of his as she twisted the ring he'd given her. He was tense. Well, so was she. "You caught me off guard, is all."

"That ring's exactly what I said. A souvenir." He sighed. "I mean, it's not like we're in high school and I'm asking you for a promise of anything."

She stilled. His voice held a chill she hadn't expected.

"It's a nice gift, Tennessee." She lay a hand on his arm. "Thank you."

His shoulders didn't relax. "What are we doing, Cor?"

"What do you mean?"

He leaned into her and put his hand on the small of her back. She could feel its warmth through the thin cotton of her dress.

"I mean I'd like to think someday, I'll give you a ring that's not made of shells."

She sucked in a breath and bit her lip.

"But you didn't factor me into your plans." He withdrew. "I'm going to head home." Coolness seeped between them. "Call me tomorrow if you want."

"Tennessee—" She snagged his shirt. "I'm not sure I'm ready."

"You mean you're not sure you *want* to be ready. If you want me to wait, I will. But I can't decide that for you." He took her hand and lifted it to his lips. Pressing a kiss against her palm, he held her gaze. "I love you. When that's enough, you let me know."

He clipped down the stairs before she could form her response. Cradling her hand to her chest, she curled into a chair. From inside the house, she could hear running water and the clatter of plates in the sink. She ought to go help but she stayed pressed into the chair, rubbing her palm over the armrest she'd sanded smooth with him.

The whine of the coffee grinder told her when the dishes had finished. She heard Uncle Jimmy's booming laugh through the open screens of the porch calling, "Gin!" The men must have gathered for a game of cards. As the night wound down, thunder rumbled in the distance. The storm was coming.

"Cora Anne?"

Startled, she hit her elbow on the chair's corner. "Right here, Mom."

Lou stepped into the deepening shadows. Cora Anne could just make out the teacup she held in one hand, a mug of coffee in the other. "Thought you could use this."

She sat up, crossing her legs as she took the offer. "You do like to tell me a cup of tea can fix anything."

"Learned that from your grandmother." Lou settled into the chair beside her.

She took an appreciative sip. Chamomile. She forced a smile at her mother over the cup's rim. "My favorite."

"I know." Lou's gaze tracked across the night sky. "Clouds are moving on in."

"Yeah."

"Makes it cool."

"A little."

"I brought you that cardigan you like. Found it in the laundry room after you left."

"I wondered where it had gotten to. I love that sweater."

"I know."

She rubbed her neck but the tautness refused to yield. "I guess you know a lot."

Lou slid a sideways glance to her. "I do. Especially about you."

Did she really? Cora Anne set the cup down without clinking. Another lesson from Nan.

Her mother continued. "For instance, I know that boy scared you to death tonight."

She cleared her throat. "A little." She wasn't ready for an intimate conversation with her mother either.

"I know you love him."

He didn't seem to think so. Clasping her palms together, she was grateful her mother couldn't see the flush creep up her neck. "He's a good man."

"Like his father." Lou rested the coffee on her knee. "But I guess you know that about me."

She heard the accusation in her mother's voice. She'd pried rather than asked. Still, she had to know the truth. "How long were you together?"

"One glorious, tumultuous summer."

Cora Anne lifted her eyebrows. "Oh."

Lou laughed, low and soft. "You'd painted a different picture in your head, I presume? You'll make a great historian, with an imagination like that for the past."

"The past has tight roots in us all." For a moment, she pictured Tennessee on the dock of the plantation, telling her what had driven him to stay.

"Yes, it does." Her mother exhaled slowly and turned her face to the ocean. "Patrick wanted to build his life and future in this place I was so desperate to leave."

"Why?"

"Oh, Cor …" Lou shook her head. "I couldn't find the life I wanted here. Too many expectations of who I should be."

How akin to her own feelings. "Were you ever sorry?"

Lou lifted her shoulders for a moment as though she was holding her breath. Then she released. "No." She faced Cora Anne again. "I wanted to be. But I was happy with what I chose."

Make your choice and live with it. That always seemed to be her mother's mantra. But she'd heard a tinge of regret in Lou's voice tonight. "I'm sorry life didn't stay happy."

"Oh, I don't know." Lou glanced back over her shoulder, and Cora Anne followed her gaze. Her father stood silhouetted in the window, watching them talk. "Sometimes we have to get out of the way so things can work themselves back out."

No, she wanted to argue. She'd been told to get out of the way since she was ten years old. And she knew, one glorious summer didn't guarantee happily ever after.

"I think you know what to do." Lou went back inside with the empty cups. Cora Anne stayed on the porch until the first of the rain came in over the beach. Finally, this summer, the storm had followed course.

Chapter 34

"*She doesn't love the triplets more than you, Cor. Even if she acts like it.*" *Hannah wasn't much for sympathy. They crept down the stairs, where the adults waited for her to choke out an apology she didn't really mean.*

That fit had been a long time coming and losing control made her feel better. Not worse. Any attention at all was better than none.

"Can we go look for more shark's teeth now?" Hannah bounced on her toes, and Nan nodded. "C'mon, Cor." Holding hands, they raced across the deck.

"Stay up by the dunes. Tide's coming in." Nan's warning called after them.

The dunes were fine because the line that rimmed the tide's ebb and flow consisted of shell bits and treasure. The quiet concentration of the task cooled Cora Anne's temper. Maybe she'd apologize for real when Mama got home from dinner out. Then she'd ask her nicely, one more time, if they could swim together in the morning before leaving. She'd probably say no, but there was just enough hopefulness in the cry of the gulls and the setting of that lazy evening sun to make her think Mama might change her mind.

When she shaded her eyes and looked out to see the sunset, she saw it.

The red bucket.

Bobbing off shore, almost washing in with the waves. But not quite.

"Hannah, look! That's the bucket I threw."

Her cousin grinned. "Granddaddy told you to watch for it. Probably got caught in the rocks."

"I'm getting it."

Hannah shook her head. "You'll get in trouble. Wait for it to wash in."

"You just don't want to get wet." In her sulking, she'd refused to change out of her swimsuit. But Hannah had on her favorite cotton sundress and dolphin earrings. No way she would even stick a big toe in the water.

Cora Anne glanced toward Still Waters. Nan had been on the deck a moment ago, but the babies must have started their wailing because now she was gone.

The only person who might notice if she went in the water was Tennessee Watson. He'd been helping his dad frame windows on the house next door all day, and now they cleaned up their tools with frequent glances at the darkening sky over the beach.

What if Tennessee had seen her tantrum? He'd never think her grown up enough to swim with ever, ever again.

She had to get that bucket and prove to Mama how sorry she really was about ruining their last day. Having a tantrum like a toddler and throwing all the boys' toys had gotten her a slap and time out instead of the attention she craved.

But if she brought back the toy ...

She trudged into the waves. Hannah stayed on the beach, her twirly skirt lifting with the wind. A gust whipped Cora Anne's braids into her face. She lunged past her waist.

"What are you doing?" Tennessee's shout carried over the dunes. "Get out of that water! Storm's coming!"

Shoulder deep now, but the bucket swirled just beyond her fingertips. She lifted her feet and kicked over a wave. But instead, she went under.

She couldn't come back up. Something tugged her legs, and no amount of thrashing pushed her out from under the water's weight. She churned and kicked and when she finally came up, she heard Hannah screaming. Down again and rolling— she would die in this ocean.

Would they care?

For a brief moment, her fight ceased.

Any attention was better than none.

A hook like an anchor circled her waist and forced her up. Parallel to the shore, Tennessee's dad, Patrick, towed her. He pushed against that current and shoved her hard. She clutched at a slick rock and another set of hands grasped her arms, hauling her up the piling.

She heard Patrick's yell and saw the wave that bashed his head against the rock. Saw him rise and fall, arms and legs spread wide like when the cousins played dead man in the water.

All around her, people screamed his name. "Pa-a-a-trick!" A drawling wail that culminated with a high-pitched keening when the ocean washed him back. Through a haze of tears, she saw her daddy push on Patrick's chest. Sirens sounded over the thunder and a flash of lightning lit Tennessee's face. He collapsed in the sand with her, and she rocked on the beach in the strong arms of a young man and sobbed like the child she was.

Blood from his scalp stained the sand, but administering CPR, her daddy pounded Patrick's chest and yelled.

One-two-three-breathe. One-two-three-breathe.

Over and over and over again.

One-two-three-breathe.

The crash shook the whole cottage and jerked Cora Anne awake. Blood pounded in her ears and her breath came in pants. *One-two-three—*

Hannah moaned. "What was that?"

"Thunder, I think." Cora Anne leaned back on her elbows. She'd made it past the screaming. Never had the nightmare lingered on past those piercing wails. Her heart beat with the rhythm Dad had tried to give back to Patrick. *One-two-three-breathe.*

So she did. Over and over until her heart beat quietly again.

She'd forgotten so many pieces of the accident. How slick the rocks had been. How the empty beach had suddenly swarmed with people. How her father had known CPR but the sand under Patrick's head just kept getting darker and darker.

Rain splattered the roof. The room's thin light seemed earlier than the red 6:37 on the alarm clock. There would be no picnics on the beach today.

No way she could go back to sleep. She slipped out of bed and left the room, pulling the cardigan her mother had brought around her shoulders. She tiptoed down the stairs and paused when she got to the landing at the bottom.

Nan raised her cup in greeting. "Good morning, sunshine."

"Not much chance of that."

Her grandmother nodded toward the kitchen. "Kettle's still hot."

"Thanks." A cup of tea fixes everything. "You're up early."

"I've missed our morning chats."

Cora Anne fixed her tea, dunking the Earl Gray bag up and down and watching the swirls it left behind. She could ask Nan about these memories that kept resurfacing. Nan would tell her the truth.

Curled into the corner of the couch closest to Nan's chair, they sipped in silence while the storm gathered strength against the windows. The triplets would likely make an appearance soon. J.D. had never been fond of thunder.

"Have you decided to change your plans?"

She strained to hear the quiet question. "For today? Looks like we'll be staying high and dry right here."

Nan's labored breath panted out a sigh.

She leaned in closer. "Nan, are you all right?"

"Of course, dear. Just a little overdone from yesterday."

She studied the blue eyes that were so like her own.

Her grandmother smiled wanly. "Don't avoid my question."

She could at least avoid looking at her. "My plans for when summer is over?"

"Yes." Her grandmother's teacup trembled as she lifted it and an amber splash ran down the sides. "Reality is always waiting just over that bridge."

Reality. Off this island, her life was objective, not subjective to haunting nightmares. Or fumbled summer loves.

Upstairs, a door clicked. Lou, likely. She rose early, too, so there was no point in more conversation. She took her grandmother's wobbling cup and saucer. "I think you need to lie down."

Wisps of white curls shook with her head. "I'll be fine ..." She pitched forward, her forehead striking the coffee table's glass edge as Cora Anne lunged to catch her. Blood spurted and ran in rivulets down Nan's sunken cheeks. Cora Anne staunched the flow with the sleeve of her sweater. Someone pounded down the stairs.

Lou, her reading glasses askew, ran for a towel. "I got it."

She pushed Cora Anne and the table aside and pressed the cloth firmly against the flow. The yellow-and-blue plaid soaked up the red. Cora Anne bit her lip. Nan's favorite new towels. Hannah had bought them at Williams Sonoma.

"What happened?" Her mother's voice snapped her back.

"She fell—fainted I think."

"Why was she up?" Lou kept her head down, her eyes focused on Nan's closed ones. "Why were you?"

"Storm woke me. I came downstairs and she was here. Said she couldn't sleep. She was shaky, and then she just ..."

Her mother made a choking noise. Cora Anne squeezed her shoulder but Lou shrugged her off.

"Call an ambulance." She didn't look up. "This is too much blood for a simple cut." Her voice quivered.

Cora Anne went for the kitchen phone. She dialed with eyes on her mother, whom she'd never seen look more scared.

Lou pressed the towel on her mother's head and waited. She'd woken with the feeling that something was wrong but not soon enough to prevent this. Cora Anne was right. The nightmare of this place kept repeating. One heartbreak after another.

"Lou, honey, let me take over." Carolina knelt beside her with a clean towel. One of the old ones that could stand to be bloodied and discarded. Under the pressure of her hand, a plaid section of the one she used was indistinguishable. She'd ruined her mama's new towel.

Across the room, Cora Anne sat at the kitchen peninsula with her head in her hands. Hannah stood behind her, rubbing her back. How many mornings had they shared with their grandmother and seen the signs?

Lou rose, hands balled into bloody fists. "How long has she been this sick?"

Her daughter raised her head but didn't look toward her.

That was all the answer Lou needed. "How could you? You were supposed to take care of her, not conspire with her."

John stepped in. "There's no need to yell at the girls. They may not have realized."

"Oh, they realized." She stepped around him and strode to the counter. "I asked you a question, young lady."

Cora Anne turned her face away again.

Lou grabbed her chin and turned her head back. "How long?"

"Dr. Kelly put her on pain meds the second week in June."

Lou dropped her hand. A bloody smear of finger prints covered Cora Anne's cheek and chin. "You didn't think you should tell me?"

"She asked us not to." Hannah stepped around the stool. "We respect her, Aunt Lou. This is what she wanted."

"To die here, like Daddy did? This is what she wanted?" She wheeled and faced the others. "Why isn't the ambulance here yet?"

"Louisa, calm down." John took her elbow and steered her to the sink. "She's not going to die. Not here, not today." He turned on the water and picked up the soap.

Lou let him squirt the blue liquid into her palm. She turned her hands over and over, as if she could wash away the source in her mother's blood that was eating her alive. She felt her daughter's and niece's frightened eyes on her back. Mercifully, the boys were still asleep. Maniacal laughter bubbled up in her.

"You okay?" John came back to her side.

"Ironic isn't it?" She turned off the water and dried her hand on the other plaid dishtowel left hanging by the sink. "She tells us to come bring life back to this old house, when really, she's been planning all along to tell us her life is ending."

"You don't know that." John crossed his arms.

"Oh, yes, I do." She looked at her daughter again, and this time, Cora Anne met her gaze. "Yes, I do."

Nan barely stirred when the paramedics loaded her onto the stretcher and covered her with blankets. Cora Anne dropped her head into her hands and avoided watching her mother trail behind as the paramedics navigated the slick stairs in the slackening rain.

"We'll be right behind you," Uncle John assured her as he closed the door.

The whole scene still seemed straight out of a hospital drama. Not real. But when she closed her eyes, she saw Nan's hollowed cheeks, frail shoulders, and below the hem of her embroidered nightgown, legs little more than skin and bone.

"The cancer's back isn't it?" She whispered the words around the lump in her throat. Words she'd been afraid to form for weeks.

Aunt Caro's strong arms enveloped her on one side and Hannah on the other. "Your mother and I have wondered that for a while now. Likely, it's metastasized, and now the pain is bad enough she's willing to take the medicine."

But not willing to take the treatment. Cora Anne pushed her fingers against her eye sockets. Surely she could block the image of helpless Nan if all she could see was spots.

"Why wouldn't she have told us?" Hannah turned her head to her mother's shoulder.

"Because she's good at keeping secrets." Aunt Caro's voice held no accusation, merely fact. "She misses your granddaddy."

"We know." Hannah reached for a tissue. "I think that's what she does every morning on that deck. Watches the fisherman and pretends one is him."

Aunt Caro sighed with such heaviness, her breath tickled Cora Anne's ear. "We're going to the hospital. You girls need to stay here with the boys."

Cora Anne knew there was no point in arguing. They had been in charge of Nan long enough.

Chapter 35

B y the time the boys finally emerged and ate their way through an entire box of Frosted Flakes Lou had brought, Aunt Caro had called to say Nan was stable and being admitted.

"Can we come later?" Hannah leaned against the counter and twirled the long cord of the old phone.

Cora Anne turned off the water in the sink where she was washing the boys' cereal bowls.

"Mm-hm, yes ..." Hannah heaved. "But Mom ... okay. Yes, I'll tell her. 'Bye." She rattled the phone back in its cradle. "Mom said stay here. No reason to come right now. The doctor is scheduling a CT and we can wait here as well as there." She glanced around. "Where'd the boys go?"

"Downstairs, of course. Video games."

"Right ... Well ..." She offered Cora Anne a half smile. "She also said maybe you could call your dad?"

"Oh." She turned back to the sink. "Yeah, I should do that."

"I'm surprised you haven't already called Tennessee. You know he won't be working in this weather today."

She shrugged. "Didn't want to wake him."

"Like he'd mind."

Oh, she was pretty sure he'd mind. Especially after the way he left last night. Rain splattered the window over the sink. The storm came in swells, like the ocean from where it gathered strength. Calm had come for a few moments after the ambulance left, then the gale returned in full force fury. No, Tennessee wouldn't be working.

"Cora Anne? You want me to get your cell? Or do you prefer this crackly old thing?" Hannah nodded toward the landline.

"I'll get it. Probably need to get dressed anyway."

"Not me." Hannah flipped her bangs away from her eyes. "Until they say we can come, I'm staying in pajamas and no makeup." A knock sounded on the front door and she gasped. "But I don't want to be seen." She ducked down the hall toward the bedrooms.

Cora Anne allowed a chuckle as she headed for the door. Tennessee waved at her through one of the front windows.

She paused for a moment before swinging the door open. "What are you doing here?"

He grabbed her around the middle, straight into his arms for a bear hug. He must have run fast because despite his lack of raincoat, he was barely damp. He nuzzled an unshaven cheek against hers.

"Why didn't you call me?"

She tried to pull away but he locked his arms. She went limp. "Because I figured you wouldn't be surprised."

Now he did let her go. "You think I knew how sick she was?"

"Well, you've been helping her make land trust plans for her will." She crossed her arms. "And you've hinted a few times she didn't seem well."

"Hinted, yes, because I've spent a lot of time with her over the past six months. Physically, she definitely wasn't the woman who hired me."

"Then you should have said something."

"Said what? 'Hey, I think Nan has cancer?' I'm not a doctor. I'm not family. I'm just the hired help."

The words stung but she lifted her chin anyway and met his eyes. "How do you even know what happened this morning?"

"Your mom called your dad."

"She did?"

"Yeah, I guess even divorced, they have better communication than we do."

She tucked her chin against her chest. "I can't do this today."

"Do what? Be around someone who loves you?" Tennessee threw up his arms. "Fine. Retreat. I knew you would. It's what you do best." She gaped at him, but he kept going. "The world's not out to get you, Cor. There's good mixed in with the ugly all the time. I just pray you realize that before you push everyone away."

He strode out the door and back into the downpour. She hugged herself. What if he'd spoken the truth? Lightning cracked and with a shudder, the house plunged into darkness. She ran to the open door and looked out. Tennessee's truck disappeared around the corner, the red of the tail lights her only guide.

Tennessee forced himself to unclench his jaw before it went numb. His eyes locked on the water-washed road ahead. If he didn't keep staring at the yellow line and navigating his way through this monsoon, he'd hydroplane for sure. Or just turn the truck around and go back to Still Waters.

No way. Let Cora Anne pick herself up this time. He squeezed the steering wheel tighter.

Except she was right and he had seen this coming. He had tried to tell her—lightning lit the cab of the truck. Aside from the storm and his headlights, there was no other light around. The houses to his right sat dark. Blackout.

He accelerated. His tires spun for a moment but found purchase quickly. Mid-morning, but the island lay darker than dusk. He took a right on the next side street and emerged back onto Palmetto Boulevard. Left would take him home to a day of rest he'd more than earned in the past week. The extra job was finally finished. But right would take him back to the Point, to Cora Anne and her stubbornness.

He crossed the lanes slowly. No point in making this any worse. She needed support. And he could give it.

The darkness lifted some as he drove. The storm would push its way on inland, and crews of linemen would restore the power soon. At the house, he took the steps two at a time and barged in the back door.

Cora Anne jumped from the corner of the couch. A blanket hung around her shoulders and Hannah stood beside her. "What are you doing back here?"

"Get dressed. I'm taking you to the hospital."

Chapter 36

Under the glare of hospital-grade fluorescent lights, the pallor of Nan's skin tinged blue. Cora Anne pressed one of her grandmother's withered hands to her cheek and breathed through her mouth. The smell of alcohol and hand sanitizer mingled with something more putrid. Her stomach churned.

Tennessee had proven her right. He always came back. Because he was good at forgiveness and she was not.

He hadn't even asked for an apology, though she'd feebly offered one. But she couldn't worry about him now. Nan had to be her only concern.

Nan's eyes fluttered open. For a moment, confusion clouded their blue, and she shifted her gaze from left to right, finally settling on Cora Anne. "Oh, good. It's just you."

"I'm so sorry. I should have done more to help you—"

"And then you'd have been spending time with an old woman out of duty and not out of love." Nan licked her cracked lips and Cora Anne reached for the small plastic cup of water with its bent straw.

"Never." She watched the effort it took for the now frail woman to sip and lie back against the inclined bed. "We could have made this easier for you."

"Having you, and then Hannah, with me was ease enough." She lifted the right corner of her mouth in the crooked smile Cora Anne had come to know so well. "You girls reminded me of all the wonder life and love bring. We've had a good time, yes?" She turned her head on her pillow and Cora Anne ducked her eyes from Nan's probing gaze.

Over the lump in her throat, she spoke the words her grandmother needed to hear. "Yes, we've had a good time."

Nan's hand pressed hers. "It's good to love, dear, precious to have someone you trust. Don't ever forget that."

"I won't."

Nan grimaced as she shifted in the bed.

Cora Anne sat straighter and glanced at the clock. "Time for your medicine."

"Not yet." Her voice still carried authority. But despite that will, the pain was evident.

"You're hurting—"

"I'll be fine for one more moment." Her chest barely lifted as she took a breath. "I want you to do something for me."

"Anything, you know that." She hoped her mother would return from the cafeteria soon, so she could escape to a bathroom stall and weep in private.

"I want you to marry Tennessee Watson."

She jerked and the metal legs of her chair scraped the linoleum. She forced calm into her voice. "You need your medicine."

"Just promise me you'll think about it."

She released her grandmother's hand and pressed her own to her tight chest. Should've never gone into that water with Tennessee Watson. Not when she was a child and not now. They wanted different things. For the first time, she realized how much it must have cost her mother to choose.

Because when she left Patrick, she also left behind this part of her life. And Cora Anne needed to leave all this behind to believe she could be more than that selfish child. Nan should want that for her—not this life where love might not ever be enough.

"I am capable of making my own decisions." But her voice trembled. "I'm also old enough to understand life's not a fairy tale."

Nan groped for her hand, gripping it tighter than she should have been physically capable of doing. "But that's just it, dear. Sometimes it is."

And for all their happily-ever-after, every fairy tale had hidden darkness.

"One more thing …" Nan's voice drifted, and her eyes closed.

She stroked the vein-lined hand. "Shh, you can tell me later."

"Don't be angry …"

"I could never be angry with you."

"With him …"

"Why would I—" For a moment, she thought her grandmother's breath had left her. But her frail chest rose and the green lights of the monitors remained steady.

"Hey, there." Her mother entered, shoulders slumped.

Cora Anne tucked her chin into her shoulder and met her Lou's gaze. "I think she needs more medicine."

"I'm sure she does. She's stubborn about it because it makes her sleep." Lou passed Cora Anne a plastic cup of iced tea. "Here."

A peace offering. She took it. "Thanks." A long swallow cleared her throat. "Where is everyone?"

"On their way. Carolina called Matthew so they were taking turns talking to him. I've already checked in with your dad and the boys. They were getting a pizza and playing cards."

"Sounds fun." Pizza and game night was an old family tradition. When they'd been a whole family. "Tennessee still hanging out with them?"

"Dad didn't say." Lou studied the clock over the door. "The doctor should come by anytime and give us the results of the scan."

Her grandmother's small form was almost lost among the wires and tubes. "I guess we're not expecting good news."

Lou lowered her head and ran her finger around the rim of her paper coffee cup.

A light knock on the door broke the silence, and a tall doctor with a stethoscope around his broad neck came in. "I'm Dr. Thomas." He pumped sanitizer from the wall and rubbed big hands together. "Dr. Kelly is out of town." He extended a handshake to Lou first and then Cora Anne. Brisk shake, but strong grip. His olive-toned skin made him appear young, but the wrinkles at the edge of his brown eyes negated youth. How many times had he told a family how long they had to plan a funeral?

"Cora Anne, go find your aunt, please." Lou's voice tightened.

The others were at the end of the hall, so she waved them to come. Hannah reached her first and slipped an arm around her waist. "Doctor?"

She nodded. They crowded into the small room.

Dr. Thomas had bent one knee at Nan's bedside and coaxed her awake. "Mrs. Coultrie? I've got some news if you're ready."

She blinked her eyes open and studied the doctor. "Well, aren't you a dish."

The laughter was soft but freeing. Cora Anne shook her head. Cancer may eat Nan's body, but it couldn't steal her soul.

Dr. Thomas smiled. "Thank you, ma'am. Now, are you ready for me to share the results of your scan?"

"Didn't need that fancy machine to tell me and everyone here that I'm dying."

He raised his eyebrows and nodded. "All right, then. Do you want to know how soon?"

"Have you been talking to my Jesus about that?"

"No, ma'am. But I can if you'd like."

"Better just talk to Him about this family of mine. I've been ready for a while." Her eyes fluttered shut again.

He patted her hand gently and stood. "She's a fine lady."

Her mother nodded, and Aunt Caro spoke. "We know."

"I'd give her four, six weeks at the most. The tumors are in her lungs, her stomach ..." He sighed. "Basically all her essential organs."

Lou pressed a fist to her mouth. "Excuse me." She pushed her way from the room. Aunt Caro leaned into Uncle John.

"I am sorry." Dr. Thomas extended his hand again and Cora Anne took it. "Let us know when you're ready to discuss options."

"I think ..." Cora Anne licked her lips. Her mouth felt full of cotton. But she knew. "I think we will take her home."

At that, Nan opened her eyes. "Yes ... it's time to go home."

Chapter 37

On the deck of Still Waters, Cora Anne sat, her feet propped on the railing. J.D. had made her an Arnold Palmer—tea and lemonade—before they all retreated downstairs for the night. Normally, the drink would be relief against the muggy heat the storm had left behind. Instead, she trailed her finger through the condensation on the glass and stared at the waves that rolled and crashed the beach below. She wondered how, if at all, she should pray.

She could pray selfishly for healing, but she was sure that wouldn't be answered. Nan had been adamant this was her time, and she was ready. She could pray against suffering and pain, but that seemed like a request to hasten the process, and she couldn't fathom letting go any sooner.

Four to six weeks. The end of summer into the beginning of fall. When the roses were at their peak and the last of the tomatoes were ripe on the vines, when the garden was just ready to shed its summer glory, that's when they could expect a funeral. Nan would accompany her beloved flowers into sleep.

The storm had passed fully now, and no clouds streaked the sky. Dusk lingered over the beach and stars popped out as beacons against the dark. An old story she'd read in high school came back to her. Something about the stars forming a path that leads the dead to their final resting place beyond the moon.

Despite the oppressive heat, she shivered.

She wanted to rage like the storm and shake off the fear. But she simply sat, and stared, and played with condensation droplets that looked like tears.

From the foot of the stairs, Tennessee watched her. He'd come, despite the heat and her text saying she was fine and wanted some quiet time. He feared he was last on her priority list, but she wasn't last on his, and he intended to let her know.

He climbed the stairs quietly. "Cor?"

She looked up, eyes like dark sapphires. Tennessee grabbed the railing. The last time he'd seen that look she was ten years old and sobbing in his arms on the beach. He gripped the rail tighter. Even then, he'd known he would do anything to keep that expression from ever crossing her face again.

Back then, she'd been a reckless kid. Now she was a tortured woman. And they weren't children anymore.

Drawing near, he bent, cupped her chin in his hand, and kissed her gently. Her lips were salty-sweet with lemonade and tears. He rubbed his thumb along her jaw until a small smile started.

"I told you I'd be all right alone." She covered his hand in hers and turned her head to press a kiss into his calloused palm. He smoothed back the tendrils of hair that always escaped her messy bun.

"Yeah, but I know what a liar you are." He dropped another kiss on her forehead and pulled a chair over next to hers. For a few long moments, they sat in silence.

"What do you think happens?" The question burst from her.

"What do you mean?"

"When we die? What do you think really happens?"

He leaned over and turned her to face him. She'd tucked her arms across her chest. The desolation he saw on her face concerned him more than the question itself.

"Cora Anne, you believe in Jesus. He's what happens when we die. Why this fear?"

She turned her face to the ocean and closed her eyes. He waited with the patience of a man who understood life's ebb and flow. This conversation had been a long time coming.

When she finally spoke, he had to lean in to hear the whisper. "I just want to know what to expect, is all. I'm not good with the unknown, you know that."

"Our plans are really good for nothing more than scratch paper, Cor. It's all unknown."

"It's all faith."

"Yeah, it is."

Her voice lowered. "She's been sitting out here all summer watching fishermen. Am I crazy to believe she's waiting for my grandfather?"

He pulled her arms away from her chest so he could grasp her hands. They were cold, so he enveloped them in his and silently asked the Lord for wisdom.

"That's not crazy. No one knows what the end is really like." He massaged her fingers with a firm gentleness. "I like to think there's really just a thin veil between this world and that one. Those who could tell us what it's like, they've already passed behind it. But because of Christ, sometimes we get just a fleeting glimpse too, like a curtain blowing in the breeze. Maybe you're right. Maybe Nan has been seeing your grandfather." Her hands twitched in his. "It's not angels and mansions and streets like everyone wants to sing about, Cor. It's about love, great unconditional love. Like what your grandparents had." *And what I hope we can have.* Would she ever be ready for that?

"I don't understand." She tucked her knees under her chin. "Why does it have to hurt so much? Why leave us here to suffer?" Her face clouded. "That night your dad died … I wanted to die with the guilt of what I'd caused. I went in the water on purpose you know …" She swiveled and faced him and the words burst from her. "And I've wished over and over a hundred times since then I had been the one who drowned." She pressed a fist to her trembling mouth. "Then, somehow, Nan showed me how to live again and now …" Her chest heaved and her face smoothed.

For a moment, he truly saw the young woman she'd become—a master at living fake composure.

Her control crumpled, and her voice hitched. "I can't see this as part of some great plan."

He grabbed her hand again. "We're limited by what we see here, by what we believe we can control. But this life's only temporary."

Her shoulders hunched and sobs racked her body. He pulled her from the chair into his lap and cradled her just as he had twelve years ago. But this time, he promised himself he'd never let her go.

Chapter 38

"I think the bedroom off the kitchen will be the best bet." Lou spoke in clipped tones, and Cora Anne wrapped the long cord of the phone around her arm, leaning on the counter while she listened. At the kitchen table, her father mimed writing notes. Yeah, she should do that.

Lou added, "Have Tennessee paint it today if he can, and if not, then I guess she'll have to be all right with it the way it is."

"It's rose wallpaper, right? Nan likes roses." Cora Anne pulled a notepad from the caddy under the phone.

"It's peeling and nearly as old as your Uncle Jimmy. That's the last time it got any real attention, you know."

"Mm, hm." She scrawled 'paint bedroom' on the paper.

"I've ordered the bed. It should be delivered tomorrow, so he'd have to paint today." A hospital bed in the back bedroom off the kitchen that had once belonged to the housemaid. That was what Nan would come home to.

"Got it, Mom."

"And bring down some of those crocheted afghans she likes from her room. And pictures. Don't forget the pictures."

"We won't." She dashed *afghans, pictures* on her list.

Lou sighed. "I'm sorry you have to do this."

"I don't mind, really."

"Strange, isn't it?"

"What?"

Lou huffed. "Well, she's had you working on the beach cottage all summer, when the farm is where she really wants to be now that …" Her voice choked, but when she spoke again, it was brisk. "Just get done what you can. Your aunt, and uncle, and I, we'll take care of the rest."

"It's okay, Mom. I got this." She hung up with a sigh of her own.

Dad lay down his paper. "She's in crisis mode, I take it."

Picking up her tea, she joined him. "Evidently. Sure wish Hannah hadn't been needed back at the shop. Family crisis ought to trump Bridezillas." Her dad snorted, which made her grin. "Guess I better call Tennessee and have him meet me there."

Dad raised his eyebrows. "You're sure he's okay with dropping everything else?"

She shrugged. "He told me to call him today and let him know what he can do." She looked around the cottage with its fresh paint and furnishings, the sun streaming in through the windows she and Hannah had scrubbed. "But Mama's right. Nan sure had him put a lot of work into this place when she wasn't planning to come back."

Dad folded the paper and a frown creased his forehead.

"What?"

He shook his head. "Nothing, honey. Just a nagging feeling that your grandmother didn't fix this place for just the family."

Him too? She sat back and crossed her arms. "What are you saying? She plans to sell?"

He lifted one shoulder. "I don't know. I'm not part of these decisions anymore, remember?"

She bit her lip. Right. "So, what are you and the boys going to do today?"

"Go fishing for dinner."

Laughter bubbled up, and she welcomed it after her night of grief. The last time Dad took the boys fishing, her mother had forbidden him from ever doing it again.

Dad grinned. "I didn't say we'd actually be *catching* dinner."

She hugged him. "Just keep the hook out of Mac's scalp this time, Dad."

"Will do."

Her sister was insistent. Lou stirred another of those tiny creamers into tar-black hospital coffee and leaned her hip against the counter while they talked.

"I can stay." Carolina's elbows steadied the plastic table in the family lounge.

"But how long can you take off at a time?" She knew how busy summer was for weddings. Caro had only told her a million times.

"Season slows down in August. September's pretty booked, but I think Hannah can handle it."

Open calendars, phones, and hospice care paperwork covered the tiny table. Lou took her seat. Now was not the time for grieving or savoring. Now was the time for logistics and planning. She removed her glasses and pinched the bridge of her nose. "I can be here full-time through the first week of August. But then I have to go for pre-planning, at least, and line up a long-term sub."

Beside her, Jimmy fidgeted. He hadn't said so, but she'd bet her new phone he wanted something stronger than that coffee. He also hadn't volunteered his schedule, but neither she nor Carolina intended to ask him for it. For him, it would be hard enough to come by for hours at a time and see their mother in such a degenerative state. He wasn't strong enough for this, and they all knew it. Better he keep the gardens tended and the business thriving than sit inside and watch Mama wither away.

"What about the boys?" asked Carolina. "I don't have to worry about young ones like you do, Lou."

"David said he'd take the boys for as long as I need."

Carolina widened her eyes. "And you're going to let him?"

John chuckled. "Good for you, Lou. It's time to relinquish some of that control."

Lou spread her hands on the table. "I'd say nothing is in mine—or anyone else's—control anymore."

The others nodded.

"All right, then …" Carolina trailed off studying her calendar squares marked with neatly penciled names and tasks. "You stay with her full-time right now, and I'll come in and out. That way, I can finish out these brides and turn the others over to Hannah."

John squeezed her hand, and Lou looked away from the loving gesture. She would have to be content with David's offer to help.

"Hon, don't forget that Clemson orientation is in August." John slipped his arm around Carolina's shoulders. "Your mother would want you to be there with Matthew."

"Yes, I would."

Everyone started. Wrapped in her favorite blue robe, Mama stood in the lounge doorway and glared. Lou flashbacked to family conferences when they'd been children. She'd sit them all down at the kitchen table for interrogations. Who exactly set the fire in the tomato field? Where in the world would anyone get the notion to drive the tractor without permission?

"Mama, you can't be getting up without help." Caro sprang to her feet.

"I'll walk around by my own self for as long as I have the strength." Mama turned an icy blue stare on each of them. "Don't think I don't know you're in here piecing together some sort of rotation for who has to stay and take care of me. You figure to wash me and medicate me and keep me resting. Well, I'm going to have plenty of rest time ahead, and I don't need you dropping your own lives to take care of my dying one."

"Mama, we're not doing anything we don't want to." Lou looked away as her mother shuffled to the table. The woman was stubborn as a mule. Jimmy offered

Mama his chair and she allowed him to take her elbow and help her sit.

"Look at you all, so sad." Mama's glare eased into a smile. "You're already filling my last moments with grief when you should be rejoicing I'm going home."

Carolina sniffled, but Lou pressed her knuckles to her mouth. She would not cry anymore right now. There would be plenty of that later.

"When we're home on Edisto, I want you to be with me. Not taking care of me. I want to talk of old times and hopes for the future. You can cook if you want, make bread, or start putting up those heirloom tomatoes Jimmy's been babying all summer. But I don't want you doing anything harder than sitting beside me when it's time. I'm not asking for anything more."

"Well, we are asking for more." Lou winced when Carolina kicked her under the table, but this needed to be said. "You kept us away all summer, let Cora Anne and Hannah in to help, but didn't tell them what was really happening. That wasn't fair, and you know it."

Her mother twisted her hands and looked away. "I wasn't ready to tell you all yet. There were things that needed taking care of first."

"Yes, and one of those things is you. Not the beach cottage. The girls are young, easily distracted—" Her Mama snorted and Lou sighed. "You gave them a beautiful last summer, and now we're just asking for the same courtesy."

Her mother tilted her head slowly, and Lou dropped her eyes. Mama had always seen right through her.

"You're always welcome on Edisto. It's a place that calls back its own."

John chuckled. "You're getting poetic on us, Annie."

Lou pressed her hands on the table. This was enough. "Mama, you need to lie down. We're working this out and we want to be the ones who take care of you."

"I just want you to tell me one thing about those schedules." Mama's blue eyes probed them all. "While you're busy with me, who's going to be taking care of you?"

Carolina reached across the table for Lou's hand. "We've got each other."

Lou nodded. That would have to be enough.

Her Civic bumped and shook over the ruts in a road that was no longer dusty. The puddles left by the storm had not yet dried, which was a sure sign the ground had gotten a good soaking. She passed perky fields of corn and tomatoes and she figured Nan's roses would have burst out into an array of colors by now, fueled by the gift of water.

Cora Anne swallowed hard, her throat as parched as the land had been. How was it she hadn't made it out to the farm all summer?

Tennessee's truck was already parked in the yard between the house and barn. She pulled beside him and waved. He leaned against a porch post. Rather than his standard work clothes of paint-splattered jeans and old Citadel t-shirts, he wore cargo shorts, a pale blue polo, and Birkenstocks. Cora Anne climbed out of the car, puzzled.

"Did you not get the memo this is a work day?" She indicated her own tank top and shorts, the same outfit she'd worn to paint Nan's Adirondack chairs at the beginning of the summer.

He came down the steps toward her and closed the gap between them in a few short strides. He dipped her and kissed her, and she let herself surrender and be lost in the moment. The sun and his hands heated her cheeks, and when she opened her eyes, the sky sparkled.

He set her on her feet. "We have to talk."

Such curtness after such affection. "What's wrong?"

He held her shoulders. "I kept a secret from you." His words hit like a punch in her gut. "You were right—I knew a lot more than I let on. Please understand."

Her lungs felt like she'd just run her morning five miles. Breathing slow would help.

"We don't have to work on the farmhouse today because I've been working on it since before you came back."

She held up a hand. He needed to stop this charade right now.

"Cora Anne, your grandmother told me she wanted this place ready for her last days. She swore me to secrecy. We weren't anything then, and honestly, once we were, I wasn't sure if you could handle the truth."

Turning her back on him, she strode to the porch. She'd show him what truth she could handle. He called after her, and she didn't stop. She bounded up the steps and jerked open the screen door. Crossed the kitchen and went into the small bedroom in which her grandmother had chosen to die.

The walls were robin's-egg blue and the trim a fresh white. It smelled new and clean, rather than musty with the tinge of tobacco and mildew that permeated the rest of the house. The furniture Nan had requested was already in the room with ample space for the hospital bed to fit. It only lacked the personal touches she'd want—the pictures, afghans, and rugs. But someone—she still couldn't believe him—had hung one picture over the low dresser on the wall beside the door. Her grandparents' wedding portrait, brow to brow as they bent over their wedding cake. In the old picture, Cora Anne could see the shiny satin of young Annie Jenkins's dress and nearly hear the laughter as she beamed at Thornton Coultrie.

Tennessee had followed her into the bedroom and when she stepped back, they collided. He grabbed her arm. "Talk to me, please."

Her whole body trembled. "I can't." She pulled her arm away and felt a shrillness creeping into her voice. "You let me carry on believing she would be okay, when I could have been helping her. And for what? So you could keep it a secret she wanted a bedroom painted?"

Back out the screen door into the blinding sunlight. She held onto the porch railing, hoping for something solid. Something that would ground her. Yesterday, she'd held onto him. Her mind ticked through her mother's list of worries. Bedroom. Done. Bathroom. She bet he had. "I guess you did the bathroom too?"

Behind her, he cleared his throat. "Yeah. Walk-in shower, handicapped toilet, wainscoting."

"Of course." She faced him. "The details make it special."

His jaw tightened, but he still didn't fight back. She welcomed the hot surge of anger flooding her limbs. This wasn't about Nan or the houses or their past. This was about right now. And he wouldn't meet her eyes.

"What else?"

He lifted his chin. "She wants your family to have a strong inheritance."

"Like we care about more *money* when she's gone. This is inheritance enough." She swept her arm over the expanse of field and woods, but then, as realization set in, Cora Anne lowered her arm and turned away slowly. "She signed over an easement."

"The fifty acres between here and the highway." His voice was low.

She wrapped her arms around her middle. The anger was fading. Instead, a heaviness settled. Disappointment. She'd rather have the anger. Steadying her voice, she said. "You knew all along."

"We've been working on this since long before you came back. It's a valuable piece of land, and she's had five different offers from developers. It's huge that she's signing it over to the trust." He put his hands on her shoulders. "Don't you see? She's preserving *your* history."

"You know what?" She recoiled from his touch. "I don't care if she signs all this land over to your trust, and then sells Still Waters. Gives me every reason to *never* come back to this place." She breathed in but not out. "I can't believe I was stupid enough to fall into this." She looked at him until he lifted his head and met her eyes. "What was I to you? The liaison between my family and your precious plans?"

His face flushed with what she could only hope was shame. He'd used her, and the sting of that was like a thousand cuts from those tiny shells rimming the shore. "One more question. How much quicker will you and Ben be able to flip the cottage since we've already done all the work?"

"We didn't buy it for a flip."

"You're lying."

His eyes flashed. "I am *not* a liar."

"Well, I think you just proved yourself wrong."

"I kept a secret from you. I gave my word to your grandmother, and I didn't tell you everything I knew, but I didn't lie. She never told me how sick she was or her timeline. I made some assumptions, so yeah, maybe I should have shared those with you. But all I ever wanted was to give you a summer of beautiful memories. I sure didn't bank on hoping this would last."

"Well, I guess you don't have to worry about that anymore."

"What are you talking about?"

She laughed. "Seriously? Did you think we would just have a fight and make up? It doesn't work like that."

"Of course it doesn't work like that for you. You're incapable of forgiveness, Cor, even when it's been extended to you."

Her heart hammered. "I can't believe you just said that to me."

"Believe it. You can believe something else too." She stared at him through a shimmer of tears. "Someday, love's going to be enough, but you'll have pushed it all away."

Chapter 39

Cora Anne stayed on the porch steps with her head on her knees for a long time after Tennessee left. When she lifted her face and wiped away the last of her tears, the sun had reached its height, and she could feel the burn on her neck.

In the house, she trudged up the stairs with leaded legs and gathered photographs and blankets from Nan's bedroom. With precision, she set the heavy, old-fashioned frames of thick wood and porcelain atop the mahogany dresser in the downstairs room. Afghans piled in the corner rocker gave the room a burst of color.

Outside, she cut roses and watered the beds like one in a trance. After arranging the yellow and pink blooms in a crystal vase and setting it in the center of the frames, she went and sat in the porch swing, looking across the farmland.

Fifty acres. What would Uncle Jimmy think? But, he hadn't depended on the harvest from these long leaf pines for years. His own property closer to Walterboro was a more practical choice for the nursery, but still. This land had started a legacy.

A legacy you've been running from …

She shifted. Stupid conscience. It was just an old family farm and a rundown cottage on the beach. She pushed her foot against the porch floor and the swing creaked.

You wanted to cut these ties …

"Yeah, I did." She spoke to the sky. Let God hear her words instead of just her thoughts. "They all told me I'd find peace with the past. Well, I've got it, so let's just move on, huh? Nan's purpose in life is up."

She pushed harder and the chains squealed in protest. Stupid Tennessee Watson. He could fix up a secret room but didn't think to put some WD-40 on the swing. What if Nan wanted to sit outside?

Her head jerked up at the sound of tires on gravel. But it wasn't his white truck. Instead, her mother's minivan spun into the yard.

Lou leapt out before the engine died. "What are you doing? I've called you five times!"

She planted her feet and the swing stopped. "Sorry."

"Did you finish? Where's Tennessee?"

"I don't know."

"You don't—" Lou blew at the damp hair on her brow. "Cora Anne Halloway, what is wrong with you?"

"What is wrong with me?" She leapt to her feet and advanced on her mother. "How about what is wrong with you? You send me here even when I don't want to come, and then you're mad at me when I actually have a good time. You wanted me to help Nan but when I do, you're mad we didn't clear every decision through you."

"I don't—"

"You don't want to be wrong." Shaking, Cora let every emotion she'd kept in check spew forth in the soft Lowcountry dirt. "Admit it. Dad left because you were wrong, because despite what you say, you loved Patrick Watson more than him. You let me believe that accident was all my fault because you didn't want to admit you were wrong to ignore me, wrong to push me aside and let me figure everything out on my own. Well, I've finally figured you out." She stepped toe to toe with her mother. "You're a coward. You run away when things get tough. And God help me, I'm exactly like you."

She expected Lou to crumple, that once again, she would have to hold her mother. But instead, the arms that grabbed her were strong and tight. "I'm sorry, I'm sorry, I'm so sorry …" Her mother's choking sobs reverberated in her ears. They stood together in that old farmyard under the warm sunshine, weeping for what they had lost.

Aunt Caro had called while Lou and Cora Anne rocked in the swing and talked. Dr. Kelly had checked on Nan and admitted that a few weeks was an ambitious thought.

"I'll see if your father can stay with the boys, or just take them on back. You'll stay?" Her mother's eyes were hopeful, and Cora Anne nodded.

"Of course."

"You were wrong about Patrick, you know." Her mother confided. "I didn't love him more than I love your father."

Cora Anne twitched at her mother's use of present tense.

Lou's gaze focused on the weeping willow tree with limbs that just brushed the ground. "I loved the idea of Patrick, of what we might have had."

Her mother's words hung in the air, and Cora Anne rubbed her sweaty palms against her shorts. She didn't love the idea of Tennessee. She loved him—his steadiness and tender heart. The way he always put her needs before his. Her stomach knotted remembering the words she'd flung at him.

"That was a bad time." Lou's voice cracked. "We were drowning in diapers and finances and exhaustion. Did you know your father actually suggested I quit my job?"

"Oh, Mom …" She sighed into the thick air. Lou's pride came from her career. She'd always thought of her mother as more defined by her title of teacher, rather than the one motherhood entailed. Had Dad really missed something so profound?

"That summer was the first time I'd thought—*what if*? What if I'd stayed, been closer to Mama, loved a man who knew a different version of me? What if I'd lived in this place that encourages slow?" Her mother smoothed a tendril behind Cora Anne's ear. "But then I wouldn't have had you. And I know I was too hard on you when the boys were born, but you were my proof I would survive. My saving grace."

She lay her head on her mother's shoulder, tucked into her collarbone like she had long ago. "I wish you had been mine."

"Me too." Lou rested her chin on Cora Anne's head. "But he's a good man, even if he did keep all the secrets."

She sat up. "I wasn't thinking of Tennessee, I was thinking of Nan."

Lou shook her head. "It wasn't her, hon. She had an inkling, but she would never have pushed. He had to help you find forgiveness. It's the only way to come full circle."

Full circle. But she was stuck halfway around, shaky about taking that last curve.

Nan came home the next day, summer's hottest of the season. Cora Anne opened windows in the farmhouse, a vain effort to harness a cross breeze. Uncle Jimmy planned to bring window units over later so that the family wouldn't melt while they sat vigil. Hannah had driven back over early, before the heat set in, armed with iced coffee and more scones, though these were store-bought.

Her cousin glided into Nan's room with another vase of roses for the nightstand. "Think she'll say there's none left to see out the window?" Hannah positioned the vase next to Nan's worn Bible and a photograph taken the day Granddaddy bought his first boat. "I'm so glad you unearthed this." She picked up the simple frame and traced her finger over the faces of their young grandparents with three children gathered around their hips and smiles wider than the ocean. They were in front of the modest fishing boat parked in front of Still Waters.

"I thought she'd like it, and those ones of Granddaddy fishing." Cora Anne nodded toward the dresser. She'd gone back to the cottage and brought over more pictures. They crowded the dresser and the round table in the other corner, but the presence of all that life warmed the coldness of the hospital bed.

Granddaddy holding Jimmy for the first time with Lou peering over his shoulder. Nan in a floral sundress beaming with her trophy the year she won the Garden Club's prize for heirloom roses. The whole family gathered around Caro and John on the steps of the farmhouse for their wedding day.

Hannah lifted that one and squinted at the sepia tones. "Mom was barely older than us. Could you imagine getting married right now?"

Tennessee's angry words flashed through her mind. "No, I can't."

Hannah handed the picture to Cora Anne. "Do you think I look like her?" Aunt Caro was in the middle, her dress swirled around her feet, holding a bouquet of summer flowers, a lace veil draped around her shoulders. She was flanked on one side by Uncle John, who looked bashfully proud. Nan held Aunt Caro's other elbow with the same joy on her face that was in her own wedding picture.

Mama had always said Aunt Caro was the beauty of the family, and it was true. The girl in the picture had long blonde hair and a heart-shaped face and a perfect smile, but it wasn't those attributes that made Caro shine. It was the delight Cora Anne felt just looking at her on that day. That same kind of unabashed joy for life radiated from Hannah. She shared her mother's coloring and jawline and narrow frame, but it was that capacity for happiness that made her Carolina's daughter.

"Yes." Cora Anne set the picture carefully beside the one of Granddaddy in his Air Force uniform at age eighteen. "I think you have all of the best of her."

Her cousin looped her arm through Cora Anne's. "You have the best of them all. Don't ever doubt it."

"Girls, they're here." Aunt Caro's call came through the open window.

Cora Anne cast a last sweeping glance around the room. The smell of the roses mingled with the pound cake cooling in the kitchen, and despite the heat, a breath of a breeze stirred the lace curtain. It wasn't Still Waters with the ocean's rhythm in the background, but this was the home Nan had chosen. The beach cottage had been her respite. The farm had been her life.

Chapter 40

Annie remembered crossing this same threshold as a young bride. She'd told Thornton to bring her in the side door, straight to the kitchen, rather than pretend with the pomp and circumstance of the front entry. Their life would be built here, side by side at the old oak table, over coffee in the mornings and teacups at night.

Her son and her daughter's husband edged her gently up the steps and into that kitchen. It still looked the same. She'd told Tennessee with all his renovation ideas to be content with the just enough. Changes had to come small if they were to be accepted in this place.

The girls had been baking. The sweet scent of lemon cake made her inhale deeply and then wince in pain. How could she have gone downhill so quickly? She blamed the stress of the hospital. That cold and sterile place was enough to make anyone sicker.

"Mama, let's get you into bed." Lou took John's place and Carolina took Jimmy's. Annie let herself be led. The room was exactly as she had requested. Walls as blue as the sky, her cozy blankets, books nearby, and her loves all around. There were even shells among the African violets on the windowsill and propped against the frames on the dresser.

"Ah ..." She pulled away from the girls and leaned her face into the bouquet on the nightstand. "Always stop to smell the roses."

Carolina smiled. "Yes, Mama. We know."

They eased her onto the side of the bed but she shooed them away and lifted her legs herself. "Just get my sandals off, girls. Bending that way got hard over ten years ago."

Lou slid the worn leather sandals to the floor, and Annie sighed. She wouldn't be putting those back on. Her favorites too. So dainty with their narrow little straps but good arch support.

"Just give me one of those afghans, Carolina. I don't need to go to bed yet. Just rest a bit."

"Whatever you want, Mama."

She leaned back and closed her eyes. "What's for lunch?"

Her daughters chuckled, and she knew she had eased their fear that tonight she'd fade away. She just might, but she intended a few bites of one last good meal first.

"What would you like?" Lou tugged at the pillow behind her head and Annie relaxed a bit more. Perhaps it wouldn't be so bad to let them care for her. Perhaps they really were ready.

"Some fresh shrimp would be nice. Sautéed in butter and just a bit of garlic, perhaps?"

"I'll send the girls out to Flowers to pick some up."

She forced her eyes back open. Gracious, she didn't need to be this tired at midday. She still had things to say. "Where are the girls?"

They leaned their heads around the doorway.

"Right here, Nan." Hannah grinned. "Like your room?"

"Don't be pretending you did all this, Miss Wedding Planner. I know your mama packed you back off to handle some irate bride."

"She did indeed." Hannah crossed to her bedside. "But I settled that girl right down, got her married off, and came back this morning. Left the assistant manager in charge." Hannah winked at her mother. "It's why we pay her the big bucks."

"I'll bet. The price of weddings these days is scandalous …" Annie focused on Cora Anne, lingering in the doorway. "My girl, are you coming in or not?" All this talking made her breathing labored. She tried to slow it down. They'd all be in a tizzy if she didn't.

Cora Anne came to the bedside, twisting her hands. A nervous habit she'd started as a child. "I'm glad you like your room."

"I'm sorry I kept it from you."

She looked away. "You don't have to be sorry."

"Yes, I do. I made him keep it from you too. You're angry."

She shot a look at her mother and Lou faintly shook her head. "I'm fine. Really."

Annie sighed. "Let's talk more after I have a nap, all right? Want you to understand …"

Her granddaughter crossed to the bedside and dropped a kiss on Annie's temple. "I do. I'm just working on acceptance is all."

Annie tried to smile but sleep pulled her under, and the sunlight and their faces washed away in the soft dark.

Tennessee tilted back on the wobbly legs of a plastic chair outside Flowers

Seafood. The tiny picnic area huddled under the shade of live oaks that bordered the highway wasn't anywhere close to five-star seating. But the fresh seafood cooked to order from the food truck behind the store kept this place high in the rankings with visitors.

Sweat rolled between his shoulders and he shifted his Citadel cap over his face. Scorching heat just meant more work. He'd sent out two crews that morning to rentals with air conditioning complaints and fielded three calls inquiring how much to roof the deck. People loved the sun on their back when they were five feet from the ocean, but not so much when they were having their evening drinks before dinner.

Another car rumbled to a stop at the old blue store.

"I haven't been here in ages."

That voice he knew. Tennessee lifted his cap. Hannah and Cora Anne crossed the small lot and went into the store. Good, they were buying to cook. Maybe he could remain unseen. Cora Anne clearly wasn't ready to make a decision, and he wasn't ready to push her again.

He pulled the cap back over his face then sat up abruptly and pushed it back. He'd forgotten she'd worn it one day he'd taken her crabbing, which explained why a coconut scent lingered on it. Stupid senses. Now he'd have to wash it. No way was he hanging onto the smell of her shampoo if she wasn't willing to hang onto him.

He crossed his arms. Maybe he'd go tell her that. He huffed. Not likely. He'd already proven he couldn't be trusted with words around her.

"Watson!" The cook called from the trailer. "Come get your food."

He picked up the Styrofoam box, thankful she was still inside and he'd ordered his flounder to go. He'd eat in the cool of the truck, driving over to his afternoon job on Jenkins Street, and ponder how to undo the tangle they'd gotten themselves in.

Cora Anne exited the store talking over her shoulder to Hannah. He quickened his pace but she walked right into him anyway.

"Oh, I'm—Tennessee?" She stepped back, and he sighed. All he'd wanted was some lunch.

"Hey." *Keep it light.* He eyed the bag of shrimp in her hand. "Nan know you're not buying down at the docks?"

"This was closer." She eyed his box. "Ben know you're patronizing other restaurants?"

He snorted. "You know the Hideaway's not open for lunch."

"Hey, y'all, let's move this out of the doorway." Hannah took Cora Anne's elbow and steered her toward the car.

Cora Anne handed her the bag of shrimp. "I'm going to talk with Tennessee for a minute."

Hannah's eyes darted between them. "Sure thing."

He headed toward his truck and Cora Anne followed. He put the box inside and cranked the air before turning back to her.

She twisted her fingers together, her lips tight. "Nan came home today."

"That's good. She happy with the work?"

Her gaze drifted away. "Seems to be."

He leaned on the closed door of his truck. The hot metal burned his shoulder but kept his emotions in check. "I'm glad. She was very specific."

"Well, it's nice she's that way with some people."

He stood back up and shoved his hands in his pockets. "What do you want, Cor? I don't think this is the time or place to have the conversation we need to have."

"What conversation do we need to have, exactly?"

The idea of grabbing her and kissing her senseless struck him and he sucked in a deep breath. Passion only got a person so far.

"Look, I told you I'm sorry I kept things a secret. If you're ready to accept that apology, then we can get together and talk. If not, then I guess we're done."

"Done talking right now?" She clasped her hands to her stomach and ducked her head. He lifted his eyes to the sky in a silent prayer.

"Yeah, we're done talking right now." Best they do this later. Outside Flowers Seafood was no place to break both their hearts. And Cora Anne didn't seem to know how to live any way but broken.

She whispered something.

He leaned in to hear her over the idling engine.

"I'm sorry." She didn't lift her head. "I'm sorry I can't give you what you want."

He touched her against his better judgment. Slipped his hand under her ponytail and lifted her head. "I'm sorry you don't believe *you* are all I want."

She turned her head away and stepped back.

He let his hand fall. "You staying until …"

This time, she met his eyes. "Yes. Then it will be time for me to go. I can't … I just can't, Tennessee. I really am sorry."

He swallowed over the lump forming in his throat. Nodded. "Keep me updated, please. Anything y'all need, let me know."

"I will." She walked away with her shoulders hunched and her arms clasped tight across her body. She looked frail and vulnerable, and all he wanted was to hold her and be the barrier between her and this awful pain.

Edisto gives and takes away. Her words that first morning they'd had a real conversation. He'd have said Edisto itself was the gift. He stayed because every roof tile and porch board put down under that hot sun kept his father close. He'd hoped she would come to realize that about Nan. This island would forever be her place, a constant reminder of life.

Instead, she seemed determined to only remember the loss.

Chapter 41

Cora Anne slid into the car with Hannah who placed a tentative hand on her shoulder. She waited until Tennessee drove away toward the beach before she put her head between her knees and sobbed. Great, choking cries tore from her chest. Tears, salty as the Atlantic, dripped on the rubber mats of Hannah's floorboards. She gripped her ankles and pressed her head lower, giving in to this gut-wrenching break.

Hannah gently rubbed her back. For once, she said nothing, and Cora Anne cried until her sandals were damp. Hannah slipped a wad of fast-food napkins into her hand.

She swiped at the snot and tears and lifted her head. "Okay. We can go now before the shrimp starts to smell."

Hannah leaned back in the driver's seat. "So that's it, then? You're done?"

She wadded the napkins into her fist. "We both knew it was coming." She looked out the window. "We always knew it was a summer fling."

"Maybe you knew, but I don't think anyone else did."

She angled the air to blow on her hot face. "Just go, please. I don't want to talk about this anymore."

"So then she sits up and says it's over. Dries her eyes, and she's done. I don't get it."

Lou listened as Hannah recounted the afternoon with her and Carolina at the kitchen table.

"Why'd she do it?" Hannah resumed her task of dish washing. "We all know she loves him."

Lou stepped beside her with a towel to dry. "Sometimes, love isn't enough. You're old enough to know that."

"Yeah, but we're not talking some passionate romance that burns out with the kindling. Those are the girls who come in for one consultation and then send me an email cancelling their event because they realize how little substance the relationship has." Hannah rubbed a glass with more vigor than necessary. "Cora

Anne and Tennessee, they could have made it for the long haul. They're beautiful together."

Lou nodded. Tears constricted her throat. Her daughter wasn't ready for that kind of love, and she might never be. Wounds may heal but the scars ran deep.

Carolina stepped up and took the towel from Lou's hand. "Go check on Mama, would you?"

Lou skirted around the kitchen table to her mother's small bedroom. She glanced over her shoulder at her sister and Hannah, hip to hip with their heads bent together. Love uncomplicated by secrets and denial.

Lou eased open the door in case Mama was sleeping. Her mother sat up against an eyelet-trimmed pillowcase which softened the angle of the adjustable metal bed. Her Bible lay open on her lap but her eyes were trained on the window.

"Hey, Mama. Need anything?"

"Some company would be nice."

Lou slipped in and shut the door gently behind her. Best that Mama not hear Hannah's tirade. She opted for the rocker between the bed and the window and her mother smiled as she eased into it.

"It's not so old you'll get dumped to the floor."

"I didn't say it was, Mama."

"No, you just sat like you're the one whose bones are being eaten."

Lou smiled. "It's not in your bones, those still look good."

Mama huffed. "Well, tell that to my legs and arms that think they're too tired to hold his Bible or walk in the garden."

Lou rocked slowly. The sun through the window was just warm enough to be pleasant for a short while. But only a short while because they'd turned off the ceiling fan when Mama said it made her cold.

"What's wrong with Cora Anne?" Her mother's voice had a warble now.

Lou stopped rocking and looked through the window. Her daughter climbed the porch steps with a watering can. The hanging ferns needed attention. She considered evading the question but her mama had always read her like a book.

She relayed a little of what Hannah had told her.

"Mm …" The groan came from deep in Mama's throat. "I was afraid of this."

Lou hitched the rocker closer to the bedside. "It's not your fault. She just doesn't trust easily." She tilted her head toward the window. "And she's stubborn like someone else I know."

"It'll be that stubbornness that breaks her heart, not that boy." Mama's breathing came in short puffs that never seemed enough.

"Why didn't you just tell her?" The question had been nagging for two days. She almost regretted asking it when a single tear slid down her mother's cheek.

"I'd hoped to hang on until she'd already decided to stay."

"Did you really think she would?"

Mama blinked and another tear fell. "I've been praying that girl here a long time. Figured she was no match for me, Tennessee Watson, and the Good Lord."

Lou took her mother's hand and rubbed the soft knuckles of thin skin. "Summer's not over yet, Mama. There's still time for that prayer to work. Maybe even on more than Cora Anne." She met her mama's gaze with a smile but then faltered and looked down.

Mama nestled herself more comfortably in the bed and withdrew her hand. "Still time … Yes, Edisto is gracious with that gift."

For some, Lou added silently as her mother winced in pain. "Let's get you another dose of medicine so you can take a nap. Then, you might feel like that walk. It'll be cooler in the evening."

Mama turned her head away but Lou uncapped the bottle on the nightstand anyway. Keep her comfortable, the doctor advised. When the care became too much, they could ask for a home nurse, but should consider the hospice home. Would be easier on them all.

Lou had no intention of letting her mother die anywhere but here. No matter what that might mean for the rest of them.

Mama swallowed the pill with a grimace. Lou's hand trembled as she set the water glass down. Vials of liquid morphine waited in the kitchen. Mama would need these before long, Dr. Kelly had said.

"Did you tell her?" Mama rasped and turned her head back to Lou who picked up the water glass again.

"Here, drink a little more." She lifted the glass and straw, then used a handkerchief with edges embroidered in pastel scallops to wipe Mama's chin. "Tell who what?"

"Cora Anne … did you tell her about Patrick?"

Lou looked away. Her daughter was still on the porch, yanking dead leaves from the fern fronds. "I told her enough."

"She's very angry."

"And it probably won't help if I tell her the whole truth, Mama."

Her blue eyes softened under a mist of tears. "And what is the truth, dear? I think you've run from it for so long you've forgotten it yourself."

Lou pushed her hair behind her ears and studied the fine cracks in the ceiling. Mama had let Tennessee Watson give this little room a makeover, but even he hadn't been able to conceal the evidence of a settling foundation. This home was built to last, but it sat on land that shifted with the sea. There would always be cracks.

"He didn't want me, Mama. Not like his son wants my daughter." Lou smoothed her hands over the bed's eyelet coverlet. "How ironic life is, hm? That now I'm the one thinking of staying?"

Mama reached for her hand. "There's a box at the beach house I want you to have. It's in the closet. Cora Anne knows which one. Ask her to bring it to you tomorrow."

"What's in it?"

"Just a little something I've been saving for you. You'll want it if you decide to come back home." Mama closed her eyes. "Ah … I feel better …" She faded off while Lou held her hand and wept quiet tears.

Chapter 42

Cora Anne climbed the steps to the back deck as though she carried the weight of Lenny's shrimp nets. Really, she only had her bag and a plastic container of pound cake.

She pushed open the back door—it didn't squeal. Tennessee had been there. Unsure what to think of that, she bumped the door shut with her hip and dropped her goods on the table.

"Mom sent cake."

The boys, clustered around the bar with Dad, whooped.

He grinned and closed his laptop. "You just saved them from the potential fires I cause when making slice and bake cookies."

"She said to tell you to get a piece, too. It's Aunt Caro's lemon."

"My favorite." Dad furrowed his brow. "You okay there, kid?"

She shrugged, and he held out his arms. She went into them and wrapped hers around his waist. He hadn't hugged her like this since the divorce. Because she'd never let him. When she pulled back, she'd left a damp spot on his t-shirt.

So much for pulling herself together.

"Better?" He handed her a tissue. "You hungry?"

"For burnt cookies?"

"No, for my almost famous spaghetti that barely requires any work. We were about to get it started, right, boys?"

The triplets crammed the last of their cake in their mouths and saluted their father as one unit. Now Cora Anne really did feel better. Silly boys with their impish grins. A few extra days hanging at the beach house with Dad had made them all browner and possibly taller. Must be the nutritional effects of bachelor food.

J.D. swallowed. "I'll brown the meat. Dad always burns that too."

Cora Anne cocked an eyebrow at her dad. "Really?"

"Boys, what happens at the apartment stays at the apartment. Wasn't that the agreement?"

Three heads bobbed and Cora Anne laughed. "I'll be sure Mom doesn't find out about your lack of cooking skills."

Dad went back into the kitchen. "It's more that we don't want her to know how often Waffle House is patronized." He opened a cabinet and peered inside. "Um, Cor, where would I find a pan?"

She chuckled and pointed. "Next cabinet. Bottom shelf. And Nan's aprons are in the pantry."

"Ha, ha." Dad retrieved a frying pan and set it on the stove. "You go take a load off. We got this."

But the boys had reopened the laptop and Cole was the only one who gave a thumbs up before settling back on a barstool.

"What are y'all looking at anyway?" She leaned on the counter beside Mac.

"Braves schedule. Dad says we can go to a game next week, maybe."

Cora Anne shot a look over Mac's shoulder to her father. "I thought you were staying here."

Dad peeled the plastic wrap from a tray of ground beef. "We're just looking at the options."

"Guess what's said at the beach house, stays at the beach house, huh?"

Dad broke up the meat with a spatula and kept his back to her. "Tennessee was here earlier, fixing the door."

She propped her hands on her hips. "And?"

Dad glanced at the boys. "Guys, go downstairs and play video games if you want. I need to talk to your sister."

J.D. hung back while Mac and Cole clumped down the stairs. He shoved his hands in the pockets of his board shorts and peered up at Cora Anne under straight, dark hair that had gotten long. "How's Nan?"

She sighed and put her arm around his shoulders. "She's really sick."

"She's going to die, isn't she?"

She looked sharply at her father. How could he have not told them? She clenched her jaw and tightened her arm around her little brother. "Let's talk about it after dinner, okay? All together."

J.D. leaned into her. "I really love her, you know."

"She knows, J."

He squeezed her quickly and then dashed down the stairs. Cora Anne crossed her arms and faced her father.

"Your mother should be the one to tell them." Dad concentrated on the jar of sauce.

"That's no excuse. They deserve two parents who can be serious with them, not one who's full of rules, and one who's nothing but fun."

He set the jar down with a thud and turned around. "That's a low blow, Cor.

You don't know what it's been like the past four years. You entrenched yourself at UGA and never came home. Your mom and I are doing the best we can, and if that means our styles are a little different, then so be it. The boys are fine."

"The boys are goof offs who know exactly how to play you both. This is a family crisis, and they don't need to be sheltered from it."

"Well, that's interesting to hear since it seems your problem has always been we didn't shelter you enough."

She turned her back on him and pressed her knuckles to her mouth. It was all disintegrating. Again. Life here bursting like the bubbles of sea foam at the shore's edge.

The floorboards creaked as he came to stand behind her. "Cora Anne …"

She crossed to the table for her purse.

"What are you doing?"

"I've got to get out of here."

Dad took her elbow with a gentle, but firm, pressure. "You don't need to run off when you're upset. Let's talk."

"About what? About how none of us are compatible? About how no matter what we do to fix up this house, it's still going to be the place where all our lives fell apart?" She pulled her elbow free. "I talked to Mom. I know about Patrick and what they were to each other. I know when life got hard and you both started to give up. That night. Down there," she jerked her head that direction. "On that beach we all love."

Dad's nostrils flared and he pulled in a deep breath. "Your mother and I had more problems than Patrick Watson. It's more complicated than that."

"No, Dad, it's not. This place." She sighed. "It just tricks us all into thinking we know what we want. Then it's over at the end of the summer." She shook her head. If only she could shake off the memories. "It's best she sells it."

Dad stepped back. "Let's sit down and talk. You, me, the boys. We'll talk like a family should."

"No." She looped the purse over her shoulder. "I'm not interested in any more family time right now."

"Where are you going?"

She paused with her hand on the doorknob. "You know, for once in my life, I don't have a plan."

Chapter 43

She drove in circles for the first ten minutes before parking under the trees that sheltered Beach Access 34. Shoving the keys in her pocket, she walked the worn planks of the access boardwalk with sand squeaking under her Chacos.

Evening quiet had settled over the island. A few families soaked up the last of their vacation under umbrellas on this quiet section of sand along the Sound. Here, the water was the true stillness that had always evaded the waves in front of the beach cottage. The tide was out and the expanse of sand stretched in front of her, rippled by tide pools and ribbons of shells.

She took off her shoes and waded down the beach into one of those pools. Puffs of sand obscured her feet like the secrets Tennessee had kept from her and the ones she'd kept from everyone else.

At the end of the beach, the sun hung on the horizon, dipping its edge into the water. She dropped cross-legged in the sand and sat as if she had finally learned the art of stillness. But guilt kept her heart pounding and her mind racing.

Finding forgiveness had come with a price. And losing Nan wasn't what she wanted to pay. Sand trickled through her fingers. She should've told her mother earlier. Not been so selfish about her time. She palmed another handful of sand.

Tennessee should've told her about the jobs.

She scrubbed her hands together, but the residue clung. Forget it. Tomorrow, she would pack her bags and go stay at the farmhouse until … until it was over. Then she'd leave her guilt and sadness behind, for good this time. She'd never have to worry about seeing Tennessee Watson when she was buying shrimp because Louisiana was three states away.

But who would she make Lowcountry boil for with all that uncompromised shrimp? Cora Anne pushed to her feet. This aimless walking and quiet grieving was ridiculous. She'd go be around people. For a little while, she'd let herself forget.

She cut through the beach access for Marsh Point Villas and intercepted the bike path. She knew where she was going.

Tennessee's white truck was nowhere to be seen in the parking lot of The Hideaway. She stamped her sandy feet before jogging up the steps. Her pocket held a five, change from buying shrimp. How far would that get her?

Christy waved and left a family settling on the porch. She steeled herself for the questions.

"Hey, Cor." Christy hugged her. "I'm so sorry about Mrs. Annie."

What else did she know? She searched Christy's face but her brown eyes showed only concern and compassion. "Thank you. It's hard."

"I'm sure." Christy picked up a menu. "Tennessee meeting you?"

"Um, no. Not this time. He had a pretty long day."

Her brows drew together. "You're alone? Where's that pretty cousin of yours my brother is so enamored with?"

Cora Anne shoved her hands in her pockets. Fidgeting betrayed nerves. "She's at the farmhouse. Helping our moms with Nan. Shifts, you know?" She lifted her shoulders in an attempt at nonchalance.

"Right. Well, you want something to eat? You can sit at the bar if you want. Service is quicker and no one wonders why you're all by yourself."

"Sure, the bar sounds good." They started across the room, and Cora Anne fingered the bill in her pocket. "Hey, Christy?"

"Hmm?" She set the menu on the counter.

"I sort of left without my purse."

Christy smiled and patted her shoulder. "You're family, Cor. Just order and we'll take care of it."

"Thanks."

"Least we can do."

After washing her hands, she hitched herself up on the high-backed bar stool and rested her toes on the rung. She bent over the menu but glanced at the hostess desk from the corner of her eye. Christy straightened menus and greeted another couple. She didn't seem to find this appearance out of the ordinary, thank goodness.

"Cora Anne, right? Tennessee's girl?" The bartender, a young guy with hair in his eyes like the triplets, set a glass of water in front of her. "What can I get you?"

She grasped the cool glass, ignored the reference, and said with a definitive nod, remembering Hannah's last order, "I'll have a glass of the Tara Gold."

"Sure thing. Still have to ID you, though."

"Oh, um…" She faltered and bit her lip. "Well, I forgot my purse, but —"

"Hey, Cora Anne!" Ben slipped in the seat beside her, and she exhaled. "Where's your entourage?" He didn't give her a chance to answer. "Paul, get me a

Corona so my friend doesn't have to drink alone. What are you having?"

"Glass of wine if you don't mind my lack of ID. I told Christy my purse was a consequence of leaving in a hurry."

Ben thumped the bar. "Get the lady whatever she wants, Paul. I'll vouch for her even if she has just about got my best friend on the ball and chain."

She flushed and looked down. Tennessee hadn't talked to anyone today, apparently.

"On it, Ben." Paul, the bartender, turned to his work.

Ben squeezed her shoulder. "How you doing with it all?"

She almost snorted into her water. If only he knew. "Pretty terrible, I'd say."

"Yeah, life's cruel sometimes." He kept his face averted, but she saw the quiver in his jaw.

"Tennessee told me about your dad." The words weren't right but they came out anyway. Anything to steer the conversation from herself.

The corner of his mouth tilted up. "Exhibit A. Man was meaner than a cornered gator at the end." He tossed his head toward his sister at the hostess desk. "Some of us are better at forgiveness."

Paul set the beer and wine down in front of them. "Enjoy. Anything else I can get you?"

"Have you eaten?" Ben asked.

She shook her head.

"Get her some crab cakes and grits, Paul. Bring us a basket of hushpuppies, too. Thanks." Ben lifted his beer and raised his eyebrows at her. "To comfort food and alcohol. Sustainers of a hard knock life."

She matched him with her glass. "I'll drink to that."

They sipped in silence. Cora Anne closed her eyes. The wine was tart and almost thick. For a moment, her empty belly burned. She drank again and this time, it just felt warm. She'd never been a drinker. A glass of wine here or there with friends, a margarita when the local Mexican restaurant in Athens sold them half-price, one beer at a party in college that had made her sick.

She sipped again, relishing the idea that if she drank this glass and then another, eventually, her mind would stop racing. Paul set the basket of golden-fried hushpuppies on the counter and the smell made her stomach rumble. Food would slow the alcohol's effects, but that would be fine. She'd just sit here all night if she had to. No thoughts beyond that.

"You want to talk about it?" Ben dipped his hushpuppy into the dish of white sauce in the basket.

She grabbed one and winced at the heat. Cornmeal goodness, fresh from the fryer. "Nope."

"Fair enough. Want me to track down Tennessee?"

"Nope."

He drank his beer without comment. She broke open the hushpuppy and steam wafted out. Paul put a set of silverware wrapped in a linen napkin on the counter and she unrolled it to wipe her fingers.

Ben spoke again. Less jovial this time. "Y'all doing okay?"

Cora Anne concentrated on eating without burning the roof of her mouth. No luck. She bypassed the water for the wine though it did little to cool the sting.

"We're fine."

Ben tipped his chin and passed his bottle from hand to hand. "He told you about the job, huh?"

"The secret job fixing Nan's hospice room? Sure, he told me." She drained the glass and ignored Ben's look.

"You know he wanted to tell you, but she begged him not to." He grabbed another hushpuppy. "I tried to warn him."

"Here you go." Paul set down a plate. "Refill that for you?"

"Sure." She pushed the empty glass toward him and didn't look at Ben. He was no one to judge.

"So you're mad, huh?"

"I'm not mad." She dipped a spoon into the grits.

Ben scoffed. "Been my experience that when a woman says she's not mad, usually means she's shooting fire."

"I'm fine."

"Yet another phrase that means the opposite of what it's supposed to."

She lay down her spoon. "He should have told me. She'd have forgiven him, and I would have been prepared. That's all." She picked up a fork to cut the crab cake. Ben's chef knew what he was doing. Little filler, just lump blue crab meat and complementary flavorings. The way Nan made them.

"That's her recipe, you know."

She grabbed her wine. Now he was a mind reader? "Nan's? They published it in the Baptist cookbook a few years ago. That what you're using in the kitchen?"

He handed off his empty bottle to Paul. "Now I could say a lot of things about Baptists, but the number one would be, they know how to cook." He winked. "Enjoy your dinner. I'll leave you alone."

"Thank you." She picked up her fork and set it down again as he rose from the stool. "Ben?"

"Yeah?"

"Really, thanks. I'm sorry I'm not good company right now."

He put his hand on her shoulder again. A brotherly touch. "Don't apologize.

We're always here if y'all need anything."

She nodded and looked down. She had no right to lean on Tennessee's support system when she'd made him the scapegoat for all her guilt. After tonight, she'd better find her own.

Ben headed out on the deck to schmooze diners, and Cora Anne picked at her dinner. Paul filled the glass again even though she felt warm and relaxed enough to recognize she should probably go. But she wasn't driving, so she had one more.

He brought her a piece of key lime pie with a small smile as she finished her third glass. "Want a cup of coffee with this?"

Key lime pie. Tennessee's favorite. She trailed her fork along the outer edge, watching it cut deep ribbons in the filling. "No. I'll stick to the wine."

Paul refilled her glass but brought her the coffee anyway. She ignored it and fiddled with the pie as she watched the restaurant put away the evening. Servers reset tables with new linens, glasses, and flatware. Votives were extinguished and thin wisps of smoke floated in the air.

She remembered their first date. How nervous she'd been and Tennessee had held her hand across that white cloth. Stilled her heart and made her vulnerable.

She drained the glass and rested her arms on the counter.

"You ready for that coffee, now?" Paul lifted her plate and wiped the bar in one smooth action. "I'll freshen it up."

She leaned her chin on her hands. "Coffee's a stimulant ... I'd rather just float away."

His eyes flickered across the room.

She laughed. "It's okay, Paul. I'm not drunk or anything ... just tired."

He leaned on the bar, eye-level with her. "Why don't you let Ben call Tennessee to come pick you up?"

She pushed back, shaking her head. "No, no, I'm good. Walked here, anyway, so I'll just walk back home ..."

"It's a long walk in the dark back to Point Street."

She pushed to her feet and braced her hands on the counter when the room whirled. "Whoa."

Paul grabbed her arm. "Sit back down. Let's get you a glass of water."

"I am fine." She felt the need to articulate better. "You can get me another glass of this." She pushed the wine goblet at him, but Paul shook his head.

"Water first."

Water dribbled down her chin when she tilted the glass. She swiped her chin and frowned. "I'm a hot mess, Paul. Where's Ben?"

"I'm right here."

She spun around too fast and almost fell off the stool and into Ben. "I knew you'd be watching me. Making sure I'm okay. This is the only place people do that, you know."

She tried to stand again but her legs seemed wobbly, so she dropped back down. "I need to spend the night here. Paul says it's too far to walk home." Not that Still Waters was home.

Ben sat next to her again. "Why don't you let me drive you?"

"No. I. Am. Fine." She tried to straighten her spine in proof but for some reason, it gave her no support. Ben grabbed her waist before she fell off the stool.

"Drink this water."

"Water tastes funny at the beach ..."

"Not this kind." He pushed the glass into her hand and she took it. Cold and slippery. It crashed to the floor and water sprayed his khakis and her sandals.

"Uh-oh."

"I got it." Paul came around the counter and Ben reached in his pocket. "Sit tight, Cor. I've got to make a call."

"Okay ... but don't call my mama. Or Nan. Better call Hannah. She's used to drunks." She knew she should stop, but this was too funny. These past few days kept making her lose control. "Because of the weddings, you know, people always get drunk at weddings." She kind of liked reveling in the emotion instead of shutting it down.

Ben stepped away and she continued talking to Paul who mopped the floor beneath her dangling feet. "I think people should get drunk at funerals, too. Don't you, Paul? I mean, a wedding is a happy time, but a funeral, well, those are just sad."

"I hear you, Cora Anne."

She put her head back down on the bar. Sad. Yeah, that's all a funeral was. She didn't go to Patrick's funeral. Her mother wouldn't let her. Said it would be too hard because she was a child and should try to forget what happened. The bar top was cool beneath her cheek. Maybe she would close her eyes and stay here after all. A dull throb began under her skull.

"Cora Anne?" His voice filled the room, and she winced. Ben had betrayed her.

She lifted her head that now felt heavy as wet sand. "What are you doing here?"

Tennessee sat on the stool to her right and waved off Ben on the other side. She hadn't realized he was still there. "I heard you tried to drown your sorrows."

"It was working too."

"Yeah, it usually does the first time."

A new glass of water had been set in front of her. She lifted it, carefully, and drank a swallow. "What do you want?"

"Figured I'd drive you home. Paul's right. Point Street's a haul in the dark when you've had a whole bottle."

"I didn't drink a bottle." Cora Anne drank the water again. Her stomach swirled. So did the dining room.

"Doesn't matter how much, Cor. You're toasted, so let's get you home in bed."

"Sure, let's go to your place." She leaned into him. He smelled so good, like Old Spice and suntan lotion.

He grasped her forearms and eased her back. "Your bed, with a bucket beside it."

"For what?" Then she knew. "Oh—" She clapped her hand over her mouth and Tennessee jumped up. He leaned over the counter and emerged with an ice bucket. Shoved it under her chin and she retched.

His hand tangled in her hair, holding it back as the wave of nausea ended. She spat to clear her mouth and coughed. Tissue, she needed to wipe her nose. Someone shoved a wad into her hand and she gratefully turned away to mop her face. If she didn't feel so sick, she'd be mortified.

"Sheesh, Paul, how many did you let her have?"

Voices made her head hurt. She wanted to go to the bathroom and throw up again but lay her forehead on the counter instead. Maybe if she just didn't move…

The voices argued. "You said give her whatever she wanted. How was I supposed to know she's not used to alcohol? She held it pretty well for a while."

Despite the pounding in her head, she found it funny that even drunk, she'd been able to hold it together for a while. She forced her head up. "That's me … always together." Her head wobbled and she put it back down, giggling. But—

"Oh …" With a groan, she leaned over the bucket again.

"Get it on up, Cor." Tennessee rubbed her back.

This time, when she finished, she looked at him through her tears. "Don't tell my mama …"

"I won't, now come on. Let's go wash your face and get you home."

He led her as she stumbled to the bathroom and he followed her in. She bent over the fancy porcelain bowl that set atop the counter and twisted the knob so the water streamed out warm. Without a word, he dumped the contents of the bucket in the toilet and flushed.

She scrubbed at her face with her hands and refused to look in the mirror. She knew what she'd see anyway. All the signs of defeat.

He led her back out with his arm around her waist and handed the bucket to Ben, who wrinkled his nose. "Well, I knew it was only a matter of time before these were put to their best use."

"Sorry, Ben." She tried to shake her head but that made stars dance before her eyes.

"It's okay. I should've kept a better eye on you." He grinned. "Not usually my policy to let pretty ladies drink alone."

Ben waved them off. Tennessee tightened his grip as they crossed the dining room and descended the steps.

"How'd you get here?"

"Um …" She tried to make sense of the evening's events. How had she gotten here?

"Ben said you walked?"

"Oh, yeah …"

He opened the truck's door and she almost fell in.

"Hang on." He put his hands under her arms and boosted her into the leather seat. The warmth seeped through her skin and she leaned back.

"I love this truck. It's so comfortable." Her head lolled and she closed her eyes. Smelled like sand and sawdust and him.

"Here." He wedged something between her knees and the dash. She opened her eyes. A five-gallon bucket. "Just in case."

She wanted to melt into the interior of the truck and forget this happened. He came around and climbed in. "So, where's your car?"

Good question. She remembered the beach but not where she'd left the car. "Um …"

"Okay, I'll find it. Doesn't matter anyway, because you're not driving."

She closed her eyes again as the truck rumbled and Tennessee backed up smoothly. Surely this nightmare would be over soon.

Chapter 44

Sunlight stabbed Cora Anne's eyes. She squinted at her surroundings and didn't recognize this room. Sand-colored walls and sheer curtains. She turned her head slowly on the pillow. Four-poster bed and vistas on canvas of mountain sunsets and Lowcountry oaks. She pushed her arms out from under the floral duvet.

After she'd lost it completely on Tennessee and cried the whole time he drove down that dark country road, she remembered throwing up again, this time in a bathroom with cool tile … She glanced at a door on the wall. Maybe in there?

She pushed herself halfway up with caution and tried to fathom where she was. Not at Tennessee's bungalow, for sure. Not at Still Waters or the farm. Maybe he'd brought her to Christy's? She cocked her head and listened.

All quiet. Christy's house would have noise. Her impression of little Colby had not been one of serenity. Cora Anne pulled up her knees and hugged herself. Christy was a person who had it all together.

A gentle knock sounded on the door.

"Y-yes?"

"Cora Anne, sweetheart, I've got breakfast," a gentle voice called. "I really think you should eat something."

She bowed her head. Of course he did. Tennessee had brought her to his mother's house.

She pulled in a deep breath. "You can come in, Grace."

The door opened and with it came the smell of bacon and coffee. "Glad to hear, because I've got you a little something before you get on your feet." She bustled in, blonde curls tucked back with combs, already dressed for the day in a peasant skirt and ruffled top. She set a tray on the nightstand, and without asking, bent over Cora Anne to fluff the pillows and scoot her back against that support.

Like being eight again with the stomach flu. Lou had positioned her the same way and brought tea and toast. Which, Cora Anne noticed, was on Grace's tray.

"Now, there." She settled the wicker tray on Cora Anne's lap. "You try some of this and just sit here for a few minutes, and then we'll get some real food on your stomach."

"Thank you."

"No problem." She winked. "I have lots of experience with hangovers."

Cora Anne choked on her sip of tea.

Grace thumped her on the back. "Sorry."

She blinked back tears. "No, I'm the one who's sorry. I can't believe Tennessee brought me here and you …" She gestured at the tray and herself. "I guess this gown is yours?"

Grace smiled. "It's just an extra I keep on hand."

She sipped more slowly this time. The tea was good. Peppermint. "Thank you."

Grace patted her leg under the duvet. "I fixed this room up for anyone who needs a little respite. You, my dear, more than qualify."

She nodded. The next question made her stomach quiver. "Do they know I'm here?"

Grace pursed her lips. "I called your mother and told her you'd had a late night and didn't feel well. Assured her you'd be here with me and Tennessee would be across the property."

"Did you tell them …" She picked up a piece of toast and put it back down.

"That you had an encounter with a bottle of Charleston's finest that didn't end well? No, I did not. That's for you to say."

She looked out the window where sunlight filtered through the gray strands of Spanish moss hanging in the trees. Did she have to tell them? Her parents would be so disappointed. Hannah would think it hilarious, and Nan … no way was she telling Nan.

Her head throbbed and she closed her eyes and pressed her free hand against her eyelids. Sometimes, the external pressure calmed the internal.

"Here, sweetheart."

Pills rattled in a bottle and Cora Anne opened her eyes. Grace held out her palm. Ibuprofen. Cora Anne swallowed and chugged from the glass of water also on the tray. Grace did know her way around hangovers. She closed her eyes again. How embarrassing.

"I'm telling you, some food will make you feel better. Gives your stomach and mind something else to chew on." Grace rubbed Cora Anne's shoulder. "Pun intended."

She squinted at this woman who had every right to resent her presence, especially in her and her son's life. She didn't deserve anyone's caretaking. Least of all Grace's.

"You want to tell me what's on your mind?" Grace propped her arms on the bedside.

Her mouth felt dry and her tongue thick. Why in the world did people do this over and over? She wasn't so sure her momentary lapse away from worry had been worth the morning after. She sipped the water again and turned away from Grace's probing gaze. "I don't deserve this."

Grace heaved a sigh. "I think it's time we had a talk. Eat that toast, girl. I've got something to show you as soon as you can stand without falling over." She left.

Cora Anne stared at the ceiling. The slow moving fan made her nauseous. So did the thought of facing the music back at the farm. She closed her eyes. She'd almost confessed everything to him that night he kissed her on the beach. How her desire for attention—from her parents, her grandparents, from Tennessee himself—had caused the accident and spiraled them all into this tailspin of despair.

Now she had everyone's attention and she'd never deserved it less.

Despair had kept her family away from home for too long. The tears came quickly and tasted like the ocean. Rivulets of salty fear that splashed the toast and the linen napkin laid by Grace.

"You ever been out to Botany Bay?" Grace drove with one hand on the wheel and the other trailing out the open car window. The day was overcast, but the humidity thinner and more breathable.

Cora Anne shrugged. "I don't think so."

"Well, you'd remember it if you had. There's nothing like it. Tennessee's land trust buddies say Botany Bay is the crown jewel."

"Another owner talked into an easement?" A note of bitterness edged her voice. She, the preserver of history, angry that her grandmother had given away a piece of heritage sown with pine trees and her grandfather's sweat.

Grace shook her head. "Oh, no. Botany Bay isn't part of the land trust protection. It's a much better story than that. The owner—and he was a character, you should ask Tennessee the stories his dad used to tell about that man—deeded it over to the state with the stipulation it be kept as a wildlife preserve."

Cora Anne leaned back. The road they traveled was canopied with live oaks, like so many others on the island, but these entwined their branches overhead. The light dimmed and only shafts of sunlight filtered through. The air had stilled, pierced only by the cries of birds and the soft hum of the car across the sandy dirt. A sanctuary.

Perhaps Botany Bay was less crown jewel and more cathedral.

The trees ushered them to an open area where a land bridge stretched across a marsh.

Grace parked on the side of the road. "C'mon. We walk from here."

Cora Anne unbuckled and stepped out. Her Chacos sank in the soft dirt and she wondered if the road back would be passable if a storm hit.

Grace was already ahead, arms spread wide. "Isn't it gorgeous?"

She crossed her arms and bent her head against the breeze that swept the fertile smell of marsh across her face. "It's nice."

"Nice?" Grace turned and grabbed Cora Anne's arm. "Sweetheart, this place is another world. You wait and see."

They hiked across the land bridge and under another canopy of trees along a sandy path to the beach. When they emerged, Cora Anne stopped.

Her heart skipped as she took it all in. Grace was right. This was another world. No play place beach but a relic of history. Trees stripped bare and washed white shone like bones against the slate gray skies. Sometime during the last century, the ocean had crept up the land, and those trees stood like sentinels in its waves. Guarding this precious place. Sea foam rimmed the shores and bubbled on the branches.

She slipped off her sandals. Hallowed ground.

Grace closed her eyes and pulled in a breath of the sea. Cora Anne imitated her. The air was tinged with salt and brine and something richer.

"They call this place Boneyard Beach."

"I can see why."

Grace walked the sand with reverence and stood in the water's edge. Thick bubbles of foam washed over her feet and clung to her calves.

"This is where I found my peace."

Cora Anne waded in beside her and hugged herself against the breeze that was becoming a wind.

"If God can keep all this here, despite man's attempts to bend nature to himself, I figured, well, then, He must know what He's doing keeping me without Patrick."

The water lapped over their feet and ankles, but she didn't move, even when the salt spray splashed up her thighs and dampened her shorts. Grace stood silently beside her. Despite the wind, the sun struggled through the low hanging clouds and lit the bare bones of those trees.

The eeriness dissipated with the fiery glow.

She'd run from places on this island since she was ten years old. Shut her eyes to the beauty every time she'd come back. Opened herself to other people's stories, but not her own. Guarded her heart from love, and hidden herself from feeling.

The water surged over her knees, and she let herself remember. "He was so strong. I always think of his arm like an anchor. He pushed me up over the waves and towed me, like I was nothing more than one of our rafts that had drifted out too far. He got me to the rocks, and Tennessee hauled me out. Then—he fell."

"A wave caught him off balance. He hit his head on a rock."

"He drowned because of me."

Grace's breath sounded strangled. "No. He drowned because he was unconscious. An accident, Cora Anne."

"An accident I caused because I was a selfish, stupid little girl." She could still see him rise and fall, arms and legs spread wide like when the cousins played dead man in the water. The water enveloped her when she collapsed, sitting in its edge, letting it lap at her shoulders, her chin, her hair as her own tears splashed down.

She'd cost Grace her great love. But this woman crouched beside her, pressing a shoulder into hers. "Patrick made a choice that day, and even if he could have foreseen, he'd have chosen to save you again and again."

"Even though I didn't deserve to be saved."

"Especially because of that." Grace waved her arm toward the bare bones of the trees on the beach. "We're all like those trees—dead despite our beauty. We don't deserve the grace that saves and gives us life." She patted Cora Anne's cheek. "You know there's only one way to return that favor."

Cora Anne lifted her face to the sky. The words caught in her throat but didn't tighten her chest. "Live under forgiveness."

"Amen." Grace whispered the word.

Childlike faith. She'd had that before. When life had been simple and she'd loved her mama despite her shortcomings. When she'd believed her daddy was strong enough to hold them all together. When she believed she deserved love, even from the Creator of the universe.

She closed her eyes and let the wind and the salt and the gray-green surf loosen the burdens she'd carried so long. Here, on this haunted strip of beach, she listened for forgiveness, and she let the surety that her life was bigger than one choice made twelve years ago settle into her soul.

"They say this is one of the hardest places to find, but the easiest to lose yourself in." Grace still stood beside her.

Cora Anne opened her eyes and drew in a deep breath of the thick air. The scent of decay and brackish water hung over the marshes, but here, at the ocean's edge, there was a tinge of freshness too. Long ago, salt purified wounds. Seemed like that practice still worked. She dug her toes further into the sand beneath the murky water. Anchoring her feet as well as her soul.

The wind died as the tide washed out, this time carrying with it the darkness that had long marred her soul, like that old tradition Edisto slaves had believed. If one washed in the ebbing tide, your sins were carried out as far and wide as the sea.

Chapter 45

"How's Annie faring?"

Phone to her ear, Lou sat the kitchen table. "As well as can be expected." Of course cousin Gloria would call now. She lived on the outskirts of everyone's life, hemming and hawing through the good and the bad.

"And how's your girl? Saw her at that new restaurant last night." The woman's voice dropped to a whisper. "Anyone who had that many glasses of wine is sure to be feeling the effects this morning."

Lou bit the inside of her cheek. So that's why Cora Anne hadn't come home. And of course, nosy Gloria wanted to know all the details. Well, Lou'd quite like to know them herself.

"Any-hoo, I'll be over with a banana pudding and congealed salad this afternoon. Your mama always liked my orange salad."

She spoke the appropriate, "Now, Gloria, you don't have to do that—"

Cora Anne's car pulled in the long drive, her father's behind her.

"But thank you so much. We'll see you then." Lou hung up—possibly, Gloria was still talking—and stepped out onto the porch, catching the screen door before it slammed behind her. Mama was sleeping.

She crossed her arms and waited against the porch post. The wall between them had fractured the other day but hadn't crumbled. Otherwise, her daughter would have called on her instead of the bartender at that restaurant.

Lou uncrossed her arms and shoved her hands in her apron pockets as the car came to a rest. The triplets bounded from the backseat but Cora Anne waited for David. They crossed the yard together.

At the porch step, David squeezed Cora Anne's shoulder and headed inside. Lou waited until the screen door bumped shut behind him.

"Thank goodness Grace let us know where you were because he was worried sick."

Cora Anne met her eyes, gaze steady. "I apologized."

"What did you think you were doing?"

"Finding peace."

"At the bottom of a bottle? Trust me, it's not there."

Her gaze faltered and she stepped back down. "How did you hear?"

"Cousin Gloria. Apparently, she had dinner at the Hideaway last night."

"Dad made me mad." She sat on the bottom step and drew her knees up under her chin.

Lou heaved out a sigh. "Well, I can understand that."

"He didn't tell the boys, you know."

Lou's back stiffened. "No, I didn't know."

"And they were talking about going to a baseball game and making all these plans like Nan's just going to get better and life's going to go on. I couldn't take it." Cora Anne wrapped her arms around her knees and spewed everything toward the big oak tree with its ancient tire swing. "And Tennessee and I both kept secrets from each other, but all this time …" She pulled in a deep breath. "He knew Nan was sick and I'd feel guilty if anything happened, but he didn't even warn me. Then Ben has to go and call him—of all people, call Tennessee to come get me when I'm sloshed half out of my mind, and oh, Mama, I threw up so many times." She hiccupped and buried her face in her knees.

Lou rubbed Cora Anne's flushed neck. "Guess he's pretty much seen you at your worst, then, huh?"

"Pretty much. Then he takes me to his mother's house …" She turned her head, her cheek still on her knees. "And she took me to Botany Bay."

Lou pressed her lips together. Botany Bay. She hadn't been out there since Patrick asked her to marry him.

"She's never hated me, you know." Cora Anne's voice was small. "And she could have."

Of course she hadn't. Grace had always made the right choice. But …

Lou sighed. "She never hated me either. And she should have."

Cora Anne studied her like she wanted to ask more, but instead, she sat up straight. "I need you to forgive me."

Oh. Lou smoothed damp wisps of hair from her daughter's face. The child must have cried all the way here.

"I forgave you a long time ago." She cupped her daughter's face. "I just did a miserable job of showing you."

Cora Anne nodded and gulped air as though she hadn't drawn breath in ages. "Everything isn't my fault."

"No, it's not." Lou smiled. "I tried to tell you, it's just life."

"And I can choose joy."

Lou pulled her close. "Yes, yes, you can." She gripped her daughter's shoulders and leaned back. Maybe it was time. "Do you have a question you want to ask me?"

"Did you love him? Even then?"

She wasn't talking about her father. Lou let go and pressed her palms into her own knees. Felt her heart squeeze.

"I guess I did." She tipped a half-smile at her daughter. "But I didn't realize it until he didn't come out of that water with you."

"Did you love Dad?"

That one was easier. This was the demon she'd wrestled to the ground over the last few years. The guilt she'd finally put to rest. The reason she could even think about changing.

"I love your dad, even now. I loved him then, but like I told you, life was hard with triplet babies. For the first time, I missed this place. I wanted to come home. Then, after … in my grief, he felt betrayed. I had made him believe that what we had wasn't good enough." She glanced at her daughter. "And I think he felt guilty, too, because he should have been the one."

"To save me."

Lou nodded. "Patrick's death broke my heart all over again. But I forgot your father helped me heal the first time, and he'd have done it again if I'd have let him."

"Are you sorry?"

"Every day."

"Are you going to tell him?"

She stared out over the pastures to the woods beyond.

Cora Anne stood and dropped a kiss on her head. "It's okay, Mom. It's enough you told me."

The porch creaked as Cora Anne crossed it, so Lou knew the words she spoke out over the land of her childhood were lost. "I don't know how to tell him."

Chapter 46

Hannah dropped another potato, slick with water and freshly peeled, into the colander in the sink. Her shoulders shook, and Cora Anne could see her lips squinched together as she fought against the laughter in her chest.

"Oh, go on. Laugh." Cora Anne said. "I'm a hilarious drunk, I know."

"Can't you just—" Hannah paused and wiped her eyes with a dishtowel. "Can't you just picture their faces? Tennessee handing Ben that bucket—" She chuckled again. "Classic."

"Yeah, unforgettable for sure." She picked up another potato and scraped the peeler over the brown skin.

Hannah sobered and hip-bumped her. "Hey."

Cora Anne glanced at her sideways.

"Everyone falls apart sometime, Cor. It's best if you do it with those you love."

"Then I guess you should have been there."

She shook her head. "Nope, I've had my share of liquor-induced hilarity. Cured by hangovers and Jesus."

Cora Anne stopped peeling. Hannah never talked faith. "Really?"

Her cousin grinned and shook her blonde bangs—lighter from their days at Still Waters—out of her eyes. "Yeah. Finally read that Bible Nan gave me for my eighteenth birthday."

She'd forgotten about those. Hers was probably still tucked in its tissue paper on the shelf of her bedroom back in Marietta. "Why didn't you tell me?"

"It's not like I'm a thumping evangelist. I'm still figuring things out, you know." She reached for the last potato. "I want a faith that's mine, not just that of my parents."

Aunt Caro and Uncle John. So steady and reliable. More like Nan and Granddaddy than anyone else. No wonder Hannah had found that a lot to live up to.

"And besides." She turned the potato deftly and the peel came off in one long curl. "You've been so angry for so long, I didn't know how to talk to you about peace."

"I was really that bad?" Guess she hadn't kept herself as in check as she'd imagined.

"Well, yeah." Hannah peeked at her. "You've been uptight and tense for years, Cor. Afraid that if someone is close, you'll do something to make them leave." She grabbed a towel.

"That's why I was over the moon to see you with Tennessee. When you were with him, it was like I had my old cousin back. The one who laughed with me and hunted shells and rode waves and—" She took a deep breath. "Wasn't afraid to show love."

Cora Anne bit her lip and held Hannah's gaze. Stepping away from the counter, she pushed her fingers through her hair. The kitchen's thick air stifled. Beyond the screen door came hollers, ensuring the triplets had put the tire swing to good use.

"Are you mad?" Hannah asked.

Her words had stung, but they were true. "I'm not mad. I'm sorry."

"Me, too." Her cousin smiled. "I should have nagged you more to come back instead of defending you for staying away."

"Nah. I wouldn't have come until I ran out of excuses. Nan knew that. That's why she waited."

Hannah glanced over her shoulder at the closed door to Nan's hospice room. Aunt Caro sat vigil on the other side. She'd been reading Psalms when Cora Anne stepped in with fresh tea earlier. "Wish she hadn't waited quite so long, though."

She wrinkled her forehead. Something nagged. Had been for weeks, though she wasn't sure until now. "Hannah, did you ever see any fishermen down on the beach at Still Waters?"

"Mm ..." Hannah cleared her throat. Her worried sound. She often made it when they were on the phone just before a difficult bride came in the shop. "Not really. I mean, maybe once or twice." She shrugged. "But the doctor asked us about hallucinations, remember?"

"Yeah ..." Cora Anne needed to let Lou know it was time to start the chicken. Her mother, in a fit of nostalgia, had declared tonight would be Saturday supper. Like Nan had served all her life. She had no doubt, if Lou had been able, she'd have bought live chickens and wrung their necks herself. Just like Nan and the housemaid had once done. But Lou had to settle with buying small roasting hens and cutting them into pieces now soaking in a buttermilk bath.

"Cor?"

She looked at Hannah.

"You think she was seeing things?"

"I don't know … maybe she saw Granddaddy."

A vehicle crunched over the gravel drive. She looked out the screen door as Tennessee's truck parked under the trees.

Hannah propped her hands on her hips. "Well, if I ever get sick, I hope that's who I see last. The person who loved me most."

Stupid. Should've gone home to change first, but his truck just kept going. Turning off the highway and bumping over the old dirt road. Heading straight for her.

Tennessee parked at the farmhouse. Shoved his hands in his work worn jeans and stamped the sawdust from his boots before he crossed the yard.

The heavy air muffled the cry of a heron as it soared overhead in search of the marsh. He'd always loved how dusk and silence came hand in hand to the Lowcountry. A brief respite in the day before the night sounds took up their symphony.

"Hey." Cora Anne stepped out the screen door and caught it behind her so it didn't slam.

He stopped at the bottom step. "I wanted to check on you."

She drew her brows together and looked at him. He knew he was a sight. They'd gutted another house today. Not a flip this time, a remodel for a couple who had just retired and were over the moon about their big purchase, a two-bedroom hidden back on Jungle Street.

A fine layer of dust covered his arms and neck, his face only spared because he'd worn a mask and goggles. His damp shirt smelled of sweat and drywall. No wonder Cora Anne looked at him like he didn't belong anywhere near her grandmother's porch.

But then she smiled, and it lit up her face.

That grin broke over him like the perfect wave. His mama had been right. She had found her elusive peace. For real, this time.

"I'm all right, no thanks to you," she teased, and sitting on the top step, patted the space beside her. "What were you thinking, leaving me at your mother's?" Her tone held gratefulness, not chastisement.

He sat with elbows on his knees. "Seems like that worked out just fine."

She hugged herself and smiled again. Her eyes danced, and he linked his fingers together. He wanted to embrace her, make everything between them right again, but instinct told him to wait.

"I'm forgiven." She spoke softly, with reverence, and this time, he couldn't resist. He took her hand in his, twining their fingers together like he had on their first date.

"Feel lighter?"

"Oh, yes." She leaned over and kissed his cheek. "Thank you."

His heart flipped. No more secrets. He tightened his jaw and took her other hand. The shell ring he'd given her was nestled on her finger.

"I have to tell you something."

She didn't pull away, just straightened her back. "I have to tell you something too."

Not what he'd expected. "All right."

She looked down, hesitated, then took a deep breath. "Tennessee, that night your dad drowned, I didn't go in the water just to grab the sand bucket I'd lost. I went because I was mad at my mom, because I thought I had something to prove, and because I was a stupid little girl seeking attention. I went in those waves deliberately, and I heard you telling me not to ..." The words tumbled together, and when her head came up, her lashes flicked back tears. "But maybe ... there was a part of me that wondered if I did drown, would they even notice?"

Memories of that night jumbled around in his head. How he'd yelled at her to stay on the shore, how she'd waded past the breakers, how he'd started after her but his father had caught his arm and jerked him back.

"I noticed."

"You always have." Tears slipped down her cheeks as she added, "That's why I don't like to call it an accident. I caused it, Tennessee, and I *deserved* to go down with those waves. And I've never been able to accept forgiveness for that ... until now." Her shoulders quivered.

She'd gone in on purpose. But ... he'd always known that. No matter the reason, Cora Anne had chosen to go in the water, and his father had chosen to go in after her. So now that she'd spoken the truth out loud all that remained was *his* choice.

He leaned his forehead on hers and heard her hiccup back a sob. "I forgave you a long time ago, Cor. I meant what I said, and I stand by it now. So this confession, it better be for you, because I've never needed an explanation."

Her head nodded against his. "No more secrets."

"No more ..." He blew out his breath and looked across the field. The tire swing swayed. The triplets had been on it when he'd pulled in, but they'd scampered off to the barn.

Mrs. Coultrie had told him all about the farm, how Thornton's family had sacrificed to keep it during the depression, how he'd brought her here as a young bride. This was the legacy she'd chosen. He'd do his best to honor it.

So he told her. "It's your turn to forgive me."

"Keeping her secret wasn't wrong. It was honorable. I was too messed up to see that."

A muscle jerked in his jaw, and he clenched his teeth until it settled. "Still Waters."

She nodded. "Nan plans for us to sell."

"Not exactly." He heaved out another breath. "She sold it already."

"What?"

He held her hand tighter. "Listen, I didn't know you. But if I'd seen this—us—coming, I'd have waited. Let you decide."

"What are you talking about? She wants you to flip it?" Her eyes swept his face.

He kept his gaze fixed on hers. "She didn't sell it to me for a flip. She sold it to me because I asked."

She was shaking her head and those wisps of curls were flying. "When?"

"In May. We closed the deal the day before you arrived."

"So all that work, that was because you wanted it done? Not because Nan needed me?"

He'd promised. But … he glanced toward the house. Mrs. Coultrie would understand.

"She asked me not to tell you. To let you believe it was all her, and honestly, most of it was. I'd given hardly any thought to changing that place. It means as much to me as it does you—it's the last place I saw my father alive and happy. Of course I wanted it."

She drew a deep breath, and he released her hands. This time, please …

"But why did she sell it without even asking us?" Her voice was small and cut his heart. "I know why she wouldn't believe I'd care, but my mom might have … or Aunt Caro."

"I'm sorry." This was too much. He could sense it in the tiny shake of her head that rippled down her body.

She pressed her palms flat against her knees and sighed. "What's done is done." A small smile lifted the corner of her mouth then. "You'll give us plenty of time before …"

The words trailed and he wrinkled his brow. Time before what? Did she mean—

"Cor, as far as I'm concerned you all can leave the cottage as it is. I didn't buy it to make money. I simply didn't want to see it sold on the open market."

"To someone who wouldn't know." She nodded. "Yes. Okay, then."

He didn't know what to make of her calm resolve. He'd expected anger, resentment even. Not this simple acceptance. Especially since she'd finally made her peace with the place.

He wanted to offer it to her, hand over the deed and beg her to make it hers with a little corner for him. But instinct and his mother's words kept him in check. *Don't push,* she had said. *Let her come back to you. It has to be her choice.*

Her choice.

"Thank you." She whispered the words and put her hand on his cheek. He turned his face to kiss her palm.

She smiled that radiant smile again. "Why don't you get cleaned up and come back for supper? Mom's frying chicken."

"How's Nan doing?"

She glanced back at the house and her eyes clouded. "She's worse every day."

He nodded. Nature of the beast. In so many ways, he could be grateful his dad didn't suffer.

The living, left behind, they struggled the most.

"You know why she wanted to come back here, right?" He'd hesitated to tell her this, but surely by now she had figured it out.

She looked from him across the stretch of pasture to the creek that rimmed the farm's edge. "This is her home."

Tennessee stretched his legs over the expanse of worn steps and tilted his head back. The porch ceiling was painted blue. Lowcountry superstition said the color kept away the haints.

"She told me your grandfather would meet her here."

Cora Anne's eyes widened slightly.

He lifted his mouth in a half smile. "I don't believe in ghosts, Cor. But I do believe in the mighty power of God's love. Who knows? Maybe He does usher us home with a reminder of the good gifts he gave us here."

Chapter 47

"You get your mama that box like I asked?" Annie coughed out the words, so the girl reached for the water glass on the nightstand.

"Sh … Nan. We don't need to talk. You just sit quiet and I'll read. Here." Her granddaughter fit the bent straw between Annie's dry lips. Yesterday, she could drink without it. This morning when she'd tried, water just dribbled down her chin. The straw wasn't much easier. She never realized how much energy one expended to get a sip of water.

"It's important …" Was Cora Anne listening? Did she understand?

"I know it is. That's why we're going back over there this afternoon. And the boys will come back tomorrow if you're up to it."

Tomorrow … Annie couldn't picture tomorrow. Her mind floated only through images of yesterdays. Lou needed to remember. Cora Anne needed to believe.

"I believe you now, Nan."

Annie rubbed her head against the pillow and watched her girl. Thornton had told her once how much Louisa's daughter reminded him of her when they were young. All that dark hair and those watchful blue eyes.

Serene … Today, her eyes were softer. Calmer. Not turbulent like the waves.

"Something's different …" Annie knew the words slurred a bit. She tried to swallow and clear her throat. Nothing simple worked right.

But she could still see. Out her window, roses climbed.

"I had a talk with Grace a few days ago." Her girl's face blurred. "She took me out to Botany Bay."

"Lose …" What was it people said about Botany Bay?

Her girl took her hand. "Hard to find, easy to lose yourself." The squeeze tingled Annie's fingers. "She told me. I didn't realize I'd lost myself, Nan." Her granddaughter's eyes shimmered. "But you were right, Edisto healed me."

"Now you can stay …"

She laughed. Just a little. Just enough for Annie to hear there was still fear. But there was joy, too. Annie knew which was greater.

"We'll see. Maybe I'll go for a little while and then come back."

Annie's tongue lolled and wouldn't form the words she wanted. She tried again, and Cora Anne leaned in close. Nodded. "Of course, you'll always be here."

Annie shook her head. No, that wasn't what she wanted to say. That young man waiting on her. *He'll* always be here.

Like Thornton had been for her. On the beach with his fishing pole. In the garden with her roses. At the fence, where he leaned now in his old work clothes, so young and vibrant and waiting to take her home.

"She's fading fast, Mama."

Her mother's fingers tightened on her pencil. She was at the worn kitchen table, scrawling out lesson plans. Her mouth became a thin line, and her eyes remained fixated on the yellow legal pad. "Carolina called hospice after she refused to eat last night." When Cora Anne gripped her hand, Lou pressed the point of the pencil down. It snapped.

Her mother jerked away and stood, shoving the chair backwards. "I need to finish these. I can't—" She gulped. "I can't right now."

Her eyes darted from side to side, seeking escape.

"It's okay." Cora Anne reached for the pencil. "I'll sharpen this for you."

Lou shook her head. "There's another in my bag." Her voice steadied. "Just let me work."

"Of course." Cora Anne stood and righted her mother's chair. "Can I help?"

Lou sat on the chair's edge. "No, I just have to write up something they can give the substitute to get her started. I've got it."

"Sure." Cora Anne moved back to the cabinet. She'd pour her a glass of tea. Keep her own hands busy. But she couldn't help but ask.

"How long do you think—"

"She has?"

"No, not that …" Cora Anne reached for the ice tray in the old fashioned freezer. She didn't want to know Nan's timeline. "How long do you think you'll stay after?"

Her mother lay down the new pencil. Cora Anne twisted the cubes loose from the tray while her mother twisted her hands. Shouldn't have asked. Mom wasn't ready.

Neither was she.

"I haven't talked to your father." Her mother's hands stilled and stared at the old clock as its hands ticked away the seconds of Nan's life. "But Carolina and Jimmy and I … We've talked about it, and someone has to stay with the farm."

And Still Waters, Cora Anne wanted to add. Someone needed to clear out the family memorabilia. The gallery wall. The platter from Great-aunt Amanda. The past passing on.

"I thought you wanted to rent it." Wasn't that what her mother had discussed with Tennessee after dinner last night? Keep their name on the deed, but let some other woman tend Nan's garden. Then, maybe someday, a Coultrie would come back.

Her mother smiled. Under the blue kerchief, her eyes glistened like the Atlantic on a perfect summer day. "Maybe ... or maybe, I'll stay. With the boys, of course."

Cora Anne's jaw slacked. Seriously? Lou must have sat on that old porch swing too many nights in a row.

"Don't look so shocked. This is my home, you know. It's not easy to imagine someone else living here."

She closed her mouth. Tried to work out something to say.

Lou raised her eyebrows. "I'm not asking you to stay, of course."

She swallowed hard. "Of course not."

"Tulane starts in three weeks?"

"Two." She'd counted the days yesterday. Wondered.

"Your grandmother wants you to be happy."

"I know." She moved to the sink. Filled the tray with water. Placed it on the shelf in the freezer. She stopped after closing the door, fingers wrapped around the handle.

"You'll make it on time." Lou's voice quaked. "If that's what you want."

Make it on time. Because by the time fall semester started, Nan would be resting with Edisto.

The boys had hung their beach towels out to dry over the front porch railings of Still Waters. Orange and green flapped in the breeze alongside the red, white, and blue of Nan's American flag.

"I'm thinking if they left towels on the front porch, how much sand did they track inside first?" Cora Anne pushed a damp curl behind her ear. The humidity at the coast wasn't any better than the farm.

Lou groaned. "Why won't they use the line?" She climbed from Cora Anne's car, tugging at her cotton shirt stuck to her back. "And you need to get this air fixed. That would be a good use of the money Nan gave you."

She shrugged. "I'm used to it, though."

Lou wagged her head. "Let me tell you something, daughter of mine. You are not going to enjoy this car in the bayou."

Another reminder Tulane loomed in the near future. Evidently, the good Lord wasn't going to use her mother as a staying influence.

The quiet house startled Cora Anne. If she hadn't seen her father sitting on the back deck, she'd have believed for a moment the last two weeks were a nightmare she'd finally woken from.

But Nan wasn't piecing a quilt on the screen porch and Tennessee wasn't holding down the lid on a stockpot of blue crab.

"Hmmm …" Lou crossed her arms and turned a half-circle. "They haven't destroyed the place."

She laid her keys on the kitchen counter. "I'm going to get that box Nan keeps insisting about."

Her mom glanced toward the deck. "Will you get me a Pepsi and meet us outside? I'm going to talk to your dad."

"Sure."

Lou exited in one fluid motion—the door hadn't stuck. Cora Anne smiled. Little things could always be fixed.

She grabbed a can of Pepsi and a bottle of water from the fridge. Left the soft drink on the counter and drank deeply of the water before crossing to the entry closet.

Nan wanted that battered green shoebox tucked in the corner. The only box she hadn't let Cora Anne unpack. She tugged it free from its resting place under the stack of *Southern Living* her grandmother wanted to keep.

Through the picture window, she saw her parents, heads bent together. The box held secrets. Maybe about the woman Lou had been when she'd been young and in love and passionate about more than her career.

She crossed the room with long strides, snagged the can of Pepsi, and went outside.

They were laughing.

Mama and Daddy. They hadn't laughed together in years.

"Hey, sweetheart." Her dad rose for a quick hug. Took the Pepsi and handed it to her mom. "Can't believe you drink those things."

"I wasn't raised in Atlanta, remember. We learned about options other than Coke." Lou popped the tab and took a drink. "Ah … tastes like home."

Dad shook his head. Cora Anne just stood, holding the box. Were they really getting along? Bantering like the old days?

Had Lou told him she was staying?

"Is that what my mother was going on about?" Lou held out her hand, and Cora Anne handed over the memento.

Nan knew what she was doing. Right?

Lou set down her drink and lifted the warped cardboard lid. "Oh my goodness …"

Tucked inside from corner to corner, yellowed with age, were letters. Cora Anne cocked her head.

The historian in her nudged. "Who are they from, Mama?"

"Maybe me." Dad wiggled his eyebrows. "Once, I was quite the writer."

"Sure," scoffed Lou. "You wrote me directions once on a napkin you'd already used."

"Environmentalist, too." Dad grinned. "Why I get along so well with Tennessee. He came over and fixed the door, by the way."

"I thought he must have." Cora Anne sat on the bench and sipped her water. Lou probed the letters, tugging them out to read the return addresses in the corners before she shoved them back.

Dad glanced at her, a question in his eyes.

She shrugged. Those letters were Lou's business, not hers. "Where are the boys?"

"I think they finally had enough sun and retreated to video game paradise."

"That explains the quiet."

"You going to tell us who all those letters are from or just make us guess?" Dad reached over to snag an envelope.

Lou smacked his hand away. "They're mine. Letters I wrote Mama during college and when we were first married, mostly." But she glanced at Cora Anne, who looked away.

College-era letters from her mother meant Patrick Watson was in there, too. Had he begged Lou to stay or let her go, hoping she'd come back?

She heaved out a sigh. This shouldn't be her focus now. Nan hadn't eaten for two days. The little blue book the hospital gave them so they could prepare for the end listed that as one of the first signs.

Time to let Still Waters go.

The tide had washed out and the beach stretched before the cottage unmarred and waiting. No wonder the ocean was such a metaphor for life. Everything had its ebb and flow.

And still waters ran deep until one waded in and learned to swim.

Her parents were talking again. Cora Anne closed her eyes and listened to the rush of waves, the cry of gulls, her mother telling her father she wanted to stay, and miracle of miracle, her father agreeing.

Chapter 48

Annie's eyelids fluttered but cracked open enough that she could see the woman bending over her. Smooth chocolate skin and warm dark eyes. Nell?

Her voice didn't work. She couldn't talk to her beloved housekeeper. Nell, who'd changed as many diapers as she had and wrung chicken necks and made her sit down on occasion so that baby wouldn't come too early.

A moan escaped her throat. The pain riddled her body if she moved, but if she slept, it went away. She'd sleep again and when she woke, she and Nell would have a talk.

"I got the morphine in her." Melanie, the efficient nurse the home care group sent over, reminded Lou of their old housekeeper, Nell. She'd looked after her and Carolina when they were just barely starting school. The farm work and a third baby had been too much for Mama to take on alone.

Oh, sweet Nell. Like this nurse, she'd been broad and strong, but her cool hands knew how to soothe and her wide smile never faltered.

"I wonder what ever happened to Nell?" Carolina voiced the thought as they watched Melanie smooth the bed covers and their mama's hair.

"Daddy helped her get a little house up in Walterboro so her boys could work at the nursery and be closer to school." Lou scooted the rocker a little closer to her mother's bedside. "They both went up north to college, you know."

"Excuse me." Melanie fixed her gaze on them both. "You girls ready for this? Your mama is, and I don't reckon it will be much longer."

Lou's chin trembled as her sister laid a hand on her back.

Carolina answered for them both. "We'll never be ready, but we'll be all right."

Melanie nodded. "I'm going to let your family be with her and I'll sit in one of the other rooms. You holler if you need me. But she's gonna sleep now. Just listen for that breathing like I told you."

Lou bit her lip. She'll sound like a fish gasping out of water—that was the description Melanie had given. How ironic that one could drown even on dry land.

Carolina rubbed small circles on Lou's back. "We'll all stay with her."

"You'll get Jimmy?" Lou asked. Their brother was hiding in the barn. Like he had as a child when something scary had happened.

"Yes, but why don't you go on out and tell your boys goodnight. They should probably go back to the beach with David."

Yes, they should. She didn't want them to see … Unlike Cora Anne, who had seen too much.

In the kitchen, all her children and their father, and Hannah and her brother Matthew, who had driven in from camp that afternoon, were gathered at the kitchen table with a faded game of Monopoly.

"Hey, Mama, want to play?" J.D. rolled the dice and whooped. "Doubles!" A swift glance from David caused him to clap his hands over his mouth.

"Nan's sleeping. We already told you like a million times." Cole punched his brother lightly on the shoulder.

"It's okay, boys." Lou came between them and ran her hands over their honey-brown heads. Like they had when they'd been little, they leaned in to her and she gave herself over to the embrace. Across the table, Mac propped his chin on Cora Anne's shoulder.

Maybe if they all held tight enough, they could will away the angel of death that loomed so near. Through the screen door, the night beckoned, a gentle Lowcountry evening that sounded of cicadas and smelled of honeysuckle. Weeping may endure for a night …

"David, it's about time to take the boys back. Y'all can come on in the morning." They didn't pout or protest. She nudged J.D. and Cole and nodded at Mac. "Now go on and kiss your grandmother, please."

They shuffled out of the kitchen and into the small bedroom together. She stood in the doorway and watched them bend over the bed one by one. The rustling behind her meant the others were packing up the game.

A hand touched her arm. "We'll stay if you want. I'll keep them upstairs."

David. Over the past few days, the solid man she'd married had returned. But she had no right to lean on him right now.

"It's best if they're not here." Her eyes glistened. "I'll be all right."

David squeezed her arm and nodded. "C'mon boys. Let's head back. I'll take you down to the beach and we can watch for turtles."

"Really, Dad?"

"Remember that story Nan told us?"

"About the soldiers who thought the turtle was the enemy—"

"Sh." Cora Anne hustled the boys out of the doorway. "Nan got that story out of her Edisto book. It's on the coffee table. Go read it."

Lou watched her daughter hug the boys in a fierce group hug and then kiss her father on his cheek. They ducked out the door quickly to avoid the June bugs swarming the porch light, and the house was left with a gaping silence.

"Coffee, Aunt Lou?" Hannah asked, reaching for the can on the counter.

"Yes, please." She glanced at the screen door where Cora Anne stood, watching headlights cut swaths of light through the long, dark night that stretched ahead.

Cora Anne had fallen asleep in the rocker by Nan's bedside, with the old Bible spread across her lap. When her mother nudged her shoulder gently so she'd wake, she heard the sound.

Nan gasping for breath. She had breathed like that once, too. In the water, in the nightmare that no longer haunted her.

Aunt Carolina and Uncle John sat on the other side of the bed in the same ladder-back chairs they'd brought in hours before. Hannah and Matthew were on the floor, arms and heads draped at Nan's feet.

Uncle Jimmy had taken the foot and he was bowed over, shoulders quaking. Susan stood behind him with a white-knuckle grip on that old armchair.

A rose-colored sunrise peeked over the horizon and shamed the glow of the lamp. No artificial light would carry Nan home.

They'd sat all night and listened to her breath. Watched the rise and fall of her chest. Held her hands that had gradually grown colder. Seen her lips take on a tinge of blue.

Like a bullet-pointed list, they'd mentally checked off all the signs.

Now it was here.

Death comes rapidly slow. Cora Anne knew. One moment you struggled, and the next, you let go and the descent was gentle into the waters.

It was the coming back, the living through, that was hard.

Wordlessly, she knelt by the bed and offered the rocker to her mother. Lou eased into the familiar chair that had rocked her as a child, and reached for Cora Anne's and her mother's hands.

Nan gasped.

The sun rose with her dying breath.

She was lost on Edisto Island. The narrow dirt road she'd mistaken for her turn took her past fields of corn and tomatoes. Then both sides of the road closed in and skinny pines towered overhead and shadowed the sky.

Ahead, the young man tossing bundles of pine straw into the back of a Ford pickup looked harmless. He paused his work when she stopped the car, and to her amusement, eyed her warily when she emerged.

Apparently, she wasn't the only one with stranger anxiety. She flipped her hair over her shoulder and gave him the smile she'd learned could get her the world.

"I was wondering if you could point me in the right direction. I think I'm lost."

He leaned against the dusty truck and nodded. "Sure thing, m'am. Where were you headed?"

"Cooper Creek Plantation. I'm supposed to meet my—someone." The word fiancé had suddenly choked in her throat. She swallowed and glanced away from this man's piercing stare. Butterflies danced in her belly.

"Well, m'am, you're a little turned around. I could lead you there, if you'd like."

"That'd be wonderful, Mr ..." Her voice trailed off, and he filled in his name.

"Coultrie. Thornton Coultrie." He pulled off his worn leather glove and held out his hand. "But most folks call me TC."

They shook, his grip firm but gentle. Warmth spread through her fingertips and tingled up her arm.

She locked her blue eyes on his hazel ones and smiled. "Anne Jenkins, but most folks call me Annie."

"Jenkins, huh? That's an old Island name." He tossed his head and held her hand. "Fact is, their old plantation, Brick House, is just down the road. I could take you there, too, if you'd like to see it. Even as a ruin, it's one of the prettiest sights on the island."

The flutters in her stomach churned. What was she doing? She pulled her hand away. "Thank you, but I best be getting on. My ... friend will be worried."

"You aren't a bit curious about a piece of your past?" A smile quirked at the corner of his mouth, and she fought against smiling back. Instead, she delivered the words she'd taught herself to believe.

"Mr. Coultrie, I'm not so much concerned about where I came from, as where I'm going."

"Well," he drawled, cocking back his straw hat. "You never know. Maybe we're headed in the same direction."

Chapter 49

They held Nan's service at the little white Presbyterian church where so many who loved this island and its ways had found respite. Tennessee, at Cora Anne's request, played "Come Thou Fount of Every Blessing" and this time, the words washed over and reverberated into her soul without fear.

She whispered with him, "Tune my heart to sing thy praise ..."

Hannah squeezed her hand.

Choosing the life-giving bounty of family and love, recognizing the good Creator who gives and takes away would be the legacy Cora Anne lived out for her grandmother.

Nothing significant for the history books. Just a life of well-lived simplicity.

Family and friends and all those who had ever known Annie Jenkins Coultrie came back to the farm after the service. Food had begun appearing the afternoon Nan passed, and the spread of Southern comfort filled the kitchen and topped the dining table and buffet.

"I've never seen so much fried chicken in all my life." Her aunt filled another platter and handed it over to Matthew. "Go help Mrs. Grace find someplace on the table for this."

The triplets wandered throughout the house with wide eyes and full plates. Cora Anne leaned on the doorjamb to the living room and watched them navigate wet kisses from Cousin Gloria and war stories from old cronies of Uncle Jimmy.

"That's a lot of congealed salads." Tennessee slipped up behind her.

She leaned her head back against his shoulder. "Don't you love how when people don't know what else to do, they feed you?"

His breath tickled her ear. "Don't you love that it works?"

She glanced down at her plate with its half-eaten slice of caramel layer cake. Six ribbons of homemade boiled caramel in that one slice. Must have taken second cousin Rose two hours to concoct. Knowing Rosie, she'd prayed over every swipe of her knife.

Cora Anne picked up the delicate silver fork—no plastic for this day and occasion—and savored another small bite. Any more would put her into sugar-induced coma. Tennessee watched her, grinning.

She offered him a small smile. "The food's not what works, it's the love."

"Amen to that."

Lou extracted herself from the tentacles that were Cousin Gloria's well-meant sympathy with the excuse she was needed in the kitchen.

Her sister-in-law took one look at her when she came through the swinging door and pointed to the porch. "Go take a break. I've got this."

"Thank you." Today, she'd never been more grateful for the woman who loved her brother.

A host of church ladies were running her mama's kitchen and encouraging folks to eat up—because truth was, the family could only take so many leftover casseroles.

Ben, with his mother and his sister, had brought baskets of hushpuppies, a steaming dish of those grits her mama had raved over, and gallons of tea. Lou's stomach rumbled, thinking of their kindness. Those people didn't know her ... but they knew her daughter and her mother.

She moaned and dropped into one of the old metal chairs in this corner of the porch. They *had known* her mother. She rubbed her chest over her hammering heart. Would time really ease the ache?

"Lou?" David leaned around the screen door. She offered him a flick of her wrist, unwilling to form words. He offered her a full plate. "You need to eat something."

Her stomach grumbled again and she straightened up in the chair, smoothing the loose skirt of her dress—black with tiny cream-colored vining flowers, tasteful but not formal. He handed her the plate and a fork he'd wrapped in a paper towel.

She unrolled it slowly. "We run out of napkins?"

"Nope, I just think a paper towel covers more, especially when you're eating with food in your lap."

She had to smile. David had always been even more practical than she, a trait she'd once loved.

"Where are the boys?"

Her ex-husband set a plastic cup filled with tea on the small table between the chairs and sat. "They might've escaped to the barn. I saw them conspiring with your brother a little while ago."

She glanced toward the barn door, which stood open, gaping at the yard full of dusty trucks and SUVS. "I guess they're fine."

"If this is going to be their home, Lou, you might as well get used to them exploring the barn and everything else."

She sighed.

"Did you tell them yet?" David leaned back and crossed his legs easily. He'd toned himself in the past few years. More time for the gym, she supposed.

"Not yet."

"Mm." He nodded and chewed on his upper lip. Another trait that had once been endearing, but now she knew it to mean he was evading something.

"What?"

He tossed his head, and she noticed his hair had lightened in the days he'd spent at the beach house. How was it he was growing more youthful while she only grew older?

"Nothing, Lou. We can talk later. Today's already hard enough."

Apparently, it was about to get harder. She lay down her fork. "What."

Not a question this time.

"Look, it occurs to me we entered teaching about the same time. In fact, I've got one year up on you." He clasped his hands. "So if you're eligible for early retirement, then so am I."

Her spine relaxed and she leaned against the back of the chair. "You're going to retire?" What was he saying?

David shrugged. "You are."

"But I'm coming here—and we've got to handle all this—" Lou swept her arm at the woods and pastures.

"I'm thinking your mama left this good and handled. You and Caro will need to take care of the house and yard, but otherwise ..." He lifted his hands. "Have you talked to Tennessee?"

She picked up her fork again. She needed food for this. "He told me about the easement, said it's detailed in her will."

"You okay?"

"What's done is done. Protects the island—and us—from too much development. Tell you the truth, I'm surprised my daddy didn't do it."

David chuckled. "Me too."

"So what are you saying, David?"

He leaned back now, propped his right foot on his left knee, and laced his fingers behind his head. "I'm not sure. All I know is I'm enjoying being here, so I'm thinking, maybe, I'll retire in December and come back."

She couldn't believe what she was hearing. "You'll come here?"

"Well, not here exactly, but Tennessee said he's got some sweet little townhomes perfect for a small family." He winked. "Or an old bachelor."

"So you'll be here. The one place you never wanted to live."

David shook his head. "You aren't remembering your history. You're the one who didn't want to live here. I always said we could entertain the idea."

"Until later when the boys were little and I wanted to be closer to my parents."

He dropped forward. "I know, and I was wrong. I can't go back and change that, but I can fix this." He spread his hands on his knees. "I don't want to be so far away from the boys or my daughter. Not anymore."

"What makes you think Cora Anne will come back here?"

He huffed. "I'm pretty sure you know why she's likely to wind up back here."

"He's a nice boy."

"Like his father."

She shot a glance at him, but his gaze was frank and open. No malice.

"So you want to be near the kids." She sighed. "We share custody, David. That's your right, and your choice. I just appreciate you understanding mine."

He reached over and squeezed her knee. The intimate gesture caused her heart to leap, but she kept her breathing in check. He hadn't touched her in so long …

"It's not just the kids I'd like to be near, Lou." He rose then and, crossing the porch, went on into the kitchen. He caught the screen door from slamming behind him and left her to wonder—what on earth just happened?

Cora Anne had thought when the house emptied that evening, the void of Nan's death would return. But it hadn't. With the day finally, blessedly over, and night settled again over the farmhouse, they gathered on the porch. Fueled by the food and fervor of those who had loved Nan, the family talked and laughed and cried.

Her mother and Aunt Caro sat in the creaking porch swing, sipping coffee, and Uncle Jimmy leaned on the railing with a pipe. Uncle John and Dad rocked to the pace of conversation, while the older cousins sat on the porch steps and watched the triplets chase fireflies.

The verse Lou had read over her mother's ashes lodged itself firmly in Cora Anne's mind. *Therefore do not lose heart. Thought outwardly we are wasting away, yet inwardly we are being renewed day by day … So we fix our eyes not on what is seen, but on what is unseen. For what is seen is temporary, but what is unseen is eternal.*

In that moment, she let herself revel in the eternal.

The next afternoon, Hannah and Matthew helped her load the Civic while her dad popped its hood and checked the oil. He'd taught the triplets to use a tire gauge, so they squatted and measured the tires' air pressure, except for Cole, who felt he had to lie prostrate on the ground to get the best reading.

Cora Anne stepped over his legs and lowered her duffel into the open trunk. "Looking all right down there?"

Her brother squinted up at her, shielding his face with his hand. For once, his blue eyes were serious. "You need to take better care of these tires, Cor. Louisiana's a far piece off."

She bit her lip to hold back the giggles. Her brothers had definitely been spending too much time with Uncle Jimmy.

"I think that's the last of it." Matthew added a laundry basket to the full trunk and Hannah dropped a small tote bag in beside it.

"That's not mine." Cora Anne reached to remove it, but Hannah grabbed her hand.

"It's just a little something from me."

She looked from her cousin to the bag and then back to Hannah's glistening eyes. "Are you trying to make me cry?"

"Oh, go on."

She pulled out the bag—a woven one with strong leather straps she'd admired at the Edistonian a few weeks ago. Inside was a t-shirt. Soft blue with a scattering of shells across the front and Edisto Beach in script underneath.

Hannah shrugged. "You can't leave without an Edisto shirt. Summer rules."

Cora Anne tucked the shirt back in its bag and embraced Hannah. "Thank you. For everything."

She shook her head and brushed her tears away with the back of her hand. "I can't believe you're really going. Nan's hardly gone and now ..."

"I have to. Classes start Monday, and I need the weekend to get settled."

Hannah nodded, sniffling. "Okay, well, we'll see you at the beach. At least we have one more night." She brightened. "Come on, boys. I think I need a slice of that pound cake I saw your mama unwrap."

The triplets abandoned their task and followed her like obedient puppies into the farmhouse.

Cora Anne shut her trunk just as her dad slammed the hood. "All good under there?"

David nodded. "Yup. You need a change when you get down there, though, hon. Find a nice place that does a ladies' special, all right?"

"I will, Daddy." She needed to do this alone, and he'd understood.

He rubbed his hands with a rag and leaned his hip against the car. "You going on down to the beach?"

She opened the door and the beeping began. Her keys were already in the ignition. The tank was half-full, but she'd fill up before she hit the interstate in the morning.

"Yes. I'm meeting Tennessee for a little while."

Her father glanced toward the sky. A perfect late summer blue with only wisps of clouds scattered across it. "Sunset, huh?"

"That's what she said."

He grinned. "That grandmother of yours always liked a metaphor."

Cora Anne tugged at the braid she'd looped over her shoulder and smiled. "She's not the only one. The apple doesn't fall from the tree, I guess."

He stepped around the open car door and gathered her for a tight hug. "No, it doesn't, sweetheart."

"I'll see you later." She pulled free and climbed into the car before emotion got the best of her.

The drive to Still Waters had never seemed so quick—or so long. She noticed every landmark between the farmhouse and the beach house, every memento of an Edisto summer.

When she pulled in the drive of Still Waters, she cut the engine and sat. The house looked the same. Nan's wreath on the door and the waving flag on the porch. Her dad had run it up every morning and taken it down every evening as a reminder that the house was occupied. He'd kept the geraniums watered, too, though maybe they didn't look quite as perky as they had three months ago.

Even flowers thrive on more than basic necessities. Cora Anne shook her head. The car was loaded down with all her basics, but she'd need more than that. Upstairs, she'd gather her books and some photographs. Save her mama and aunt the task of sifting through what she'd already gleaned cleaning out closets that summer.

Oh, Nan. She leaned her head on the steering wheel. How could Nan really be gone? How could she bear to leave?

Cora Anne shivered when she walked into the house. The air conditioning raised gooseflesh on her arms. The sight of Tennessee sitting on the back deck raised butterflies in her stomach.

"Hey." She pushed open the back door with ease.

"Hey, yourself." He nodded at the chair beside him. "Found you something."

She sat and picked up the creamy welch shell, rubbing her fingers against its points. Rarely were they found unbroken along this strip of beach. "Thank you."

"All packed?"

"Yes."

Tennessee didn't look at her. She sighed and fought back tears that pricked her eyes. He didn't understand.

"I don't have to like it, Cor." He linked his fingers together, elbows on his knees, earnestness in his voice. "But I do understand."

She reached over and ran her fingers through the blond hair he'd let grow long enough to tickle his ears. He caught her hand in his and turned his lips into her palm.

She savored that contact. "I have to go this time."

He nodded against her fingertips that grazed his stubble.

"I have to go," she pulled in a deep breath and pushed it out, gaining strength from the scent of the sea, "so I know I can come back."

He brought her hand down and held it loosely. The choice mattered. She knew he got that. He was here now when he could have gone anywhere else.

When he stood and tugged her arm, she drew herself up with him. He slid his arms around her waist and rested his forehead against hers.

"I can't promise you there won't be any more sadness. Just that when you come back, there's going to be joy too."

When. He trusted her. He trusted them. She lifted her lips to his and let herself sink into the surety of this moment. They stood and swayed together as if dancing to those old healing breezes sweeping in from the sea.

Nan had asked to be divided between all those places and people she'd loved. So they'd scattered her ashes under the weeping willow in the farmyard, buried an urn beside Granddaddy, and gathered at Still Waters.

"I want the girls to do it." Lou's statement met with nods of agreement from her brother and sister, but Cora Anne and Hannah exchanged glances that said, *really?*

Her mother cupped her palm and spilled the ashes into Cora Anne's hand as Aunt Caro did the same for Hannah.

With low tide, the beach had emerged, but it was deserted this late in the season and the evening. A dusky sunset had already begun to streak the sky over the Sound. Cora Anne and Hannah waded in up to their knees, waves lapping at the hems of their cotton sundresses.

Cora Anne glanced back over her shoulder at Tennessee. He stood on the sand, his arm around his mother's shoulders. When he caught her eye, he lifted his chin. Go on.

"Ready?" Hannah used her other hand to keep her hair from blowing in her face. The wind whipped tendrils around Cora Anne's eyes.

Like driving with the windows down in anticipation of a summer at Edisto Beach.

She caught Hannah's free hand with her own. "For Nan and snail shells and shark's teeth—"

"—And ghost stories and bedtime prayers." Hannah cast the handful of dust into the sea.

Cora Anne mimicked her, but the wind didn't let the ashes completely settle in the waves. Caught in the swirling air, some of the dust lingered in the sticky salt residue the ocean spray left on their arms.

She cupped water and washed, but Hannah dove into an oncoming crest and emerged on the other side.

Rivulets of water trickled down her face. "C'mon, Cora Anne!"

Could she?

She plunged under water that didn't fill her lungs or burn her throat. Popped her head up next to Hannah's.

"What in heaven's name are you doing?" Her mother's voice shrilled across the waves, hands propped on hips.

But Aunt Caro, her smile wide, grabbed her sister's arm and her brother's hand. "They're giving Mama a proper send off." She drug them laughing and protesting into the waves, and everyone else followed.

Off the shore of Still Waters, where the water never stilled and life always happened, they bid Nan goodbye with the ebb of the waning tide and the echoing joy of summer.